Beryl Kingston is a [...] [...]
many years she taugh[...] [...]
London and Bogno[...] [...] [...]. She stopped teaching
several years ago to write full time. Her previous titles
include *Two Silver Crosses*, *Maggie's Boy*, *Alive and
Kicking* and *Laura's Way* and *Gemma's Journey*.

AVALANCHE OF DAISIES

Beryl Kingston

ARROW

Published by Arrow Books in 1999

3 5 7 9 10 8 6 4 2

Copyright © Beryl Kingston 1998

First published in the United Kingdom in 1998 by Century

Arrow Books Limited
20 Vauxhall Bridge Road, London, SW1V 2SA

Random House Australia (Pty) Limited
20 Alfred Street, Milsons Point, Sydney,
New South Wales 2061, Australia

Random House New Zealand Limited
18 Poland Road, Glenfield, Auckland 10, New Zealand

Random House South Africa (pty) Limited
Endulini, 5a Jubilee Road, Parktown 2193, South Africa

Random House UK Limited Reg. No. 954009

A CIP catalogue record for this book
is available from the British Library

Papers used by Random House UK Limited
are natural, recyclable products made from wood grown in
sustainable forests. The manufacturing processes conform to
the environmental regulations of the country of origin

ISBN 0 09 927098 6

Typeset by Deltatype Ltd, Birkenhead, Merseyside
Printed and bound in Germany by Elsnerdruck, Berlin

When George Bernard Shaw got married, reporters asked him his opinion of married life. He replied that he and his wife, being middle-aged and childless couldn't possibly know anything about it.

'Real married life,' he said, 'is the life of the boy and girl who pluck a daisy and bring down an avalanche on their shoulders.'

I dedicate this book to the young couples who married in the late thirties and early forties as a tribute to their courage and endurance, for the avalanche that fell on their shoulders was the Second World War.

CHAPTER ONE

We were waiting. All of us. All over the country. All
across Europe and the United States. Soldiers, sailors,
airmen – and civilians too because we were all involved
in this war – from the arsenals of California to the
battlefields of Kiev and Leningrad, from the bomb-sites
of London to the terrible, secret torture-chambers of
Belsen and Buchenwald. There had never been such a
wait. It was almost as if our lives had been temporarily
suspended. We were hanging on, that's how it was,
from one month to the next, our minds focused towards
one, long-desired, meticulously planned, all-important,
much-dreaded event – the Allied invasion of Europe
that we called the Second Front.

The war had been dragging on for more than four
years and we all knew it wouldn't stop until the
Germans had been driven out of occupied Europe. We
knew what it would cost too, that thousands of young
men would be killed in the fighting before it was over.
But now it was the beginning of 1944, the plans were
complete and the invasion was coming no matter what
our feelings about it might be. The signs were all there.
There were US bases all over south-east England;
military convoys roared along the main roads everywhere you looked; equipment and supplies arrived by
the day to stand in the fields in long, reassuring rows;
and, to cap it all, the famous Desert Rats had been
brought back from Italy and were billeted in Norfolk
waiting to lead the invasion and strike terror into their
old enemies.

The Desert Rats! What extraordinary men they were!
It lifted our morale just to see them, with their tough

1

brown faces and their foreign slang and the Africa Star brave on their battledress, victors of Tobruk and El Alamein, the men who'd defeated the invincible Rommel and seen off the dreaded Afrika Korps, heroes to a man. They had a wonderful disregard for petty rules and seemed to be able to wear whatever they fancied, silk scarves, gaudy pullovers, corduroy trousers, even suede shoes, which they claimed were 'scuffed by the sands of the desert'. And why not? Knowing what lay ahead of them. Within days of their return they came swaggering into the local towns and took possession, laying claim to all the pubs, cinemas, dancehalls and women that were most desirable.

The nineteen-year-olds, like Steve Wilkins and his oppo Dusty Miller, who'd been sent to replace the men who'd been killed in the Italian campaign, were mere boys compared to them – and they knew it and looked it. They had a rough time in such company, for although they would soon be facing the same dangers as the rest of the army, for the moment they were scorned for their youth and inexperience, mocked for their pale faces and white knees and advised to 'get some in' whenever they made mistakes. Most of them kept their heads down and accepted being ribbed as the price they had to pay for being part of such a famous army. For as Steve said, 'If I've got to fight, I'd rather fight in their army than anyone else's. They know what they're doing.' Only a few, like Dusty, who was small and quick-tempered, took their teasing personally. As he did that Saturday night.

'Bloody sergeant!' he growled, kicking into the Nissan hut in his army boots and trousers. It was mid February and very cold, so his dash across the compound from Ablutions had brought him out in goose-pimples. He had a towel draped round his neck but that was more for decoration than warmth and his chest was blotched pink from the combination of night air and quick scrub. He shivered into his vest and shirt,

2

frotting the khaki cloth against his arms to warm them.
'I can't help havin' a white skin! To hear him goin' on
all the time, you'd think I done it on purpose.'

'But you're lovely with it!' Steve said. 'I mean to
say, look at you. Clark Gable in khaki! You've got the
same ears. You going dancing in your boots?' Unlike
the old hands, he had the knack of teasing to soothe.

'Don't you start!' Dusty grinned. 'I got enough with
Shit-Features. It's all very well for you, lying there. I
suppose you're gonna say you're ready.'

The hut was a swarm of preening activity and
clouded with cigarette smoke as the other twenty-two
men who lived there prepared for their night on the
town, struggling into shirts and tunics, polishing shoes,
anointing hair with brilliantine, squeezing spots, fighting to admire themselves in their one small pock-
marked mirror. But Private Steve Wilkins wasn't part of
it. He lay sprawled on his bed, peacefully reading, with
the book balanced on his tunic.

'I don't take all night tarting myself up,' he said
amiably.

Although he'd only been with the 7th Armoured for a
few weeks, his calm was already legendary. His
appearance could easily have singled him out for special
teasing – for he was a very noticeable young man, over
six foot, slim and long-legged with auburn hair, large
brown eyes and a very handsome face – but it didn't.
Composure is invaluable in wartime, as soldiers are
quick to discover, and a man whose self-control actually
increases under stress is a rare breed. His mates were
already calling him 'old Steve' and passing on tales of
his dependability. And that, combined with a touching
innocence, an occasional other-worldliness and a complete lack of vanity, was enough to shield him from the
taunts of the old hands and to make him something of a
thing apart among the newcomers. The way he prepared
for a night out was typical of him – wash, dress, run a
quick comb through his hair, and he was ready.

3

Dusty snorted in mock disapproval. 'You won't get yerself a bint if you don't make an effort. I'll tell you that for nothing.'

Steve shrugged and grinned. 'I'm easy,' he said. He didn't particularly want to '*get himself a bint*'. The very word put him off. It sounded coarse and cheap, like '*a bit on the side*' or '*a bit of skirt*', the sort of girl you picked up, went as far as you could with and then dumped. If a bint was all they were after, good luck to them. Privately, he knew he wanted a great deal more than that. But he had to accept that he was too shy for all the chatting-up you had to do to get any girl interested in you in the first place. Too shy and too ignorant. He hadn't learnt how to flirt, that was part of it, and flattery had always seemed dishonest and rather despicable.

He turned a page, deciding, yet again, that he would wait until the right girl came along. He'd find her somehow. He had no idea how or where but two things were certain – it wouldn't be until the war was over, because it wouldn't be fair to get involved and then shoot off and leave her; and it wouldn't be in a dancehall. The one they were going to that night was no better or worse than the others. It would be entertaining there. It would pass the time. But it was just a dancehall. Not worth getting into a lather about.

In fact the Saturday hop at King's Lynn was held in the Corn Exchange, which was a prestigious place had anyone stopped to consider it. But nobody did. The locals were too used to it, the soldiers were too busy looking for talent, and it was always much too crowded. It had been crowded even before the Desert Rats moved into the area and now there were suddenly three times the number of men about and most of them were soldiers. The local girls were thrilled by their sudden popularity but the local lads were put out in every sense of the word. Unless they were already comfortably attached to the girl of their choice, they mooched in and

4

out of the hall in disgruntled gangs trying to appear nonchalant and scowling at their adversaries. There were three of them glowering at the entrance when Steve and his mates strolled in.

'Punch-up?' Dusty said hopefully. He was still angry from his brush with the sergeant and a scrap was just what he needed.

Steve glanced round the hall. Hordes of girls might make him feel ill at ease but he enjoyed a brawl. As a schoolboy he'd been in enough street fights to know what to expect. It gave him a chance to use his height and strength and he liked the sense of being part of this invincible army. But there was no likelihood of any trouble that night. There were Desert Rats everywhere he looked and three locals were hardly likely to provoke trouble with that sort of opposition about. 'No,' he said. 'Don't think so.'

'Pity,' Dusty grimaced. 'I could've taken them on, no trouble.' He pulled a cigarette from Steve's proffered packet, lit it and began to size up the talent. 'Boy, oh boy. Get an eyeful a' that!'

That was a dark-haired girl in a red sweater and navy-blue trousers who was doing an energetic jitterbug with a languid GI. To Steve's eyes, she wasn't a particularly pretty girl but she was certainly vivacious. Her hair swirled as she danced, her feet leapt, her breasts bounced. Now they *were* pretty. Soft and full and tip-tilted and . . .

'Boy, oh boy!' Dusty groaned. 'Will you look at that redhead!'

'There's fickle you are!' Taffy Jones yelled at him above the noise of the band. 'I thought you was after the sweater gel.'

'You know me,' Dusty shouted back. 'Play the field, me.' He went on enjoying the sights on offer, smoking happily. By the time the jitterbug crashed to an end, he'd decided on four possibilities. He said, 'Tally ho!' to Steve, stubbed out his cigarette and plunged into the hunt. The next dance was a waltz so the lights were turned down as he moved and the silver mirror ball set spinning above his head. Soon he was lost in the swirl.

This was the moment in any dance that Steve enjoyed the most, when he could stand with his back against the wall, have a quiet smoke, dream vague dreams and watch without having to be involved. The waltz was soothing. It reminded him of the wireless back home, Dad mending shoes by the fireside, nails between his lips, Mum darning, her work-basket open beside her, the smell of home-cooking . . . What wouldn't he give for a plate of her bacon and eggs! Or bacon and tomatoes. Or just fried bread.

Soft light and drifting music gentled the hall. The dancing couples gyrated dreamily beneath the long beams spinning from the mirror ball. Discs of white light dappled their shadowy faces. The obscenity of bombs and bullets was a long way away.

One day, Steve promised himself, with a bit of luck, when I know a bit more, when this war's over, if I'm still in one piece, I shall have a girl and we'll dance like that, cheek to cheek. The words of the song filled his mind with hope. '*I'll be loving you. Always. With a love that's true. Always. When the things you've planned need a helping hand . . .*'

At that moment, there was a commotion on the other side of the hall, somebody being pulled off the floor by the looks of it, somebody shouting, arms waving. Dusty appeared at his side as if by magic.

'Now *that's* a punch-up,' he said, eyes gleaming. He cracked his knuckles, crick-crack, left hand, right hand, like a boxer flexing his muscles. 'Let's have a shufti.'

The rest of the gang had gathered round him too, all eager. 'Yeh! Come on! Let's.'

They pushed their way through the crowd, shouldering people aside, avid for action. But it wasn't yobs versus the army after all, just one of the local lads shoving a girl about. Dusty was visibly disappointed.

The lad was a stocky-looking individual about three inches shorter than Steve, dark of hair and eye, with brawny arms and big hands that he was using with unnecessary force to push the girl backwards away from the dance floor. She was fighting him off valiantly, twisting her body out of his reach and shouting at him to leave off, but he was too heavy for her and too insistent.

'You came here with *me*,' he shouted, pushing at her again. The words rose into the languid sounds of the waltz, staccato as bullets.

'No I didn't,' she shouted back. 'I come on my own.'

'You're *my* gal,' he insisted. 'My gal ... so you dance with me, properly, or you go home. You'll get yourself a reputation.'

'I don' care!'

'Well I do!'

The girl kicked out at him viciously, catching him on the shins, so that for a second he staggered back, temporarily off guard. 'You don' own me, Victor Castlemain,' she said. 'I hain't your gal an' thass no good you think it. Don't talk squit!'

Kicking him made him worse. He seized her by the shoulders and shoved her against the wall, his handsome face dark with rage. 'All this hossin' around has got to stop. Do you hear me?'

No, Steve thought, this is too much. I can't let this go on. Even in the heat of her anger, there was something vulnerable about this girl, something about the expression in her eyes, the tilt of her chin, the way she stood her ground. It roused him to an instant and protective tenderness. She was too small to fight a great gawk like that. Too small and too skinny, her wrists fragile against the brute fists of her aggressor. Without thinking any further, he stepped forward to defend her.

'That'll do,' he said to the gawk. 'Leave her be.'

The young man barely looked at him. 'Buzz off,

7

soldier!' he said. 'That's nothing to do with you. That's between me an' her.'

'I don't think so,' Steve said, putting his height and strength between them.

For a prickling second, the two men bristled at one another, challenging, eye to eye, Steve using his height to intimidate, the other standing four square, jutting his chin. Then the young man spoke again. 'Buzz off!' he warned. 'I told you. This is private.'

'In a public dancehall?' Steve mocked. 'Oh I don't think so. Anyway, she's dancing with me.' He turned to the girl. 'Aren't you?'

She looked straight up at him, and now she had a devilish expression on her face. Daring? Delight? He couldn't interpret. 'Thass right,' she said, and held out her hand to him.

The young man scowled at her. 'You're not. Don't be stupid.'

'She is,' Steve told him, taking her hand and leading her away from trouble. 'D'you want to make something of it?'

Now, and a bit late, the young man realised that he was surrounded by hostile khaki. 'Now look here,' he said.

Dusty moved happily into the attack, fists clenched. 'No, you look, sunshine,' he said, thrusting his face at his enemy. 'Seems to me you need to cool down.' Steve and the girl were already dancing their way towards the centre of the floor. 'Seems to me you need to take a little walk. Bit a' fresh air. Whatcher think fellers?'

'You can buzz off too!' the young man said, standing his ground. 'I'm not going anywhere and you can't make me.'

They had his arms pinioned behind his back before the words were out of his mouth.

'D'you wanna bet?' Dusty mocked as they shoved him forwards.

Out on the dance floor the girl was laughing, her face

transformed, cheeks rounded, eyes gleaming, lips spread wide, small teeth catching the light. 'I shouldn't laugh,' she said, 'but you got to admit thass funny. He onny start hollerin' because a' me dancing with someone he knew. Thass what start it. And now I'm with you an' I don't know you from Adam. You got to admit . . .' Laughter overwhelmed her.

'I'm Steve,' he told her, adding with some pride, 'Private Steve Wilkins, 7th Armoured Division.'

'I can see that,' she said, looking at the divisional badge on his shoulder. 'I'm Barbara.'

Two other dancers nudged past them and the girl reached out to pull at Barbara's red sweater. ''Lo Spitfire!' she said. 'What was all the hollerin'?'

'Onny Vic,' Barbara told her easily. 'You know the way he go on.'

The girl grimaced and was gone.

'Spitfire?' Steve asked.

'Thass my nickname.'

'Suits you,' he said, admiring her. Small, quick, spitting fire, it was just the right name for her. Full of life and movement, like mercury. Now that they were so close to one another he could see how attractive she was, her features finer than most of the other girls in the hall. She had a funny little nose, like Bob Hope's, but her eyes were large and almond shaped and shadowed by amazingly thick lashes and her mouth was quite the most delicious he'd ever seen, her top lip wide and lusciously curved, her bottom lip so full it was almost as if she was pouting. Then he noticed the red sweater and realised who she was. The jitterbug girl. Good God! I'm dancing with the jitterbug girl. Wonders'll never cease.

'I could have seen him off myself, you know,' she said.

'I don't doubt it,' he told her. With that bold face she could see anybody off.

'I don't need rescuing. Not really. I got three

brothers. If I can cope with them I can cope with anyone.'

Instincts sharpened, he recognised threatened pride and realised that he would have to disguise his noble intentions. 'Actually,' he said, 'I did it for my friend. He was looking for a punch-up.'

'Thass all right then,' she said, and grinned at him, her face devilish. 'What'll they do to him?'

'Depends how lippy he is,' he said and was going to suggest a few lurid possibilities when another young man manoeuvred his partner into position alongside them and leant towards them to talk to her.

He wore the navy-blue jersey and serviceable trousers of the merchant seaman, but his calling would have been obvious even if he'd been wearing civvies. Everything about him proclaimed it, from his mop of dark curly hair, his tanned face and sea-blue eyes, to his rolling gait and his jaunty air and the strong smell of salt and cheap cigarettes that blew in upon them as he talked.

'You all right, kid?' he asked, looking at Barbara.

''Lo Norman,' she said. ''Course. What d'you imagine?'

He grinned at her. 'Just checkin'. He didn't hit you or nothin'?'

'He wouldn't dare,' she said, grinning back.

'We heard him hollerin' the other side the room,' the girl put in.

'I kicked him in the shins.'

'You would,' Norman laughed. 'You lead him a dog's life, poor ol' bor.' And they danced away.

'Who was that?' Steve asked. They looked so alike he was sure this one was a relation.

'My big brother,' she said proudly. 'He's in the merchant navy. Atlantic convoys mostly. He's home on leave for a few weeks. He thinks he's got to look after me when he's on leave. Daft ol' bor! The girl he's dancing with is our cousin.'

Steve felt compelled to ask his next question. 'Is Vic a cousin too? I mean, you're not related or anything are you?' It didn't seem likely but the gawk *had* been acting as though he was a boyfriend. All that business about 'you're my gal'.

She stiffened in his arms and leant back to frown at him. How quickly and entirely her expression could change. She was never the same two minutes at a time. Now, with her lips pursed and her eyes narrowed, she looked like a vixen. 'No,' she said. 'We ain't.'

'My mistake!'

'He live round the corner,' she explained. 'We were at school together – till he went to the grammar. That was half his trouble, goin' to the grammar. Gave him ideas. Made him big-headed. I went out with him a few times. Last summer. Now he reckon he owns me. Which he don't.'

They danced without speaking for a minute or two, or to be more accurate, they swayed gently from foot to foot. The floor was too crowded for anything more adventurous and in any case the waltz was slowing to a halt. Her expression was changing again, growing dreamy.

'How about the next one?' he offered when the music stopped. He couldn't just escort her from the floor and say goodbye to her. Not now.

They were announcing the next dance and it was a quickstep. 'Yes,' she said. 'Why not? D'you jitterbug?'

He didn't. Couldn't. The mere idea made his heart jump. But the need to go on talking to her was stronger than his alarm. 'I'll have a go,' he said.

It was a disaster. The music was too quick, he didn't know which way to turn or what to do with his feet or his arms, he trod on her feet and bumped into everybody within range. Within seconds she was laughing at him, her face spread and lifted the way it had been when she first joined him on the floor.

'Sorry!' he apologised. 'I'm not much of a dancer.'

11

'You can say that again,' she agreed cheerfully. 'You're like an elephant.'

This time he wished she wasn't quite so outspoken. 'Thanks!'

She laughed at him again. 'Never mind. I'll teach you. I'm good with elephants. There's nothin' to it once you get the hang of it. Watch my feet and do what I do.'

He allowed himself to be led, following the beat. She put her hands on his shoulders and pushed him in the direction she wanted him to go, twisting his body first this way and then that. Then she seized his hand and made him turn her, ducking underneath his outstretched arm as if he were leading her and grinning up at him as she turned. There was no possibility of talking. It was all he could do to follow the moves. But the excitement of dancing this amazing dance with this amazing girl more than made up for it. By the end of it all he wasn't simply out of breath, he was bewitched.

'There!' she said, as he walked her back to her friends. 'What d'you think? Four more dances an' you won't know yourself.'

'Can I have four more dances then?'

She gave him her daring expression. 'If you like.'

'I thought you'd say, "*Never again*." I mean after the way I trod on you.'

'You're a challenge,' she laughed at him. 'I'm a great one for a challenge, me.'

They were almost at her table, where four or five girls were waiting for her, all questioning eyes. He'd have to be quick. 'Next waltz then,' he asked.

The next waltz it was, and the next, and three more valiant attempts at the jitterbug, each one marginally better than the last. Then, and a great deal too soon for his liking, it was the last waltz and the lights were dimmed so far that he couldn't see anything except the gleam of her eyes, the tender sweep of those long thick eyelashes and the outline of that expressive face. She was dancing dreamily again, her lips slightly parted. It

12

would be the easiest thing to lean towards her and kiss them. Oh the easiest, most wonderful thing.

'I'll walk you home,' he offered, and was annoyed that his voice was suddenly so husky that he had to cough to clear it. 'I mean, that feller might be hanging around.'

'He'll be with his mates,' she said easily. 'Thass where he'll be.' She didn't sound, or look, the least bit troubled.

'I'll walk you home,' he insisted. 'See you to your door.'

'Thass only round the corner,' she said. 'I usually go with my friends.'

'I'll walk you all home then,' he said. Better to be one of a crowd than to end their evening now. 'Safety in numbers.'

She laughed at that. 'Wait till you seen 'em till you start sayin' things like that,' she warned.

They were a noisy lot and there seemed to be dozens of them, all milling about and joshing one another as they waited for her to get her coat. 'Hassen you up!' they called after her in their Norfolk burr. 'We hain't got orl day!'

After half an evening spent in her company, the coat was just what he expected her to wear. It was a scarlet wraparound jacket, with a hood to cover her wild hair and a tie-belt to pull about her waist, bright, bold and very suitable.

'Red Riding Hood,' he teased, as they inched towards the exit.

She grinned at him. 'Onny *I* eat the wolf!'

I'll bet you do, he thought. But there wasn't time to say anything because she'd gone on ahead of him.

He followed her through the double barrier of the blackout and into a sudden slap of cold air and total darkness. As always on a black night, it took a few seconds for his eyes to adjust. He could just about see that his truck was waiting in front of the hotel where it had dropped him off but the buildings round the square were simply black silhouettes against the Prussian blue of the sky. After the noise and warmth of the dancehall the square was cold and all sound either distant or diffused. Chirruping voices retreated, calling good night, army boots scuffled the pavement, high heels squeaked and clicked, and somewhere to the right of them, unseen bicycles rattled over the cobbles and someone was cranking a car.

'Right then,' he said. 'Which way?'

'Follow the others,' Barbara said. Her friends were already heading north out of the square. She thrust her hands deep into her pockets, and shivered as she strode off. For a second he wondered whether he could hold her hand or put an arm round her shoulders, then he decided he'd better ask first.

'I suppose I'd get thumped if I was to offer you my arm.'

'Yes,' she said. 'You would. I'm an independent spirit, I'll have you know, not some ol' lady with a walkin' stick.'

So they walked on sedately, side by side, she still shivering, he struggling to think of something to say. Something non-committal. Or a joke maybe. She didn't seem to notice his silence. Or perhaps she just wasn't troubled by it.

In fact the expression on his face was making her feel guilty. Well not exactly guilty. That was too strong. Aware that she might have hurt his feelings. It was a novel sensation. Usually she rebuffed advances without giving a thought to the consequences. But this time it was different. This time she felt she had to make amends.

Presently she turned her head towards him and asked him a question. 'You come from London, don't you?'

Relieved to be talking again, he was happy to admit that he did.

'Whereabouts in London?'

They were halfway across the square. 'New Cross,' he told her.

'Where's that?'

'South-east. Near Greenwich.'

'Ah!' She'd heard of Greenwich. 'I've always wanted to go to London. Never have, with the war an' everything. What's it like?'

He was at a loss to know how to begin to tell her. 'Big,' he said, at last. 'Friendly. We live by the station. My dad's a signalman. Well one of the stations, I suppose I should say. We've got two.'

'So have we,' she said, not to be outdone.

'Not in the same road though. Not side by side in the same road.'

That she allowed. 'An' now you're going to France.'

'That's the plan.' He tried to sound as though he was making light of it, but it was a moment of pride to admit it, just the same. It reinstated him.

Her friends were turning a corner, giggling, their dark silhouettes disappearing into the shadows.

'I think you're very brave,' she said. 'Knowin' you got to go, knowin' you got to fight.' And she thought, knowing you might get killed.

'I've known that since the start,' he told her seriously. 'I mean, I was fourteen when the war broke out so I knew I was bound to be in it, sooner or later. After Dunkirk, I mean, well we all knew then.'

'I was twelve when it started,' she told him. 'Still at school. I suppose you were out to work.'

They turned into the dark lane. He would have to admit to his education now and, after what she'd said while they were dancing, he was afraid she might disapprove of it. 'Well no,' he said. 'I was at school too. I stayed on till I was eighteen. I was at grammar school.' And when she didn't comment, 'It doesn't give us all the wrong ideas. I mean, we don't all throw our weight around like that Vic feller. Some of us are quite nice.'

15

'You mustn't mind what I say,' she told him looking at him seriously. 'That was just sour grapes talkin'. I was better'n him when we were at St Nick's. I used to come top a' the class most weeks. Drove him crackers. He wasn't the only one to win a scholarship. I got one too. Only he went to the grammar an' I didn't. Thass the difference.'

He was shocked to hear such a thing. 'But that's terrible,' he said. 'D'you mean to say you won a scholarship to a grammar school and didn't take it?'

'Couldn't afford to,' she said, shrugging her shoulders. 'Anyway girls don't. Leastways, girls what live in the North End don't, an' thass about all there is to that.'

'Well it shouldn't be,' he said hotly. 'It's a waste. And it's not fair. If you had the brains to go to a grammar school, you should have gone.'

'Well it's done now,' turning her face and her mind away from the subject. 'No use cryin' over spilt milk. There's nothing I can do about it.'

'Not now, maybe. But when you're twenty-one you can do something.'

'Like what?'

'Like vote for a different government,' he told her. 'One that'll make some changes.'

They'd reached a dark alleyway. 'We're here,' she said. 'I live just up the alley.'

'Come on then,' he said, turning into the darkness. The offer felt like an intrusion. 'You don't have to come all the way,' she said. 'I can make my own way now.'

'I'm taking you to your door,' he said firmly.

'But this is the North End,' she warned. 'I mean . . .'

'To your door,' he said, leading the way.

'Wait till I light my torch then,' she said. 'Thass a death-trap along here. I don't want you walking into bike or nothin'.'

The alley led into a yard, very dark and evil-smelling, like a cross between a fish shop and a dirty public

16

lavatory. Two rows of small houses stood facing one another across the uneven cobbles. There was a runnel down the centre where he caught a glimpse of water, and odd dark shapes in every corner, mangles, buckets, bicycles, tin baths, an old pram, a ladder, swathes of nets. She was right about the need for a torch.

She led him through the yard, round the corner alongside one of the houses into another, and through that into a third.

'Thass a proper ol' rabbit warren,' she said, stopping at last in front of one of the dark doors and speaking in a whisper. 'I did warn you.'

He whispered too. 'Is this where you live?'

'Yup. This is where I live. This is Rag's Yard.'

He was almost as horrified by the yard as he'd been by her deprived education. 'What, all of you?' he asked, wondering how they all fitted in. 'You and your brothers and . . . everything.'

'No, not my brothers and *everything*,' she said, stung by his implied criticism. 'Just me an' my aunt. I had to move out when Jimmy was born. There wasn't room for all of us at home.'

He was more horrified than ever. Fancy being moved out of your own house because there wasn't room for you. But he didn't say anything because he'd annoyed her enough already. And besides, he was trying to find the words to ask her to go out with him again.

'Look,' he said, forgetting to whisper. 'You don't have to work tomorrow or anything, do you? I mean being Sunday . . .'

She put a finger to her lips in warning and answered him very quietly. 'I help my aunt with the housework of a Sunday.'

'But not all day,' he urged, this time remembering to whisper. 'I mean, I could get a couple of hours off in the afternoon. I could get a bus over. We could go for a walk or something. Or the pictures. I mean if you'd like to.'

17

She was caught between annoyance at his criticism and curiosity about what it would be like to go out with him. She looked up at him for such a long time, while she considered it, that the wait made him breathless. Then curiosity won. 'All right,' she said. 'Where d'you want to meet?'

'By the Corn Exchange. Half past three.'

It was agreed. This gorgeous, extraordinary girl was going to see him again. He'd made a date. He was so happy he wanted to leap about and shout. It took all his self-control to restrict himself to shifting his feet.

'Yes. You'd better go,' she said misinterpreting the signs. 'Take my torch, or you'll never find your way out.'

But even with the torchlight to guide him, he was in a state of such clumsy elation, he tripped over a bucket and stumbled into a mangle.

Her whispered query breathed across the alley. 'You all right?'

'Two broken legs,' he joked back. 'Few cracked ribs. Never felt better.'

'Idiot!' she laughed. And opened the door.

CHAPTER TWO

It was very dark inside the house, for the blackout curtains were drawn, the oil lamp was out and the fire had dwindled to a single coal which was little more than a pink glow in a heap of whitening ash and gave out no light at all. Fortunately, being in the dark didn't worry Barbara Nelson. Not that she would have admitted to it if it had. Having grown up in the North End, with a harsh-tongued fisherman for a father, she'd learned to keep her fears hidden from a very early age. In fact, it was her mother's proud boast that 'our Babs' was the toughest thing in shoe-leather. 'Blust gal!' she would brag to her neighbours. 'She don' turn hair fer nothin'.'

Until that evening Barbara had shared her opinion. Now she wasn't quite so sure, for her hair was bristling from nape to forehead and her head was so full of unfamiliar emotions that she felt quite giddy under their impact. Had she really agreed to go out with a soldier? She, hard-to-get, wise-cracking, independent Spitfire Nelson, the girl who made mincemeat of wolves? What on earth had got into her?

She picked her way through the furniture to the mantelpiece, scrabbled her fingers along it until she found the candlestick and matches and produced a light. But then, instead of removing her coat and tiptoeing upstairs to bed as she usually did on a Saturday night, she stood before the hearth, candlestick in hand and leant forward towards the mirror. She'd never been vain. She was too busy and too sensible for that. So it was most unlike her to spend time gazing at her reflection. But everything she'd done that evening had been unlike her – at least everything she'd done after

19

she met Steve Wilkins. Just talking to him had made her feel special. And the look on his face when he'd asked her out had been the best of all. That had made her feel beautiful. To remember it made her blush, even there in the chill of that small cold room.

She put her free hand against her cheek to hold back its rising warmth, and thought how silly she was being. She wasn't beautiful. She was just Barbara Nelson who lived in the North End and was very ordinary.

But the person who gazed back at her from the mirror was unlike any image of herself she'd ever seen. The funny face she'd accepted until then, with its odd-shaped nose, its rough skin and its mop of uncontrollable hair, had been transformed. What she saw now was almost ethereal, heart-shaped and dreamy and set off by a halo of thick, dark, contented curls, with skin the colour of apricots, brow and cheekbones gilded by candlelight, eyes huge and lustrous. She gazed and gazed until her breath misted the glass. How could she look so serene when her thoughts were in such a turmoil?

And come to that, how could she look so innocent when she'd just been telling lies? Well not exactly lies perhaps, but not the whole truth, and she'd always been a stickler for the truth. But tonight, when Steve had asked her whether she and Vic were related, she'd said no, at once and without thinking, and that wasn't strictly true. And it wasn't fair to Vic either. Until that evening, she'd accepted that they were as good as engaged. Not committed, with a ring and everything, but sort of understood so that she knew what sort of direction her life was going to take – a few years earning her living and larking about with her friends, dancing and going to the pictures, keeping her admirers at arm's length, a little while in the army if the war was still going on when she was eighteen, and then she and Vic would get married and settle down and raise a family the same as everyone else in the North End. They'd been going out, off and on, since she was sixteen and although she didn't exactly love him, she liked him well enough, they got on all right, they were well matched. And she knew how to handle him, which was half the battle when it came to being married. Now she wasn't so sure that that was what she wanted to do. In fact, she wasn't sure about anything. I don't know what's got into me, she thought.

But that wasn't true. She *did* know. It was because Steve was so attractive. Because he wouldn't take no for an answer. Because he was tougher than she was. Not tough in the way she was used to in the North End, all fists and mouth, but in a gentle way. Strong and silent, leading her away from trouble, with his hand under her elbow, insisting without saying a word. She'd never been treated like that before, not in the whole of her life. And especially by such a looker. The way he laughed, throwing back his head, brown eyes shining. You could like him for that alone. And she did like him. There was no doubt about that. She liked him very much. He couldn't jitterbug for toffee nuts but waltzing with him had been terrific. She'd fancied quite a lot of young men in the last couple of years but always in a rather cerebral way, aware of their charm but physically unmoved by them. Now it made her blush for the second time that evening to remember what she'd been feeling as she danced with this one.

Behind her, the room was in its usual evening order, clean, tidy and swept speckless, but for once that was an irritant to her rather than a comfort. It wasn't right for the world to be so ordinary and predictable when she had changed so much. She could still smell the sausage and chips that she and her aunt had eaten for supper although the gate-legged table had been cleared, folded down and stood against the wall, all crumbs had been burnt, the frying pan scoured clean, and the remaining food carefully stored away, marge in its dish, bread in its tin. Her aunt Becky was a careful housewife and did

21

constant battle with cockroaches and 'other such vermin'. Even the rag rug had been given a beating before she settled for the night. The red circle at its centre might keep out any devils that happened to be looking down the chimney but lack of dust and crumbs was the best deterrent to black beetles.

The two rules of the house were *clean as you go* and *a place for everything and everything in its place*. Even now, excited as she was, Barbara was careful to take her coat upstairs to put it away and she carried the candle guardedly, shielding the flame with the palm of her hand so that it wouldn't splutter and drop wax.

Like most of the cottages in the North End, Becky Bosworth's was a basic two-roomed dwelling with no hall, no kitchen, no bathroom, no running water, no means of cooking other than the open fire and no sanitation. The two rooms were built one on top of the other like a pair of boxes and the stairs were in one corner, closed off by a door at either end and rising in a very steep spiral and complete darkness. So a candle was a necessity. As was a chamber-pot under the double bed to save you having to run out to the privy in the cold. And a stone hot-water bottle for warmth in the winter.

The one in the bed that night still had quite a bit of heat in it. Barbara eased it over the mattress until it was underneath her cold feet. Now that she'd blown out the candle and opened the curtains to let in the moonlight, she could see that frost ferns had already grown halfway up the window and that her breath was pluming before her in the cold air of the room. She heaped the bedclothes round her shoulders and tried to settle to sleep. But she was as wide awake as if it were early morning. Steve, she thought. I wonder what you're doing now. Halfway back to base, I s'pose. And she wondered whether he was thinking of her.

The minutes flowed pleasurably by, rich with remembered delights. Aunt Becky snored companionably. The last of the night's revellers made their noisy way back to the North End. There was quite a racket going on in one of the adjoining yards, a gang of boys horsing around and hollering, singing rude songs at the top of their voices, '*Roll me oover in the cloover* . . .' kicking the dustbins. They go on like that, Barbara thought, someone'll be down after them an' they'll get a whack round the lugs. I bet you never see Steve kicking the dustbins – even if he did trip over the mangle.

On which thought, she finally drifted into sleep.

Three rows of houses away, over in Cooper's Yard, Vera Castlemain was waiting up. She always sat up on a Saturday night, to keep the fire in until her son came home. When her husband Shrimpy wasn't at sea with the fishing boats, he spent his evenings in the pub and took himself off to bed as soon as he got in, usually grumbling that she spoilt the boy and that she was wasting good coal. But she sat on, her head bent over the book she wasn't reading, her ears strained for the first sound of her returning darling, eager for his company.

Even when he came home after midnight, she was glad to see him and got up at once to brew him a mug of tea or Camp coffee and to say, as she did that night, 'Did 'ee have a good time, lovey?'

Vic settled in his father's seat before the fire, propped his feet on the fender and smiled at her. 'You know me.'

'Was your Barbara there, my lovey?'

He smiled again. 'Of course. I took her, didn't I?'

She couldn't help admiring him. He was such a good boy, so strong an' clever an' handsome, an' head over heels in love with his Barbara. Had a picture of her on the ol' wall upstairs an' everythin'. Though she didn't always treat him right, bad little mawther. Teased him ragged sometimes. 'Be nice when you're married,' she said, handing him his mug of coffee.

23

'Yes,' he agreed. 'It will.' There'll be a bit less of this silly nonsense in the dancehall then. He'd spent the last half of the evening in the pub with his friends drinking a pint of bitter and talking himself out of his ill-humour, but the memory of being manhandled still rankled.

He looks a bit down, poor lad, Vera thought, settling back in her own chair on the other side of the fire. And she tried to cheer him up by reminding him of how popular he was. 'I s'pose all your friends was there.'

'Yes,' he agreed. 'They were. Matter of fact, I went off to the pub afterwards with Spikey and ol' Tubby.'

'That was nice.'

'We been planning our futures,' he said. Actually they'd been bragging about their ambitions – but that was planning in a way. 'I'm not going to be desk clerk all my life. You watch me, Ma. In five years' time I shall have business of my own. Staff, big car. There'll be no holding me then.' And no frogmarching me out of a dancehall either. 'You just watch. Then I'll come back here an' build you a big house by the river with a garden and a summer house, an' you can sit out in the sun an' eat strawberries all day an' be a lady of leisure.'

Vera didn't doubt it. He was so clever he was capable of anything. 'That'll be lovely,' she purred, round face beaming. 'Drink your coffee, lovey. Don't let it go cold.'

'I think I shall have a bit of a lie-in tomorrow,' he decided, as he sipped the coffee. His father was at sea till midday so the luxury was possible. 'I'll probably nip round an' see Barbara in the afternoon.' She might need talking round a bit after all that stupid nonsense with the soldiers but she usually went out with the gang of a Sunday and he was part of the gang. 'We might go to the pictures. There's a cowboy on.'

'Thass right, bor,' Vera approved. 'You like good cowboy.'

The sight of her bland doting face was making him feel irritable, the way it so often did, reminding him of how badly he'd been treated. Under the muddling haze of hurt pride and ignominy, grievance still swelled and prowled, a dark pirhana in a murky pool. 'There's too many soldiers in this town,' he complained.

She agreed with him automatically. 'Too many on 'em. Yes, my lovey, thass the size uv it. Millions so that say in the paper. Off to France, poor boys. An' then what'll happen to 'em out there? Thousands'll be killed so that say in the paper. That don't bear thinkin' about.'

Vic was lost in his complaint and paid no attention to her. 'Far too many,' he said. 'You can't move for them. Great feet everywhere.' He looked down at his own neat size eights and remembered the great feet of that soldier, walking out onto the dance floor with Barbara. Just because he's tall and he's got great big feet, that doesn't give him the right to walk all over us and he needn't think it.

Back in the barracks, the big feet were propped up on the bedrail while their owner stretched out on the inadequate length of his mattress and smoked his last cigarette of the evening – like everybody else in the hut. Their twenty-four, companionable red fireflies glowed and eddied in the darkness around him. It was long past lights-out and they were gradually settling for the night in a diminishing murmur of voices and a fug of stale sweat, beery breath, discarded socks and dying cigarette stubs. Despite the discomforts of army life, Private Steve Wilkins was supremely and utterly happy. Not for him the surprise of his dancing partner, far less the jealousy of Victor Castlemain. He had found his girl.

CHAPTER THREE

That Sunday morning was the longest and most enervating that Steve Wilkins had ever dawdled through. It was intolerable to be stuck in camp when the sun was shining as though it were already spring and his girl was a mere ten flat country miles away. There were newspapers to read and routine chores to get through but neither occupied him for long. By mid afternoon, his renowned calm was being sorely tested.

He climbed aboard the bus to Lynn in a scramble of boots and impatience and began to crane his neck for his first sight of her long before he reached Tuesday Market Square. And then to tangle his eagerness into frustration, she was late.

Woman's privilege, he told himself, trying to stay calm and be sensible about it. But his heart was racing as if he were on manoeuvres. He leant against the wall of the Corn Exchange, fished in his battledress for his umpteenth cigarette of the day and settled to wait, one foot on the pavement, the other resting against the base of the central column, his face serious in the pale sunlight of the afternoon.

Which was how Barbara saw him as she came briskly round the corner and set off at a stride across the square. He looked so handsome that her heart gave a sudden lurch at the sight of him. And it leapt again, when he turned his head, smiled, stubbed out his cigarette and strode towards her. Oh the rhythm of those long legs, the strength of that face, the warmth of that smile. It lifted his entire face, widening his eyes, rounding his cheeks, stretching his mouth. That's a Cupid's bow, she thought, gazing at it. And, before she could stop herself, she imagined being kissed by it. And that took her breath away. So naturally she took instant refuge in ribbing.

'Don't start,' she warned, her face bold with daring. 'I know I'm late.'

He held up his hands in mock surrender. 'Did I say anything?' he laughed. 'I appeal to you, your Honour, did I say a word?' His face was glowing with the delight of seeing her again, brown eyes shining, skin flushed with so much happy colour he could have rivalled the tan of the Desert Rats.

'You can look words,' she said.

They were so close he could feel the warmth of her body. And her eyelashes were wondrous, so long and thick and tender that he was weak with desire just looking down at them. Then she lifted them and looked up at him with those amazing eyes . . . Seen in daylight the impact of her eyes was extraordinary. In the dancehall and on their magical walk home, he was sure they'd been brown. He'd dreamed of them as brown, sleeping and waking. But they weren't. They were green, like the curve of a sea wave just before it breaks, a stunning, gorgeous, translucent, radiant green.

'You've got green eyes,' he said, inadequately. And was then confused.

Now it was her turn to laugh at him. 'Yes. I've noticed. One on each side of my nose an' all.'

He wanted to tell her how beautiful they were, how beautiful she was, but it was too early for that, so he simply asked, 'Where're we going?'

'The pictures?'

'Which one?'

'There's a musical on at the Majestic.' She knew some of the gang would be there and she'd get ribbed rotten when they next saw her. But living in a small town that was something she had to expect. There'd be people she knew wherever they went and at least it was supposed to be a good film.

27

'The Majestic it is then,' he said and wondered whether they could sit in the back row. And that made him aware of how much he wanted to kiss her.

'Hassen you up then,' she ordered. 'Thass too cold to be standing about.'

'You're such a bully!' he laughed. 'I'll bet you bully the cat.'

'We hain't got a cat,' she said.

'But you would if you had. Look how you thumped that Victor feller.'

As they strode off to the cinema, she wondered whether they would bump into that Victor feller and hoped they wouldn't. It surprised her to realise how much she wanted privacy that afternoon.

As it turned out, the cinemas had to do without Vic's custom that day because his bit of a lie-in lasted until his father came bellowing home for Sunday dinner and by the time the meal had been eaten and he finally got to Rag's Yard, the light was already fading and Barbara had been gone for over an hour.

That was the trouble with that gang of hers. They were too quick off the mark. 'Where've they gone?' he asked Mrs Bosworth. 'Did she say?'

Becky Bosworth pushed a wisp of grey hair back inside her hairnet and gave him a quizzical look but she didn't enlighten him. 'No,' she said.

'Who'd she go with, then?' he insisted, scowling at her. With that foxy face and those boot-button eyes looking at him so sharply, she could be very off-putting. 'Was it Mavis and Joan and that lot?'

'No.'

'Who then?'

'A friend.'

His heart sank so suddenly it was painful. She couldn't have gone with a friend. All sorts of people asked her out but she always said No. It was never just *one* friend. If she wasn't going out with him, she always went round with her gang, hordes of them, giggling and horsing about. Safety in numbers, she said. The stupid old mawther was making a mistake, or making it up.

'What friend?' he asked and his face was dark with suspicion.

Becky didn't know who it was except that it was a feller. That much was obvious. You only had to see the way she'd gone rushing off, in her best blouse an' all. Not that she was going to tell Victor Castlemain *that*. ''Ers,' she said.

A combination of hurt pride and monosyllabic answers drove Vic to insolence. '*A friend! Hers!*' he mocked. Some of these old women round here were so dumb, it was all you could do not to holler at them. 'Which one? Hain't she got a name?' A girlfriend he could tolerate. But his head was spinning with remembered images and all of them wearing khaki. No, no, no, it *couldn't* be a soldier. She was scathing about soldiers. It couldn't be. Mustn't be.

Becky decided to give him the benefit of a sentence. 'Git you off uv my doorstep, bor,' she said. 'You mek the 'ol place look untidy.' If Barbara was going to annoy him by going out with someone else, let *her* deal with it when he hollered.

So he had to leave her none the wiser. He stormed out of the alley dark with temper, his fists in his pockets. Dusk was already masking the debris in the yards and the sky was full of turbulent clouds. If he had any idea where she'd gone he could have followed her and seen for himself who she was with. But she could be anywhere.

There was a squashed tin can lying in the runnel directly in front of his shoe. He kicked it viciously into the wall. Bloody war! Bloody army! Bloody Desert Rats! She *couldn't* have gone out with a soldier. Not his Barbara. Not Spitfire Nelson. But where was she? And who *was* she with?

*

29

She was in the back row of the Majestic, blissfully warm and sharing Steve's last cigarette. They were being terribly well-behaved. He hadn't even put an arm round her shoulders or anything. But she was so aware of him it was as though there was an electric current crackling between them, linking them together. Neither of them had paid much attention to the second feature, which was pretty ropey, but the main film had been diverting in its technicolored, all-singing, all-dancing, totally incredible way and now the familiar globe was spinning on the screen and British Movietone was about to *bring the news to the free peoples of the world*. And that had to be watched no matter what they might be feeling.

'*Monty visits the famous Desert Rats*,' the voice-over said. And there he was, surrounded by men in khaki, as the snow fell steadily upon them, flecking his familiar black beret with white. And it wasn't just the beret that looked familiar.

'Why thass Lynn,' Barbara said, leaning forward for a closer look. 'Thass the station. I didn't know he was down here. That must ha' been las' week, when it snowed.'

'That's right,' Steve said, his voice proud. 'It was.'

'Were you there?'

He tempered his pride with self-mockery. 'I'm the third beret along on the left.'

'Oh yes,' she teased. 'I can see you. The ugly one.'

They watched as the great man addressed his troops.

'Why don't he wear his jacket in all that snow?' she asked. 'You know, that ol' sheepskin of his. He look a right fool standin' around with no coat on.'

'He wanted us to see his medal ribbons,' Steve explained. 'That's what the tankies said anyway. They were bellyaching about him for hours after.'

'Why?'

'He had the wrong badge in his cap. See it? The one this side's the General Staff badge. That's all right. But

30

the other one's the badge of the Royal Tank Regiment an' you're not entitled to wear that unless you're a tankie. They were up in arms about it.'

That intrigued her. 'I thought he was their hero.'

'He is,' he told her. 'That's why they rib him. We go by opposites in the army. The more popular you are, the more you get ribbed.'

'Do you get ribbed?' she asked, thinking, I bet he does. I bet he's one of the most popular men on the camp.

Steve was torn between an undeniable desire to let her know how well-liked he was and an equally powerful compulsion not to show off. Fortunately, there wasn't time to answer because the newscaster had turned his attention to the war in the Pacific.

'American troops storm ashore at Los Negros in the Admiralty Islands,' he intoned, as the screen filled with approaching landing craft and hundreds of soldiers leapt into the water and began their dangerous wade ashore, rifles held above their heads, faces seamed and grim beneath their rounded helmets.

They're going to be killed, Barbara thought, and she was filled with a yearning pity for them. They're going to be shot down and killed the minute they get on that beach. Thousands of them. It was something she'd known all through the war in a vague, generalised way but now the knowledge was immediate and personal. These men, struggling through the water, were going to be killed. Were dead already in all probability, poor devils. That's what happens when armies invade. Men get killed. That'll happen when the Second Front begins. They'll be killed on the beaches in France too. Men like these. Men like Steve. And that made her heart contract with a new and personal distress.

'I hate this war,' she said, passionately.

He turned to look at her in the light reflected from the screen and was torn by the distress on her face. 'Let's go,' he decided. 'We don't want to see the rest, do we? It's only General MacArthur poncing about.'

The narrator was continuing his commentary. '*From a warship somewhere off-shore, the landings are watched by General MacArthur.*' And the plump general was holding a pair of binoculars to his eyes, watching the carnage he'd commanded. No, she didn't want to see any more.

They struggled along the back row, past the outstretched feet and busy hands of all the snogging couples, and emerged into chill air and the monochrome of ordinary life. Barbara put up her hood and tied her red coat tightly about her waist, and they set off as if they knew where they were going. In fact they were walking aimlessly, away from the thought of death and injury, heading east into the wind and feeling decidedly cold after the fug in the cinema. It was evening and extremely dark, for although the moon was almost full, the clouds were still low and fast-moving, so its light was intermittent and unpredictable.

Barbara tried to make conversation as they walked because she was still upset. 'My ma loves the pictures,' she said. 'Specially musicals. She say they take her out of herself. I ain't so sure that's a good thing.'

'Why?'

'I suppose thass because you come back with such a bump afterwards. I mean, all that colour an' everythin' bright an' a happy endin', an' then we come out to this, everythin' grey an' run-down an' dusty. Nothing changed. The war still goin' on. The Second Front coming.' She'd always thought her mother's escapism was pretty childish, now, shuddering with pity for those poor marines, it was an affront.

'It won't last for ever,' he tried to reassure. 'Once we get going.'

But that didn't comfort her.

They'd reached an open space where bare trees

rustled their branches and a footpath led into the darkness. 'What's this?' he asked. 'Is it a park?'

'Thass the Walks,' she told him, pulling her mind away from death and invasion. 'There's a tower bit further up.' And to prove her right, the clouds suddenly blew away from the moon and there it was in the moonlight, the Red Tower, stolid and hexagonal and faintly pink on its grassy mound. 'Used to be part of the ol' city walls,' she said, as they walked towards it. 'Part uv the ol' defences. War again, you see. There's never an end on it.'

'When this lot's over,' he told her seriously, 'the first thing we'll do is to find a way to stop the next one before it begins.'

'Thass all very well,' she said. 'But what about this one? Thass the one what ought to be stopped. I hate this war.'

Her voice sounded so wild that he stopped walking and turned to look at her. She had an odd, taut expression on her face, as if she was fighting back tears, and the sight of it made him feel as if someone were pinching his heart.

'Please don't look like that,' he begged.

She blinked and scowled, angry to be so near tears. 'I can't help it,' she said. 'It's all so awful. People gettin' bombed an' shot an' blown to pieces an' drowned. An' all for what? Thass what I want to know. All for what?'

'To stop the Germans,' he told her earnestly. 'They won't stop till they're beaten and if we don't stop them they'll get worse and worse.'

She knew the truth of it. She'd always known the truth of it. But that didn't stop the anguish. 'Why hain't there another way?' she said wildly. 'There ought to be another way.'

'We'll find it,' he promised. 'Once there's peace.'

'Once there's peace!' she echoed, mockingly. 'Oh yes, I've heard all that.' Her eyes were dark in the

33

moonlight and lustrous with tears. 'But when will it be?'

'Soon,' he said. 'Really.'

'Not soon enough. When our Norman's at sea we never know what's happening to him from one week to the next . . . An' there's all these soldiers bein' killed an' people bein' bombed . . .'

There was no time to think of the proprieties. He put his arms round her, wanting to protect her and comfort her, acting instinctively. 'Please!' he implored. 'Please don't be upset. I can't bear it.'

She didn't scold him for taking liberties, but her expression changed in the abrupt way he'd come to expect. Now it was a question, eyebrows raised, eyes wondering. Why not? it said. What's it to you?

The answer was in his mind and very nearly spoken. But he couldn't say it. Not yet. It was much too soon. Instead he pulled her towards him and kissed her full on the lips.

It took them both by surprise, he because it was done so easily and naturally and because she answered it and didn't move away, she because it was the first time in her life that a young man had kissed her without asking permission first. By the time he lifted his head, they were both out of breath.

The silence effervesced around them, as they stood quite still and gazed at one another, his face full of affection, hers questioning. 'Do you believe in love at first sight?' he asked.

The words spun like Catherine wheels in the little space between them, sparking disbelief and hope and amazement.

'I don't know,' she admitted. 'Thass what people say . . . I mean you hear of it, don't you.' Was he going to tell her *he* loved *her*? He couldn't. Could he? They'd only just met.

He cupped her face in his hands, drinking in the sight of her before he kissed her again. I love you, he thought. I shall love you for the rest of my life. But he couldn't say it. Not yet. Not so soon. And in any case, there was no need for words. Desire was speaking for them, leading them on, gently, steadily, inevitably, like a field of daisies opening to the sun. And as the clouds drifted away from the face of the moon, he kissed again, this time with passion. Oh yes, they could say everything that needed to be said with kisses.

Afterwards they had no idea how long they stayed in the Walks that night. There is no such thing as time when you are caught up in the powerful magic of sex, especially when it's for the first amazing time. There is no such thing as place, either. They were vaguely aware that there were bare trees rattling and creaking in the shadows of the park but they could have been any-where. There was no reality beyond the circle of their arms and within that circle it was all sensation.

Eventually they were called to their senses by the sound of a church clock striking the hour. But the significance of those repeated strokes didn't penetrate Steve's consciousness until they were an echo. Then he stopped between kisses to wonder what time it was.

She was dreamy with desire, her eyes half closed. 'Midnight,' she said.

His tone and expression changed. 'Oh Christ!'

She opened her eyes at that. 'What is it?'

'I'm late. I've missed the last bus. I should've been in camp a minute ago.'

'Is that bad?'

'Could be,' he admitted. 'I don't know. I've never been late before.'

She was instantly full of practical concern. 'How will you get back?'

That wasn't a problem. 'I'll walk.'

She lay back in his arms again, enjoying their support. 'Have you got to go now?'

It was too great a temptation. 'Not yet,' he decided. 'I'm so late another ten minutes won't make much

35

difference. I'll walk you home.' Whatever was going to happen would happen. There was no point in thinking about it. Not when her mouth was so close he could taste her lips before he kissed them.

They strolled back to the North End as though they were taking part in a slow three-legged race, thigh to thigh and holding one another about the waist.

'I *must* go now,' he said as he kissed her for the last – or almost the last – time. 'I'll see you tomorrow evening, if I'm still a free man.'

'I'll be at the Corn Exchange seven sharp,' she promised.

And she was. But it wasn't Steve who came tumbling from the truck to sprint across the road towards her. It was a small, skinny soldier with mouse-coloured hair who said his name was Dusty, handed her a letter, and watched her as she read it.

And was watched in his turn by Victor Castlemain, from his carefully chosen vantage point on the other side of the square, half-hidden in the doorway of the Duke's Head Hotel. He'd followed all the comings and goings that evening, had seen Barbara arrive and watched her as she waited. Now he peered out to see what she would do when she'd read her letter.

It was short and to the point and didn't take her long.

Dear Barbara,
   I'm sorry about this but I'm on jankers so I shan't be able to get out until Thursday. Can we meet then, same place, same time? Just tell Dusty yes or no.

'Yes,' she said, casually. 'Tell him that'll be all right. And thanks for bringing the letter.' Then she tucked it into her pocket and strode off to see if any of her friends were in the queue for the pictures. She was disappointed but she certainly wasn't going to show it.

Victor, following at a discreet distance, was relieved

to see that the company she chose was female and that she was in cracking form, laughing and teasing.

'Thought you were off with some ol' soldier,' Joan called out to her.

'No,' Barbara said, her voice mocking. 'Course I hain't. What would I be doin' with some ol' soldier? I'm in the pride of my youth! You took root on that pavement Mavis, or is there room for me?'

They made way for her, giggling and horsing around and telling her what a laugh she was. They sounded so cheerful that Victor was tempted to stroll across and join them. But he thought better of it. He was quite sure now that the 'friend' *was* a soldier and that the skinny one had been a messenger. I'll watch every evening, he decided, and just see what happens next and who it is. The trucks always parked in the square at the same place and the same time, so it shouldn't be difficult.

Thursday was a very long time coming for all three of them, and when it did, it was one of those dark dank days when there is so much moisture in the air that your clothes are damp the minute you step outside the front door. Victor was cold in his doorway and by the time Barbara reached the square her hair was spangled with moisture.

But Steve was there, standing beside the column, smoking a damp cigarette and trying to look patient. This time there was no ribbing about being late. This time they hurled themselves into one another's arms and two kisses later they were heading off to the pictures, eager to be in the back row again. Neither of them noticed that they were being shadowed.

'Was it bad?' she asked as they walked.

He'd forgotten all about his punishment. 'What?'

'Bein' in prison. Jankers.'

He was delighted by her mistake, delighted to be able to explain to her. 'They don't lock you up for being late back,' he said, cuddling her into his side.

'What do they do then?'

37

'Make you march up and down all evening in full kit.'

'Thass daft!' she said scathingly.

'That's the army for you,' he said, enjoying her scorn. 'Anyway it's over an' done with now. I shan't have to do it again.'

Although he was sorely tempted to run the risk – that night and every subsequent evening that they spent together. To be parted from her after such a short time in her company was agony. Waiting had taken on quite a different meaning for him now. He waited from one date to another, reliving the last and looking forward to the next, lost in a tumescent dream of the most exquisitely unresolved pleasure, the world and the war pushed into the shadows.

On Saturday he took her to the Corn Exchange and they spent the entire evening together and danced every dance except the tango, much to the interest of her friends and annoyance of Victor Castlemain, who danced every dance too, with somebody or other, and did his best to be good company and not to mention what was going on even though he was thinking very dark thoughts.

On Wednesday, when Vic was at the pictures with Tubby and Spikey, they returned to the Walks and spent the entire evening kissing under the trees.

'This is probably a daft thing to say,' he confessed, 'but I feel as if I've known you all my life.'

'That ain't daft,' she said. 'I feel the same. I tell you things I've never told to no one else in the world.'

'Do you? Like what?'

'Like wishin' I could ha' gone to grammar school. That was a secret till you come along.'

'Secrets and dreams,' he said, remembering his own. 'Do you dream?'

'Oh yes.'

'What about?'

'All sorts uv things. Sailin' an' flyin' in aeroplanes. Bein' in the army sometimes.'

'The army? What makes you think of that?'

'I shall have to join the army, or somethin', won't I, if the war's still on when I'm eighteen an' I have to register.'

The news stuck pins in his heart. He didn't want her anywhere near this war and certainly not in the army. 'When's your birthday?' he asked, hoping it wouldn't be too soon.

It wasn't. 'January 6th,' she said. 'When's yours?'

'April 23rd. I'm nearly three years older than you.' Nearly twenty to her seventeen. It was perfect.

'I wish we could stop the clock,' she sighed. 'I'd like to stay here like this for ever an' ever.'

'So would I,' he said devoutly. And kissed her to prove it.

But the clock moved on despite them. Spring and the invasion were coming and much, much too quickly. February lengthened its stride into March, March winds blew them all breathlessly into April, with days so warm and peaceful and bright with sunshine that it seemed incongruous for him to be in uniform and even more incongruous that they should be strolling arm in arm under a sky full of bombers heading out to northern France. Soon daffodils nodded in every flower bed and the gardens were yellow with forsythia. And then, two weeks into April, he arrived one Wednesday evening to tell her he was off on manoeuvres again and that they wouldn't see one another for ten days.

The thought of being parted tightened her chest and caught at her throat so that her expression changed and clouded, before she could prevent it. There was nothing to be done about it. They both knew that. If he'd had orders that's all there was to it. He would have to go – just as he'd have to go when the invasion started. And they would have to accept it and be sensible about it.

'I'll write every day,' he promised, holding her face between his hands.

'See you do,' she teased. 'Or I shall have something to say when you get back.'

'It's only a little while,' he said, comforting them both. 'I mean what's ten days? It'll be over before we know where we are. Anyway, let's not think about it. What's on at the pictures?'

So, like everyone else in wartime, they didn't think about it. When they kissed goodbye on their last evening together, they were both deliberately bright and cheerful. But it was a bitter-sweet moment for all that.

CHAPTER FOUR

Victor Castlemain had spent a miserable morning at the bank, totting up recalcitrant figures and trying to make sense of the situation he was in. Normally the sight of one of his nice accurate columns gave him a pleasant sense of achievement, especially when the manager came by and praised him for it – as he often did – but now it was just an irritation.

It had been six weeks since Barbara started going out with that soldier – damn nearly seven – and he couldn't be off knowing it, for there they were, night after night, strolling about the town with their arms round each other or lurking under the trees in the Walks, kissing and cuddling and being stupid. He felt sure people were beginning to talk about it, and the misery of being so publicly and obviously rejected was tying his innards into a perpetual knot of anguish and jealousy. It wasn't as if he could complain about it either, even to Spikey Spencer and Tubby, who were his best and oldest friends, because he'd look a fool if he did. He just had to get on with things and pretend it didn't matter. It was the hardest thing he'd ever had to cope with.

Sighing, he dipped his pen in the ink and tried to settle to work. Another five minutes and he could cut off for dinner. Spikey and Tubby had invited him to join them at their works canteen and, although the food would be foul, he'd agreed for want of anything better to do. Food was foul everywhere these days, and at least old Spikey would make him laugh.

As it turned out old Spikey did a great deal better than that.

'Got some news for you, Victor,' he said happily as

41

they clattered their trays onto the nearest table. 'The Desert Rats are off on manoeuvres.'

It was like a great light being switched on. Heaven-sent. Couldn't be better. It cheered him up at once. 'When?' he asked, setting his plate on the table. 'How long for?'

Spikey pushed a chunk of wet white cabbage towards his forkful of Woolton pie and considered it before he lifted it into his mouth. 'Went yesterday,' he said, chomping. 'Whole kit and caboodle. For a fortnight.'

'Smashing, eh?' Tubby beamed, trellising his portion of the pie with ribbons of HP sauce. 'Now we can have our gals back.' He spoke as if they'd been torn away from him in droves although, in fact, he'd never persuaded a single one to give him so much as a glance. 'Be a different story this Sat'day night, bor.'

Vic could already see himself dancing with Barbara again. How quickly things change in wartime! With that lot out of the way, they could all get back to normal. The Woolton pie was almost palatable – if you swallowed it quickly. 'Wizard!' he said. He'd get Ma to wash his white shirt – there wouldn't be time to send it to the laundry – and he'd wear his blue tie with the red and orange flowers, because she always teased him about that one. Have a haircut, maybe. Buy her some chocolate if he'd got enough coupons left. He'd been a bit heavy on the sweet ration this month, being in a low state, but Ma would help him out. Roll on Saturday. In the meantime – while the cat's away – he might just go and see old Ma Nelson. Drop her a few hints about what was going on. In case she didn't know. Be a kindness really. Public spirited. And it would do Barbara some good too in a roundabout sort of way. All gals needed warning about the way soldiers went on and she wouldn't listen to him. Glowing with righteous concern, he decided he'd call in at the yards on his way back to the bank.

Dodger's Yard was full of people that lunch hour, for

the fishing fleet had come in on the morning tide so the women were all out cleaning and untangling the nets, and just to complicate their lives, the kids were home from school. They sat placidly on the doorsteps eating hunks of bread and jam or prowled the yard in arguing gangs or played football as well as they could among the nets, dodging the dripping water, the seaweed and their mothers' irritation.

Maudie Nelson was hard at work in the middle of the mêlée, with a sacking apron over her skirt, a navy-blue gansey over her ample bosom and one of her husband's caps on her bush of greying hair, worn back to front to protect her neck from the drips. She looked up mildly at Vic as he picked his way towards her.

'You come to give us 'and, bor?' she asked, pulling a lump of weed from the net.

He moved his legs deftly out of the way, struck, yet again, by how completely unlike her daughter she was; she so dumpy and slow moving, Barbara so skinny and quick; she all beige and navy blue except for her grey hair, Barbara all bright colours and bright eyes. 'Not in my working clothes,' he said. 'Good catch, was it?'

'Middlin'. What d'we owe the honour then?'

'I've got some news for you,' he said and told her about the manoeuvres.

She wasn't particularly interested. 'Sort a' rehearsin', I s'pose,' she said mildly. 'How's your mother goin' along? She still got the rheumaticals, hev she?'

Vic wasn't interested in his mother's 'rheumaticals'.

'Be glad to see the back of them,' he said.

'You hain't got rheumaticals an' all, have you bor?'

'No,' Victor said struggling to stay calm. 'I was talking about the soldiers.'

'Thass on account of gettin' wet all the time on those thing-a-mees.'

Victor stifled a groan. 'What I *mean*', he said heavily, 'is Barbara won't be seeing so much of them.'

'Not if they hain't there, bor. Stands to reason.'

43

Was she deliberately misunderstanding him? Vic thought. Or can't she help it? He would have to spell it out to her. 'Your Barbara's been going round with one of the soldiers.'

Maudie Nelson took the news with perfect aplomb and total disbelief. 'Don't you worry about our Barbara,' she said easily. 'Thass just the way gals go on. She'll marry you in the end, you see if she don't. She's a good gal.' And she shook out a swathe of net so suddenly that weed and water spun out all over his jacket before he could dodge it.

'I'm off back to work', he said, making a joke of it, 'before I get drowned.' And went at once, thinking what a waste of time it had been. Silly old mawther. She should've been glad I came to tell her. Not shook water all over me. Still, the great thing is *they* won't be at the dance. And *I* will.

He couldn't wait for Saturday night and grew short-tempered with impatience at its slow approach, arriving at the Corn Exchange before the doors were open, even though he was perfectly well aware that he would lose face among his friends if he appeared too eager. He'd managed to get the chocolate, he was wearing his clean shirt and his flash tie, he'd even polished his shoes. Come on! he urged, as he waited beside the band. Hurry up and get here! But the hall was full before she arrived.

She was wearing the same dress she'd worn the previous Saturday, when she'd danced with that damned soldier all the time, a sort of wine red which looked gorgeous on her. And she was the old bold Spitfire again, dancing with everybody, doing the jitterbug with one of the Yanks and the foxtrot with Spikey, wise-cracking and laughing all the time. That's more like it, he thought. I'll wait till the end of this one and then I'll stroll across and say hello.

But in fact he was misreading the signs. Barbara's gaiety was a shield, deliberately held up to her friends to protect feelings that were suddenly and achingly raw.

44

She was in the oddest mood, unaccountably listless one moment, irritably restless the next, as if there were a great weight pressing down on her shoulders that she couldn't shake off. If it hadn't been for the fact that a change of routine would have provoked questions, she would have stayed at home with Becky Bosworth that evening. She certainly had no appetite for the dance and no desire to go anywhere if she couldn't be with Steve.

The first three days without him had been unexpectedly difficult. True to his promise he'd sent her a letter every day, but she missed him all the time, dreaming of him most erotically by night and suddenly remembering his kisses as she stood behind the counter by day, so that it was a struggle to pay attention to her customers. On the second day, the sun had been obscured by cloud and a cold wind roistered through the town, hurling the blossom from the boughs and stripping the new spring flowers to tatters. It was the first time she'd ever felt disturbed by the destructive force of nature. Until then she'd simply accepted it. Now the sight of all those shattered flowers made her separation from Steve seem unnecessary and destructive too. Still, it wasn't in her nature to complain, nor to stay at home and mope. That Saturday night she brushed her hair, put on rather more lipstick than usual and went off to the Corn Exchange with her friends, horsing around and laughing so much that she felt sure that one of them would see how false she was being.

None did. They all said what fun she was. 'Thass our Spitfire. She's a one.' And when Vic came strolling round the edge of the floor to say hello, they greeted him with the news that she was 'on form tonight'.

'I can see that,' he said. ''Lo Spitfire.'

''Lo Vic,' she said, smiling at him brightly. 'When you gonna put that ol' tie out fer jumble?'

'Like a dance?' he offered hopefully and was delighted when she said, 'Why not?'

They danced energetically, he concentrating on the

perfection of his steps, she enjoying the beat and glad
that there was no need to talk while they were bouncing
about the floor. It was like old times for both of them.
But when the music stopped, the lights dimmed for a
waltz and she walked him off the floor before he could
offer to dance *that* with her too.

'Nice to see you two together again,' Tubby said,
looming in upon them. 'You soon forgot that ol' soldier
then.'

She swung round to face him and even in the dim
light he could see how bright her eyes were. 'What?'

'The one you been hossin' around town with,' he
elaborated. 'Off on manoeuvres, so they say.'

'Thass none of your business,' she told him sharply.
'Careless talk costs lives or ain't you heard.'

He wasn't the least bit abashed. 'Thass no secret,
though, is it?' he said. 'Like a dance?'

She looked him up and down with disdain. 'No
thanks. I got more respect for my feet.' Then she was
off to join her friends, pushing through the crowd at the
edge of the dance floor, hair bouncing, red dress
flicking like a flag in a gale.

Vic turned on his friend in fury. 'Why don't you keep
your big nose out of things?' he said.

'Well thass nice,' Tubby said, looking aggrieved. 'I
onny asked. I mean to say . . . Thass a free country.'

'Hang on!' Victor called after the red flag. 'I bought
you some chocolate.'

But she was lost behind a mass of uniformed backs
and he didn't find her again until the waltz was over and
the floor was clearing. Then he heard her laughing on
the other side of the hall.

'Sorry about that,' she said, when he pushed through
the crowd to join her. 'But that Tubby's such a know-
all, him an' his big mouth. He get on my nerves.'

'Mine too,' he told her, happy to be her ally even
against his oldest friend. 'I've give him what-for. Like
some chocolate?'

That was what was so nice about Vic, Barbara thought. He might holler a bit now an' then but he took your side when you needed it and he was really generous. She was touched to be offered part of his sweet ration especially after the way she'd treated him these last few weeks. 'Keep it for on the way home,' she said, smiling her thanks at him. 'We'll eat it then.'

So they danced again – and again – and joked with their friends in the old easy way, and when the dance was over the entire gang walked back to the North End together. But although she seemed to be herself again, he wasn't such a fool as to think that the soldier was out of her memory. He noticed that she hadn't danced a single waltz with anybody and there was something different about her, even when she was laughing and horsing around. Bright but too bright, laughing with her mouth but not her eyes. He'd have to play his cards very, very carefully if he was to win her back.

'Pictures Wednesday,' he suggested, casually, as they reached the North End.

There was general agreement. 'Yeh!' Joan approved. 'You comin' an' all, Spitfire?'

Barbara considered it, but only for a second. 'Yes,' she said. 'Why not?'

It wasn't until later that night that she faced why not. Although she'd exhausted herself at the dance, she couldn't sleep for troubling thoughts. She lay, wide awake beside her snoring bed-mate, and tried to make sense of them. It infuriated her to think that she and Steve were being gossiped about. Her love for Steve – if it *was* love, she wasn't even sure about that yet – but if it *was*, it was simply theirs, a world of their own, too precious and private and delicate to be made a public display. The thought of being watched by a great fat oaf like Tubby was like standing in a gale while all the lovely bloom of it was stripped to tatters. How dare he spy on them! Horrid creature. Well I'll soon see about that, she thought. Just watch if I don't. He got no business prying into my affairs. We'll go somewhere private from now on, somewhere out of town where he can't see us. We made it too easy for a spy, always meeting in the market square and going to the same places.

It was horrible to think that they were such public knowledge. She hadn't told *anyone* how she felt about Steve, not even Joan and Mavis, and they'd always known everything there was to know about old Vic. And that was another thing. She knew quite well she wasn't being fair to Vic. He'd been really nice that evening, buying her chocolate and sticking up for her and asking her to the pictures and everything, and all the time she'd been thinking of Steve and wishing he'd been there to waltz with her. If she'd seen anyone else going on like that, she'd have said she was giving him the run around. I ought to tell him, she thought. But what could she say? She wasn't sure enough of her feelings to tell Steve. It was impossible. And yet she *did* miss him. So much. She simply couldn't wait to see him again. It made her yearn to think of it. But was that love? Six more days, though. A whole working week. It was an achingly long time. Just as well we're going to the pictures. At least that'll be something to do.

They went to all three pictures that week, safe in the gang with lots of giggling and teasing and no chance to talk to anyone seriously. And Steve sent her a letter every single day, just as he'd promised, joking about the mud, the iron rations and sleeping in the open, and saying over and over again how much he was looking forward to being back in Lynn. '*I can't wait to see you again. Roll on Saturday night.*'

That Friday, when there was just one more day to endure without him, she went to the shops in her lunch hour and blew half a crown and four clothing coupons on a new short-sleeved blouse, made of cream cotton, embroidered all over with little green flowers, with a

48

row of little pearl buttons all down the front. It was a wicked extravagance, which made it all the more pleasurable. With her green skirt and her green clogs, she'd be worth looking at. And it was important to be worth looking at, when he couldn't wait to see her again.

It took her a lot longer than usual to get dressed that Saturday night. Her restlessness was so bad it was making her clumsy. She smudged her lipstick and had to do it all again, broke a comb in her hair and spent several painful minutes disentangling it, and finally snagged her last remaining pair of stockings, swearing as she watched the ladder run inexorably from calf to ankle.

Becky Bosworth laughed at her. 'You'll jest have to dance bare-legged, thass all gal,' she chuckled. 'Good job thass a warm night.'

It had been pleasantly warm all day, almost as though it were already summer. Now it was a gentle evening and the dusk was pearl pink. And she would see him again in a matter of minutes. Half an hour at the outside.

Joan and Mavis were waiting for her at the band-stand. The warmth of the day had left the hall decidedly stuffy. They'd made themselves fans from folded newspaper and elastic bands and were flapping them energetically.

'You look glam,' Joan said approvingly. 'New, is it?'

'Thass like an oven in here,' Mavis complained. Her dark hair was stuck to her forehead with sweat. 'D'you wanna fan?'

'No ta,' Barbara said, 'I'm not hot.' And was then caught up in such a rush of heated pleasure that her cheeks burned with it. For there he was, striding towards her, looking tanned and wind-blown and heart-stoppingly handsome. Oh the rhythm of those long long legs. The set of that jaw. The love in those brown eyes, smiling, smiling.

He caught her about the waist and pulled her towards

him as if he was going to kiss her, there and then, in front of everyone. 'You look gorgeous!' he said.

They were held in a trance of delight and desire. 'Do I?' she asked breathlessly.

'Good enough to eat,' he told her. He was breathless too but he remembered his manners. 'Hello Joan. Hello Mavis.'

The greeting brought Barbara back to her senses and allowed her to move again. She seized his hand and ran into the crowd on the dance floor, pulling him after her, and then they were in each other's arms, which was all right because it was a waltz. 'Oh I *have* missed you,' she said.

He kissed her hair as they swayed. And remembered the dream that had woken him yearning for the last ten lonely nights, lying beside her, both naked and kissing and . . . It took an effort of will not to tremble. 'Me too,' he said.

The waltz swung them together for delicious minutes, she with an arm round his neck, breathing in the scent of his skin, he with both arms about her waist, holding her close, aware of the lovely length of her body, the swell of her breasts, her breath against his cheek.

'Let's go out,' he said. 'There's too many people in here.'

They went to the Walks – where else? – and stood beneath their favourite elm as the dusk lapped about them, silky soft and secret as water, and kissed until their lips were sore, immersed in the sharp, sweet, endless pleasure of sexual feelings fully roused and tantalisingly ungratified. It wasn't until they paused for breath and realised that the clock was striking eleven that she remembered her plan.

'Let's not meet in the square tomorrow,' she said.

He was too taut with desire to care where they met. 'Um. Kiss me.'

'I'll be on the quay,' she said, struggling to be sensible, 'by the Custom House. D'you know it?'

50

'Um.'

'Three o'clock?'

'Um.'

'I thought we'd go somewhere different.'

He accepted that too. He would have accepted anything. They had less than an hour now and he hadn't kissed her for thirty seconds.

Sunday afternoon was as warm as summer and the air was so still that the river Ouse was as pale as milk and flowed without a ripple.

'Where to?' he asked as she came tripping towards him, bright in her green skirt and her new blouse, bare-legged and bare-armed and glowing in the unaccustomed sunshine.

'What you reckon to a country walk?'

'Smashing. It's too nice to be indoors.' And the country was quiet and private.

They took the ferry across to West Lynn, sitting side by side in the stern and apart from the other passengers. Then they walked through the village hand in hand, past the two pubs and the church until the road petered out and became a footpath and they were all on their own in the open country, free to stroll arm in arm through fields of green corn, between hedgerows that chirruped with nesting birds, busily darting back and forth with beaks full of insects for their young. The sky was summertime blue, there were bees buzzing in the blossom, and from time to time a swarm of midges rose from the rankness of a stagnant ditch to dance about their faces, once so thickly and incessantly that Steve had to beat them off with his beret.

'It's too warm for this sort of caper,' he said, folding the beret and tucking it into his epaulette.

Barbara was comfortably warm – but then she hadn't been fighting off midges and she wasn't wearing a coat. 'That uniform's too thick,' she said. 'Why don't you take your tunic off?' Which he did, and rolled up his shirtsleeves for good measure.

51

He looked devastating, his forearms brown and sinewy and covered with soft golden hairs. Being the only girl in the family, she was used to the sight of hairy males. Norman had so much dark hair on his arms and legs that she used to kid him he was related to a gorilla. But this hair was different, not bristling and dark and threatening, but soft, tender and strong, all at the same time. And wondrously sexy. She put out her hand and stroked it gently.

It was too much for his fragile control. He threw his tunic to the earth, pulled her into his arms, and kissed her with such passion that it made them both breathless. Now that he'd removed his battledress, she realised how much the thickness of it had been getting in the way. With just a shirt and blouse between them, she could feel his heart thundering as he kissed her, could run her fingers down the length of his spine, from the sharp short hair at the nape of his neck all the way to the leather barrier of his belt. Oh the wonder of being kissed like this. By the time he finally lifted his head she was panting and so giddy that she had to cling to him for support.

'We should be sitting down,' he said. Or lying down. But where could they lie in this huge open landscape? 'There ought to be a grass bank or something somewhere.'

'Let's look,' she suggested.

He picked up his tunic, holding it over his shoulder with one hand while he cuddled her with the other, and they strolled on along the empty footpath, clinging together and kissing at every other step, following their instincts – and the curve of the path. And there, in the shade of a burgeoning oak tree, was a half-used haystack, one side straight and neat and thatched, the other scooped into an untidy straw cavern. It was just the thing.

They scrambled up, dislodging straws with every movement, and he threw his tunic inside the cave and they tumbled into it together, mouth to mouth, rolling over and over in an ecstasy of sensation. He was unbuttoning her blouse, kissing her throat, her breasts, her nipples – should he be doing this? probably not, but oh, how she wanted him to – his lips hot and searching as she held his head between her hands. 'Steve, Steve, oh my dear darling Steve.' And then everything happened too quickly to weigh up the consequences or even to give them a thought. He was inside her, and they were moving together, fitting together, made for each other, sensation growing and growing, higher and higher, until it exploded into such a crescendo of pleasure that she caught her breath. And at that he made an odd groaning noise and after a little while he stopped moving too.

She lay where she was with her eyes still closed. It was amazingly peaceful. The sun was warm on her head and her bare arms and she could hear a dog barking a long way away and a mouse rustling in the straw next to her ear. And doubt rustled into her mind. We shouldn't have done that, she thought. Now that she was reasonable again, she knew it quite well. I should have stopped him, said no, before we . . . She remembered the warnings. Nice girls don't go all the way. Nice girls keep themselves pure until they're married. She wasn't even sure whether nice girls were supposed to enjoy it.

His voice came to her blurred and from a distance. 'Are you all right?'

She opened her eyes and looked at him for a long thoughtful second. His face looked so happy and so satisfied, although there was a shadow of anxiety in those brown eyes. My darling Steve! Whatever her worries she couldn't say anything about them. Not to him and certainly not now. 'I'm wonderful,' she said, trying to speak lightly. 'Why shouldn't I be?'

He leant over her, supported on one elbow. 'No reason,' he said, gently picking straw from her hair. 'I just wondered.'

'You're sayin' we shouldn't have done it. Is that it?'

'No,' he told her seriously. 'That's not it. I just didn't want you to be upset. I wouldn't upset you for worlds. You're too precious to me.'

It was necessary to reassure him. To reassure them both. 'Look,' she said, arguing against the warnings, 'I know they say you shouldn't till you got a weddin' ring on your finger but I think thass a load of ol' squit. If thass all right when you're married, thass all right when you're in love, ain't it? What's the difference? Thass love what matters.'

'Oh,' he said, kissing her fingers, 'I do love you, Spitfire. So much. More than ever now.'

It was the time for declarations. She couldn't doubt her feelings any more. Not after all this. 'An' I love you,' she said, knowing it was true and that it would always be true. 'Very, very, very much.'

'Oh my dear, lovely girl!' And he pulled her towards him to kiss her again.

The movement made her aware that she'd lost her clogs and that the straw was scratching her feet. Then she realised that she was lying on the pocket of his tunic and that it was full of small, bulky objects. 'Just a minute,' she said, shifting her body to a more comfortable position. 'What you got in your pockets?'

'Fags,' he remembered and that made him yearn for a smoke. 'Would you like one?'

'They'll be squashed,' she laughed.

They were, but he picked out the two least battered, lit them both and handed the best one to her. And they tasted all right. They lay side by side on the straw and smoked companionably, like film stars. But the mouse and the doubt were still rustling.

'I s'pose other people would say I'm a fallen woman,' she mused. It was a good description because that wonderful exploding feeling was just like falling. Not falling down and hurting yourself but falling up, as if you were flying through the sky, lifted up on great surging wings of pleasure. A fallen woman.

The words upset him, because that was exactly what he'd been worrying about, that she'd feel sullied or ashamed, that she'd regret what they'd done. And he simply couldn't allow that. Fallen women were the lowest of the low, the sort that went with anybody, the sort they made coarse jokes about after lights out. She was beautiful and pure and entirely his. 'No you're not,' he said hotly. 'You're not to even think it. You're my own dear, darling, beautiful, wonderful Spitfire and you're going to marry me as soon as I can arrange it and stay with me for ever and ever.'

Marriage hadn't entered into her scheme of things at all until that moment. 'We can't get married,' she said. 'Can we?'

But he was in command now, seeing everything with total clarity as if making love had sharpened his wits. 'I've got seven days leave owing,' he told her. 'I been saving it up for when they move us to the ports. A last holiday, sort of thing. To say goodbye.' That thought cast a shadow into his mind too so he shrugged it away at once and began to make detailed plans. 'So. I'll write to my mum and dad tonight and let them know, and then I'll put in for my leave first thing tomorrow and we'll call the banns, or whatever it is we have to do, tomorrow evening. I can wangle an hour or two after work so we can go together. It might be better to get a special licence and I expect we'll need permission being under twenty-one. But that'll just be an extra form to fill in. What do you think?'

He was making her feel so protected and special that she could feel herself drifting into a sort of dreamy satisfaction. 'Um,' she said. 'Yes.' It was the right thing to do, the natural thing. They loved one another. They belonged to one another now. But she couldn't take it in. Not fully. Not yet.

He was busy making plans. 'We'll get a room or a

flat or something. In Lynn probably. Then I can stay there whenever I get any leave. We'll have our own bed and our own wireless and a shelf for our books. And we'll cook our own food and have breakfast in bed . . .'

'Um.'

'Did I ought to see your father?' he wondered. 'Ask his permission sort of thing? That's what you're supposed to do, isn't it?'

That question woke her up. 'No,' she said. That wouldn't do at all. 'Let me tell Ma first. He can be pretty horrible when he likes. We don' want him hollerin'.'

He allowed that but pointed out, 'He'll have to be told.'

'I'll work him round to it,' she promised. 'He's at sea at the moment so we can't tell him yet anyway.'

He kissed her gently and lovingly. It was all possible. One short ceremony and they could be together whenever they liked. Until he had to go to France. But there was no point in thinking about that. 'That's settled then,' he said, smiling into her lovely green eyes. 'I'll arrange it. I'll write to my mum tonight and we'll tell your mum when we've called the banns. It'll be a piece of cake.'

CHAPTER FIVE

'It's a joke,' Heather Wilkins said, holding out the letter to her husband in disbelief. Her nose was sharp with distress, her mouth downturned. 'He's having us on. He must be. He *can't* be getting married. He'd've said something before. I mean, you don't just write to your mother out the blue and say you're going to get married. We don't even know who she is.' She'd been clearing the breakfast things when the letter arrived but now she stood by the kitchen table with her right hand splayed against the oilcloth, looking down at the faded blue and yellow checks, noticing how frayed the edges were, too upset to move. 'It's so unlike him,' she complained. 'He's such a sensible boy.'

Bob Wilkins took the letter and let her run on while he read it. This was the moment he'd been half-expecting ever since Steve had been called up. The boy was too full of life not to fall in love sooner or later. You had to expect it. But he'd always known it would upset poor Heather when it happened. She was so bound up in him. Always had been. Being the only one, that was the trouble. He glanced at her now, standing by the table in her flowery apron, her long face set and stubborn. Poor old gel. She'll be better once she's got the first shock out of her system. But no matter what she might hope, he knew Steve wasn't joking. He could see that by the strength of the handwriting, even before he digested the words. *'I have met the girl I am going to marry. There is not much time now before we go. A matter of weeks. I have got a 36 hour pass on Wednesday. I will tell you all about it then. Love to you both.'*

'You see what he says,' Heather said, her face anguished. 'A matter of weeks. He's going in a matter of weeks.'

So that's it, Bob thought, and he moved towards her at once to comfort her. He was due at the signal-box in ten minutes so he'd have to set off soon otherwise he'd be late, which was unthinkable because he'd never been late in the whole of his working life. But he couldn't leave her. Not when she was in a state. 'He'll be all right,' he said, putting his arms round her. 'You'll see.'

That only made her worse. 'Oh talk sense for crying out loud,' she cried. 'How can he be all right when the Germans'll be firing shells at him? An' bullets an' bombs an' God knows what else. You don't imagine he'll be able to get out the way a' *that* do you? It's a bloody nightmare. Bad enough he's got to go, without springing this on us at the last moment.'

How grey she's getting, Bob thought, kissing her hair and remembering how it had been when it was young and auburn. He was aching with pity for her. 'She's probably a very nice girl,' he soothed. 'I mean you couldn't imagine our Steve picking anyone who wasn't, now could you?' And when she gave him a wry look, 'Well there you are, you see. He's a good lad. An' he's bound to marry sometime. I mean it's only natural. Let's not be hasty. Wait an' hear what he's got to say about it. That's the best plan.'

'Say?' she cried, looking up at him, blue eyes wild. 'What's the good a' saying things? It don't matter tuppence what you say. Not in the middle of a war. I mean who's going to listen? It's all *"Grin an' bear it." "See it through." "We can take it!"* Be just the same if we couldn't. We're stuck with it. We just got to sit here and take whatever's slung at us. An' I tell you Bob, I'm sick to death of it.'

'I know,' he said, stroking the nape of her neck, the way he always did when he was trying to console her. 'I know. It'll be over soon.'

58

Her face was wrinkling towards tears. 'It's all so unfair.'

'I know,' he said again, his voice so full of tenderness the words were a caress.

She blinked away the need to cry. 'Anyway,' she said taking refuge in renewed irritation, 'he's too young to get married.'

'He was twenty last week,' Bob pointed out. 'You've only just sent him his parcel. Don't say you've forgotten *that*! Well then. Not much younger than I was when I met you.'

'There's no comparison,' she said. 'You were twenty-four. You'd been at work nearly ten years. In an' out the army. You were in the signal-box by then. An' I was twenty-five. He's barely out a' school. Much too young.'

'I can remember your mum saying just the same thing,' he reminded her. And he quoted, ' "Ain't got the cradle marks off yer bum the pair of yer." '

His mimicry was so accurate it made her smile.

'That's better,' he said, cupping her face in his hands to kiss her goodbye. 'Look on the bright side, eh?' And when she smiled again, 'I got to go or I'll be late.'

She began to tidy her outburst away, smoothing her apron, tucking stray hairs back into their restraining kirby-grips, resuming her workaday self. He was right. There was no point in making a fuss. But it was hard not to, just the same.

'Don't go worrying your head about it,' he advised as he picked up his snap. 'Concentrate on how nice it'll be to see him again.'

She turned her attention to the breakfast things to show him she'd recovered. 'I got much too much to do to waste time worrying,' she reassured him. Which was true enough for she worked behind the counter at the butcher's and there'd be queues there today because the offal was due in. And when he looked at the clock again, 'You cut off. I'll be all right.'

'Sure?'

'Yes. Go on.'

He left her slowly, smiling at her before he closed the door behind him. He's such a good man, she thought, touched, yet again, by how patient and gentle he was. I shouldn't've gone on at him. It's not his fault. I'll see if I can sneak a bit of liver for supper Wednesday. He'll be on late turn by then so he'll be home too. We can all have it together. I wish there was some fruit around. Bit too soon for that. Still I could make potato cakes for tea. They like potato cakes.

But despite her most determined efforts to be practical, irritation seethed in her chest all the way to the butcher's. Who *is* this girl? she thought crossly. We don't know anything about her, who she is, or what she does, or where she comes from, or what her parents are like, or anything. We don't even know her name. It seemed ominously significant that Steve hadn't told them anything about her. She'll turn out to be some brazen hussy who's been setting her cap at him because he's away from home and feeling low. One of those tarty women you see hanging around with the Americans. There's a darn sight too much of that going on. The more she anguished about it, the more agitated she became. I've half a mind to take a day off work, she thought, and go up there and see for myself. Girls like that need putting in their place. She needn't think she can up an' marry my son without someone having something to say about it. Horrible girl.

The horrible girl had been uncomfortably idle that day and just at a time when she had more energy than she knew what to do with. Since cloth and clothing had been rationed, trade at the draper's shop had fallen steadily. Now it was so low that the manager complained there were days when he wondered why they bothered to open the doors at all. But sales – or the lack of them – were the last thing on Barbara's mind that day. Her life had changed so dramatically and at such speed that she was tangled in the sheer pace and wonder of it. It hardly seemed possible that a mere ten weeks ago she hadn't even met Steve Wilkins and now they were lovers and engaged to be married and, once this boring day was over, they were going to call the banns. She was in a state of such confused happiness that she felt as though she was growing out of her skin.

Outside the shop, the street was as restless as she was. Rapid cloud dappled the pavements with a shifting pattern of sunshine and shadow and the sea breeze was so strong that it flicked coats and skirts like flags, tossed hats into the air and bowled them along the road, lifted the shop blinds as though they were sails so that they heaved and strained, cracking like whips. At twenty to five, she caught sight of Steve, striding along the windswept High Street and watched him as he stood in a doorway to light a cigarette, cupping the flame with his left hand, the pink desert rat brave on his shoulder.

Now that she could see him, standing there, a few feet away from her, having to wait another twenty minutes was intolerable. On an exuberant impulse, she asked the manager whether they couldn't shut early for once. 'Seein' we ain't 'xactly overwhelmed with custom.'

He was tempted – but only momentarily. 'No, no,' he said, smoothing his bottle-brush moustache neatly back into obedience. 'Duty to the customer, you know.'

So they all had to stick it out until the empty end. And the last ten minutes took twenty-four hours. But eventually the shelves were tidy, the floor swept, the door shut, locked and given a last little shove to make sure, and she was free to dart across the road and into her lover's arms, back where she belonged.

'Come on,' she said, dancing with impatience. 'Where we got to go to?'

'Registry Office,' he told her, as the wind pushed them in the right direction. 'I've put in for my leave.

61

Seven days with an extra forty-eight tacked on. Piece a' cake. I told you didn't I?'

It impressed them both that registering their intention to marry was such a simple business and took so little time – fifteen minutes from start to finish. And even though they were warned that they required their parents' written consent before the date could be fixed and notice posted, neither of them could foresee any difficulty with that and Steve promised that they'd be back on Friday. They emerged into the bright air of that April evening feeling that the deed was as good as done.

'I'll go straight round to Ma soon as you've caught your bus,' Barbara promised. Which, twenty kissing minutes later, she did.

Her mother was standing by the fire, frying sausages for the boys' tea. The room was in its usual chaotic state but there was no sign of her father and both her little brothers were out in the yard, playing marbles. It was an ideal time. ''Lo Ma,' she said and unbuttoned her coat against the heat of the fire before she sat at the table.

Maudie paused to wipe the sweat from her forehead. Her bare forearms were mottled from being too close to the fire. ''Lo Bar'bra,' she said mildly. 'What's brought you?'

'Got a form for you to sign,' Barbara said happily and handed it across.

Maudie took it vaguely and in her left hand while she continued to prod the sausages with her long toasting-fork. The smell of frying meat rose succulently into the usual mixture of smells that clogged the room: salt-encrusted clothes, dust, sweat, salty nets, dead fish. 'Thass always forms,' she complained, her voice still mild. 'I hates forms. What they want this time?'

'Thass for me to get married,' Barbara explained, happiness welling into her chest at the mere sound of the words. 'You don't have to fill it in or nothin', you just have to sign – to give consent.'

Maudie narrowed her eyes, partly against the heat of the fire and partly against her own incomprehension. 'What you on about gal? You hain't getting married.'

'Yes I am,' Barbara said, her face glowing. 'We've just fixed it.'

'Oh come on, gal,' Maudie said. 'Don't talk squit. You're too young. Both of you. I thought your Vic had more sense than that. What's got into his fool head?'

It was a horrid moment. Like running into a brick wall. She'd been so happy she'd forgotten all about Victor Castlemain. I've done this wrong, she thought, her heart sinking. I should have told her about Steve first. And she rushed to put things right. 'It hain't Vic, Ma.'

Her mother's face changed at once, suspicion corrugating her forehead, annoyance reducing her lips to a pursed crescent. 'What d'you mean, it hain't Vic?'

Keep going! Tell her quickly! 'He's a soldier. One of the Desert Rats. The ones what are going to the Second Front. His name's Steve Wilkins. He's the nicest man I ever met. An' so handsome you'd never believe.'

Maudie wasn't impressed. 'Do Becky know all this?' she asked. 'She met him, hev she?'

'No,' Barbara said. ''Course not. I wanted to tell you first. I mean, you're my ma.'

But it was too late to josh her mother back to good humour. Maudie's suspicion had already hardened into denial. She was remembering Vic Castlemain's warning, her fury fed by the twin facts that he'd known more than she did and that she'd been fool enough to ignore him. He got no right to know so much, she thought. An' *she's* got no right to get engaged. Not without tellin' her family.

She tossed the form onto the table, snorted and returned to her cooking. 'You've gone off your head, gal,' she said, spearing a sausage as though it had done her some injury. 'Blust if you hain't. Married at your

63

age! I never heard the like. Git you off 'ome to your Aunty Becky an' don't talk squit.'

This is the scholarship all over again, Barbara thought. Only this time I'm going to make her agree. She hunched her shoulders and set her jaw against the struggle to come. 'That ain't squit,' she said stubbornly. 'Thass the truth. We're gonna get married. He's asked me. I've said yes.'

Maudie lifted the frying pan from the coals, straightened her back and looked her daughter in the eye. 'More fool you,' she said. 'Well now you'll have to say no. You hain't marryin' him. Nor no one else neither. You're too young.'

'I'm seventeen,' Barbara said hotly. 'I been at work three years.'

'Thass what I mean. You're too young. You don't know what you're lettin' yerself in for. Well I do gal. An' let me tell you, thass a mug's game, gettin' married. Bloody slave labour thass all that is, believe you me. Non-stop work, day in day out, kids forever under your feet, scrimpin' and savin' an' makin' ends meet all the time, an' your ol' man comin' home with a thick head, nine times outta ten, hollerin' an' roarin'. Bloody slave labour. You don't know the half of it. You wanna keep out of orl that sort a' squit long as you can.'

Barbara looked round at the squalor of the room. The breakfast things were still congealing on the stained oilcloth, the dresser was heaped with rubbish, newspapers, knitting, empty packets of fags, bits of rope, chipped cups full of buttons and bent cigarette cards, there were crumbs and cigarette ends and broken toys all over the floor and, in the usual corner, the usual heap of crumpled boots and darned socks, stiff with dried sweat and sea water. 'That'll be different for us,' she said.

'Don't you believe it, gal,' her mother said, taking a fork to a saucepan full of boiled potatoes and mashing them vigorously. 'Thass like it for everyone. Stay you single till you marry our Victor, thass my advice.'

'I don't want to stay single,' Barbara said, trying to keep her patience. The determination in her mother's stocky figure was rousing a dreadful and familiar anger. Why does she have to oppose everything all the time? This is the most decisive moment of my life. Why can't she try and understand for once? 'An' I don't want to marry Victor. I want to marry Steve.'

'Well you can't. 'Cos I hain't signin'.'

'Ma! Please! You don't know what this means to me!'

Such a direct appeal made Maudie relent a little. But only a little. 'Wait a coupla years,' she said. 'Then we'll see.'

'We hain't got a coupla years,' Barbara told her. Irritation was altering the tone of her voice but she couldn't help it. 'He's going to France. Don't you understand? He's goin' to France an' he might not come back. He might be one of the ones what get killed. We onny got a couple a' weeks. We got to get married *now*.'

'He ain't got you into trouble, hev he?' Maudie said, looking more suspicious than ever.

'No he hev *not*,' Barbara said hotly. That was too close for comfort and embarrassed her terribly. He couldn't have, could he? Not the first time. Joan said you were safe the first time . . .

'Well thass orl right then.'

'No. Thass not "orl right". We want to get married. How many more times I got to tell you? He's goin' to France an' we want to get married before he goes. He's asked me. I've said yes. All you got to do is sign. It won't cost you a penny. We'll pay for it.'

'Well I haint signin'. An' there's an end on it. An' don't think your father will neither. Thass out the question.'

'Look,' Barbara said. 'We shall get married in the

65

end. Once I'm twenty-one you can't stop me. So why not now?'

''Cos you'd regret it.'

'I wouldn't. I love him.'

That didn't impress Maudie at all. She sloshed milk into the mashed potatoes. 'You'll get over it,' she said.

Her thoughtless complacency made Barbara rage. 'How can you *say* such a thing? I shall love him for ever, till my dyin' day. Don't you understand?'

'Better than you do gal. As you'll find out.'

There's no getting through to her, Barbara thought. She was shaking with fury and frustration but she hung on to her control for a last despairing attack.

'All right then,' she said, enunciating the words so savagely that she could feel her tongue hard against the back of her teeth. 'I'll leave home and go to London an' get a job there an' you won't never see me again. You can't stop me doin' that.'

The threat caught Maudie by the throat. She wouldn't, would she? Not all that way with a war goin' on. 'Don't talk so stoopid,' she said. 'Go to London! They're bombin' people in London. Or don't you read the papers? They been bombin' 'em since January.'

Barbara was too wild to hear what she was saying. 'I don't care!'

'Don't care was made to care,' her mother warned, beating the potatoes, to ease her anger. 'Don't care was hung. Don't care was put in a pot an' boiled till he was done. Be a different story when they're bombin' you, gal.'

But her daughter had snatched the form from the table and was out of the house, striding through the yard, pushing her little brothers aside, hot tears stinging her eyes.

Her youngest brother, Jimmy, who was ten and didn't take kindly to being flung to the ground, picked himself up and ran into the house to see what was going on. 'Whass up Ma?'

Maudie was dishing up, and apart from a rather red face, she seemed to be her placid self. If she'd learnt nothing else in the back-breaking years of her marriage, she'd learnt not to take anything too seriously. Most quarrels blew over, sooner or later. Best thing was to let them roll off, water off a duck's back like. Barbara *had* upset her, silly little mawther, but it was over an' done with now. Just so long as she don't go marryin' some stupid soldier.

'Your sister's hollerin', thass all,' she said, pushing the dirty breakfast things to one side to make room for the dinner plates. 'Hassen you up an' git our Wilfred. I got your tea orl ready for you. You can have it soon as Norman gets back.'

Norman was on his way home at that moment, striding through the yards, whistling in his tuneless way, with his cap on the back of his head and three cheerful pints under his belt. He was very surprised to see his sister running towards him with tears streaming down her face, especially as she didn't seem to see him. He stood in her path and opened his arms wide to catch her and hold her. 'What's up, kid?'

She fell against his chest, crying into the rough wool of his gansey. 'Oh Norman! She won't let me get married. Thass the scholarship all over again ...'

'Easy on!' he said, patting her shoulders. 'Git your breath. You don't want world an' his wife to hear you.' And he led her away from the gawping eyes in the yards, out onto the quayside where half a dozen dinghies lay moored and empty, waiting for the fishing fleet to return, and there were only gulls to hear them. 'Now then, tell me orl about it.'

If there was one thing he knew about this volatile sister of his, it was that she wasn't the sort to fall in love lightly, but it took a long time to make sense of her story because she was in such a temper and crying so wildly that everything she said was hot and muddled and half finished.

'Thass the scholarship all over again,' she wept. 'I knew it the minute she started. She won't let me live my own life. She never has an' she never will an' I love him so much. I can't tell you how much. He's the nicest man I ever met.'

'Yes,' he remembered. 'He looked a nice feller.'

'He is. He is.'

'Thass all a bit quick though, you got to admit.'

'I know,' she agreed. 'Thass it. We hain't got any time at all. He'll be gone to France in a week or two. Oh Norman, what am I gonna do?'

He took off his cap, gave his shock of hair a thorough scratching, and put it back on again. It was quiet out there on the quayside, with the tide slapping the wall and the gulls wheeling and mewing above their heads. 'You still got the form, hev you?'

She handed it to him, flicking the tears from her eyes, and waited while he read it in his methodical way. 'Thass hopeless, ain't it? If she won't sign, I can't marry him. I shall run away. I told her so.'

'Hang about,' he said, still ploughing through the text.

So she hung about.

'Well now,' he said when he'd finally made sense of it. 'I'll tell you what. I think there's more than one way to kill a cat. Thass what I think. Fact, I can see another right here on this ol' piece a paper.' He spread the form on his navy-blue knees and prodded it with a blunt forefinger. 'Parent or guardian so that say,' he pointed out. 'See for yourself. Parent *or* guardian. Well then, if Ma can't bring herself to do it, Aunt Becky can. You been livin' in her house long enough. Seven years come September. If that don't make her a sort of guardian, I don't know what do. To say nothin' of her bein' Pa's second cousin once removed.'

Surprise dried Barbara's tears. Surprise and hope. 'Yes, she could, couldn't she? D'you think she would?'

'No harm tryin'. Might not be legal though.'

'I don't care. Just as long as I can get married. It's only a piece of paper.' She'd recovered enough to grin at him. ''Sides, you have to cut corners. There's a war on.'

'I don't s'pose you could get married here neither,' he warned. 'Case they was to make a scene.'

That wasn't a problem. 'We can marry in London. He's goin' there Wednesday to tell his parents. He can fix it for us. I'll write an' tell him.'

'Better get ol' Becky to sign up first,' he laughed at her. Wasn't this typical of this sister of his? Floods of tears one minute, all smiles the next.

'D'you think she will?' she asked as they set off, arm in arm, for Rag's Yard. 'Oh she will, won't she?'

'Leave her to me,' he advised, 'an' I'll see what I can do.'

Aunt Becky was sitting by the fire, with a sheet of newspaper on her lap, carefully peeling potatoes for their evening meal and gathering the peelings into the paper ready for the pig-bin. But she put down her knife and got up at once when Norman walked through the door.

''Lo Norman,' she said. 'Thass a nice surprise. What's brought you round?'

He came straight to the point. 'I got a favour to ask you.'

She gave him one of her long shrewd looks, her face fox-sharp. 'Oh yes?'

So he told her, speaking slowly and reasonably, and she listened and nodded. And when he'd finished and Barbara had agreed that everything he said was true, she stood by the table for a long time and pondered.

'Well I don't know,' she said at last. 'I thought you was going to marry Victor.'

'That was boy an' gal stuff,' Barbara told her.

'You told him, hev you?'

'Not yet.'

'Poor boy. He'll be ever so upset.'

'He'll git over it!' Norman said, answering before Barbara could say something she'd regret. 'Worse things happen at sea. So what about this ol' form?'

Becky frowned. 'Maudie won't like it.'

'She'll come round to it,' he said, with perfect confidence. 'She ain't axactly 'pposed to it. She'd uv come round to it gradual. You know that, now don't you? In her own time sort uv thing. You know how she is. Onny they ain't got the time to wait for her to do it. Thass the long an' the short uv it.'

'When's he going?' Becky asked.

'Matter uv weeks,' he told her. 'No more. We're all goin', one way or the other with that ol' Second Front a-comin'. I shall be off messell tomorrow.'

'Again?' she mourned. 'I thought you was home for weeks.'

'Weeks is up,' he told her cheerfully. 'So there you are. You gonna send a poor sailor off to sea happy an' content or hain't you? Orl you got to do is sign this ol' form. What d'you think?'

She sighed, gave him another one of her looks, frowned, sighed again. But she picked up the form. 'I s'pose so,' she said. 'Seein' thass for you. I wouldn't uv done it for no one else mind. I hain't at all sure thass right.'

He threw his arms round her and gave her a smacking kiss on the cheek. ''Course thass right, you dear ol' thing. Hain't I jest told you?'

As a pen was found and the form was signed and shaken dry, the clock on the mantelpiece tinged half past six. Barbara looked up at it, surprised that so much had happened in such a short time. 'Thanks Aunt Becky!' she said. 'You're a brick.'

'I'm a fool to messell,' Becky said. 'I onny hope I don't live to regret it.'

'I'd better be off,' Norman said. 'Or the ol' lady'll be after me for bein' late.'

'I'll walk you out the yard,' Barbara said. Which she

did so that she could hang on to his arm and kiss him goodbye and tell him he was the best brother in the world.

'Write that ol' letter,' he reminded her.

'Don't you worry,' she said, earnestly. 'That'll be the first thing I do.'

The letter was dropped into Steve's hand just before he went on duty the next morning. He answered it there and then, telling her not to worry and to leave everything to him. Then he left the hut, still digesting the news. He couldn't believe any mother could be so cruel as to refuse consent, let alone Barbara's. Just as well her aunt obliged. And just as well his old darlings were sensible.

His sensible mother was hard at work in the butcher's shop when he came breezing in on Wednesday morning. He thought she looked rather tired, but she cheered up at once when she saw him and giggled and protested when he lifted her off her feet to kiss her. Which delighted her customers. 'This your boy then, Mrs Wilkins?'

'Soppy thing!' she laughed, admiring him. He looked very brown and very dashing, with his beret on sideways, his battledress unbuttoned, his tie all anyhow. He hasn't changed a bit, she thought. All that nonsense about getting married *was* a joke. Thank God for that. 'Put me down do you daft happorth!'

He lowered her to the ground, grinning at her. 'When's Dad home?'

'Should be there now,' she told him. 'He's on late turn.'

'Perfect!' he beamed. 'See you teatime.' And he kissed her again and was gone.

'Always in a rush, these young things,' one of the customers said. 'Can't wait fer anything.'

'That's the war,' another chipped in. 'I mean, what's the point a' waitin' when there's a war on? We might

71

all be dead by termorrer, let's face it. Live life while you can, that's what I say.'

'Gaw dearie me!' the butcher said, wiping his hands on his apron. 'You're a cheerful lot this morning! Now then, Mrs Harris, what can I do you for?'

Fried onions, Heather thought, as she weighed out half a pound of scrag-end for Mrs Harris. And her mind leapt forward to the scene there would be round her table that evening, the three of them together again, just like old times, three plates, three bottles of beer. Oh it *was* good to have him home.

But when she got back to Childeric Road, he wasn't there. Bob had put the potatoes on to boil and was sitting in his armchair in the corner reading the paper and looking a bit sheepish but there was no sign of Steve.

'Did you see him?' she asked.

Bob nodded. 'Yep. Caught me on the 'op. I was still in my pyjamas.'

She took off her coat and put on her apron, tying the strings firmly round her waist. 'I hope he's not going to be late for supper,' she said. 'It'll spoil if he is.'

Bob looked more sheepish than before. 'No, no,' he said. 'He should be back directly.'

'I'll get on with the onions then.'

But when the meal was cooked and ready to serve and her lovely Steve finally came bursting through the door, he hardly gave the onions a sniff.

'It's all fixed,' he said. '13th a' May, half past ten. I know it's a bit early but it's the only space they had. There's a rush on. Anyway, I've booked the hall, an Charlie's going to take photos, an' I went round to Aunty Mabel and Uncle Sid. Didn't see him but she was there an' it's all OK. She can stay there Friday night. They're going to put their camp bed in with the girls. Bit of a squash but it'll be all right for one night. The girls came in from school while I was there an' they say they'll see to the flowers. So it's just the invites, that's all. I got two sets a' cards, with wedding bells on.' And he took them out of his tunic pocket and laid them on the table beside his father's plate. 'I thought they'd do.'

'May the 13th?' Heather said weakly. This couldn't be happening. It couldn't be true.

'That's the day,' Steve said and gave her a smile of such rapturous happiness it made her heart contract to see it. How could she tell him off when he looked like that? But she had to say something.

'And where's it going to be?'

'Here. In the Town Hall.'

She felt giddy. Why here? Weddings were supposed to be at the bride's place. And why in such a rush? What was going on? She took a breath to steady herself and tried another tack. 'Don't we have to give consent?'

'Yes,' he said cheerfully scathing about it, 'if you ever heard anything so barmy. I'm old enough to die for King and Country apparently, but not old enough to get married unless my daddy says so. Don't worry. Dad's seen to it.'

So that's why he was looking sheepish, Heather thought, and turned towards him, her face stern with rebuke. But he was wearing his warning expression.

'Her name's Barbara,' he said quickly, 'an' before you ask, he hasn't brought us a snap or anything but she's gorgeous.'

'She would be,' Heather said.

Her sarcasm was lost on Steve. 'There wasn't time for snaps,' he explained, all smiles. 'It's all been a bit of a rush. We haven't got much longer, you see Mum. It could be any day now. I was surprised I got leave, to tell you the truth.'

I can't deny him, Heather thought. Not when he says things like that. He's making a terrible mistake and he'll live to regret it but we'll have to let it happen. 'Tell us while we're eating supper,' she said, suggesting him to the table. 'I got liver an' bacon.'

'You're the best mum in the world,' he said.

So he went back to King's Lynn with everything arranged to his happy satisfaction and that Friday evening Barbara handed in her notice. A fortnight later, with all her worldly goods packed in Becky's battered suitcase, and all his army kit packed in a standard army kitbag, they were on their way to London and their new life.

CHAPTER SIX

The next fifteen hours passed in a blur. The train to
London was crowded with servicemen, every seat
taken, string racks crammed to the ceiling and with so
many kitbags and cases piled on the floor and so many
people squashed together in the corridor that Steve
could barely find a space for them both to stand in. Not
that they cared. Travelling was always uncomfortable in
wartime. You had to expect it. They were together and
that was all that really mattered. When the train swayed
over the points, he could put an arm round her waist to
hold her steady, when a sudden jolt threw her against
his chest, she could stay where she was until the roll of
the rails pulled them apart again. Desire carried them
sensuously from moment to moment.

'By this time tomorrow,' he said, brown eyes
lustrous, 'we shall be married.'

Fields of green corn and sugar beet spread like a
dappled sea beyond their criss-crossed window, clumps
of trees whooshed by, the wheels beat their familiar
rhythm over the rails, fiddledy-dee fiddledy-dum. By
this time tomorrow we shall be married. They stopped
at Cambridge and more passengers squeezed into the
throng so that they were pushed even closer together.
The air was blue with cigarette smoke. By this time
tomorrow we shall be married.

Then they were racketing through London, past rows
of dishevelled back gardens and terraces of soot-stained
houses, stolid under slate roofs the colour of battleships.
It wasn't long before Barbara noticed the gaps and the
piles of rubble.

'Is that the bombs?' she asked, awed by how many there'd been.

'That's the bombs,' he told her grimly. 'Don't worry. They'll pay for it.'

'Too right,' an Australian soldier agreed. 'You're with the Desert Rats, ain'tcher mate?'

Steve agreed that he was, proudly, and was soon deep in a conversation that rapidly involved all the soldiers and airmen around them.

Barbara didn't understand what they were saying but she felt honoured to be in their company. Fighting men, she thought, the ones who are going to win this war. And she felt such pride and terror at what that implied that it made her chest ache. She was quite relieved when they pulled into Liverpool Street station and the talk had to stop.

They struggled onto a wide platform, joined the great crowd of blue and khaki figures all moving in the same direction, emerged into a street so huge and dusty and full of people that for once in her life she was glad to have an arm to cling to.

A bus took them through the City – such buildings! – and over London Bridge – imagine! – to a place where trams clanged along the middle of the road one after the other in a long wine-red convoy and there were cars and lorries everywhere and people were talking in quick rough voices in an unfamiliar English and all sorts of other languages she couldn't understand. A tram buzzed them through endless streets to New Cross, which looked exactly like all the other places they'd driven through, with shops along both sides of a wide main road, crowds thronging the pavements and streets and streets full of houses.

'It's so big,' she said, as they set off down one of the side turnings. The size and assurance of it were making her feel like a country bumpkin.

He was so happy to be home that he didn't notice how discomfited she was. 'Isn't it,' he said happily. 'Here we are.'

They'd reached a long terrace of Victorian houses with bay windows hung with net curtains and posh front doors shaded by porches and little front gardens edged by privet hedges and little brick walls.

She was stunned by such affluence. 'Do you live here?'

'No,' he said, knocking at one of the doors. 'This is where my Aunty Mabel lives, where you're going to stay the night.' And before he could tell her anything else, the door was opened by two skinny girls who fell upon him and pulled him into the house, both talking at once and leaving Barbara to follow them.

Steve introduced them, 'My cousins. This is Joyce.' Waving at the older one. 'She's a Tartar. You'll have to watch out for her. And this is Hazel. This is Barbara, girls.'

'We know!' they chorused, staring at her.

'You coming in?' a woman's voice called. 'I expect you'd like a cup a' tea, wouldn't you.' Plump, smiling, with Steve's brown eyes. 'I'm Steve's Aunty Mabel.'

So they had tea and a meal in her warm kitchen, and Barbara sat facing a dresser full of plates and cups patterned green and orange, and listened as they swapped family gossip that she couldn't understand, and felt out of place and uncomfortable with four pairs of identical brown eyes watching her every movement. Then, to her alarm, Steve said he'd better be off.

She couldn't believe her ears. Surely he wasn't going to leave her? 'Now? I mean, straight away?'

He smiled at her. ''Course. It's tradition. Bride and groom have to be kept apart on the wedding eve otherwise it's bad luck. Come and see me out. Bye Aunt Mabel. Bye girls. Thanks for supper.'

The entire family followed him to the front door, his aunt and cousins happily, Barbara with growing anxiety. 'Hain't I gonna meet your mum an' dad?' she asked.

'Tomorrow,' he said and kissed her goodbye, a very proper kiss with all those eyes looking on. 'Must go. My mates are waiting for me.'

She wanted to keep him there a bit longer, to argue that she really ought to meet his parents before the wedding, to beg him not to leave her alone, but he'd opened the door to the darkness outside and was already striding down the little path and hurdling over the gate. 'The girls'll look after you, won't you girls,' he called. 'See you tomorrow.'

She didn't want the girls to look after her. She wanted to be with him, not on her own in a strange house with strange people. How can he do this to me? she thought, staring into the darkness. Don't he realise how I feel? But apparently not, because he didn't even look back.

'He's off drinking with his mates,' the big one explained, and she shut the door and adjusted the blackout curtain. 'He always does that when he's home on leave. Come on. We got to show you round.'

The tone upset her. 'You don' have to,' she said. 'I aspect I can find my own way.'

'You want to know where you're going to sleep don't you?' the big girl asked, her glasses glinting in the half-light in the hall. She was nearly as tall as Barbara, and with that tightly permed hair and those round specs she looked and felt like an opponent.

'Show her the bathroom first, our Joyce,' the smaller one said. 'She might want to spend a penny.'

So she had to follow them and be shown. First they took her back to the kitchen, where their mother was clearing the table, and from there to the bathroom, which was a narrow room leading out of a scullery at the back of the house. She was impressed by it despite herself. Imagine having a lavvy inside the house! And a bath with a geyser for hot water. What luxury! They must be rich. But she didn't use the toilet, even though she wanted to. That would have been too embarrassing with them waiting outside. So they led her upstairs to the front bedroom, which overlooked the street and was full of beds, a high double, a lower single, a camp bed virtually on the floor.

'That's yours,' the little girl said. How pert she was with her short bob and that straight thick fringe. 'That'll do, won't it.'

Be all the same if it wouldn't, Barbara thought as she nodded. But it was only for a night. Just one night. That was all.

'You can put your things in here,' Joyce said, opening a drawer. 'We cleared it out for you.' And she looked at the battered case that her guest had carried upstairs. 'You won't need more room than that, will you?'

Barbara unpacked, as that seemed to be expected and the two girls sat on the double bed and quizzed her.

'How long you been going out with our Steve?' Joyce began.

'Ages,' Barbara told her, trying to slide her cheap underwear into the drawer before they could get a look at it.

It was a wasted effort. She'd never known two girls with such sharp eyes. 'You should've got yourself some parachute silk,' the little one remarked. 'You only need a panel and you can make all sorts a' things. Molly up the Co-op had petticoats and french knickers an' all sorts. You should've seen 'em.'

The bombardment went on. Was her hair natural or did she have it permed? Did she have any brothers or sisters? Were they coming to the wedding? Was that clogs she was wearing? 'Look at that Hazel. All made a' wood. They must be ever so heavy. Are they heavy?'

'Not parti'cly,' she said, daring them to disagree with her, and she folded her new blouse into the drawer and closed it quickly before they could make some disparaging remark about *that* too. 'We going down now?'

'Not yet,' Joyce said. 'We got you a wedding dress.'

'What?'

'It's second-hand but it's only been worn the once,' Joyce said, pulling a large cardboard box from the top of the wardrobe. Then she giggled. 'Well it would be, wouldn't it? It was Molly's up the Co-op. She says she was ever so happy when she wore it an' she hopes you'll be the same.' She took off the lid and removed two layers of tissue paper. 'There you are. What d'you think?'

It was an ivory-coloured dress, short and silky with a straight skirt and a bodice covered in lace, and Barbara could see at a glance that it wouldn't fit her or suit her. 'Well,' she said. 'I don't know whether . . .'

'Try it on,' they insisted, lifting it from the box. 'See what it looks like. There's a veil there an' all. An' a tirrarra. You'd never get a new one, would you? Think of all the coupons.'

So she tried it on, as there didn't seem to be any way of refusing without being rude to them. And it didn't fit. 'Thass ever so kind of you,' she said, relieved that she'd be able to escape from the awful thing so easily. 'But thass too big. You can see can't you.' And she pinched the excess cloth in the bodice and held it away from her.

'Oh we'll soon have that fixed,' Joyce said briskly. 'Stand in front a' the mirror an we'll pin it to size. We can do what we like with it. She said.'

There was a pin cushion on the dressing table hedgehogged with pins. Within seconds she had half a dozen of them clenched between her lips and was busy at work nipping and tucking, while her sister hovered and gave advice. 'Bit further over our Joyce . . . Little tuck under the bust . . . Not that much. You're pullin' the seam.'

'There y'are,' they chorused when they'd finished. 'Put the veil on. Get the full effect. You look smashing. Like a film star.'

But when Barbara turned to the mirror to see what they'd done to her, she didn't look smashing. She looked ridiculous. Stiff and awkward and unrecognisable. Like a badly-dressed doll with her bodice pulled over sideways and her hem uneven. I can't wear this, she thought, staring at her reflection. I simply can't.

'Well ain't that lovely!' a voice said from the landing and there was Aunt Mabel, smiling approval. 'Well done you two. It's a transformation.'

But I don't want to be transformed, Barbara thought. I want to be me.

'That's the borrowed bit taken care of,' Hazel said, as she and Joyce pulled the dress over Barbara's head. 'An' the old. That veil's ever so old. And the ring'll be new. Now we've just got to work on the blue. Bit a' blue ribbon'ud do. We could make a garter or something or tie it round the flowers.'

'What flowers?' Barbara asked shaking her head free.

'We're gonna cut the lilac,' Hazel told her. 'It's lovely this year. It'll be a bit heavy but you won't mind that, will you.'

'Dad'll find a bit a' broom handle to hold it up,' their mother said. 'Right. That's all settled then. We'll hang that up in the wardrobe for now. It's almost time for Bebe Daniels.'

'Can't miss that,' Joyce agreed. 'Then I'll have to do my hair or I shall look a fright in the morning. What time's our Betty coming home?'

So there's another one of them. I thought two was bad enough.

'Late,' their mother said. 'She won't wake you. You can have another hour listening to the wireless and then you'd all better turn in. We've got a lot to do tomorrow.'

So they had another hour, which Barbara found difficult even with the wireless to keep them entertained. Then they went to bed.

The two girls bounced into their double bed and were asleep in minutes but Barbara couldn't settle. The camp bed was as uncomfortable as it looked, the house was unfamiliar, and the dress loomed in the wardrobe like a threat. What have I let myself in for? she wondered as she tried to turn over without waking her new cousins. Do I want to belong to this family? To be here in this huge town, where I don't fit, with all these people who give me funny looks an' don't like me? She wasn't even sure she wanted to get married. Not now. And not here. Oh dear, she thought, what have I done?

Presently she could hear someone tiptoeing up the stairs and along the landing and she lay very still in the camp bed with her eyes shut pretending to be asleep, as another girl came in and undressed quickly and eased into the single bed. Our Betty. Should I say something to her? she wondered. And decided against it. This is all a mistake, she thought as sleep dragged her away, an' I shall have to say so in the morning.

But the next morning her new cousins let her lie in and didn't wake her until nine o'clock when Joyce arrived with tea and toast on a tin tray and the news that it was a beautiful day and that she was to have a bath 'all to herself' because she was the bride.

'We share ours', she confided, 'to save water. But Mum says you're the special one today. And she says you're to borrow Bet's dressing gown because there's all sorts in the kitchen.'

Never a truer word. By the time Barbara came downstairs to take her promised bath, swathed in the prescribed dressing gown and feeling very self-conscious, the kitchen was full of people. 'Here's the bride!' they called. 'How are you duck?' The dresser was mounded with cut lilac and Betty and Hazel were hard at work in their petticoats making buttonholes and an enormous bouquet, neighbours ran in and out with boxes, her new aunt was pouring tea, there were two women by the table gossiping and making sandwiches, Joyce was standing in the hearth, half an inch away from the mirror, wincing as she took the curlers out of her hair, and a man in his shirtsleeves who said he was 'your new uncle Sid', was sitting in the corner patiently cutting the end off a broom handle.

So the bath was rather an uneasy luxury. It was blissful to be able to lie out full length in scented water – for the first time in her life what's more – but her thoughts were spinning with anxiety. What if someone was to come in to use the lavvy? Why hadn't Steve taken her to meet his parents? What if her mum had found out and came up to London to stop them?

Presently she became aware that the two girls were in the scullery and that they were exchanging scurrilous confidences in the low, slightly shocked tones reserved for these occasions. So naturally she listened. And realised with a shock of anger that the person they were disparaging was her.

'She's taking for ever in that bath,' Hazel was saying. 'What you think she's up to?'

'Expect she's dirty,' Joyce confided. 'I don't suppose they have baths where she comes from. Out in the country.'

'D'you see her knickers?' Hazel giggled.

'Weren't they *awful*!'

'Ghastly. An' those clogs! Fancy wearing them round town. She looks a proper clodhopper. I'd die if it was me.'

'I don't know what our Steve saw in her. I mean, she's nothing to look at and the way she talks! All that oo-ar stuff. *Thass* this an' *thass* that.'

'Oo-ar, oo-ar, the country bumpkin,' Hazel said. And they both giggled as they walked away.

Their mockery stiffened Barbara's resolve. Right, she thought furiously. Thass it. I hain't wearing that rotten frock an' you needn't think it. I *would* be a country bumpkin in that.

She climbed out of the bath, dried quickly and swathed in the dressing gown, strode through the kitchen and straight upstairs to dress as she pleased.

It took quite an effort because her skin was still damp

but she was ready – in her green skirt, her pretty blouse and her country bumpkin clogs – before anyone came up to see how she was getting on. And then, mercifully, it was Betty and not her two horrid sisters.

She was carrying an enormous bouquet of white lilac and was watching it carefully as she walked in. 'No one's to see you till the car comes,' she said. 'Otherwise it's bad luck. Hazel says to tell you your blue ribbon's in the lilac. Tied round the handle.' Then she looked up and stopped, her eyes widening. 'You're not wearing the dress then?'

'No,' Barbara said boldly. 'That makes me look a freak.' And she waited, prepared to be mocked or scolded or argued with.

But Betty smiled at her. 'Quite right,' she said. 'You wear what you want. I know I would.'

She understands, Barbara thought. I've got a friend in this family. She's an ally. 'Thanks,' she said and smiled.

Betty smiled back. 'I'm Betty by the way,' she said. 'Came back too late to be introduced last night. You were asleep.'

'I wasn't actually,' Barbara admitted. 'I was pretending. I'd have known who you were anyway. You're ever so like Steve.' The same brown eyes, the same smile, the same thick hair only brown instead of auburn and fashionably long, in a page-boy bob to her shoulders and mounded above her forehead in two elaborate scrolls. A face with strength and honesty in it, the scarlet mouth firm and shapely, nose straight, eyebrows unplucked. A friendly face.

Betty was thinking, brown eyes clouded. 'Would you mind if I asked you something?'

'No, of course not.'

'Well then. Have you got a hat?'

'No,' Barbara admitted. 'Didn't have the coupons.'

'Hang on a tick,' Betty said and ran out of the room, her blue cotton dress swishing with the urgency of her stride. She was back in seconds, carrying a hat, which she held out to Barbara balanced on the tips of her fingers. It was a very pretty hat, made of cream-coloured straw with a trimming of blue forget-me-nots around the brim.

'You can borrow this if you like,' she said. And when Barbara hesitated, 'It's all right. It's not some old second-hand thing like that dress. I bought it new.'

'But don't you want to wear it yourself?' Barbara asked. 'I mean, if you bought it new . . .'

'That's right,' Betty said, understanding her completely. 'I bought it for the wedding. But I've got another one and you're the bride. Go on, borrow it. I'd love you to. If you like it, I mean. Try it on.'

So it was tried and as Betty said, it set everything off a treat, the forget-me-nots matching the blue flowers embroidered on her blouse, the straw echoing the creamy blooms of the bouquet, which was heavy, just as they'd warned her, but very sweetly scented. The two girls stood side by side in front of the mirror and admired the effect they'd created.

'Well?' Betty asked.

'If you're sure you don' mind,' Barbara said. And to her surprise and delight was given a kiss by way of answer.

Then Joyce was yelling up the stairs that the car had come and was she ready. And from that moment on the day picked up such speed that she barely had a chance to register one impression before the next was pressing in upon her, although she was horribly aware of how annoyed they all were when she came down the stairs not wearing that awful dress.

But the drive seemed to be over before it had begun. She was still settling in the seat when they were all tumbling out again. She caught a glimpse of a large building rising from the pavement, with soot-stained columns, a clock tower high above her head, an imposing door, and then they were all inside. There were crowds of people waiting in the foyer – the man called Uncle Sid, Becky Bosworth in a new hat, a fat woman dressed in red, smoking a cigar and beaming at her, the girls from work, Joan and Mavis giggling, two of Steve's oppos, the mousy-haired one who'd delivered his first letter and the one called Taffy. She scanned the crowd, trying to take them all in and aware that she couldn't do it. If only Norman wasn't at sea, if only he could have been there to give her away. She *did* miss him. But then Steve was striding through the mêlée towards her, looking very smart in his uniform, holding out his arms. And the day shifted and became possible.

'Hello gorgeous!' he said. 'Have you missed me?'

Her face told him one thing and her mouth another. 'No 'course not.' If only she could kiss him. She'd never needed to kiss him as much as she did then. But there were more introductions to face.

'This is my mum,' he said, reaching out a hand to pull a middle-aged woman towards them. Long face, greying hair, lumpy sort of figure, wearing a flowered dress with very square shoulders, and a wary expression. Not a bit like Steve. Am I supposed to kiss her?

Apparently not for she was holding out her hand, rather stiffly. 'Pleased to meet you,' she said. But she didn't sound as though she was.

'And this is Dad,' Steve was saying.

'Yes,' Barbara said. 'I can see.' The same nice warm brown eyes, the same smile.

'Welcome to the family,' he said and kissed her cheek. Now that's better, I'm going to like him.

But there wasn't time to say anything because they were being ushered into a brown room and asked to sit in front of a table polished like glass, where the registrar, who was very old and wore pebble-dash spectacles, brought the meeting to order. 'I call upon these persons here present . . .'

Afterwards neither of them could remember what

they'd promised, nor when or how they'd signed the register. One minute Steve was easing the ring onto her finger and the next they were running down the steps towards the waiting car under a shower of confetti.

And if the ceremony was a blur, the wedding breakfast was total confusion. There were speeches, and everybody laughed a lot, and a man called Charlie took pictures. They seemed to be drinking a lot of wine, and there were certainly things to eat but apart from the cake, they didn't really notice any of it. The cake was different. It was so enormous that it took two people to carry it into the hall. And when she and Steve had posed in front of it knife in hand and the ceremonial pictures had been taken, the fat woman stepped forward and lifted the icing into the air to mocking cheers, to reveal a small fruit cake standing rather forlornly on the silver stand. And as Barbara looked up in surprise, she saw that the icing was made of cardboard and had plainly been used on several occasions, for the inside was chipped and stained and covered in pencil marks. But it was a tasty cake for all that and just big enough to go round.

Then and abruptly it was time to catch the train to London Bridge. It wasn't until the engine was picking up speed and the waving guests had been left behind and Barbara was shaking the confetti from her hair to the amusement of the other passengers, that she thought to ask her new husband where they were going.

He looked like a purring cat. 'You'll see,' he said.

Back on the platform, the wedding guests were going their separate ways. Hands were shaken, hats adjusted, congratulations offered, train times checked.

'That orl wen' off very well,' Becky Bosworth said to Heather Wilkins. 'Considerin' what a rush job it was, you done wonders. They make 'andsome couple.'

Heather had been steadfastly polite all day. 'Yes,' she

said. 'Thank you for coming.' And turned her eyes towards the next farewell.

Thass a funny sort a' woman, Becky thought, sharp eyes missing nothing. Don' she see what a catch our Barbara is? Being Becky, she kept her thoughts to herself. But Mavis, who was waiting her turn to say goodbye, caught the impact of her expression and on the journey back to Lynn, she started to put two and two together – London wedding, all done in a rush, no sign of the Nelsons, not so much as a telegram from them.

'Did Barbara tell her Ma?' she asked Becky. 'Or hain't she s'posed to know?'

'Not yet awhile gal,' Becky said. 'Thass a secret.'

'What about Vic? Did she tell him?'

'No. Thass just us what knows,' Becky told her. 'Don' you go sayin' nothin' to nobody, thass my advice.'

Mavis and Joan exchanged glances, Mavis warning, Joan questioning. She don't mean it, surely? Joan thought. We can't keep a weddin' secret. Thass not right. Can't be. Not from Vic anyway, the way he go on about her. He'll be really upset. They'd talk it over later on. At the dance, maybe.

The two girls from the draper's were still lost in the romance of the wedding. 'Did you smell that lilac?' 'Didden she look bootiful?'

'Yes,' Becky agreed. 'She did. An' richly deserved, thass what *I* say. She's a bootiful gal.'

That was Bob Wilkins' opinion of her too but, given his wife's brittle temper, he wasn't sure it was safe to express it. He had a nasty feeling that the two women had taken against one another. Nothing he could put his finger on, because nothing had been said. A matter of looks really. The frozen look on Heather's face when they were introduced and the changing expression on the girl's. Not dislike. It wasn't as strong as that. Sort of shrewd at first. As if she knew she wasn't welcomed.

And then bold, sticking her chin in the air, challenging. Or accepting Heather's challenge. Not encouraging either way. Perhaps it would be better just to keep quiet and concentrate on getting home.

Heather seemed to have the same idea. She didn't say anything until they were walking up Childeric Road towards their flat. Then she burst into complaint. 'All that work,' she said. 'Well I hope it was worth it, that's all.'

''Course it was,' he said, putting his key in the lock. 'It was a lovely wedding.'

'Lovely,' she said. 'It was dreadful. I don't know what she thought she looked like! All that trouble to get her a wedding dress and she gets married in old clothes and green clogs. Green clogs! I ask you. And did you see her hat?'

He thought it looked very pretty.

'Well of course it looked pretty,' she said scornfully. 'Because it was Betty's hat. The one she bought specially. Betty's lovely hat with green clogs. Words fail me!'

'Steve didn't seem to mind.'

'Steve's got the stardust in his eyes,' she said. 'He'll see through her in the end. You notice her parents didn't turn up. Only that hideous old aunt. Joyce thinks she's run away from home. And I wouldn't be surprised. She looks the sort.'

He tried to demur. 'Aren't you being a bit hard?'

'No,' she said. 'It'll end in tears, you mark my words. Do you know how old she is? No I thought you didn't. Seventeen. That aunt of hers let it slip. Didn't tell me, mind. I overheard her. Seventeen. It's ridiculous. And did you see the way she looked at *me*? I never saw anything so bold. Sticking her chin up, daring me. She's a nasty bit a' work.'

'She could have been nervous.'

Heather snorted. 'Nervous? That one! Don't you believe it. She's a hard little thing. There's not a nervous bone in her body. I can't think what he sees in her.'

'He loves her,' Bob said, defending his son.

'Oh I don't doubt *that*,' she said, following him up the stairs. 'But there's a lot more to marriage than love. As he'll find out.'

'Not when you're newly-weds,' he said.

'You can't be newly-weds for ever,' she said, brisk with distress and anger. 'You've got to live with one another when you're married. Be a different story then. You mark my words.' And she went off quickly to change into her ordinary clothes. The sooner she got this day back to normal the better.

They might never get the chance, poor little devils, Bob thought. This honeymoon might be all they'd get. The Second Front was necessary and unavoidable, they all knew that. It was going to be a very great event, a valiant endeavour, a moment of history. But at that moment it loomed over his household like a monster avid for blood.

CHAPTER SEVEN

When Steve and Barbara arrived at their destination, they were so far out in the depths of the country that they could have been at sea. There was no station, just a halt with two wooden platforms and a gap where the name-plate had been, and no roads either, no convoys, no Jeeps, no staff cars, and apart from Steve's uniform, not a trace of khaki anywhere. An earth track ran alongside the halt and out into the fields, which spread peacefully east and west across rolling countryside, growing fruit trees and wheat and an odd sort of crop that needed a network of strings to support it. Barbara could see a farmhouse in the distance and a building with two fat chimneys, which seemed to have been built leaning over sideways, but otherwise the landscape was empty. After the speed and noise of London it was blissfully, soothingly quiet. And wondrously private.

As soon as their train had disappeared round the bend, Steve put his arms round his new wife and kissed her so long and lovingly that her borrowed hat fell from her head and lay in the dust of the platform, quite forgotten.

'We made it,' he said, looking down at her with splendid triumph.

She wound her arms round his neck as they stood close together in the gentle silence. 'I do love you,' she said.

He smiled into her eyes. 'Likewise,' he said. 'Come and see our house.'

She looked round at the fields. 'House? Have you got us a house?'

'Wait till you see it. Come on.'

They picked up their luggage, retrieved her hat, and set off with their arms around each other, walking in unison in their lovely three-legged way, and following the track between the fields. The sun warmed their shoulders; the sky was clear blue and full of cotton wool clouds; there was no such thing as war.

'How d'you know where it is?' she asked. He didn't have a map but he didn't seem to need one.

'I used to come down here every September when I was a kid.'

'For holidays?'

'No,' he grinned. 'Hopping.'

So that's what those funny plants are.

'Had to stop when I went to grammar school. Went up in the world. But it was fun while it lasted. The whole family came down. Me an' the girls an' Aunty Mabel and Mum and Aunt Sis. Half the street. Dad said it was like moving a regiment. They ran a special train for us out of London Bridge. Terrible old thing. You should've seen it. Packed to the gunnels. People brought all sorts of things down with them. Aunt Sis used to bring her canary.'

'Where did you sleep?' she asked. 'Was it in this place we're goin' to?'

'Good God no,' he said. 'We were in huts. I wouldn't take you to a hut. *We*'ve got a bungalow. Only the best for you and me!'

So naturally she had to stop and kiss him, even though it meant losing her hat for the second time, and as the kiss went luxuriously on, a skylark rose from the distant corn and trilled into the air, its joyous song rippling over them as it spiralled higher and higher, free and passionate and untrammelled.

'I know exactly how that bird feels,' she said, looking up into the sky at the black speck above their heads. 'I'm *so* happy. I'd like to stop the world an' stop time an' stay here like this for ever an' ever an' ever.'

'I wouldn't,' he said cheerfully. 'I want to get to bed.'

She laughed with delight, picking up her hat. 'You would!'

'And you don't?' he dared her.

The answer was clear as sunshine on her face. 'You know I do.'

'Well then. Come on. We're nearly there. See that clump of trees by the bend. It's just behind them.'

There were three ramshackle buildings behind the trees, set higgledy-piggledy round a small scruffy green, each made of roughcast and with a corrugated iron roof, and all obviously empty.

'Which one is it?'

'The one at the end,' he said. 'With the tiles.'

She'd seen red tiles from the corner of her eye as they rounded the bend, but she'd assumed it was the roof of a shed. Now she realised that it was a fourth house, that it was standing in a hollow and that it was made entirely of red tiles. The low roof was rosy with them and the front was hung with brick-red pantiles, warm against the black paint of the three square windows and the door.

'Well?' he said hopefully. 'What d'you think?'

She was already running down the slope, hat in hand, too excited to wait. 'Thass smashing!' Fancy spending your honeymoon in a little house!

But when they reached the doorstep, they couldn't open the door. The lock took the key easily enough but the door wouldn't budge. He pushed it, she pushed it, they pushed it together.

After the third attempt, his face was dark with frustration. 'Bloody thing! What's the matter with it?'

She was surprised to see him in such a temper over something as trivial as a door. 'Thass been shut a long time,' she said calmly. 'Thass what 'tis.'

'All through the war,' he said. And remembered his army training. 'Oh well, I'll just have to kick it open.'

Which he did, taking a short run and kicking it so violently that it swung wide with a crash, much to her admiration. Inside was a narrow L-shaped hall with very thin walls covered in faded wallpaper and four doors leading from it, all covered in flaking brown paint. Little drifts of dust lay heaped on the brown lino and there was an odd musty smell like a cross between a broom cupboard and a coal cellar. A row of iron coat-hooks protruded from one side wall and there was a huge gas meter on the other, both grey with dust. But Barbara was thrilled by it. Four doors, she thought, four rooms. Four rooms. Imagine! It was like being offered a box of chocolates. She didn't know which to choose first and, while she dithered, Steve opened the right-hand door.

'No,' he said, as she stepped inside. 'Wrong one.'

She was torn between desire and curiosity. It was such a pretty room, a real living room, the sort of thing she'd seen at the pictures. She caught a glimpse of a fireplace made of brick, a tiled hearth and a tin fender with two tin coal-scuttles at each end, with brown leather lids that made them look like little stools. There were wicker armchairs, a wooden dresser covered in dusty china, a deal table and two plain chairs by the window, gaslights with pretty pink shades, a divan covered by a hand-made blanket, crocheted in lopsided patterns of brightly coloured wool. And wonder of wonders, just inside the door, pushed right up against the wall, the dearest little piano, half the size of an ordinary one and covered in carvings and decorations.

'Oh!' she said. 'Thass like a palace. Fancy living in a place like this!'

He was too busy kissing her neck to look at it. 'Come and see the bedroom,' he urged, gentling her back into the hall. 'It's got a double bed.'

The delight of such a thought. No more snatched kisses. No more scratchy straw. Just peace and privacy in a bed of their own.

They went through another brown door and it *was* a bedroom. She was vaguely aware of an iron bedstead painted black, and a high bed with a beige cotton coverlet, but then they were both tumbling down onto it and there was nothing in the world and nothing in the room except their hunger for one another.

Afterwards, as they lay dishevelled and satisfied, sharing a cigarette, she became aware that the coverlet was marked with brown rust stains and felt decidedly damp.

'We shall have to air this bed 'fore we sleep in it,' she said.

He was easy with gratified desire, his skin glowing and his eyes half shut. 'Who said we were going to sleep in it? I've got other plans.'

She turned back the bedspread and pressed the palm of her hand against the mattress. 'Thass soaking wet.'

'I don't care.'

'Is there a clothes line?'

He pretended to groan. 'Five minutes married and she's going all housewife on me.'

'I haint sleepin' in a damp bed,' she told him. 'I had enough of that at home.' Her younger brothers had wet the bed she'd had to share with them every blessed night, and she'd always hated it.

He groaned and sat up. 'Oh come on then,' he said. 'We'll find you a clothes line. I expect it's round the back in the garden.'

It was and the blankets and pillows were soon hung on it. But the mattress was too heavy to haul into the garden and too damp to dry in the sun.

'We need a fire,' Barbara said. 'Nice big one. If we prop that up in front of a fire, that'll be dry in no time. Is there any coal?'

There was a coal-shed in the garden full of it and a box full of old newspaper and enough twigs for kindling lying about on the grass. 'I'll have that going in no time,' she promised. 'I'm good with fires.' And although this one took a long time to catch, she coaxed it alight eventually. They heaved the mattress from the bed, lugged it through the hall and stood it in front of the blaze to steam. Soon their pretty living room was full of the musty smell of its stale, damp flock.

'Phew!' Steve complained. 'What a stink!' And went to open the windows. 'Let's get out of here.'

So they explored their kingdom and discovered that the fourth door led to a front bedroom crammed with furniture – a double bed covered by another rust-stained bedspread, a black travelling box, a deal washstand painted pale blue and a dressing table painted white – and that the kitchen, which they'd rushed through to get to the garden, had a larder and a broom cupboard, a sink complete with tap, draining board and plate-rack, and standing on its own, looking extremely modern and grand, a grey and white gas cooker.

'I'm sorry about the bed being damp,' Steve said. 'I wanted everything to be perfect for you.' He grimaced. 'Didn't make a very good job of it, did I? We have to kick the door down to get in and the bed's running water and God knows what else we shall find.'

He looked so downcast that she flung herself into his arms and peppered his face with kisses. 'It *is* perfect,' she said. '*We*'re here. That'ud make anywhere perfect.'

'You', he said, overwhelmed by such a fierce, loving, perfect reply, 'are my own dear darling.' And when she beamed at him, 'This is better though, isn't it? This kitchen, I mean. Every mod con, as they say.' And he looked at the cooker hopefully.

'I've never used one of them,' she admitted.

'Never?' Now it was his turn to be surprised.

'We cooked on the fire at home. Don't worry. I'll get used to it.'

He was himself again. He'd provided a touch of luxury for her. 'There's nothing to it,' he said, demonstrating. 'You just turn on the tap and light the gas and Bob's your uncle. Simplicity itself.' Talk of cooking reminded him that he was hungry. 'Where'd we leave the shopping basket?' Aunt Mabel had pressed it upon him as they got into the train, saying it was '*a few things to be going on with*' and he'd carried it down without giving it much attention.

Now neither of them could remember where it was. Out in the hall probably.

It was still on the doorstep beside his kitbag and her hat, where they'd flung it before they ran inside. And now that they weren't in such a rush, they noticed that there was a card lying on the doormat beside it. '*Passengers' Luggage in advance in shed.*' That was a puzzle because their luggage was limited to a change of clothes in the kitbag and there'd been nothing in the coal-shed except coal. So they went back to the garden to investigate.

This shed turned out to be a lean-to propped against the brick wall at the end of the garden and obscured by an elderberry bush and a profusion of nettles and couch grass, and the luggage was a wooden trunk lashed shut with two leather belts and yards of elderly rope and boldly labelled '*Mr and Mrs Wilkins*'. It took the pair of them to haul it through the back door into the kitchen.

'Aunty Sis,' Steve said, as they unfastened it.

'You got lot of aunts. Which one was that?'

'The fat one. Had a red suit on. Smoked cigars. Her friend owns this place. That's how I got it. She said she was sending something down for us. I didn't think it would be a trunk.'

It was a treasure trove. Packed across the top were a pair of white sheets and two old fashioned pillowcases with a note attached '*They're not new but they'll do a turn!*' Then came two towels, one blue and one green, four tea towels neatly darned, and a checked tablecloth. Then two pairs of plimsolls with another note. '*They might be a bit on the big side for you, Barbara but you can stuff them with newspaper and they'll save your shoes.*' Then an army blanket and a cardboard box full of goodies – a tin of stewed steak and a tin of spam, a jar of home-made marmalade and a small tin of condensed milk – Nestle's what's more, very grand – a bag of potatoes, flour, part of a string of onions, a packet of salt and another of tea, a jar of pickles and a bottle of vinegar both wrapped about with several protective layers of newspaper, even an Izal toilet roll, a large box of matches and a packet of soap flakes. And tucked in one corner were two flannels made out of an old towel, a bar of scented soap and a leather strap for sharpening Steve's razor.

'She's thought of everything,' Steve said, holding the strap in his hands. 'This was Uncle Percy's. She must have kept it.' And when Barbara looked a question at him. 'He was killed at Dunkirk. I thought she'd thrown all his things away. And look at all this food. She must have spent her coupons on those tins.'

But Barbara was scowling. There's altogether too much of his family, she thought, looking at the tins. What's the matter with them? 'Don't they think I know how to feed you?'

He changed the subject, deftly. 'How long's it going to be before that lot's dry? I haven't kissed you for ages.'

'I thought you were hungry.'

'So I am,' he said, stroking her bare arms. 'I just don't know which appetite to satisfy first.'

She wasn't in the mood for love at that moment. 'Well I need food if you don't,' she said. 'I'm starvin'.' And she unpacked.

'We can't eat in that stink,' he pointed out, admiring her as she filled the kettle and rinsed two cups and saucers and two plates under the tap in the sink.

'We'll have a picnic.'

So they ate their first meal together sitting on the rough grass out in the garden. Bread, cheese and pickles and one of Aunt Sis's onions – which turned out to be very tasty despite Barbara's misgivings – and all washed down by their first pot of tea, sweetened by condensed milk. And the sun went on airing the blankets.

When they'd eaten every last crumb, Steve tore himself away from her for five minutes to make up the fire. He returned to report that the mattress was still steaming and the room was like a Turkish bath.

'I had a bath this morning,' she remembered. 'Bath salts an' all. Seems like years ago. I lay there thinking what if Ma comes down an' tries to stop us.'

'There's no stopping us,' he told her happily. 'We're invincible. We're married.' He paused, looking at her closely. 'Promise me something?'

'Depends,' she said. She'd recovered enough to tease him.

'Don't let's talk about our parents.'

She didn't agree with that. 'Why not?' she said. 'We shouldn't have secrets from one another. We should talk about everything.'

'But not now,' he urged. 'Not on our honeymoon.'

For the first time in her outspoken life, she saw the need for caution. 'Well . . .' she said. 'Maybe not now then.'

'Or the war?' he said. 'Or the Second Front or anything like that?'

That was easier to agree to. She didn't want to talk about the war either. 'All right,' she said. 'I promise.'

So they pushed all unquiet thoughts from their minds and gave themselves up almost entirely to the pleasure they needed. That night they slept – eventually – on a warm mattress under Aunt Sis's sheets and their sun-dried blankets. And woke late to love again and to plan their meals for the day. Toast and marmalade for a very late breakfast, tinned steak and mashed potatoes for supper.

By Monday morning their food stocks were running low. They had condiments in plenty but no bread and butter. So they found their emergency ration cards, walked to the nearest road and caught the morning bus to the nearest town. The bus stopped at the station, where, feeling very virtuous and far-sighted, they arranged for the trunk to be collected in a week's time. Then they strolled into the centre of town and did their shopping – two large loaves, chump chops, bacon, sugar, butter, marg, cheese and another packet of tea. They also discovered that there was a milkman who would deliver the odd pint to their door now and then *and* a travelling greengrocer who did his rounds on Tuesdays and Fridays.

'We shan't want for anything,' Steve said, as the afternoon bus rattled them home.

Only time, Barbara thought, but true to her promise, she didn't say so.

The ease of the next six days stretched enticingly before them. For a week at least they were unassailable. For a week at least they could love when they wanted, eat when they wanted and be totally and utterly private.

On Tuesday they stayed indoors all day because it was raining and having found a dust-shovel and brush, an old cloth and the remains of a tin of polish in the cupboard and an old broom in the shed, they set about putting the house to order, working together as Steve said happily, 'like an old married couple'; on Wednesday evening when the sky cleared, they strolled the half mile to the local pub for a couple of pints; on Thursday when the sun was blazing again, they put on their plimsolls and went for a walk in the fields where they met the farmer who was out inspecting his crops and stopped to talk to them, amiably but for much too long.

But for most of the time their world was shrunk to the four thin walls of their red-tiled kingdom, to the warm, musty nest of their well-used bed. As dusk fell, they drew the curtains and lit the gaslight and returned to enchantment.

'Your eyes are like mirrors,' he told her. 'I can see my face in them. Like a little photo.'

'I'd like a photo of you,' she said. 'Just as you are. To keep for ever.'

He was in the full pride of a splendid erection. 'Just as I am?' he demurred.

'Just,' she told him, and when he grimaced, 'well head an' shoulders then. I wouldn't show it to no one else. It'ud be mine.'

He ran a loving hand down the long curve of her naked spine. Without the boxiness of her clothes, she was all luscious curves, her flesh golden in the gaslight. He was bewitched by the sight and scent and sensation of her, those rounded arms so soft about his neck, those lovely sloping shoulders – which he hadn't suspected when they were squared by shoulder pads – that belly so wondrously rounded, those tip-tilted breasts so full and beautiful that he grew taut with desire simply to see them.

'And you're mine,' he said, pulling her towards him. 'All mine. I still can't believe it.'

'I know,' she said, lifting her mouth to be kissed again. 'Thass like a dream.'

From time to time, as they lay in one another's arms, the dream was interrupted by the steady drone of Allied bombers heading out to France and Germany, but neither of them spoke of it. Once they saw a squadron of Hurricanes hurtling through the sky on their way to strafe the German defences, but they watched without comment. They were out of the war for the time being and sated by pleasures great and small. And that was all they needed.

On Saturday it was so warm and they were so exhausted that they spent the morning out on the green, lolling about on the grass.

'This is our first anniversary,' he said. 'D'you realise that? We've been married a week.'

She smiled at him lazily, replete with happiness. 'Happy anniversary!'

101

'Yes,' he said, admiring her. 'It is. You've caught the sun.'

'So have you,' she told him, returning his admiration. 'You got freckles all over your nose.'

'I have *not*,' he protested and leant forward to kiss her into silence. But as he moved, he caught sight of a distant figure heading towards them down the footpath. 'Hello,' he said. 'There's somebody coming.'

'There can't be,' she said, turning to look too. 'There's nobody here but us an' nobody knows that, do they, except the milkman an' the greengrocer. An' your aunt Sis.'

But she was wrong. There was a postwoman peddling towards the green and she was waving a letter.

Steve's heart sank. 'Maybe it's not for us,' he said, hoping against hope. 'I mean, it could be for someone in one of the other bungalows. They could be coming down. For the weekend.' But of course it *was* for him, as he knew only too well, and it was in an official brown envelope, OHMS. He held it in his hand, waiting for the privacy to open it, afraid of what it contained.

Unfortunately the postwoman was chatty. 'Here on holiday?' she asked.

'Yes,' Barbara told her, after an anxious glance at Steve. 'Thass right.'

'You're not from round *these* parts, are you,' the postwoman observed. 'I can tell.'

Barbara confessed to her Norfolk origins, and as the cheerful questioning continued, acknowledged that King's Lynn was a long way away, explained that they'd had a week's holiday and agreed that they'd 'got the weather for it', while Steve withdrew further and further into his thoughts, holding the letter between finger and thumb and tapping it absent-mindedly against his leg. But he didn't open it until the postwoman had trundled round the bend in the path and was out of sight.

Barbara watched him as he read it. 'Thass bad, ain't it?'

'I been called back,' he told her, proud that his voice was calm. 'I've to report to the Rail Transport Officer at Liverpool Street station by eighteen hundred hours tonight.'

Her face crumpled into distress. It was as if they were suddenly surrounded by guns, as if jack boots were kicking into their quiet house, trampling their lovely, fragile, short-lived happiness, as if he were being physically torn from her arms. 'That ain't fair! They've took our last day! Our very last day. They could've left us *that*. What's a day to *them*?'

He pulled her into his arms to comfort her but now that she'd begun, she couldn't stop. 'This bloody war!' she raged. 'This bloody awful bloody war! Pullin' everyone apart. Turnin' us inside out. They don' care. They could've let us have our honeymoon. That wouldn't have hurt. One more day. Thass not so much to ask, is it? One more day. But no! They got to pull us apart. That ain't fair!'

He let her weep, kissing her hair and wiping away her tears with his thumbs, touched and torn and infinitely tender. Being sent to France was as intolerable to him as it was to her. 'It has to be done,' he said.

'I don' see why!'

'You do,' he said gently. He wasn't rebuking her. It was a statement of fact, spoken most lovingly. 'We all do. It's got to be done.'

She admitted it, even in the throes of her distress, sniffing back her tears, struggling for control. 'Yes, all right. I know. I know I shouldn't be goin' on like this . . .'

He kissed her salty mouth. 'Come to bed,' he begged.

So they retreated to their kingdom to make love for the last time, as much for comfort as desire. But this time, they were driven by an anguished greed that left them both unsatisfied and weeping.

103

'Don't cry,' he begged, hiding his face in her hair so that she couldn't see his own tears. 'There'll be other times. They won't send us straight away.'

But neither of them really believed it and when he made to move away from her, she clung to him, begging him not to move, her face anguished. 'Cuddle me! Please! Don't go.'

'We shall miss our train,' he said, trying to be sensible.

'There'll be another one. Please!'

He'd worked out exactly what train they had to catch so that he could escort her back to New Cross and call in and say goodbye to his parents. If they missed the next one, it would be a scramble, and he might be late reporting to the RTO. But how could he leave her, when her cheeks were damp with tears and she was clinging to him with such passion? So they stayed in one another's arms until they were both quieted and they'd heard the missed train come and go.

Then they got up and made their last pot of tea together and took refuge in chores, working in harmony and saying little, contained in a protective gentleness. They did the washing up, packed the trunk and the kitbag, folded the blankets, swept the floor, gathered the remains of their food into the shopping basket, took one last look at their pretty living room and left, locking the door on their dreams.

It was a sad journey back to New Cross. They sat side by side, holding hands like children, while he told her what he planned.

'You can stay with Mum and Dad till I know where I've been sent. You'll get your wife's allowance – you cash it at the Post Office – and I've arranged for an extra seven shillings a week to be taken out of my pay for you, so you'll be all right. I'll write as soon as I get there. You'll have a letter first post on Monday, I promise. And as soon as I know where I've been posted, we'll find a flat or a room or something near where I am, an' we can be together when I get time off.'

'Yes,' she said. 'Yes.' Trying to smile. But she could barely understand what he was saying.

They were still holding hands as they walked into his parents' flat in Childeric Road.

His father was in the kitchen sitting in his chair in the corner mending his work-boots. There was a card half full of blakeys on the table beside him and the air was sharp with the smell of newly cut leather. 'You're back early,' he said. 'We weren't expecting you till tomorrow.'

Steve explained, quickly and without emotion, suggested that Barbara could stay with them 'for the time being. That's all right isn't it?' while Barbara stood by the kitchen table clutching the basket before her like a shield, remembering the way his mother had looked at her and knowing that this wasn't a good idea. But how could she tell him? In a matter of minutes they would be saying goodbye.

'Leave it all to us, son,' Bob Wilkins said. 'She can have your old room. She'll be all right with us, won't you Barbara. Now have you seen your mother, Steve?'

Steve admitted that he hadn't, explained that he had to catch the next train to London Bridge, avoided his father's eye because he was ashamed to be rushing off like this. 'I've got two minutes to change,' he said, heading for his bedroom. 'Give her my love. Tell her I'll write to her.'

Before Barbara could make up her mind whether she ought to go with him, he was back in the kitchen in full uniform with his kitbag over his shoulder. Then they were running down the road to the station, rushing to buy a platform ticket, struggling through the barrier, as the train steamed in.

She stood on the running board and he leant out of the window to kiss her goodbye, quietly and tenderly but without making a fuss. It was far too public for that and there was too much noise, whistles blowing, doors slamming shut, people shouting at one another above the racket. But when the engine huffed into action and the train began to move, her face crumpled into misery no matter how hard she tried to control it.

'Jump down, sweetheart,' he warned. 'It'll be dangerous in a minute.'

She clung to him for the last torn seconds. 'Write soon,' she begged.

'It'll be the first thing I do,' he promised. 'You'll be all right with Mum and Dad.' And he tried a joke. 'I've left you plenty of reading material.'

'What?' she said, as she jumped back onto the platform.

But it was too late for him to explain. The train was picking up speed, pulling them apart, the distance between them growing too far and too fast.

'I'll see you soon,' he called. 'I promise.'

But the engine was shrieking and she couldn't hear what he was saying.

There was nothing for her to do now but stand on the platform and wave as the train swept him away, shrinking his tanned face until it was nothing but a pale oval framed by the window. 'I hate trains!' she cried into the noise of his leaving. He was out of earshot so she could say what she liked. 'I hate trains an' I hate stations an' RTO's, an' platform tickets what won't let you leave the platform an' go with him, an' officers what won't let you finish your honeymoon, an' being left with your mother-in-law, an' everythin' to do with this bloody, bloody war.'

It was suddenly much colder and the sky above the station was ominous with rain cloud. Now that the train had gone the track was revealed in all its squalor, grease-black and full of litter, dog-ends, crushed cigarette packets, bits of paper so ancient they were as brown as dead leaves. They shouldn't allow that to get in such a state, she thought. Thass not hygienic. The sight of it reminded her of the yard at home. And, suddenly and unaccountably, she was miserably homesick.

Now stop that gal, she said to herself. There haint no point standin' round in this nasty ol' station feeling sorry for yourself. You got a new life to lead now and you'd better get on with it.

CHAPTER EIGHT

Heather Wilkins was most upset when she got back
from work that Saturday evening, hot, sweaty and bone-
weary, to find that her son had come home a day early
and left without seeing her. She knew instinctively that
this was the invasion coming. It had to be. So how
could he have gone without saying goodbye? When she
might never see him again.

'Why didn't you stop him?' she said angrily as she
turned on the tap to wash her dirty hands.

The excuse sounded feeble even to *Bob*'s ears. 'He
was in a rush.'

'Rush?' she said, scrubbing hard to subdue her
anxiety. 'What d'you mean rush? He's never in a rush.
Not our Steve. He has everything planned down to the
last little detail. Always. He could've nipped in and
seen me on his way to the station. That I *do* know. It
wouldn't've taken him more than a minute.' Then she
noticed the straw hat and the shopping basket standing
beside the dresser and was suddenly and bitterly
jealous. 'I suppose *she* was with him. That's what it
was.'

'Well 'course she was,' Bob said. 'She's his wife.
And while we're on the subject, I've said she can stay
here till they know where he's been posted.'

Heather's frown deepened. 'Why can't she go
home?' she said, shaking the water from her hands.

'Her home's with Steve now,' he pointed out,
doggedly patient. 'It's only till she knows where he's
gone. Then they'll get a room or a flat or something.'

The answer was sensible but she was still irritated. 'I
tell you what, Bob, I'm beginning to think the girls

were right. She *has* run away from home. I thought they'd got hold of the wrong end a' the stick at the wedding but I'm not so sure now. If she's going to stay here . . .'

Bob picked up his repair box and put it away in the broom cupboard, hoping to placate her by tidiness. 'It'll only be for a little while,' he said.

She wasn't placated. 'That's all very well. How long's a little while?'

His next answer made it impossible for her to argue any further. 'Till they get a flat or till the invasion.'

So he'd worked it out too. 'This is it then?' she asked, her face set. 'Is that what you're saying?'

He answered calmly. 'Looks like it.'

'Does *she* know, d'you reckon?'

'She never said nothing,' he told her cautiously. 'Neither of 'em did, come to that. But like I told you, they was in a rush.'

She took her kitchen apron from its hook behind the door, put it on and started to unpack her shopping basket. 'Oh well,' she said wearily, 'I suppose she'd better stay, if that's what he wants.'

'We won't say nothing about the invasion, will we.' It was half question, half command. 'Let her tell *us*.'

'Give me credit for a bit a' sense,' she said. 'Where is she now, if I'm allowed to ask?'

'Gone with him to say goodbye.'

'*She* got the chance you notice. Which is more than I did.' Beyond the kitchen window the sky was purple with rain clouds. 'I don't suppose they thought to take an umbrella.'

'No.'

'No sense, these young things,' she said, studying the food she'd unpacked. She took her chopping board from the cupboard, picked the largest onion and counted out three rashers of streaky, comforted by the routine of domesticity. 'Good job it's bacon roll tonight. At least that'll stretch to three. I got spring greens.

There wasn't much else. I told Mr Fisher that last lot a' spuds was chronic so these had better be better. Right. That's everything.'

The bacon roll was tied in its cloth and steaming gently and she was peeling the last of the potatoes when the doorbell rang. The peremptory sound brought a renewal of irritation. 'You go,' she said, without looking up. 'I've got my hands full.' She couldn't face opening the door to the girl. Not yet anyway, and not in the middle of cooking a meal. Oh why hadn't he called in to see her, just for five minutes? It would have made such a difference.

Barbara was standing in the porch with her chin in the air and a belligerent expression on her face. Her arms and shoulders were spotted with rain and there were drops spangling her dark hair.

'You got back just in time,' Bob said, standing aside to let her in, and thinking how pretty she looked. 'It'll be chucking it down in a minute.'

She recognised that he was trying to welcome her but she couldn't respond to him. It was as if all her emotions had been turned on at full blast and then shaken together until she could barely distinguish one from another. As she followed him upstairs, she found herself observing things with a stupid intensity as if she were in enemy territory and her survival depended on it – Anaglypta halfway up the walls, dark brown and all swirls and ridges, lino on the stairs, six doors on the landing. She was quite sure there were six, because she counted them.

Bob was explaining the layout of the flat. 'This is our bedroom,' nodding at a closed door. 'An' that one's *your* room and that's the bathroom.' But although she heard the words, their meaning wasn't getting through to her. It wasn't until he opened the kitchen door and strode through saying, 'Here she is Heather,' that the full scene came into focus and she knew, with a miserable certainty, that her mother-in-law resented her arrival.

Heather decapitated a potato and wouldn't look up. 'Did he get off all right then?' she asked.

Barbara swallowed hard before she spoke. This was going to be very difficult. 'Yes, thank you,' she said politely, and added, 'He sent you his love.'

The sarcasm in Heather's voice was too pointed to be missed. 'Nice of him.'

Barbara looked at her mother-in-law's closed expression and hardened herself for a struggle. You might not like me, she thought, but you can at least give me a bit of respect.

'Look,' she said. 'That hain't my idea, stayin' here. Thass your son what want it. That hain't me. I can always go somewhere else if you'd rather.'

'No need for that,' Heather told her, stung by such a direct challenge. She tossed the last potato into the saucepan. 'We've got the room.'

'I'll pay my way,' Barbara told her. 'I shall get an allowance.'

'Well there you are then,' Heather said, salting the potatoes. 'It's settled. I'll show you where to put your things.' And she marched into Steve's bedroom as if she were on her way to a war.

The sight of his room made Barbara catch her breath as if she'd been struck. It was so exactly what she expected, four square and neat, with the bed pushed against the wall to make more room, a wall mirror at his head height, prints of cricket and cricketers arranged in ordered rows on the cream wallpaper, and three long shelves full of books ranged above the bed, Penguins mostly and grouped in order, blue to the right, orange to the left. His books. *I've left you plenty of reading material.* But oh! Below the shelves, strewn across the grey-blue bedspread, were his discarded clothes, left where he'd thrown them and still warm to her touch. It was as if he were still in the room, as if she could turn

111

and find him standing behind her, smiling at her, eager for kisses. She missed him so much she felt as if her ribcage was caving in. Oh Steve! My dear darling Steve!

'Well!' Heather said crossly beside her. 'Will you look at that. He *must* have been in a rush. I never known him leave his clothes lying about, like that. Never in all my born days.' She sounded surprised and exasperated.

'He had a train to catch,' Barbara explained. 'He had to report to the RTO.' And she began to retrieve the clothes, opening the wardrobe door to hang them up.

Heather went on complaining. 'I don't know what's got into him, leaving everything to the last minute. It's not like him. That shirt'll have to go in the dirty clothes' basket.'

'I'll wash it for him,' Barbara offered and she held the shirt to her chest. It would be a labour of love.

That didn't please her mother-in-law. 'No need for that,' she said. 'It can go in with the rest of the wash Monday. I always do a wash Monday. It's my day off.'

For a second it felt as though they were on the verge of a quarrel. Then Barbara offered a compromise. 'I'll help you then.'

Heather hesitated. She could hardly turn down an offer of help, cross though she was. It would look churlish and petty. 'Well, we'll see,' she temporised.

Thank God I shall only have to stay here a few days, Barbara thought, cuddling the shirt. I couldn't stand much of this. She cut people to ribbons. And she made up her mind that she would certainly help with the washing *and* with the washing up and that she'd get out of the house as much as she possibly could.

That first supper was an awkward meal because they were all thinking about Steve and wondering where he was. None of them could find anything much to say, and although there was a play on the wireless, it wasn't entertaining. Barbara had no appetite but she ate what was put in front of her and, when Heather cleared the table and boiled a kettle for the washing up, she took the wiping-up cloth from its hook on the wall and dried as Heather washed. Then her new parents settled down in their two armchairs by the fireplace, Heather boldly, with her knitting on her lap, Bob rather anxiously, cleaning his pipe, and left her sitting at the table feeling in the way.

The evening spread emptily before her. 'Right then,' she said. 'I'm off to see Betty. Take the hat back. Thass orl right, ain't it?'

'You must feel free to do whatever you like,' Heather told her, icily gracious. 'We turn in at ten. Take the torch. It'll be dark by the time you come back.'

Bob watched as she picked up the torch from the dresser and put it into the pocket of her red coat. 'D'you know the way?' he wondered.

She didn't but she wasn't going to ask for help. 'I can find it.'

'I'll come with you,' he decided, setting his pipe aside. And when Heather gave him a questioning look, 'I need some fags for tomorrow.'

So he and his new daughter-in-law walked off together under the same umbrella. It was raining steadily and the terraces were monochrome in the fading light, grey roofs, grey walls, grey rain.

'She's in a bit of a state,' he apologised. 'With Steve goin' off an' everything.'

'Yes,' Barbara said shortly. 'I know. I miss him too.'

He was beginning to recognise that her bold expression was a cover for distress but, having been answered so sharply he couldn't think of anything else to say, so they walked on in silence. Outside Mabel's house, as they waited for someone to answer the door, he passed the umbrella to her and on impulse, bent beneath it to kiss her cheek. 'Don't be late back,' he warned. 'She means what she says. We do turn in at ten.'

He's trying to help me, Barbara thought, warming to him. But she barely had time to smile at him before a shadow darkened the stained glass, the door was flung open and Joyce was standing before them, yelling back into the house. 'Mum. It's Uncle Bob!'

'I'll be off then,' he said. 'You'll be all right with Mabel.' And was gone before she could draw breath.

'I brought the hat back,' she explained, holding it in front of her.

'Oh!' Joyce said shortly, giving her a most unwelcoming stare. 'You'd better come in then.'

The kitchen was full of people but, to Barbara's great disappointment, Betty wasn't one of them. Aunt Mabel was sitting at her sewing machine with both feet on the treadle busily turning a pair of worn sheets side to middle, Hazel was doing a jigsaw with the pieces all over the chenille tablecloth and Joyce had been darning a lisle stocking, which she'd left on the sideboard with its needle stuck in the toe, and which she took up again as soon as she got back in the room. And sitting at the table, drinking a cup of tea, was the fat aunt from the wedding – Aunt Sis, wasn't it? – round face, shrewd eyes, snub nose, dark spiky hair, surrounded by a strong smell of sulphur and cigars, and looking fatter than ever in some sort of railway uniform.

'Hello Barbara!' she said. 'I thought Bob was with you.'

'He walked me round,' Barbara explained. 'Thass all. I brought Betty's hat back.'

'She's out dancing,' Aunt Mabel said, biting off the thread. 'I'll tell her. Everything go off all right?'

'You're back early, ain'tcher?' Sis said and nodded at the chair beside her. 'We wasn't expecting you till tomorrow.'

Barbara sat down, feeling very out of place. 'He had a letter,' she explained. 'This morning. He's had to go back. He's been recalled a day early.'

'That's the army for you,' Sis said, making a grimace. 'How was the bungalow?'

Barbara's feelings were on the boil again, bubbling

and confusing. So much had happened since she woke that morning that it was hard to realise that the day had begun in the bungalow. But she made a great effort and managed to tell Sis it was 'lovely' and to thank her for the things she'd sent in the trunk. 'I'll wash the sheets an' towels as soon as the trunk comes,' she promised. 'We ate all the food.'

'That's what it was for,' Aunt Sis said, and she took a cigar from her jacket pocket, lit it with a great deal of smoke and enjoyment and puffed on it as she went on. 'So I gather he's gone already, is that right?'

'Yes.'

'So whatcher gonna do with yourself while you're waiting?'

'That'll only be for a day or two,' Barbara hoped.

'Tell yer what,' Sis said. 'If you're still here next Saturday morning, Joyce and Hazel could show you round the shops. It's pretty lively round here of a Saturday. Our Betty works in Woolworths. Did you know that? You could all pop in after, an' see her an' have a cup a' tea. They got a caff there. You'd like that.'

Joyce and Hazel didn't look at all pleased by the suggestion, so Barbara hastened to assure them that she wouldn't need their services.

'That all depend on what he says in his letter,' she said. 'I mean, I might not be here by Saturday.'

'Be something to look forward to if you *are* though,' Sis said, 'wouldn't it?'

That had to be admitted, despite Hazel's frown. This aunt was plainly the sort of person who was used to getting her own way.

'Well that's fixed then,' Sis said and turned her attention to other matters. 'Mrs Cronin's boy got his call-up papers yesterday. Did I tell you, Mabel?'

'I know,' Aunt Mabel said. 'I met her in Davey Greig's this morning. Reckon he's going in the RAF.'

Barbara sat in her chair by the fire and felt more and

more out of place as the gossip went on. She didn't know any of the people they were talking about, Joyce and Hazel kept giving her funny looks, and Betty wouldn't be back for hours. But she could hardly stand up and walk out, not when they were all busy talking, and not when she'd only just arrived. She was relieved when Sis stubbed out her cigar, made a useless attempt to brush the ash from her uniform and announced that she'd better be off.

'I ought to go too,' Barbara said, glancing at the clock to support her departure. 'I'm s'posed to be in by ten.'

'I'll walk along with you,' Sis offered. 'It'll be pitch black out.'

So they left together and the entire family came out into the half-lit hall to see them off.

'Don't forget Saturday,' Sis said to the two girls, as they kissed goodbye.

And Barbara asked her new aunt Mabel to give her love to Betty. 'Tell her thanks for the hat.'

'I will,' Mabel assured her, brushing her cheek with an awkward kiss. 'Mind how you go.'

It was a sensible warning for, once outside the house, it was extremely dark.

'Grab an arm,' Sis instructed, offering her elbow as they walked down the path. 'Got a torch, 'ave yer?'

The rain had stopped so they carried their umbrellas hooked over their free arms so that they could hold their torches one on each side of them like headlights. The air smelt of dust and soot and the blackout was total. At first Barbara could just about make out the gleam of white paint that marked the edge of the curb but as her eyes grew accustomed to the darkness she began to glimpse the outline of roofs against moonlit cloud and to sense garden walls and privet hedges even if she couldn't see them.

'I wonder what our Steve's doing now,' Sis said suddenly.

Hearing his name made Barbara ache to be with him again. 'That won't take him long to get us a flat, will it?' she hoped.

But Sis didn't say no, the way she expected. Instead she plodded on as though she was deep in thought.

'I do miss him,' Barbara confessed.

''Course you do, duck,' Sis said comfortably. 'That's natural.'

In the darkness it was possible for Barbara to say things she wouldn't have dared in the light. 'I wish he weren't in the army. I know he had no choice but I wish he weren't.'

'I felt the same way about my Percy,' Sis told her. 'Re'glar army he was. He never had much of a choice neither, poor bugger. He was out a' work fer two an' a half years. Signed on in '32. Seven years in the colours, five in the reserve. An' then this lot come along an' buggered everything up an' they packed him off to France an' that was that. Thirty-seven he was. He'd've been forty-one last week.'

'I know what happened to him,' Barbara said, tingling with sympathy and foreboding. Wasn't that just what she was afraid of? 'Steve told me. I'm ever so sorry.'

'War, you see,' Sis said. 'Don't give none of us a chance. We just have to put up with it. I'll tell you what though, gel, once we've won, we'll make damn sure it don't happen again.'

'That's what Steve said,' Barbara remembered.

'He would,' Sis nodded. 'He's a good lad.'

'Yes.'

She sounded so bleak that Sis felt compelled to cheer her up and she did it in the best way she knew. 'It'll all be different after the war,' she said. 'We'll have full employment for a start. That's the answer. A proper job a' work for everyone. No more hangin' about street corners with nothin' to do. No more idleness. Mr Beveridge hit the nail right on the head about that. He

117

said it *destroys wealth and corrupts men*. One a' the five giants, he called it.'

Barbara didn't know what she was talking about and she was missing Steve so much she couldn't listen with any attention. The words flowed over her, 'Five giants. Giant Idleness. Giant Want. Giant Disease. Giant Squalor. Giant Ignorance . . . if we want a better world when we've put a stop to Herr Bloody Hitler, we're gonna have to fight the lot of 'em . . . You read it, have yer?'

The question was so direct it had to be answered. 'What?'

'The Beveridge Plan.'

'No,' Barbara admitted. 'I haven't. Should I have?'

'It's Steve's Bible. There's a copy on his bookshelf.'

They'd reached the corner of Childeric Road and paused to smile at one another in the torchlight. 'Well look after yourself, kid,' Sis said.

'I will.'

'Tell you what,' Sis said after a pause for thought, 'I could get you a job an' all, if you like.'

There was just enough light for Barbara to see the gleam of her brown eyes. 'Thass ever so kind,' she said, 'but I shan't be here long enough.'

'No,' Sis agreed, but her voice sounded vague. 'Well bear it in mind. Just in case it don't work out the way you've planned. Let me know when you get your letter. I'm easy to find. I'm in the booking office most days, New Cross Gate. An' if I'm not there, I live over Green's the newsagent's. Just up the top a' the road. You can't miss it.'

Barbara wasn't sure whether she was supposed to kiss her goodbye or not, but decided to risk it. And was quite pleased to be kissed in return.

Sis shone her torch onto the face of her watch. 'It's three minutes to ten,' she said and grinned. 'You'd better look sharp or she'll lock you out. Hope you get your letter all right.'

It arrived, as promised, first thing on Monday morning, just as Bob was leaving for work. And it crushed them all.

This won't be much of a letter because I can't tell you where I am or what I'm doing. The camp is sealed which means that all mail is being censored and that there will be no further leave so there is no point in looking for a flat. This is just to let you know I've arrived and to send you all my love. Stay where you are. Mum and Dad will look after you. I will write to them tomorrow but warn them not to expect any news. We are very busy here, waterproofing our vehicles. A damn sight too busy. Still at least it keeps us occupied. Write soon. I miss you more than I can tell you.
All my love.

'The invasion's coming, ain't it?' Barbara said. There was such a pain in her chest she could hardly breathe. '*No further leave ... waterproofing our vehicles.*' It could be any time. Oh dear God, any time. But not yet. Please not yet. Let me see him once more before he goes.

For a second, watching her daughter-in-law's smitten face, Heather felt sorry for her, but then that chin went up and she put on that awful bold expression and her compassion melted away. 'Yes,' she said, distress making her brusque. 'It is.'

'Write an' tell him not to worry,' Bob suggested, offering what comfort he could. 'Tell him you'll be all right with us.'

Barbara was still looking at the letter. And she was remembering what Sis had said to her. '*Just in case it don't work out the way you've planned.*' She knew this was going to happen, she thought. She was warning me, offering me something to do if I had to stay here. Thass why she told the girls to take me round the shops. And

119

fixed for us to have tea with Betty afterwards. She knew.

'What'll you do now?' Heather asked. With a bit of luck she might go back to King's Lynn.

There was no doubt about the answer to that. 'I shall get a job. I can't sit around all day doing nothing. I'd be better occupied.'

They were both surprised but Bob approved at once. 'That's the ticket,' he smiled. 'Don't you think so, Heather?'

'Very sensible,' Heather said, but she was thinking, if she gets a job here we're stuck with her, and that didn't please her at all. 'Ah well,' she said. 'I suppose we'd better get that boiler lit. We got the washing to do, an' I'm back at work tomorrow.'

120

CHAPTER NINE

That afternoon, when the washing was on the line, the flat was dank with steam and the bathroom walls were still dripping water, Barbara put on her cardigan and walked out into the summer sunshine and down to New Cross station with Steve's letter in her pocket.

Aunt Sis was in the booking office, where she'd said she would be, busy at the window with her rack of tickets behind her. She read the letter between serving passengers and gave it back with a rueful expression on her round face.

'You knew this was going to happen, didn't you?' Barbara said.

Sis nodded. 'I had a rough idea, duck. Yes, sir? Single to Crystal Palace.'

She was so calm about it that Barbara found it was possible to ask her the awful question, the one that had been filling her mind ever since the letter arrived. 'How long will it be before they . . . ?'

The answer was honest. 'Not long, I shouldn't think. It'll depend on the tides. Day or two. Week at the most. What will you do? Stay here or go back to Lynn?'

They had to wait until another passenger had bought his ticket before Barbara could answer. 'Stay here. You said you could get me a job.'

The understanding between them was quick and easy. 'That's right,' Sis agreed. 'What sort a' job d'you want?'

Barbara had considered that on the way to the station. 'Demandin',' she said.

'How about being a clippie?'

'What's that?'

'Tram conductor. It's the sort a' thing I do, only you'll be on the move. Yes, madam? Return and two halves to London Bridge.'

Barbara stood aside to allow the woman to buy her tickets and watched as her two boys kicked one another while her back was turned. 'Yes,' she said when they'd taken their quarrel down to the platform, 'sounds just the thing.'

'I'll call for you after work,' Sis said, 'an' we'll go an' see old Charlie Threlfall. He's the feller. Good union man our Charlie. Seven sharp.'

Old Charlie Threlfall worked in the New Cross Road tram depot, which was a large square vaulted building hidden behind the shops on the south side of the High Street. Trams buzzed busily in and out through an unobtrusive entrance but inside they stood in line on rows of parallel rails, patient and empty like liners in dry dock. Barbara liked the place on sight. It was important and dependable and very busy. There were drivers and clippies everywhere she looked, all in navy-blue uniforms, the drivers wearing enormous leather gloves, the clippies with wooden ticket racks full of coloured tickets slung across their chests like a row of campaign medals. If I can work here, she thought, I shall be kept too busy to sit around an' mope.

Mr Threlfall was short and stout and walked with an odd bouncing gait like an Indiarubber ball. He was checking in the latest arrivals, carrying a clipboard in his left hand and a pencil in his right, but he waved when he saw Sis and called out that he'd be with her in a minute.

'Brought you a new clippie,' Sis called, when he came bouncing across the yard to them. 'If you still need one.'

He tucked his pencil between his cap and his ear. 'Still need two, as a matter a' fact,' he said, and then turned at once to his new applicant. 'Done much a' this sort a' work have you?'

'No,' Barbara had to admit. 'Afraid I haven't.'

'She's from Norfolk,' Sis said. 'Married our Steve.'

Now he'll notice my accent and think I'm a country bumpkin, Barbara thought, and she wished her new aunt didn't have to be quite so outspoken.

Mr Threlfall smoothed his greying moustache thoughtfully, right side, left side. 'Need a bit a' training then,' he said. And before she could open her mouth to point out that she was quite prepared for it, he asked, 'When could you start?'

It was all so quick. 'Tomorrow,' she told him, covering her surprise by boldness.

The boldness pleased him. 'Capital,' he said. 'You can follow Mrs Phipps around for a day or two. See how you get on. She'll show you the ropes. There's nothin' to it really, once you get to know the fare stages. You'll soon get the 'ang of it.'

They're all so quick and confident here, Barbara thought, watching as two trams buzzed out into the evening sun, one after the other. And she made up her mind that that was how she would be too.

But the next day, when she reported for duty, she felt very far from confident although she put on a brave face. It seemed to her, as she stood beside the office waiting to be given her orders, that she was the only person in that vast place who didn't know what she was supposed to be doing, and her ignorance made her feel insignificant and small, as though she'd shrunk to half her size. But she'd made her decision and she'd manage, somehow or other. No matter what she might be feeling, there was no doubt about that.

Mrs Phipps turned out to be a small, skinny woman in her forties who brisked out of the office and told her that she'd soon pick things up, which was reassuring, and to come this way, which was aboard the third tram along. But it was a bewildering ride, for she assumed that Barbara knew the fare stages because she lived in the area, and she did everything so quickly it was hard

123

to keep up with her. I'll need a map, Barbara thought, as she followed her mentor about. But she could hardly keep looking at a map when she was supposed to be punching tickets. And as the journey continued, she was alarmed by how many passengers asked for directions and wanted to be told when they'd reached their stop. Mrs Phipps knew every stop and every street and could give directions and sell tickets at the same time. But how would she manage to do it?

That night she wrote a long letter to Steve. A long careful letter, for she'd decided not to let him know how nervous she'd been. That would only worry him and she'd soon get over it. So she told him that she'd started the job and learnt how to clip the tickets and that she was feeling quite at home on her great rocking vehicle. *'That's like a ship at sea,'* she wrote, *'the way that moves. Good job I come of a family of fishermen and I don't get sea-sick!'*

She was pleased and gratified when he wrote back by return of post to tell her he approved and to say how proud of her he was.

I knew you'd settle in. Let me know how you get on. I can't tell you anything about what's going on here. There are guards on the gates and the censor reads every letter. They've even sealed up the telephones, not that that makes any difference to you and me. Non-stop drill, pep-talk yesterday, another one this afternoon. Keep your letters coming.

So she kept them coming as her training continued – for two more bewildering days, which she spent trying to memorise the fare stages and calling them out whenever she was sure she knew them. On Thursday evening, as Mr Threlfall seemed satisfied with her progress, she was given a uniform, kitted out with a clipper and her own rack of tickets, and told that she

124

was to report for duty the next morning ready to join a driver called Mr Tinker and to take a tram out on her own. It was quite a triumph. That night she wrote to Steve *and* Becky to tell them how well she was getting on.

And even though her first day was horribly difficult, it wasn't as bad as she'd expected because her passengers were kind and made a joke of her mistakes. They showed her where to clip the tickets when she wasn't sure, and called out the stops for her when she hesitated, and generally turned the whole thing into a sort of pantomime. 'Big place, London,' one old woman said to her. 'Don't you worry, duck. You'll soon get the 'ang of it.'

By the end of her shift she was very tired and on Saturday morning she overslept and was late for breakfast, which annoyed her mother-in-law.

'Just as well you haven't got to go in this morning,' she said, rather acidly, 'or you'd have missed your shift.'

Barbara didn't know how to answer without appearing rude, but luckily, at that moment there was a ring at the doorbell which took her disapproving in-law downstairs.

Voices in the hall, Heather's surprised, a younger one quick and high trebled. Feet tramping up the stairs. Joyce and Hazel had arrived, wearing their best cardigans and hard-done-by expressions, to do as they'd been told and escort Barbara round the town.

'Isn't that good of them?' Heather said, leading them into the kitchen. And her expression said, they know how to behave if you don't.

Joyce's expression said she didn't expect Barbara to take them up on the offer. Hazel sighed, loudly. But they were out of luck, for their arrival had given Barbara the chance to get out of the house.

'Right,' she said, daring them with a smile. 'I'm ready. Where we goin'?'

They were disgruntled, but they took her on the tour, from the twin turrets of the Palais and the Kinema at one end of town to the triangle of tramlines at New Cross Gate at the other, pointing out landmarks all the way. 'That's the Town Hall. You know *that*, don'tcher! I should hope so! There's the underground shelter, see, in front the WVS shop. We got another one at the corner a' Pagnell Street. We'll show you that an' all, in case there's any more raids. There's the butcher's where Aunty Heather works. An' there's the tobacconist's. They're ever so nice. That's where Uncle Bob goes. An' there's the fish and chip shop. I bet you never had nothing like that where you come from.'

It was like a chorus and a very annoying one. 'Ain't it big?' they asked as they crossed the road. 'Don'tcher think so? I'll bet you never had nothing as big as this where you come from.'

'Oh we had plenty of good things in Lynn,' Barbara told them. 'You'd be surprised.'

But that spurred them to greater efforts.

'It ain't just shops an' dancehalls an' cinemas,' Joyce explained, nodding importantly. 'We got churches an' chapels an' all sorts. There used to be a synagogue next to the tram depot. I'll bet you never had a synagogue. Only it got bombed. They flattened the depot too, the same time. The one you're in is new. They had to build it all up again.'

It shocked Barbara to see how calmly they took all this destruction, especially when Steve was going out to France to face even worse. But she couldn't say so because they would have mocked her and anyway they were rushing her back to the station end of town again.

'This is the best part a' town,' Hazel said. 'We come here every Sat'day. Everybody does. Look at all them shops. We got everything here, Home an' Colonial, Dolcis, Davey Greig's, the UD, Hemming's, see – that's a baker's, they're ever so nice – Singer sewing machines, the Co-op, Mr Green's where Aunty Sis lives.'

'That's Pearce Signs,' Joyce said, pointing to a large building on the other side of the road. 'My friend Martha works there. They got a workshop out the back. Huge great thing.'

But the *pièce de résistance* was Woolworths, which was set on a corner site between the Co-op and a little shop that sold cards. 'Whatcher think a' *that*?' Hazel asked in triumph. 'Ain't it whopping? I bet you never seen a Woolworths as big as that?'

'Wait till you see inside,' Joyce said. 'It's so big they got a caff down the end. Aunty Sis told yer, didn't she? We'll 'ave a cup a' tea presently an' you can see where our Betty works. She's on the lipstick counter. Come on.'

Well at least I shall see Betty again, Barbara thought, as she followed them through the doors. And she realised that she was quite looking forward to it. I can thank her for the hat. But then the impact of the store rushed in upon her and pushed all other thoughts aside.

It smelt exactly the same as the Woolworths in King's Lynn, a mixture of soap and polish and packing cases, with a whiff of leather from the purses and a combination of fluff and lanoline as they passed the wool counter. For a second it made her feel quite homesick but then she gave herself a shake and decided it was nice to be in a familiar place, even with these two superior kids! And it was totally, cheerfully familiar. It had the same wooden boards on the floor, the same plain light fittings, the same trays with the goods laid out in the same neat rows, the same price cards, sixpence, thruppence, penny ha'penny, the same milling Saturday crowds, the same patient queues. There was even the same red weighing machine.

They trooped off to find Betty, who was hard at work, neat in her maroon uniform, behind a lipstick counter besieged by young women. And it was nice to see her again.

'What a morning!' she said, when the crush eased and she could pause for breath. 'We been run off our feet. The Tangee's come in. Would you like one Barbara? I kept some under the counter for me specials. I'm gonna wear mine tonight up the Palais. Give 'em all a treat. Tell you what, you could come with me, if you like. Whatcher think?'

Barbara treated herself to a lipstick but she wasn't sure about the invitation. It was kindly meant but she didn't want to go dancing. Not without Steve. 'I should miss him too much,' she explained.

'Yeh!' Betty said. 'I can see that.' The next customer was holding out a lipstick. 'Yes, miss. Can I help you?'

'You coming up the caff?' Hazel said, leaning over the counter so that her sister could hear her. 'Is it your tea break yet, our Betty?'

'Two minutes,' Betty said. 'You go ahead an' save us a seat.'

So they went ahead and found four seats round a corner table and after a while Betty came strolling up to join them and they all had a cup of tea and a doughnut, which kept the two girls quiet long enough for Barbara to thank her new cousin for the loan of the hat.

'How's our Steve?' Betty wanted to know. 'Aunt Sis said you'd had a letter.'

'I had another one this morning,' Barbara said and took it out of her pocket. 'You can read it if you like. They're still waitin'.'

'What's drill?' Joyce asked, reading the letter over Betty's shoulder.

'Guns an' things,' Hazel told her and she looked boldly at Barbara. 'He used to play with guns when he was a little boy. He come home once with all blood running down his face. You should've seen him. Aunty Heather went bananas.'

128

Barbara could see him then, wounded and covered in blood, and her expression showed it.

Betty gave her sister a kick under the table and was pleased when she yelled. 'You finished that doughnut, have yer?' she asked. 'Right then. Go an' play somewhere else. You an' all, our Joyce. Give us a bit a' peace.'

'Where we supposed to go?' Joyce said, glaring behind her glasses.

Betty took a purse from her pocket and fished out a couple of pennies. 'Go an' weigh yourselves,' she said.

And rather to Barbara's surprise that did the trick.

'They like that machine,' Betty said. 'Hazel collects the cards. Right now we can talk.'

'Yes,' Barbara said. It was a relief to be rid of them.

'No tact,' Betty said. 'That's their trouble. You don't really want to worry about our Steve. He can look after himself. Really.'

With the two girls out of the way Barbara could say what she felt. 'He'll be right in the thick of it,' she pointed out, her face creased with concern. 'I mean bein' with the tanks. They're right up in front.'

'Give you a bit of advice,' Betty said, offering Barbara a cigarette. 'Don't think about it till you 'ave to. That's what I do. Just get on with your life an' make the best of things. It might never happen an' then you'll have wasted all that time worryin' for nothin'.' And when Barbara looked doubtful, 'If it's got your number on it, it'll get you, no matter what. All the worryin' in the world won't stop it.'

It was such pragmatic advice and so courageous that it cheered Barbara up. She took a cigarette and they both lit up. 'I'm glad you're my cousin,' she said.

'Same here,' Betty told her and made a grimace in the direction her sisters had taken. 'Those two get on my wick sometimes. They're all right. Don't get me wrong. Bit silly, that's all. But it's nice to have someone me own age in the family.'

129

'I know what you mean,' Barbara told her. 'I got two little brothers at home. They can be little beasts when they like.'

So they smoked and compared notes on the annoyance of younger siblings.

'Joyce'll be all right once she gets out to work,' Betty said, as she stubbed out her cigarette. 'That'll knock her down a peg or two, which is what she needs. Hazel's spoilt, a' course. That's *her* trouble. Makes her cocky.'

'Yes,' Barbara said with feeling. 'I've noticed.'

'Have they been putting you down?' Betty asked.

Barbara was embarrassed. They had been horrid but she didn't want to tell tales. 'Well . . .' she said.

'Beastly little things,' Betty said, grimly. 'Well I'll soon put a stop to that.'

'Don't let them know I said anything.'

''Course not,' Betty grinned. 'I know a trick worth two a' theirs. You wait till they get back.'

Which they did, almost on cue, as Betty was repairing her make-up to go back to the counter.

'Now then you two,' she said to them. 'We got a treat in store for you. If you can behave yourselves, me an' Barbara are gonna take you to the pictures Wednesday. Our trèat because we're both working women. An' she's our cousin. Only no nonsense mind. You'll have to be on your best behaviour from now on.'

Quick eye messages from Joyce and Hazel. How much does she know? A shrewd stare from Hazel to her older sister. Are you friends with her? A smile of approval from Betty to Barbara. Yes, I am. A sly sideways look at Hazel. So you'd better watch it.

'Thanks!' Joyce said at last, accepting the offer and the change of behaviour. 'That'ud be lovely.'

'Don't thank me,' Betty told her. 'Thank your new cousin. It was her idea.'

So their Wednesday outing was arranged, to Betty's catty gratification and Barbara's satisfaction. But she didn't go to the Palais that night even though Betty

130

asked her again as they parted company. She stayed at home and turned in early. And couldn't sleep.

She lay on her back in Steve's neat single bed, gazing at the shadowy shapes of his furniture and listening to the cackle of the wireless in his kitchen, and turned her wedding ring round and round on her finger. They'd had one blissful week together and one hard-working week apart and she missed him cruelly. My darling Steve, she thought, if I knew where you was that wouldn't be so bad. And she wondered whether he was thinking of her and hoped he was.

In fact, Steve and his brigade were a mere six miles away, on the other side of the Thames, crammed into the stadium at West Ham. But they weren't thinking of their loved ones. They were listening to the Brigadier. Their vehicles had all been thoroughly waterproofed, their equipment checked and re-checked, they'd been through every training routine so often they could have done them in their sleep. 'And we'll probably have to', as Dusty Miller observed, 'before this lot's over.' They were armed and ready and, although few of them had expected to be brought to such a pitch, they were raring to go. And now they were listening to a personal message from General Montgomery, Commander-in-Chief 21st Army.

'The time has come,' the Brigadier read, 'to deal the enemy a terrific blow in Western Europe. The blow will be struck by the combined sea, land, and air forces of the Allies – together constituting one great Allied team, under the supreme command of General Eisenhower.

'On the eve of this great adventure I send my best wishes to every soldier in the Allied team. To us is given the honour of striking a blow for freedom which will live in history; and in the better days that lie ahead men will speak with

131

pride of our doings. We have a great and a righteous cause. Let us pray that "The Lord Mighty in Battle" will go forth with our armies, and that His special providence will aid us in the struggle.'

Amen to that, Steve thought, and found that he was stirred almost to tears by the splendour of the words. It *was* a great cause and a righteous one. And they *were* making history.

'I want every soldier to know,' the message continued, 'that I have complete confidence in the successful outcome of the operations that we are about to begin. With stout hearts, and with enthusiasm for the contest, let us go forward to victory . . . Good luck to each one of you. And good hunting on the mainland of Europe.'

'So this is it,' Dusty said, as they filed out of the arena.

'This is it,' Steve agreed. It could only be a matter of days now. Or hours even. 'The sooner we get on with it the better.'

CHAPTER TEN

King's Lynn was a very dull place on that Saturday evening. The abrupt departure of the Desert Rats had leeched all the colour from the town and Tuesday Market Square was virtually deserted. There were no lorries, no gangs of soldiers, just a baker's van making a late delivery at the hotel and half a dozen local lads on bicycles idling towards the Corn Exchange in the half light of a midsummer's evening.

Victor Castlemain crossed the square in ebullient high spirits. His rival was gone – good riddance to him – and now he was on his way to the hop to reclaim his girl. He hadn't seen her for over a fortnight because he'd had a bad cold last Saturday and felt too rotten to go out, but that only meant that there'd be more things for them to talk about tonight. She'd probably be missing that soldier quite a bit, so she'd be glad of some intelligent company. Oh yes. Everything was going to come out right now. As he bought his ticket, he couldn't help preening.

There were so few people in the hall that he saw her gang at once, done up to the nines and posing by the bandstand. Barbara wasn't with them, which was a bit of a disappointment, but he didn't mind if she was late, just so long as she turned up eventually. He ambled round the edge of the floor, where half a dozen couples were dancing in the self-conscious way of the first on the floor, and pretended to meet the gang by accident.

'No Spitfire yet?' he asked, trying to sound nonchalant. 'Hain't she comin' tonight?'

Their reaction was alarming. Instead of giggling and bridling at him the way he'd expected, they dropped

133

their eyes and looked embarrassed and said they didn't know. What's the matter with them? 'What you mean, you don't know?'

To his horror, Joan snapped at him. 'Like we said, we don't know. We're goin' ourselves in a minute, hain't we, Mavis? Thass no fun with nobody here.'

'Thass right,' Mavis said. She smoothed her hair in her usual way but she was still avoiding his eye. 'We're waitin' five minutes in case the Yanks come an' then we're off.'

There's something up, he thought. No doubt of that. And now thoroughly alarmed he went on questioning. 'You meeting her somewhere else then, are you?'

'No we hain't,' Joan said, much too aggressively. 'If you want to know.'

'Where is she then?'

'We don't know,' they chorused. And now he was sure they were hiding something and that it was serious.

'Don't worry,' he said pretending nonchalance. 'I'll find her.'

But although he roamed the town all evening and prowled in and out of the dancehall at regular intervals, the only people he found were Tubby and Spikey Spencer, who were half-cut and no use to him at all, except for buying drinks. By the time he got home he was brewing a hangover which was most unlike him, and as a result he spent most of Sunday sleeping it off. It was all rather demoralising.

However, on Monday morning, as he set off to work, the weather blew him into life again. There was a strong tide running and a strong wind howling and rain clouds were fairly scudding across the town, ragged with speed.

'Thass more like November than the first week of June,' his workmates complained, grumbling in to start the week. But it restored Victor's optimism. She might not have been at the dance but she had to be at work. He could find her there. Normally he wouldn't have dared to intrude on her during a working day but this had gone on long enough. That lunch hour, after combing his hair until it looked as slick as a wet otter, he stepped out into the gale in the High Street and fought his way to the draper's.

The manager homed in upon him at once, hopeful of a possible sale, having recognised the bank clerk's uniform. But when he heard that the young man was simply looking for Miss Nelson, he lost interest.

'Miss Nelson doesn't work here any more,' he said, already turning away. 'She's been gone more than a fortnight.'

He could feel his heart shrinking in his chest. 'Gone? Where to?'

The manager wasn't rising to that, especially as a valuable customer had just come in. 'I couldn't say, I'm sure. Ah Mrs Todd, may I be of service?'

Victor walked back into the gale seething with emotion. To have to endure being put down – and by a shopkeeper of all people – was bad enough, but to discover that Barbara had left the shop was worse. Where had she gone? Had she got a new job? Why hadn't he heard?

As soon as he finished work that evening he went round to Mrs Bosworth's house with a direct question. And got the answer he didn't want.

'Hain't livin' here no more,' Becky told him. She felt hideously guilty about all this but there was no point in pretending.

He looked at her steadily, recognising that she was embarrassed. 'Where's she gone then?'

She had to answer that too, even though she could see how much it was upsetting him, poor boy. 'London.'

'Whereabouts in London?'

'New Cross.'

'How long for?'

'Don' ask me.'

But he persisted. 'You mean she's left home. Is that it?'

Becky gave him her foxy look, tilting her head to one side. 'Thass about the size of it,' she admitted.

He couldn't bear to ask her anything else in case the answer was what he feared. He'd go to Dodger's Yard and see what Mrs Nelson had to say. Horse's mouth sort of thing. 'Well thanks anyway,' he said.

Maudie Nelson had had a bad day and was none too pleased to see him. A wet Monday was always a nuisance because it meant the washing had to be dried indoors and the room was clobbered enough without having wet clothes drip-drip-drip everywhere. And then Jimmy had been sent home from school because he'd been sick in the playground so she'd spent the entire afternoon looking after him and trailing in and out to the lavvy with his stinking chamber pot. Now he was upstairs in bed sleeping it off and the whole house was sour with the smell of vomit.

'No,' she said. 'I don' know where she is. I got enough on my plate without worryin' about our Bar'bra. Ask Mrs Bosworth.'

'I just come from there.'

'So what she say?'

He explained and was appalled to see that it was news to her too. What *was* going on?

Maudie kept her feelings under control. No point letting him know what she was thinking. 'Well there you are then,' she said. 'She gone to London. Got a job there I shouldn't wonder. Thass what 'tis.'

Her complacency made him cruel and cruelty drove him to face the thing he feared the most. 'This is all to do with that soldier,' he told her. 'He'll be behind it. You see if I'm not right. I'll bet she's run off with him. I warned you. You remember.'

She *did* remember and was annoyed to be reminded. But she hardened her mouth and her heart. 'Thass orl

136

squit,' she said. 'You don't wanna take no notice of that. Toughest thing in shoe-leather our Bar'bra. You wouldn't catch her runnin' off with no soldier.' But as soon as he'd gone sloping out of the yard, she hauled young Wilfred away from his game of marbles, left him to keep an eye on his brother and ran round to Becky's to demand to know what was going on.

Becky was standing by the fire cooking her solitary supper. The table was set for one, with two slices of bread and butter on a side plate, the newspaper folded and ready to read, and a mustard pot beside the tea things. So he was right, Maudie understood. She hain't living *here* no more.

'I've onny got a minute,' Becky warned, 'an' then I shall be eatin'.'

'Now look'ee here,' Maudie said, her face pink with fury. 'What's all this I hear about our Bar'bra? An' don't go givin' me load of ol' squit. I wants to know.'

It was the moment Becky had feared ever since she signed that dratted form, but she faced up to it at once. 'She gone to London,' she said turning the sausage she was frying. 'Got a job on the trams. Doin' very well so she say.'

'Vic Castlemain say thass on account of that soldier,' Maudie said. 'To hear him talk you'd think she'd run off with the bloke.'

She'd hoped for denial and reassurance but she didn't get either. 'Thass right,' Becky said. The truth was out now and they'd all have to get on with it. 'She has. His name's Steve Wilkins an' you'd better get used to it, 'cos she's married him.'

The information was so upsetting that Maudie began to weep. 'She hain't,' she cried. 'She can't have. She got more sense than that. I told her not to. I warned her.'

'Thass as may be,' Becky said, 'but she has. Now there's my supper ready an' waitin'. If you'll excuse me.'

Maudie didn't care about supper. 'She *can't* have,'

she insisted. 'I never gave consent. You have to have consent when you're under twenty-one.'

Becky felt cornered. But she found a possible answer. 'Special licence,' she suggested. 'Thass what it'll be. Special licence.'

'Oh my dear heart alive!' Maudie said. 'What'll Crusher say? He'll go off his head.'

'Don't tell him, then,' Becky advised, sliding the sausage off the cooking fork onto her plate. 'What the eye don' see.'

'What's the good of sayin' that?' Maudie wailed. 'He'll find out. Bound to. I mean you can't keep that sort of secret from a bloke like Crusher. How could she *do* such a thing? Stupid little mawther!'

Becky sat down at the table and poured herself a cup of tea. 'If you'll excuse me,' she said pointedly.

So Maudie left her and took her bad news home. And just as she'd predicted, Crusher lost his temper. He hollered for a full five minutes, calling his daughter every name he could lay his tongue to, berating Maudie for not keeping her under control, Becky Bosworth for letting her run wild, the army for putting temptation in her way, the church for aiding and abetting. 'They should've let into her an' sent her straight back home to me. Thass what *they* should've done.' He made such a noise that he soon had all the neighbours peering from their windows.

'She no daughter of mine,' he roared, 'an' she needn't think it. You jest tell her that. No daughter of mine. I s'pose she got herself into trouble, stupid little mawther. Thass what 'tis, hain't it. Well thass her stupid look-out. If she has a bebby she'll have to look after it. Soldiers are all the same. She should've knowd. I hain't accountable if she took leave of her senses. An' don't tell me they got a special licence because that hain't legal. That I *do* know. She needn't think she can come crawling back here an' aspect me to fergive her. You tell her that an' all. I'm done with her. She no daughter of mine.'

Then he stomped off to the pub where he went through the whole diatribe again with his mates. By closing time, the yards were agog with interest.

Shrimpy Castlemain took the tale home to his wife. 'That won't please our Victor none,' he observed as he removed his boots.

'No,' Vera agreed. And she wondered how she was going to break it to him. Poor boy.

'Hassen you up to bed,' Shrimpy advised. 'Time enough to tell *him* in the mornin'.'

So for once in his life Vic came back from the pub to a dead fire and a dark house. And the next morning, as he was adjusting his tie ready to leave for work, his mother asked him if he'd heard the news.

He knew what it was from the expression on her face but he did his best to be nonchalant about it. Whatever he heard, he was going to be sensible, and he certainly wasn't going to holler. 'That's about Barbara, ain't it,' he said. 'I did hear something, last night.' It was a lie. He'd been in a pub on the other side of town, deliberately putting a distance between himself and the news he didn't want to hear.

'Gone to London,' his mother told him anxiously. 'Working there. On the trams, so they say. Her pa's thrown her out. Well not thrown her out axactly, 'cos she gone already, but sort of disowned her. The thing is, they say she's married some soldier. Oh Vic, my lovey, I'm ever so sorry.'

'Thass all right,' he said, cutting her short before she could upset him even more. 'I know all about it, Ma. Actually I've known for weeks. She told me. Must be off, or I shall be late.' And he walked from the house and out of the yard, swaggering slightly and whistling through his teeth to show how little he cared. But his thoughts were buzzing like hornets and every one with a vicious sting. He'd begun to face up to the fact that

139

she'd taken herself off to London. It left him looking a fool in front of his friends, but he could make out a good case to explain it. Lots of people went to London. He'd go there himself if he got half a chance. The jobs were better there and so was the pay. But getting married was something else. The mere idea was an affront. It made him shrivel. How could she be married? She's my gal. She's always been my gal. We're as good as engaged, and everybody knows it. But that made him shrivel away to nothing. How could he look his friends in the eye when his as-good-as-fiancée had run off and married a soldier? A common soldier, for heaven's sake! She's only known him five minutes. It was too demoralising to cope with.

He was very glad to arrive at his desk and start work. Arithmetic was calming and God knows he needed a bit of peace. But that morning there was very little time for calm or work. He'd hardly got started when the manager came running out of his office with his hair standing on end to say that the Second Front had started.

'I just this minute heard it on the wireless,' he told his staff. He'd had a wireless in his office for months, tuned in expressly for this eventuality. 'Just this minute. Special bulletin. They went in this morning on the north coast of France.'

There was uproar in the office, as his staff cheered and said how wonderful it was and that it was about time too. But although Victor nodded and appeared to be joining in the general clamour, inside his head he was leaden with misery.

What do I care! he thought to himself. They can invade the whole of Europe if they like. It don't mean anything to me.

Barbara's tram was in the Old Kent Road and heading for the Elephant and Castle when four passengers came tumbling aboard, ablaze with the news. 'Second Front!

Ain't it grand! Early this morning. Yeh! It's official. It was on the wireless.'

Although she'd been expecting it ever since Steve's first letter, it still caught her off balance. She could feel the blood draining from her face. 'Oh, my dear heart alive!' she said, and put her hand on the back of the nearest seat to steady herself.

'You all right, lovey?' one of the newcomers asked.

The woman sitting in the corner seat answered up for her. 'You got someone there, ain'tcher, duck?'

She admitted that she had.

'What's his name?' the woman asked.

'Steve.' Oh please God don't let him be killed.

'Steve,' the woman repeated. 'I'll say a prayer for him, duck. Don't fret. He'll be all right.'

Barbara was recovering a little. She thanked her new friend, adjusted her ticket rack, advanced along the tram towards her passengers, even managed to call, 'Fares please!' as if it were a normal day. But she was taut with anxiety and, after a few minutes, unaccountably in pain, with a familiar dragging sensation pulling at her belly. I shouldn't be due on yet, she thought. But due or not that was what was happening to her. She didn't know whether to be relieved or disappointed. A baby would have been only natural after so much love, but to carry it here, in a strange town, with a war going on and being worried about him all the time . . .

'This is my stop,' the woman in the corner said. 'I shan't forget, duck. I shall go to church this evening. Steve, ain't it?'

I shall go to church an' all, Barbara decided. She hadn't been near a church for years but they wouldn't mind, would they? Not on a day like this. Not when there was such a lot to pray about.

So that evening, when she'd helped cook the supper and washed up the dishes, she put on her red coat and slipped quietly out of the house to find the nearest place of worship. She'd noticed that there was a St James's

Road on the opposite side of the High Street and as that seemed the most likely place, she went there first. And found a church crowded with people and tense with emotion.

They were halfway through the first hymn, 'Oh God Our Help in Ages Past'. The two women in the nearest pew shifted along to make room for her and gave her a hymn-book and found the place for her. But she couldn't sing. Not yet. Not until she'd said her first heartfelt prayer. 'Please God look after him. Don't let him be killed. Keep him safe and let him come home to me.'

CHAPTER ELEVEN

It seemed fitting to Steve Wilkins that there should be a strong sou'wester blowing as the 131st Brigade embarked for France. They'd been delayed for more than twelve hours because of heavy seas, and despite the wait, conditions hadn't improved. It was as cold as November, the sea was slate-grey and extremely rough, the sky bruised by rain clouds, blue-black, oppressive and threatening. Tough weather for tough work.

Now that the moment had come, his emotions were sharpened to such a pitch that he was totally calm, as if the invasion were happening to someone else and he was merely a spectator. He was aware that he was experiencing powerful feelings – the edgy excitement he always felt before a scrap, pride at being part of such an army, the strongest sense of the enormity and importance of what they were going to do, and fear too at what lay ahead, anxiety about how he would behave under fire, regret at leaving Barbara behind after such a short time together, but everything was distanced, as if he'd been anaesthetised.

The Channel was an impressive sight that afternoon. There were ships as far as he could see, some, like theirs, heading out of harbour and rolling heavily, some returning, their prows carving white parabolas of foam, warships, sleek and grey and bristling with guns, landing craft like enormous square-mouthed barges, LCT's and Liberty ships, even rusty old colliers, filthy dirty but riding the waves like ducks. He'd never seen such a fleet, let alone imagined he'd be a part of one. And once they were out in mid Channel, he'd never seen such a vast army either, deck after deck packed with khaki vehicles and loaded with men in full kit, their helmets catching the light as they bobbed and shifted like a great harvest of steel flowers. In his odd, detached state of mind, they made him think of Jason's mythical warriors raised from the teeth of dragons, teeming from the earth in their thousands, fully armed and primed for war. He felt exalted to be one of their number.

But exalted or not there was nothing for him to do while they were in transit, except wait and feel queasy as the great rollers mounded towards the ship one after the other, and his innards lifted and fell, lifted and fell, and were squeezed with every heave.

It took a very long time before they reached the French coast and by then most of them were feeling so ill they simply wanted to get back onto dry land, no matter how dangerous it might be. They could see it, clear in a sudden beam of sunlight and less than a mile away, a long sandy beach, full of men and vehicles and edged by dark landing craft from which lines of troops straggled ashore. Further up the beach were the sand-dunes they'd been told to expect, long and buff under the rain, spiked with clumps of coarse grass and topped by a row of holiday homes.

But before they could step ashore they had to be transferred from the Liberty ship to an LCT, which was an extremely difficult manoeuvre in such heavy seas. The landing craft came alongside easily enough but it rose six feet with every wave and yawed away just when they were ready to climb down. Steve and Dusty jumped when their moment came and were surprised to land on deck instead of falling into the water. Then, as they headed inshore, the battleships opened fire.

The noise of their bombardment was so shattering that it made Steve's belly shake, especially when he looked up and realised that he could see the shells streaming inland over his head. There were thousands of them. What firepower! he thought. I wouldn't like to

144

be on the receiving end of *that*. But even as the thought was in his mind, there was a sudden sharp explosion to his right and turning, he saw that one of the landing craft had been hit or struck a mine. Christ! That could have been us. Chunks of debris were being thrown into the air and he could see men in the water, some struggling, some hideously still. Not mythical warriors after all, poor sods, but ordinary men, wounded and dying. Dying! Oh dear God! Dying! Before they've even set foot on shore. Now what? Are we going to turn back and pull them out?

But no. They'd already arrived on the beach and were being ordered to wade ashore. And they obeyed automatically, holding their rifles above their heads the way they'd been trained and weighed down to a snail's pace by all the equipment they were carrying – gas masks, grenades, bandoliers of rifle ammunition, rations, water bottles. If the buggers are still here and they fire at us, Steve thought, they'll pick us off one by one. There's nowhere to run, even if we could.

But there was no gunfire from onshore and presently they strode out of the water and stumbled onto sand, their legs aching with the effort they'd been making. Now they were walking through the wreckage of the D-Day landing and they could see what a furious battle it had been. The houses that had looked so attractive offshore were either pitted with holes or were roofless ruins and the dunes were criss-crossed with tyre marks and littered with debris, bloody rags, empty shell cases, smashed tin hats, discarded vehicles, broken equipment of every kind. They were marched through it so quickly that none of them had time to gather more than an impression nor to look back at the dead and injured they'd left behind in the water. But they were all terribly aware of what was going on and they were all afraid, putting one foot after the other automatically, their throats dry and their hearts pounding.

The beach head was swarming with men and

machines, for it wasn't just troops that were being brought ashore. There were Vehicle Landing Craft all along the water's edge too. One was unloading Sherman tanks, which came rumbling down the ramp one after the other to crunch off across the sand, looking massive in that restricted space. Higher up the beach one had broken down and a mobile repair unit was refitting it with a new track which lay beside it in a huge sand-spattered coil. And weaving through the new arrivals, the mine-detectors were at work, moving cautiously, the long sticks of their detectors swinging backwards and forwards before them like pendulums.

The brigade trudged through the dunes, following the column, and pressed on through the gaps between the houses until they reached open country where they found a signpost like a pollarded tree with too many branches, newly erected and covered with unit signs and initials, among them the familiar pink Desert Rat of the 7th Armoured Division. Now it was simply a matter of following the signs, which led them to an earth track, which had once been a country lane but was now churned into muddy ridges by its unaccustomed traffic. A convoy of heavy vehicles roared past, heading inland and spraying them with mud, and as they marched on, they could see the erupting plumes of distant explosions from the bombardment.

Although they still hadn't come under fire there were signs of recent battle wherever they looked – earth pitted with shell holes, trees shattered, a concrete pill-box smashed open as if it had been hit by a giant fist. From time to time they passed a group of newly dug mounds, and realised with a *frisson* of fear that this was the temporary burial of the dead, German and British side by side with a rifle and helmet stuck at the head of each grave. Nobody spoke but they were all thinking the same thing, knowing that this was how they could end up and praying that they could avoid it, somehow or other. A hundred yards on, they came upon one of

146

the most dreaded German guns, an 88-millimetre, still in its emplacement, but with its muzzle shattered, like one of Groucho Marx's exploding cigars. The sight of it brought a cheer and a warming sense of triumph. But even so, fear brooded with them all the way to their first camp.

That night, after a solid meal, they wrote their first letters home and settled to sleep in the open air. Steve spent the first two hours of the night on sentry-go, marching about their improvised settlement with a tommy-gun in his hands and nothing but his thoughts for company. He was surprised by how still it was, even though there were guns rumbling like thunder some-where inland. Far away on the plain he could see fires burning, the flames flaring and dying and rekindling to flare again, now orange and yellow, now lurid red with a blue core. He watched with fascination, off and on, for over an hour, wondering what it would be like close to. But when his relief took over, he simply reported that it was all quiet.

He took off his boots, rolled his tunic into a rough pillow and lay down in his bedroll. But although he was dog-tired he was too keyed up and fearful to sleep. Tomorrow they would be in action. Tomorrow he could be killed, blown into the air like those poor sods in the LCT or left to die on his own while the army moved on. Wakefulness made him face up to it although he would rather have slept and forgotten. After an hour fear was gnawing at his stomach and his mouth was full of bile. He felt the need to pray but he couldn't remember a single prayer, just a few odd words from something he'd learned at school. So he said that. '*O God of battles, steel my soldiers' hearts. Possess them not with fear. Take from them now the sense of reckoning . . . Not today, Oh Lord. Oh not today.*'

The next thing he was aware of was the sound of the wind whistling through the wheels of the nearest TCV. His hair was damp with dew and when he sat up he could see that the eastern sky was pale green. It was dawn.

Daylight brought a return of common sense and a great deal to do in a very short time. Orders came through as soon as they'd been fed. They were to advance to a place called Ellon where they would join three regiments of tanks to spearhead the next advance to a road centre called Villers Bocage. And by now, with food in their bellies and the night behind them, they felt cocky enough to joke.

'Villers Bocage!' Dusty whispered to Steve and Taffy. 'They got some names round here! What d'you reckon *that* is when it's at home?'

'Good defensive territory,' they were warned, 'so keep your eyes skinned for snipers and pockets of German infantry. They're well camouflaged and some of them are armed with *faust patronen* or *panzerfaust*. It's like the American bazooka, which you know about, a hollow charge projectile on a rocket tube with a range of about seventy-five yards. Extremely effective against tanks.'

So we hit them before they hit us, Steve understood.

They were warned about a new German mine too. 'The Yanks call it the 50–50. It's like the "S" mine, which you know about, but, instead of ball-bearings, this one hits you with a sharp steel rod. If you hit with your right foot, the rod flies up past your right side. If you hit with the left, you'll be singing tenor.'

'Lovely!' Taffy joked as he lit a new cigarette from the butt of the dying one. 'I've always fancied singing tenor.' But his eyes were strained despite his grin.

And that was that. By 5.45 they were in their TCV's and on the move. Soon they'd left the open plain behind and were driving cautiously down a sunken road between very high hedges, discovering with every yard that this terrain was more difficult than anything they'd tackled in training and more fearsome than anything they could have imagined. For the *bocage* turned out to

148

be perfect cover for snipers. It was a maze of small, high-banked fields and orchards, surrounded by pollarded trees and hedges that were more than twelve foot high and so thick that it was impossible to see through them. And to make matters worse the roads weren't simply narrow and overhung with foliage, they snaked and curved so that visibility was never more than fifty yards. They could be picked off at any time and from any direction for German infantry could be anywhere.

And things got worse when they'd made their rendezvous with the tanks, for now, although they were heavily camouflaged, they were on foot and advancing into enemy territory, sometimes across fields and through dense woodland, sometimes along roads that were little more than footpaths, treacherous, narrow, overhung by foliage – and mined, probably with the new 50–50's. Steve had never experienced such fear. His heart was beating so fast it pained him, his throat was full and his mouth so dry it was difficult to swallow, and sweat was pouring from him, running down his back and his sides and streaming down his forehead so copiously that he had to shake it away like a dog freeing his coat of water.

When the first attack began it was almost a relief. Suddenly there were voices shouting, 'Take cover!', a rattle of machine-gun fire, the red trace of a sniper's bullet, somebody screaming close behind him.

Fear coalesced into anger, he remembered his training, obeyed orders although his fingers were stiff, sprayed their hidden enemy with machine-gun fire, hoping his aim was accurate. A tank crashed through the hedges just ahead of them, sending branches spinning to left and right, and roared across the pathway to smash down the opposite hedge and head out into the fields. Two seconds later it was followed by a Sexton, and Steve just had time to realise that they must have run into German tanks and called in the artillery, before he glimpsed a Tiger through the new gap in the hedge

149

and watched it ricochet as it fired. Then he was running past the gap, head down, scrabbling for cover in the ditch as another volley of fire raked the hedges.

There was a reek of petrol, a stink of cordite, an explosion that made the hedges shake, billows of black smoke and long tongues of flame, and he knew that a tank had brewed up and hoped it was the Tiger.

And then it was over, as suddenly as it had begun, and he leant against the hedge and was sick.

The pathway was littered with cartridge cases and strewn with bodies, some blown to pieces, some wounded and groaning, one trying to crawl away. And among them was Taffy, lying on his back, hideously spread-eagled in a long pool of blood. Oh Christ! Taffy!

Get to him quick! What was it they said? Shock was the worst killer. Must keep him warm. How the hell do I do that? Where's the field dressing? Chest wound. Chest wound. What did they tell us about chest wounds? Staunch the blood. 'Taff! You're all right mate! I've got you.' Struggling to undo the buttons on a tunic slippery with blood.

Dusty was crouching beside another casualty – Johnnie Taylor wasn't it? – holding a cigarette for him. 'Bloody awful mate! Don't move. They've called for the stretchers. Don't wanna disappoint 'em.'

It was totally incongruous. One man joking, the next man unconscious. 'Taffy! Open your eyes mate! Taff! Come on!'

The stretcher bearers were standing beside him. He was aware of their boots, their khaki legs, the smell of their sweat. Almost as strong as the sickly smell of blood.

'He can't hear you, mate,' a voice was saying. 'He's gone.'

'Gone? He can't be. He was talking to me a minute ago.' But they were already moving off to attend to Taylor and the Corporal was rounding up the survivors, shouting orders.

'Get up! Leave them! You can't do any more! We're moving!' Steve obeyed, although his legs were leaden with grief and his brain stuck with a single thought. Alive one minute, dead the next. But there wasn't time for pity. Ten minutes later, a private from A company came hurtling down the road towards them, white faced, waving his arms in warning and shouting that the road ahead was occupied by hundreds of Germans and to get the hell out of it.

Then they found the strength to run and legged it across the field into a thick wood, where they waited, fear returning. It was silent among the trees and they didn't come under fire, although they could hear a tank battle raging below and to the east of them.

Presently the order came through that they were to head through the woods to a line of slit trenches and regroup. And it began to rain.

And so the day continued. They were fired on so often they lost count. Time itself was an irrelevance. There was only action and reaction, deferred grief and that awful, ever-present terror. When the dusk finally arrived and they leaguered for the night, they were so tired they slept where they dropped. It was ten o'clock and they'd been in the front line for seventeen hours.

The night gave them little rest. There were still sentry duties. The hedges had to be patrolled. A watch had to be kept. So they slept when they could, and at first light, just after their supply column arrived, the battle began again.

For days they slogged it out in the damp prison of the bocage, as the rain filled their slit trenches with mud, the tankies grew more and more irritated to be cooped up in such terrain and the Germans harassed them day and night with shell and mortar fire. They were well supplied and usually well fed, but their casualty rate was alarmingly high and progress demoralisingly slow. And there was never time to digest what was happening to them. And never time to grieve.

They were simply relieved when the order came that they were to make a temporary withdrawal from Villers and its hated bocage because the RAF were going to bomb the place. 'And about bloody time too!'

They took up their positions on the reverse slope of a hill north of another shattered village called Livry and watched. It was a massive raid delivered by heavy bombers and it seemed to go on for a very long time.

'There won't be a stone left standing,' Steve said as the noise went on. 'I pity the poor buggers who live there.' And he suddenly thought of the red tiles of his honeymoon cottage and that peaceful musty bed and their first picnic out in the rough grass of that peaceful garden. 'I ought to write home,' he said.

'Do it now,' Dusty advised. 'You won't get the chance once the bombers have gone.'

But when he'd found pencil and paper, and had written '*My darling*,' he couldn't think what to say. He couldn't tell her where he was or what was happening because the censor wouldn't let it through, he couldn't tell her about Taffy – he couldn't even bear to *think* about Taffy – and he certainly couldn't let her know what he was feeling, although the words leapt into his head, straight and simple and honest. *Dear Barbara, I'm frightened. I want to come home.* The very idea of writing such things shamed him to blushing. She *would* think him a booby if he went on like that. In the end he had to settle for platitudes, like everyone else in the brigade.

> *We have been in the front line since we arrived but are having a spot of rest at the moment. The rain is incessant. We keep as dry as we can with ground sheets and gas-capes. We are all very dirty but the grub is good, tell Mum. I can't say much because of the censor. Give my love to everyone. I haven't had any letters yet but they will catch up with us eventually so keep them coming. At least*

we've got the consolation of knowing that we are keeping the Germans so busy here they won't have any planes left over for bombing London.

Love to you all.
Steve

CHAPTER TWELVE

It took five days for Steve's first letter to reach Childeric Road and Barbara worried through every minute of every one of them, waking long before the postwoman was due and prowling up and down the stairs endlessly until she arrived, stamping her feet to urge her on, 'Hassen you up woman. Where's my letter?' She knew her restlessness was making her mother-in-law irritable but she didn't care. Her anxiety was too acute.

On the first day she had a long letter from Joan, which she glanced at and didn't read. On the second, a card from Becky and a parcel addressed to Mr & Mrs Steven Wilkins which turned out to contain an album full of wedding photographs, neatly arranged from a blurred shot of their scamper up the Town Hall steps to a perfect close-up of their cardboard cake. Bob said they were lovely and even Heather approved of the group picture, although she sniffed at all the others, but Barbara simply couldn't take them in. They were pictures, that was all, of a day that had receded into insignificance under the impact of this awesome invasion and the endless, yearning need to know what was happening.

After two days, little Mrs Connelly, who lived downstairs, joined in the vigil, calling encouragement – 'She's just coming, so she is.' 'She's on her way.' 'I can see her.' – and crooning commiserations when the wanted letter still wasn't delivered. And Bob assured her every morning that it would be 'bound to come tomorrow'. But nothing made the wait for it any easier.

Its eventual arrival was greeted with relief by every member of the household, even old Mr Connelly, who

154

usually sat in the kitchen stolidly munching through his breakfast no matter what was going on.

But for Barbara the relief was very short lived. The letter had been written five days ago and, although it proved he had survived the landing, she had no idea what had happened to him since then. Even when she found his second letter waiting for her when she got home from work that afternoon, the anxiety remained. It was wonderful to see his lovely flowing handwriting twice in one day and to know that he'd still been alive and well when he wrote for the second time but now there was another anxiety. It was such a short letter. Almost curt. It hadn't told her anything really. And he hadn't said he loved her.

She read it for a second time, missing him with a new yearning. If only he'd said something personal and loving, something about the time they'd spent together. He couldn't have forgotten it already, could he?

I'll send him a nice long answer, she decided, looking at his nice long row of books, and I'll remind him.

In the middle of the row, set neatly between the blue and orange of all those Penguins, was the white spine of her new photograph album. The sight of it gave her an even better idea. She would send him a photo, not one of those blurred ones and definitely not a group, but a nice one of just the pair of them, looking at one another. There was one at the end of the book that was just right. How young they looked! And what a long time ago it seemed! She eased the little picture from its restraining corners, turned it over and wrote on the back: '*Just in case you've forgot what I look like!*'

Then she composed her letter, telling him everything that had happened since her last and adding, '*You were right about the Germans not bombing us. It's all very quiet here.*'

But she spoke too soon. The very next night she was yanked from her sleep by the sound of a massive explosion.

For a moment she couldn't understand what was happening. Then she sat bolt upright, struggling to wake and feeling very frightened. The window was rattling in its frame and she could hear the explosion still reverberating in the darkness. Oh God, she thought. Thass a bomb. And she remembered her mother's mocking words, '*Go to London? They're bombing people in London.*' And her own wild, stupid reply. '*I don't care!*' And now here she was in the middle of an air raid, shaking with fright, her mind full of terrifying images – bombs, falling out of the sky, crashing through the ceiling – this ceiling – exploding and destroying and blowing people to bits.

The noise faded and stopped, and now she could hear voices in the front bedroom, curtains being drawn, a light being switched on. I mustn't let *them* see I'm frightened, she decided. No matter what. And she made an effort to stop shaking, got out of bed and began to put on her clothes.

The light on the landing was switched on, there was a patter of feet outside her door and her mother-in-law appeared in the doorway, putting on her dressing gown.

'Don't go near the window,' she ordered. 'If there's another one you could be cut to pieces.'

'I know,' Barbara said. The thought of it made her feel panicky again but she made a great effort and spoke as calmly as she could. 'That was a bomb, wassen it?'

Heather didn't show any sign of fear at all. 'Big one by the sound of it,' she said. 'What's the time? Can you see?'

Barbara peered at Steve's bedside clock in the light from the landing. 'Nearly half past four.'

'The sirens'll go in a minute,' Heather said shortly. 'Put your shoes an' socks on. We might have to go downstairs.'

The first shock was passing and, now that the night was quiet again, Barbara realised that her heartbeat was steadying. She sat on the edge of the bed and put on her socks and shoes, her movements slow but quite controlled. Heather ran back to her own bedroom. Mrs Connelly called up the stairs to see if they were all right. 'You coming down, are you?' And Bob's voice answered, 'I think so, don't you?'

Within minutes, the five of them were gathered in the Connelly's musty front room, sitting round the Morrison shelter, dressed and drinking tea and speculating as to why the sirens hadn't gone and why the guns weren't firing. The shelter looked huge and clumsy, like a cage for some poor wild animal, but it was better than waiting to be bombed upstairs.

'I thought we'd finished with this shenanigans,' Mr Connelly grumbled, rubbing the grey stubble on the side of his face. 'Bloody Jerries! You'd think they'd shut up with the invasion an' all. Have we not had enough?'

'I reckon it was a loner,' Bob said. 'Come over on the off-chance an' they shot him down.'

'He had a bloody big load,' the old man said. 'Must've done a fair bit a' damage.'

Mrs Connelly finished her second cup of tea and set it down on the table with a crack. 'If they don't sound the sirens soon I'm off back to bed,' she told them. 'I've lost enough sleep in this war without sittin' up for nothin'. My feet are like ice, so they are.'

And as the air raid warning didn't go, that's what she did. The rest of them sat on for another half an hour but it was still quiet so they turned in too.

'A loner,' Bob said, as they climbed the stairs. 'See if it ain't. We'll hear tomorrow.'

But there was nothing about it on the wireless and nothing in the papers either. 'Too small,' Heather said. 'It has to be a big raid to get a mention nowadays, with the Second Front and everything.'

Barbara's passengers were full of it. 'Did you hear it, duck?' they asked. 'Bloody Germans. Startin' up again. They don't know when they're beaten.'

It wasn't long before the tramway bush telegraph was in action and drivers and clippies were passing on the news of what had happened. It *had* been a plane and it had come down on the railway bridge in Grove Road in Bow, blocking the Chelmsford–Liverpool Street line. 'Winders out for a quarter of a mile,' Mrs Phipps told Barbara. 'Ten killed, so they say, an' ever so many casualties. Flying glass, you see.'

It was quite a triumph to be able to come home that evening and tell her in-laws all about it. In fact Bob had heard the story that morning too, but he kept quiet and allowed her the floor, pleased to see how sensible she was being and how clearly she explained.

'A one-off,' he said when she'd finished. 'An' just as well. We don't want all that starting up again.'

'We won't tell Steve,' Heather decided. And she gave Barbara her fiercest expression to make her understand that this was an order. 'There's no need to go upsettin' him over it. He'd only think the worst. It's over an' done with now.'

But she was wrong. Three nights later they were woken by the howl of the air raid sirens and minutes later, while they were still struggling into their clothes, they heard the sound of an approaching plane. Not the laboured throb of a German bomber or the high, sweet note of a pursuing Spitfire or a Hurricane, but an alarming, unfamiliar sound, phut-phut-phut, rattling and spluttering, more like a motorbike than a plane. And before they could work out what it was, there was another explosion, exactly the same as the first one but this time nearer.

They tumbled down the stairs one after the other, dressing as they ran.

'And don't tell me *that* was a lone plane', Heather said, 'because I won't believe it. Once maybe, but not twice, an' not making a row like that.'

The ack-ack was putting up an enormous barrage.

158

'We'll wait till they ease off an' then I'll go out an' have a look,' Bob said.

Heather wouldn't hear of it. 'You'll do no such thing. There could be hundreds a' the beggars.'

And as if to prove her right, there was another explosion, further off this time but just as violent, and twenty minutes later, a third.

'Better get in the shelter,' Bob said, looking from Heather to Mrs Connelly. 'There's room for three. We'll join you if they get any nearer.'

So the three woman crushed into their protective cage. And the explosions went on and on, each one throwing Barbara into a renewed surge of fear.

If this house is bombed, she thought, wincing at the ceiling, that'll all fall down on top of us an' we shall be crushed. Or suffocated. An' there's nothing we can do about it. She'd never felt so frightened, or so helpless. And yet the others were so calm.

'Sounds as if it's over Woolwich way now,' Mrs Connelly observed. 'Or Eltham.'

Barbara looked at her in amazement. Fancy sitting there working out where the bombs were falling, when one of them could fall on *you* at any minute.

'I'll tell you what though,' Bob said. 'They're big bombs but they're few and far between. I reckon it was half an hour between the last two.'

'They could go on all night at that rate,' Mrs Connelly said. 'It's as bad as the Blitz. I'm going to lie down, so I am, an' see if I can't take a little bit of a nap.'

She was asleep in five minutes and snoring in ten.

'Is it always like this?' Barbara asked, as another explosion roared in the distance.

'It is so,' Mr Connelly told her with feeling. 'Snored every night of my married life, so she has. Winter and summer, peace and war, every mortal night the same.'

'It'll be breakfast time soon,' Heather observed to Bob. 'I'd better be getting on or you'll be late for work.'

159

But as she spoke there was a really heavy explosion, so loud and so close that the lustres on the mantelpiece tinkled in alarm and Mrs Connelly sputtered and coughed and woke up.

'Now *that* was close,' she said.

Heather crawled out of the shelter and brushed herself down. 'Eggs an' bacon,' she said. 'Good inner lining. That's what we need.' And to Barbara's amazement, she went upstairs.

'Is that safe?' she asked Bob. 'I mean, the raid's still on, issen it?'

'If it's time to cook a meal,' Bob told her with some pride, 'she'll cook it, raid or no raid. That's the way she is.'

Thass courage, Barbara thought, admiring it and adjusting her opinion of this mother-in-law of hers. 'Shall I go an' help her?'

But they all said she should stay where she was.

'She'll call us when she's ready,' Bob said.

Which she did, her voice steady as if there were nothing extraordinary about what she was doing at all.

It was a surrealist breakfast, because although it was light enough for the curtains to be opened, they kept them closed and ate in electric light. Bob and Heather made a good meal but Barbara had no appetite at all and her mouth was so dry she could barely swallow. The raid was still going on, even though none of them mentioned it. They could hear ambulances and fire engines hurtling along the High Street as they ate. But, after a while, a train chuffed along the line at the end of the garden in its usual, ordinary way and Bob put on his cap and jacket, kissed them both goodbye and went to work.

Why isn't he frightened? Barbara wondered. He might get killed, going out in a raid. But he was walking downstairs perfectly steadily, closing the door neatly behind him, whistling as he set off down the road.

160

The all-clear sounded as the two women were washing the dishes. And after that, they went to work too, parting at the top of the road with barely a nod.

Barbara was surprised by how alert she felt. After a night without sleep she should have been exhausted, but the raid seemed to have energised her. It was partly because everything was so strange. The sky was full of drifting smoke and the air prickled with a strong and distinctive smell, a mixture of bonfire, brick dust and cordite, a tang of unlit gas, damp wood, stale shit. It was the characteristic smell of a bombed house as she was to learn in the days that followed.

I've lived through my first air raid, she thought, as she walked to the depot. And she felt quite proud of herself. But it wasn't long before she realised what a devastating effect one air raid could have.

She and Mr Tinker took their first tram out bang on time as if it were an ordinary day, but they didn't get far. One of the bombs had fallen on a Deptford square and the blast had damaged the High Street and blocked Deptford Bridge, which was littered with rubble and cordoned off by the civil defence.

Mr Tinker stopped the tram and Barbara got out to see what they were going to do next.

'Run a shuttle service,' he told her. 'That's what we done in the Blitz. Go as far as we can both ways.'

Their passengers grumbled a bit, particularly about 'bleedin' Hitler', but having made their protest, they left the tram and struggled over the debris to wait for another on the other side, while Barbara and Mr Tinker drove back to the depot to report.

News of the air raid was passed from tram to tram all through the morning and the revelations grew more terrible as the day progressed. The shops at Rushey Green had been hit, and Colliers, Marks and Spencer and the Times Furnishing badly damaged. The civil defence was still clearing the site. There'd been a bomb on the railway siding at Hither Green, and two in

Eltham, one on the Cottage Hospital and the other in Castleford Avenue, where it had blown up nine houses. And the casualties had been gruesome. Scores of people had been buried alive in the rubble of their homes. One had been hurled through a plate-glass window by the blast, another had been killed by a shard of flying glass that had gone through her like a spear, another had been ripped in half.

The only mystery was where the planes were coming from and what sort of planes they were. It occupied Barbara's passengers all through the morning. Some thought they were old planes, brought out of retirement to replace the ones that were being pinned down in France, others thought they were something completely new. As one woman said, 'I mean to say. Hark at 'em. They don't sound like any Jerry I've ever heard.' And that afternoon, as the tram was whirring up the New Kent Road and Barbara was collecting fares on the upper deck, they saw one of them.

It was flying quite low over the rooftops about half a mile to the east, a squat, black, ugly looking plane, with stumpy squared-off wings and sparks of flame belching from a high tail, scarlet against the blue of the sky. The sirens hadn't sounded, there were no guns firing and, as far as they could see, it was the only plane in the air. It looked purposeful and dangerous and uncanny.

As they watched, the clatter of its engines suddenly cut out, the nose dipped and it began to fall.

'Down!' Barbara yelled. 'Get you down!' Not that her passengers needed urging. They were on the floor before the explosion, lying flat or crouched with their hands over their eyes. Seconds later the tram was buffeted by a shock wave that jerked them sideways against the legs of the benches and shattered the glass in their taped windows. The air was full of smoke and they could hear the crash of falling debris. Then it was suddenly and completely quiet. The traffic seemed to have stopped and nobody was moving or speaking.

Barbara picked herself up and dusted down her uniform. 'That was close!' she said. 'Everyone orl right?'

To her great relief – and theirs – everyone was, apart from the odd bruise and an old lady who'd spat out her false teeth and was down on her knees trying to find them.

Mr Tinker appeared at the top of the stairs. 'We'll have to take it out a' service,' he said. ''Cause of the glass.' And repeated Barbara's question. 'Everyone all right?'

They drove the tram back to the depot very slowly and carefully, just in case there was another bomb, and because they were now on the wrong side of the tracks, and they dropped off their remaining passengers wherever they wanted to be set down.

'I don' reckon that was a proper plane at all,' Mr Tinker said confidentially as he and Barbara went to report. 'If you ask me, there wasn't anyone in it. I never saw no parachute when it was comin' down. Did you?'

Barbara had been too busy looking after her passengers. 'A sort of robot, do you mean?' she asked. 'But thass horrible!' The idea of an automatic *thing* flying towards them, full of bombs, with that awful flame coming out the back of it and nobody in it, was fearful, like something out of science fiction, or something in a horror film. It filled her with revulsion. You could accept a plane with a man in it. That could be shot down or driven away. But a robot would just keep on coming, no matter what. And it could fall on anybody.

'I wouldn't put it past 'em,' Mr Tinker said. 'It's just the sort of stunt they *would* pull.'

Two days later the newspapers were agreeing with him. '*New raids on London*,' they announced. '*Flying bombs hit the capital.*' In fact they were reaching Greater London at the rate of seventy-three a day but that wasn't mentioned, being the sort of information the authorities kept hidden. Not that their caution made any difference. Within a week the size of the new attack was general knowledge and the flying bombs had acquired two mocking nicknames, buzzbombs and doodlebugs.

Because she knew her mother-in-law would disapprove, Barbara wrote a long letter to Steve every evening, describing the night raids and how they slept in the shelter, telling him what the new weapons looked like and how uncanny they were and what a lot of damage they did.

'*You got about thirteen seconds to take cover when the engine cuts out,*' she wrote, pleased that she could be so sanguine about it, and added with splendid pride, '*We don't take no notice of them unless they're directly overhead. Me and Mr Tinker take our tram out no matter what. People make jokes about them.*' And to prove it she sent him a copy of the cartoon that had appeared in the *Mirror* that morning. It showed a street full of people with a buzzbomb flying overhead. They were all standing still and all looking up and every single one of them had grown an ear as large as an elephant's. '*Now I know what they mean when they say "London can take it!"*' she finished. '*We're all in this together.*'

Then she waited for him to write back and praise her. Dear Steve. Although she knew what dangerous situations they were in, it pleased her to think that they were both sharing the same hazards.

It was another long wait. The 131st Brigade was pinned down in desperate street fighting in the ruins of Villers Bocage and if she'd seen her dear Steve at that moment she wouldn't have recognised him. The strain of three weeks living from one terror to the next, always in the open and always under threat of attack, had changed them all, fouling their clothes, hardening their faces, emptying their eyes, reducing them to such fatigue that they were little more than robots themselves. Even when the order came through that they were to withdraw to a village called Jerusalem for rest and refit they were almost too exhausted to respond to it.

They'd been at rest for two days before Steve read his letters and learnt about the buzzbombs. Then he was roused to a dreadful protective anger and wrote immediately and fiercely to tell her to get another job where she could be near a shelter. *'There is nothing noble about war,'* he wrote. *'It is an obscene necessity. It brings you to the abyss of death and forces you to look into it until you are dead.'*

Fortunately, the act of writing cooled his frightened anger and gave him time to recover. When he read the letter through he saw that he couldn't send it. It was too raw and too alarming. It would only upset her. So he wrote a second, simply telling her he was out of action for a week or two, that he was well and hadn't been hurt, and advising her to take cover when the buzz-bombs were overhead.

Then, being calmer, he added a postscript to thank her for the photograph and turning the little picture over, almost carelessly, saw her saucy message on the back. He answered it at once and seriously.

I could never forget you. You are under my skin. I remember everything about you, how you look, how you smell, how you feel. If I don't write you love letters it is because war and love are worlds apart but I could never forget you. You are my own dear darling. So please take care of yourself. It is better to run for cover and look foolish, than to brave it out in the open and get killed.

CHAPTER THIRTEEN

All through the long bright days of that summer the news from northern France was followed intently by everybody in the British Isles. The BBC Home Service went on broadcasting at the usual regular intervals, but the *Forces' Programme* put out fresh bulletins every hour on the hour and the newspapers provided daily maps and pictures, as the advance continued, step by slow and costly step.

Saloon bar warriors up and down the country were scathing about the lack of progress.

'They wanna get a move on,' Spikey Spencer said, wiping the froth from his upper lip but leaving the sneer in place. He and his friends were in the Three Tuns analysing the state of the campaign, as they did most evenings. 'They ought to 'ave been in Paris by now. Thass where I'd have been if I'd been there. Not pissin' about on the coast. I dunno what they're playin' at.'

Tubby had reached the befuddled stage of his evening's drinking and was finding it hard to focus his eyes and harder to put sentences together. 'When you think how they was . . .' he grumbled. 'I mean to say how they was when . . . when they was round here. How they was . . . Now they ain't here thass different. An' why? Cos they hain't here, bor. Thass why. Don't you think so, Vic?'

Vic was brooding and incommunicative. 'I dunno what you're on about,' he said, staring into his glass. That soldier must have been sent to France by now and yet she still hadn't come home. Becky Bosworth had said she was in New Cross and she ought to know. Her little brother was telling everyone she was working on

166

the trams in Greenwich and Greenwich was a huge place. He'd seen it on a map. Even if he went there, he'd have a hell of a job to find her. Needle in a haystack sort of thing. Still, that Jimmy was a stupid kid. What did *he* know?

'Well, well, well,' a voice said in his ear. 'Victor Castlemain, or I'm a Dutchman.'

A small, sharp, ferrety face, with a small, sharp, ferrety moustache, ferrety brown receding hair stuck to his scalp with brilliantine, watery grey eyes, new suit, white shirt, loud tie. 'Good God! Phossie Fernaway. I thought you were in the army.'

'Not no more,' the ferrety face said happily. 'Got out, didn't I.'

'How d'you manage *that*?'

Phossie Fernaway looked meaningfully at the three glasses collecting pools of beer on the table. So Victor bought him a drink and introduced him to his companions, 'This is Phossie, Johnnie Dent's cousin, used to come down here for the holidays, didden you Phossie?'

Phossie agreed that he did and when he'd taken the edge off his thirst, he preened himself ready to tell his story. 'Got out, didn't I,' he repeated. 'I said to mesself, you don't catch me heading off to France to be butchered. Sod that for a game of soldiers. I got better things to do with my life.'

'Very sensible,' Spikey approved. 'How did you do it?'

Phossie launched into his story. 'Went to the MO, didn't I. Told them I couldn't hardly see. So they set up this chart, didn't they, and they said, read the fourth line from the top, they said. Couldn't see it. Got it all wrong from start to finish. So they said, read the third line down, they said. Couldn't manage that either, could I. Got one or two right. Didn't want to overplay my hand. So they said, well try the second line then. And I thought I'd better manage that. So I just made one mistake. And they said, your sight's very poor, do you

167

know that? And I said, Oh dear, is it? And the upshot was they found me "unfit for active service". Smart, eh?'

'Did you get discharged?' Tubby asked in awe.

'No I didn't,' Phossie admitted. 'That was the one snag. But there's always ways round that. I waited till this lot got under way, didn't I? And then I took off. Don't reckon they'll miss me with all this going on. Smart, eh?'

Vic had been costing the suit and the white shirt, noticing the gold ring on his friend's little finger. 'So what are you doing with yourself?' he asked.

'Salesman,' Phossie said.

Vic sipped his beer thoughtfully. 'What d'you sell then?'

The answer was candid. 'Bit of everything, me. You'd be surprised what falls off the back a' lorries these days. Suits, nylons, coupons, bacon, sugar, tins a' meat. Matter a' fact, that's why I'm here. Brought my old lady a hamper, didn't I?'

He's a spiv, Vic thought, and he was full of admiration for the man. 'You're doing all right then,' he said.

'Not bad,' Phossie preened. 'I make a living. People are fed-up a' rations, see. Well we all like a little bit under the counter, don't we. Stands to reason.'

They agreed that it did.

'It's better than slogging your guts out in a bank,' Phossie said. 'You should come an' join me. I've just lost my last oppo.'

'I might at that,' Vic said, finishing his beer.

'There's always vacancies,' Phossie told him confidently. 'It's a growing business.'

He's nowhere near as intelligent as I am, Victor thought and he's making money hand over fist. If he can do it, so can I. This could be just the opportunity I've been waiting for, the chance to get away, to be someone, to find Spitfire. 'You're on,' he said and held out his hand to seal the deal.

Phossie shook the proffered hand and gave his old friend a sly grin. 'I'll be on the last train to London tonight,' he said. 'If you're serious you'll have a ticket. My round I think. What's your poison?'

So this is it! Victor thought. He was on his way at last! Won't Ma be surprised!

She was thrilled. 'I always knew you'd get on my lovey,' she said, smiling rapturously. 'When you gotta go? Tonight? My dear heart alive! They're keen! You got a case, have you? I'll give you hand packing.'

Which she did, producing an old carpet bag from under the bed and folding all his best clothes slowly and neatly before she packed them, while he found his identity card and his ration book, put his cherished snap of Barbara in his wallet and wrote a letter of resignation to the bank manager. Then he kissed her goodbye, took one last look at his reflection and left.

It was cold and dark on the station but Phossie was waiting. He was so drunk that his eyes were puffy and he spent most of the journey sunk into a heap in his corner seat, fast asleep and snoring. But what did it matter? Victor thought. What did anything matter now? The die was cast.

Phossie seemed puzzled when they reached Kings Cross, and asked Victor who he was, repeating the question several times as if he wasn't satisfied with the answer. Then he announced that they would have to get a cab and staggered out into the traffic to find one, waving at every car that passed. His gait was so unsteady and his speech so slurred that Victor decided he would have to take command and having found a cab, bundled his reeling friend onto the seat and persuaded him to part with an address and a pound note. He had no idea what the fare would be and didn't want to be caught without enough money to cover it.

They seemed to be driving through London for ever

but eventually they arrived before a small, soot-blackened, straight-fronted, terraced house where, after a lot of giggling, Phossie produced a key and let them in.

'Gotta lie down,' he said, leaning against the wall. 'Worl's turning round. Whole worl'.'

They were in a small square living room, unlit and musty – horsehair sofa against the wall, rocking chair by the fire, rag rug on the floor – and facing them in the shadows, a brown door which obviously led to the kitchen. Beside it a steep flight of stairs divided the two rooms and rose precipitately to the two similar rooms above them.

'Come on!' Vic said and hauled his dizzy colleague through the darkness and up the stairs. There was an unmade bed in the front room, plainly Phossie's for he collapsed upon it at once, and another in the back room which was stacked with cardboard boxes. They were piled on the floor, heaped on the only chair, even thrown on the bed. Vic had to remove them before he could get into the thing and then, just as he was settling to sleep, the air raid siren wailed and, to his horror, guns opened fire.

He was very much alarmed, particularly as he didn't know what he was supposed to do. You went into a shelter or something, didn't you? Underground. Phossie would know. But when he'd pulled on his trousers and groped his way past the top of the stairs and into the front bedroom, Phossie was no help at all. He lay on his back, dead to the world, with his mouth open and earplugs in his ears and no amount of shouting and shaking could rouse him. By this time, the bombs were exploding and there was an eerie glow in the square of sky framed by the window. So there was nothing for it but to stumble back to his room again and sit it out. And very unpleasant it was. Not what he'd come to London for at all.

'Did you hear the raid?' he asked when Phossie finally came groaning downstairs at eleven o'clock the next morning. He'd been up for over an hour himself and having found a teapot, tea, and half a tin of condensed milk had made himself an approximation to breakfast.

'Nope,' Phossie said cheerfully. 'Never listen.'

'Well I did,' Vic told him sternly. 'It was pretty rough.'

'Get yourself a good pair of earplugs,' Phossie advised. 'That's what I do, don't I. Sleep like a top then you will.'

'You don't stay here every night, do you?' Vic hoped.

'No fear. Only when there's a job on. Most of the time we're in Essex, aren't we, at the markets, Romford, Chelmsford, places like that, buying up stuff from the farmers.'

'Do you rent this place?'

'Yep.'

'Who from?'

'The Skibbereen,' Phossie said. 'Some old girl used to live here. Got bombed out I think. Went somewhere else anyway. The Skibbereen took it over. Ain't a palace, but it suits me. We don't get redcaps down this part a' the world.'

'Redcaps?'

'Military police,' Phossie explained. 'I don't wanna get picked up, do I? Gaw dearie me, Victor! Do I need a hair of the dog or do I need a hair of the dog.'

'Who's the Skibbereen?' Victor wanted to know.

But Phossie was already out of the door.

They had a pint of breakfast at the ornate pub on the corner and after burping his way back to comfort, Phossie outlined their plans. 'We'll hang around here till closing time, in case he wants us. If he don't we'll go to the flicks. Up West. Or take in a show maybe. Then we'll get some grub – there's some good restaurants up West. Cost a bit, natch, but worth it. Then we'll get back here, in case there's something on tonight.'

Vic wanted to ask what sort of something it was likely to be but he didn't get the chance. At that moment the landlord arrived at Phossie's elbow.

'Phone call fer you, Phoss,' he said. 'Usual place. Pronto.' They had been summoned.

'Where are we going?' Victor asked as they left the pub.

Phossie was off at a trot and hadn't got the breath to be communicative. 'To get the car,' he said. 'You'll see, won'tcher?'

The car was the black Humber which Victor had noticed parked outside the house. The back seat was covered with cardboard boxes.

'Hop in,' Phossie instructed. 'We gotta rush.'

And rush they did, through narrow streets, past bomb-sites and sooty terraces until they came to the cliff face of an enormous warehouse, a place of mean windows and grimy walls which looked as though it hadn't been used for centuries. One side of it had been blown open, leaving a gaping hole, and two more black cars were parked beside the rubble, which was still piled in a hillock of broken bricks and spars.

Phossie parked, scrambled out and climbed over the mound. And Victor followed, now very excited. He was vaguely aware that there was an explosion somewhere or other but it was a long way away and by now he'd learnt that you could ignore explosions when they were in the distance.

There were half a dozen men in overcoats and black trilbies standing moodily by the far wall smoking cigars. They were talking in low voices and looking out at the river through the broken shards that were all that remained of the windows. But when they heard the crunch of Phossie's approach they turned, as one man, and glared at him.

''Bout time too!' the tallest said. 'Where you been?'

A suddenly subservient Phossie explained that he'd only just got the message. And there was another explosion, this one close enough to pepper the air with dust.

'Who's this?' the tall man said, glaring at Victor.

'Old friend,' Phossie said and introduced them. 'Victor Castlemain, the Skibbereen. You said you wanted another pair of hands. Remember? Well he's them.'

The Skibbereen considered the offer while Victor studied his face and tried to read his character. He was an impressive looking man and obviously used to getting his own way for he stood with his legs astride and wore his coat over his shoulders like an American gangster. And besides being the tallest man in the group, he was also the fattest, thickset and broad shouldered, with a bull neck, a solid belly with a gold watch-chain suspended across it, and white hands with banana-fat fingers girded with thick rings. His hair was thin and grey and carefully combed and his face so round you would have thought it bland until you looked at those sharp eyes. The boss, without a doubt, Victor thought. And he's none too sure of me.

'Can he keep his mouth shut?' the Skibbereen said to Phossie.

Oh no! Victor thought. If you've got something to say you can say it to me, and he spoke up quickly before Phossie could answer. 'I can speak for myself,' he said. 'I got a tongue in my head and I know when to use it – an' *when not to*. I hain't a fink.'

'Hmm,' the Skibbereen said and he thought for a while, staring at Vic. 'All right,' he said at last. 'You can come for the ride. See how you make out. Work hard, keep your trap shut and you might do. No promises mind.'

On which terms and as a third explosion threw dust into the air, Victor was taken into the syndicate.

The ride took them to the dockside in their three

black Humbers and the work there was certainly hard and done at speed. The dockers were unloading sugar and the Skibbereen had arranged for a quantity to go missing 'providing we can have it away in twenty minutes,' as he told his team. 'So look lively.'

'Now what?' Victor whispered as the first car sped away with their illegal load. He was glad to have the job done because the bombs had been much closer in the docks, close enough, in fact, for them to hear the ambulances and fire engines speeding through the streets, which had made him feel very uneasy.

'Now we pay the Skibbereen for what we can sell and get rid of it pronto,' Phossie told him, equally quietly. 'How much cash you got?' And when Victor told him. 'Spend to the limit. That's my advice. Nothing venture, nothing gain.'

It seemed sound advice, so Victor kept half a crown for his immediate needs and spent the rest. Then he and Phossie transferred the sugar to their cardboard boxes and set out again to visit the local grocers. There was a lull in the raid so the streets were full of shoppers.

'Stick with me for the first two or three,' Phossie advised. 'I'll show you the ropes. Then you'll have to find your own patch. Don't worry. It'll be a doddle.'

He was right. The black market was everywhere. The very first grocer Vic approached on his own was only too happy to see him and asked if he could get him some eggs 'later in the week'. The next wanted to know if he'd got any peaches, the third was after corned beef.

By the end of the day, he'd made enough money to treat Phossie to a slap-up meal in a restaurant in the West End. And that was a revelation too, for although a five shilling maximum had been placed on restaurant meals in 1942, the rich obviously didn't take any notice of it and the bill that evening ran to nearly five pounds.

'Now thass what I call living,' he said as Phossie drove him back to their dingy lodgings. 'If that wasn't

174

for those ol' buzzbombs that'ud be a great life. They're the flies in the ointment.'

'We'll go to Chelmsford,' Phossie decided. 'They all been after me for eggs an' bacon today. What say we travel overnight? I'll show you how to drive an' we can take it turn and turn about.'

It was an admirable idea. The further they went from Hitler's bombardment the better. And eggs would be sure to sell.

It was a busy week and a highly profitable one. By the end of it Victor had learnt to drive the Humber – more or less – begun to carve out a nice little corner for himself and earned so much money that he'd dined out every evening, bought himself a new suit and some earplugs and decided to buy a car or rent a better flat.

'I'd rather go on the razzle,' Phossie said. 'What say we go up West Sat'day night? Few drinks, grub, bit of a laugh. We could find a couple a' tarts if you like. What you say?'

Victor could just imagine the sort of girls Phossie would knock about with. 'No thanks,' he said. 'I've got a girl actually. I don't need to find one.'

'Lucky dog!' Phossie admired. 'So *that*'s why you want a flat. Gettin' it regular, eh?'

Victor preened but didn't elaborate. He had no intention of letting someone like Phossie know anything about his private life.

'Oh well,' Phossie cut in, 'you'll cut off and see her this Sat'day then.' And he shrugged his shoulders, making the best of it. 'Not to worry. I'll find one of the others. Never short of company, me.'

But in the event they spent Saturday night working for the Skibbereen. A call came through just as they were enjoying their first beer of the evening and within twenty minutes they were in Limehouse, watching as the Skibbereen concluded his negotiations with a couple of dockers.

'You're from Whitbreads if anyone asks,' he informed his team and left the six of them to carry four dozen cartons of whisky out of the corner of the warehouse, where they were stacked and waiting, and into their cars.

'Where's he gone?' Victor asked, as he and Phossie filled their boot.

'To his club probably,' Phossie said, sliding the last carton onto the back seat. 'Too many buzzbombs about.'

The words were barely out of his mouth when they heard the familiar tinny rattle of a buzzbomb on its way towards them. It sounded as though it was directly overhead. It couldn't be, could it? But when they looked up, they suddenly saw the bright flame of its exhaust spurting into the little oblong of night sky between two warehouse walls, and before either of them had time to say anything, the engine cut out and they heard the awful rush of its fall. They flung themselves into the dirt, instinctively covering their necks with their hands, breathless with sudden terror. If the warehouse comes down, Vic thought, we shall be buried alive – if we're not cut to pieces. And his heart struggled in his chest, like a bird desperate to free itself.

The explosion rocked the ground they were lying on and the roar of it seemed to go on for ever. Then they heard a crash like a wall collapsing and the thud of tumbling debris, and that went on even longer.

But the warehouse walls didn't fall and presently the echoes died away and the debris stopped falling and they stood up and dusted themselves down and saw that they'd all survived and began to make obscene jokes to cheer themselves up.

'That could ha' been Potter's Wharf,' Phossie said, squinting up at the dust cloud.

'What do they store there?' Vic asked.

'Food,' Phossie said, still squinting.

176

'Might be worth a look then,' Vic said. 'What you think?' glancing round at the others. This was getting really exciting.

So they scrambled into their cars and drove off before the doors were shut, just like an American gangster film.

'If it *is* Potter's,' Phossie explained as he drove, 'we've got ten minutes at the most, then the civil defence'll be there. It's been a noisy night so with a bit a' luck they might be busy somewhere else, but we can't bank on it. We'll have to work like stink.'

The wharf was shrouded by clouds of brick dust and couldn't be seen but it was obviously the centre of the dust storm so they all plunged straight towards it. By now they were wild with excitement and heedless of the danger, scrambling over piles of broken brick, dodging smashed pipes, crunching over broken glass, eager for loot.

There was plenty of it, for although one side of the warehouse had vanished, as far as they could see, there were packing cases everywhere, looming out of the dust like a herd of humped beasts, some smashed open, some lying on their sides spilling tins, some virtually intact. But all of them too heavy to carry.

'We need a wheelbarrow or something,' Victor said, peering round wildly. And saw a tarpaulin, thrown across yet another heap of cases. Perfect. Grab it quick before the others see it. Then it was simply a matter of filling it with tins and lugging it back to the car, passing two of the others as they staggered out of the dust under the weight of half a broken packing case.

They'd made three trips and were on their way back for a fourth when there was a spurt of fire directly ahead of them and part of the building was suddenly ablaze, belching black smoke and scarlet flames behind dust clouds which were now eerily and dramatically brick-pink.

177

'Scarpa!' Phossie yelled and they both hurtled to the car. It was packed to the ceiling and very heavy to drive. But they got it away and the civil defence hadn't arrived and nobody could have seen them, thanks to all that dust. What a success! Fucking marvellous! They laughed and swore all the way home.

It wasn't until they were inside the house that it occurred to Vic to wonder what had happened to the others.

'That's their look-out,' Phossie said. 'It's every man for himself in this business. Let's have a look an' see what we've got.'

So they wiped the dust from their looted goods and found that what they'd 'liberated' was tinned food from the USA, corned beef, peaches, jam, rice pudding and stewed steak, all of it eminently saleable.

'We'll make a fortune!' Phossie predicted happily. 'A fortune! And we don't even have to pay a cut to the Skibbereen. That's the beauty of it. It's all Freeman's. Courtesy of Adolf Hitler. How d'you fancy a tin a' steak for supper?'

'Good old Hitler!' Victor said. Now he'd be able to buy that car. Then he'd find Spitfire – there couldn't be *that* many tram depots even in London – and he'd take her a box full of goodies or some nylons or something and see if she'd like to go out for a spin. Anything was possible now. Somewhere deep in the more honest recesses of his mind he knew that what they'd just been doing was stealing and that it was against the law, but there was no point in thinking about that now. If they hadn't taken the things, someone else would have done. Or they'd have been ruined by the fire brigade. In fact, when it came down to it, he and Phossie had shown a lot of guts running into a bombed building. Not many people would have done that. 'What a night, eh?' he said.

'That's war for you,' Phossie said happily opening a

178

tin of steak. 'There's a lot to be said for it. Gives people an appetite. They want better things. We supply better things. Profit all round. I'm all for it. They can keep it going as long as they like.'

CHAPTER FOURTEEN

'Where the fuck are we?' Dusty Miller growled, turning a filthy face to Steve, as they scrambled out of their troop carrying vehicle. 'I can't see a fucking thing in all this fucking dust.' Like everybody else in the company he was taut and irritable, afraid that they were lost or off-track, afraid that the Germans were alongside them, or ahead of them, or behind them – Christ no! Not behind them! – afraid that everything was going wrong, just plain afraid.

Steve had to spit grit before he could answer. Not that any answer was possible. Officially they were back with the 11th Hussars again and in the front line, in open country north-east of Caen, but at that moment it looked as though they were lost. 'Could be anywhere,' he said. 'Anywhere *else* preferably.'

The operation, code-named Goodwood, had begun in the standard way early that morning with a massive air bombardment. More than two thousand planes had been used, half of them RAF heavy bombers, so the destruction had been formidable – entire streets flattened, guns twisted in their mountings, fuel tanks and ammunition dumps exploded like firework displays, German tanks hurled bodily into the air. The brigade had watched with great satisfaction, saying it was 'enough to soften anyone up'. But there was a price to pay for it, especially in the long rainless days of mid July and the price was more dust than they'd ever seen in their lives. By the time the planes left the area, it was inches thick and every time the tanks advanced they blew up such a storm that the troops following in their

TCV's were temporarily blinded and cut off from one another.

Even the old campaigners said it was the worst they'd ever experienced. They'd driven through sandstorms out in the desert and stirred up a sand-cloud with every yard they travelled, but there the terrain had been open before them and the clouds had soon settled behind. Here the dust was incessant and pernicious, swirling perpetually before their eyes, thick, rust-red and foul-tasting, clogging their eyelashes and filling their mouths with grit. It obscured the road, turned trees and troops to looming ghosts, even masked the massive outline of the tanks and the TCV's. It burdened their helmets and kit, turned their boots to stone and their guts to water, for it was the perfect cover for snipers and sudden death could lurk behind every evil swirl of it.

And now the column had ground to a halt and the TCV's had caught up with the tanks and nobody seemed to know what direction they were supposed to be travelling in. And Steve and Dusty had been sent out to reconnoitre.

'A fat lot a' good this is,' Dusty said, kicking the dust with the toe of his boot. 'How're we supposed to see with all this muck in the air?'

All around them intercoms crackled with bad temper and swearing mouths spat back, tense with fatigue and fear. Apparently there was a traffic snarl-up somewhere in the rear. 'Yes, I *can* read a fucking map. I just can't fucking *see*, that's all.' 'Up yours!' 'If you did *your* fucking job we wouldn't *be* fucking stuck.'

It alarmed Steve to hear what a state they were all in. They were tense and afraid, which was fair enough, but they were taking it out on one another, which was frightening. Even the major was irritable. 'Well pull your bloody finger out,' he said into his intercom. 'We're a sitting target out here. We need some info and we need it quick.'

Steve and Dusty could just about make out the

outline of the tank immediately ahead of them. It was
inching forward again, its tracks grinding, and the tank
commander had his head out of the hatch in a vain
attempt to see where he was going. They watched him
as he adjusted his earphones, his right hand pale below
the dark cloth of his beret. To the left, the dust had
cleared enough to show that they were on a flat stretch
of plain, to the right they were passing woods. But
they'd hardly taken it in before they were suddenly and
violently under fire, the shells landing much too close –
bursts of black smoke with a brilliant scarlet centre –
red-hot shrapnel flying up and out in large jagged
chunks. Before the major could be given his answer, the
tank commander was hit, blood and brains spurting
backwards from his head and spattering the turret.

The major was in the field standing beside Steve and
Dusty, swearing and giving orders. 'Get him out, for
Chrissake! Get that bloody hatch clear! Come on! Come
on!' And they obeyed with the instant response of men
under fire and in utter terror, scaling the tank, tugging
the lead from the commander's earphones, hauling him
through the hatch, lowering him to the earth, working
so quickly it was all done in one movement. He was
unconscious and extremely heavy, his body floppy and
hard to lift, and as they lowered him to the ground, his
head left a smear of blood and brains all down the side
of the tank.

Waves of nausea rose into Steve's throat and he
turned his head away and was sick into the dust. It was
always the same when one of his mates was hit but he
knew how to deal with it now. There was no point in
trying to control it. The best thing was to get it over
with, quickly and without making a fuss, and then he
could return to the job in hand.

But once the commander was lying on the ground, it
was all too horribly obvious that there was nothing they
could do. He was dying, his legs twitching and his
breath making a dreadful quacking noise in his throat,

on and on and on. Poor bugger! Steve thought, as he crouched beside him. What a God-awful way to go, with half your head missing and making a noise like that. He ached with anguish at his inability to help. But what could he do? What could anyone do? They could hardly put a field dressing on a wound like that and it was pointless to call for the stretcher bearers.

He glanced up at the major for orders but he was simply a shadow in the dust-cloud. And at that moment, a tank four hundred yards ahead of them was hit by a mortar and brewed up.

It was the first time Steve and Dusty had been close to a tank that had taken a direct hit and they were so horrified by what they saw and heard that neither of them could move, even though they were in grave danger. Everything was exploding at once, the petrol tanks ablaze and sending tongues of flame high into the air, ammunition erupting from the sides of the tank in long glowing beads of fire, black smoke billowing in every direction. But much, much worse was the mind-numbing noise they could hear, as the crew screamed in their last terrible agonies inside the inferno.

Steve knew he was screaming too. 'Somebody get them out! Somebody do something! Christ Almighty! Somebody do something!' But it was useless because there was nothing any of them *could* do. The heat was searing them at four hundred yards.

And then all the tanks were on the move, the entire company was out of the TCV's and they were in the middle of a battle. There were commands to be obeyed and mortars to be fired, instantly and as accurately as their shaking fingers would allow. They were robots again, doing what had to be done, with no time for pity and no space for compassion, their only reality action and terror. And the dying man had to be left.

The exchange went on for a very long time but eventually the German fire diminished and a few seconds later they seemed to be retreating. The British tanks moved on, hosing the woods with precautionary fire as they left. Steve could see tracer glowing among the dust-clouds, then it faded and cut out and the tanks were gone, their motors just a distant hum. The dust finally began to settle and the brigade was left with the carnage. And the tank commander was dead.

No matter how many times he saw the aftermath of a battle and no matter how glad he was to have emerged unscathed, Steve was always shocked by the dreadful waste of it. And this time, as well as dead and wounded infantrymen to be attended to, there was also the burnt-out hulk of the tank and the horror it contained, which he couldn't avoid because it was directly in his way.

It was so badly burnt that all the paint had flaked from its sides in long ash-grey strips and the impact hole of the mortar was clearly visible. It looked like a jagged porthole and gave a dark view into the interior, a dark view he had to take whether he really wanted to or not.

Lying on the floor of the turret was what was left of the crew, five gruesomely blackened, grotesquely twisted corpses. The heat had been so intense that their flesh had melted to a black oozing tar that had fused them to the floor. Their heads were burnt to the skull, white bones pathetically visible, their teeth bared in a horrifying grin. These were men he'd known since the King's Lynn days, men he'd joked with and trained with and got drunk with – and he couldn't recognise them. The pity he felt for them was beyond sickness, beyond compassion, too far into anger to be expressed in any way at all. For a second he thought he was going to faint, but then Dusty crunched up alongside him to say that the stretcher bearers had arrived and they were detailed to assist. And having a job to do kept him going.

The stretcher bearers were professional and cheerful. 'Here we are, mate!' they called to the wounded.

'The Sheriff's bleedin' posse always gets through! Let's be 'avin' yer!'

Drips were set up, wounds given temporary dressings, fags lit and relit, and the casualties were borne away, drips and all. 'Room for one more on top! Fares please! Have the exact fare ready if you please! Regimental Aid Post and all stops to Blighty.'

Steve had never admired them so much. They were so stolid and dependable. So normal. Fancy being able to joke after such a battle!

When the wounded were gone, the mood changed abruptly. Now there were graves to dig and comrades to bury, and although they did it all as quickly and neatly as they could, it was still a sombre business. The battery carpenter made the necessary wooden crosses, the regimental padre said what he could, a few shots were fired in a last salute. And then they obeyed the next order, climbed into their TCV's and moved on.

Usually, when they were in transit, there was a buzz of talk, as they played cards, ate their 'compo' rations, told foul jokes and kidded one another. But this time they were all subdued. The air sentry sat on the roof, his feet dangling from the circular lid for the Bren gun and the rest of them crouched on their tip-up seats facing one another, smoked incessantly and miserably, and didn't talk.

By the time they leaguered for the night, the light was going. There was gunfire booming in the distance but it was too far away to bother them. Away from the dust, it was a beautiful summer's evening, the sky the colour of opal, the air gently warm, and somewhere across the fields the birds were singing.

They sprawled on a grassy bank above a ditch that would give them cover if they came under sniper fire and with their rifles close at hand, ate an unappetising evening meal. In the confusion of dust and misdirections, the supply column hadn't caught up with them, so they ate what they could find. In Steve and Dusty's case, it was cold rice pudding from a tin. They were tired and covered in filth of all kinds and their hands were still gory with dried blood and brains but there was no water to wash with and hunger reasserted itself despite the horrors of the day.

We're growing callous, Steve thought. But how could it be otherwise? When you're stuck in a situation like this it's inevitable. You fight, you bury the dead, you eat, you sleep, you fight again. Always in the present. It's not that we forget the dead – none of us will ever do that – it's because we're too weary to remember.

'If I get through this bloody awful war,' he vowed, 'I shall want to see some pretty drastic changes. We can't go on in the old way, not after this.' He looked at his hands again. 'They can't expect *us* to stand in a dole queue and rot without work. Not now. Not after all we've seen and done. I tell you Dusty, there'll be no ex-servicemen standing in the gutter selling matches, the way they did last time, poor sods. We've won the right to something better.'

Dusty was busily writing between mouthfuls. 'I can see you on the hustings,' he teased and began to sing, '*Vote, vote, vote for Private Wilkins . . .*'

His oppo's mocking tone made Steve aware of how dangerously fragile his feelings were. He changed the subject quickly. 'Writing home?' he asked.

'Nope,' Dusty said, and he held up a little card for Steve to see. 'Doin' me sums.'

It was a snapshot of a sweater-girl, dark hair piled above her forehead, smiling sideways at the camera. 'Who is she?'

Dusty barely gave her a glance. 'Some bint,' he said. 'I took her out for a coupla weeks when I was called-up.'

'Looks nice.'

'She was all right. Give me that when we said goodbye. Never wrote though.'

The mass of dark hair made Steve think of Barbara –
for the first time that day. 'She's pretty,' he said.

'She's just a bint,' Dusty said casually. 'There's
plenty more where she came from. Look on the other
side. *That*'s me sums.'

Steve turned the photograph over. The reverse side
was covered in pencil marks – six vertical strokes and
one across, like six-barred gates.

'Marking off the days,' Dusty explained. 'One more
I've got through in one piece. One more to the end of
this bleedin' war. It's my good luck charm sort a'
thing.'

That was something Steve could understand. Another
day still alive. Wasn't that what he told himself every
evening? Another day nearer going home. And he
suddenly remembered Barbara in the most vivid and
erotic detail – lying beside him with straw in her dark
hair and love in those green eyes, running down the
slope towards their little house, waving goodbye on that
hateful station, glimmeringly naked in the gaslight, her
head thrown back and her beautiful mouth lifted for
kisses. He missed her so painfully that his face was
anguished. And missing her brought anxiety into focus.
The papers were guarded about the new flying bombs
but reading between the lines it was obvious that they
were very, very dangerous. There was no way he could
protect her – or anyone else he loved come to that – but
that didn't stop him aching to be able to do it. If there'd
been some sort of bargaining counter where he could
offer to take their risk into his own life and leave them
free of it, he would willingly have done it. My darling
girl, he thought, remembering the courage of her letters.
Don't get hurt. I couldn't bear you to be hurt. I love you
so much.

187

CHAPTER FIFTEEN

The buzzbombs had been falling on London for over six weeks and although most Londoners made light of it, being on perpetual alert was beginning to wear them down. The papers called it 'war weariness' and prescribed Sanatogen and Horlicks to counteract it. Betty and Barbara preferred a weekly trip to the cinema.

Over the last few difficult weeks their friendship had progressed so quickly that they were now two best friends. It hadn't taken them any time at all to discover that, as well as their affection for Steve, their occasional annoyance at their siblings, a capacity for hard work and a stoical acceptance of their present danger, they also shared the same taste in many of the lesser things in their lives, films and food – or the lack of it – make-up and hairstyles, radio shows, popular songs, even newspapers. Betty was brandishing a copy of the *Evening News* at that very moment as she rushed into Barbara's bedroom, brown eyes gleaming with excitement.

'You seen this about Hitler?' she said. 'Someone's tried to do him in.'

Barbara had been combing her hair, standing on tiptoe so that she could see her face in Steve's high mirror. Now she paused and turned to face her cousin. 'Is he dead?' she hoped. Oh let him be dead and then the war'll be over and Steve can come home.

Betty pulled a face. 'No,' she admitted. 'Says here *"an unsuccessful attempt was made on Hitler's life."* They threw a bomb at him, apparently, but it killed someone else.'

'Pity!'

'Shows they're gettin' sick of him though,' Betty

188

said. 'I mean, we don't go takin' pot shots at old Winnie.'

'So they should be getting sick of him an' all,' Barbara said, returning to the mirror. 'The dreadful things he's done, thass onny right an' proper. Read it out while I finish my hair.'

She listened attentively while Betty read the paper aloud. 'Better luck next time,' she said, when Betty stopped reading. 'Thass all I got to say. Are the kids coming with us?'

'They're on their way,' Betty told her. 'You know how they dawdle. Had any more letters?'

'Not since Monday's,' Barbara said. 'I showed you that, didn't I?' Steve's letters were always so careful they were actually quite disappointing – apart from that one lovely PS. She kept them in a shoebox, tied with a bit of red ribbon that Betty had nicked from Woolworths for her, and she read them every night before she settled to sleep – or to a night in the shelter – but she couldn't help wishing they'd been love letters. Still at least as they were she could show them round to the family.

Betty returned to the paper. 'I been tryin' to work out where he is,' she said. 'It's full a' stuff about that Caen place. I'll bet he's there.'

Barbara didn't want to think about the fighting. It was too painful. So she changed the subject. 'What we goin' to see?' she asked.

Betty turned the page to find out and as she ran her finger down the column, the doorbell rang. 'There's the little'uns,' she said and went clattering off downstairs to answer it.

She was back almost at once to say that there was a young man on the doorstep asking for Barbara.

Barbara picked up her lipstick – coolly. 'What sort of young man?' she said. 'I don't know any young men.'

'He's a looker,' Betty told her. 'Dark hair. Talks like you.'

The only looker Barbara knew was Victor Castlemain and it couldn't be him because he didn't know where she was. But if it wasn't him, who could it be? Mildly curious, she finished off her make-up and went downstairs to find out. And it *was* Victor, wearing a smart grey suit and a brown Homburg hat and looking distinctly prosperous.

For a few seconds she stood where she was and looked at him. And he looked at her, his expression guarded. She realised that she was feeling acutely embarrassed. How could she explain who he was? Why had he come? Did he know she was married? And what on earth could she say to him?

In the end she simply sauced him, falling into the old habit of defence by bravado because she couldn't think of any other way. 'Oh!' she said. 'It's you.'

Her mocking tone reassured him. 'So they tell me,' he joked. 'Thass onny a rumour, mind.'

The burr of his accent brought Lynn back into her memory in sudden and nostalgic focus. And that made her sharp with him. 'How d'you know where I was?' she said and the question sounded like an accusation.

'Skill!' he told her happily. 'I do a bit of sleuthing in my spare time. Followed you home from the depot.' In fact he'd been hunting for her ever since he took possession of his new car, trailing from depot to depot, asking questions and soft-soaping her friends, and it wasn't until that afternoon that he'd discovered her address.

She wasn't sure whether to be impressed or cross. 'How did you know I was at the depot?'

'Working on the trams,' he explained. 'That's general knowledge in Lynn. Hain't you goin' to introduce us, then?'

She made the introduction while she thought what to do next. She couldn't invite him in or Mrs Wilkins would go mad. 'Victor Castlemain. He's from Kings Lynn. My *husband's cousin* Betty Horner.' If he was going to be upset – an' she couldn't blame him if he was – better get that said quickly.

But he was smiling at her. 'Yes,' he said. 'I heard. Congratulations. Hello Betty.'

'We're just going out,' Barbara told him.

'Can I give you a lift?' he offered. 'I just got a new car.' And he stood aside so that they could admire it.

Barbara gave the car the coolest glance she could manage, determined not to be impressed. And was impressed just the same. It was so big and black and shiny. 'Actually,' she said, offering him a get-out, 'we're only goin' up the road. To the pictures.'

But he didn't want a get-out. He'd spent weeks looking for her, and now he'd found her, he was going to stay with her as long as he could. He'd made a good start. She was pleased to see him. She hadn't sent him off with a flea in his ear. 'Tell you what,' he said. 'Let me come with you an' I'll treat you both. I hain't been to the pictures for ages.'

'There's four of us,' Betty warned, laughing at him. 'My kid sisters are coming too. That's them dawdlin' up the road. See?'

He accepted them at once and easily. Money was no problem now and it would be a good investment. Show he meant no harm. 'The more the merrier.'

Barbara had recovered her balance. He didn't seem to mind that she was married. He wasn't hollering or looking cross or even upset. He was just being himself – the way he'd been in the old days. 'You come into a fortune then?' she teased. He certainly looked as though he had. That suit must have cost a pretty penny.

He grinned at that and turned the full charm of his attention to Betty. 'So what about it, Betty?'

The little 'uns had arrived at the gate and were looking at him with great interest. 'Well, why not?' Betty said. 'Any friend a' Barbara's is a friend of ours.'

And at that moment Heather came downstairs, buttoning up her coat and with a bundle of magazines tucked under her arm. 'What you lot doing hanging about in the doorway?' she rebuked. ''Lo Hazel. 'Lo Joycey. I thought you'd be gone by now. You'll miss the start a' the big picture if you don't look sharp.' Then her face changed as she saw Victor. 'An' who's this?'

Her hostility was so extreme that it made up Barbara's mind. 'This is Victor Castlemain,' she said. 'He's an old schoolfriend of mine. We're going to the pictures with him. Victor, this is my mother-in-law.'

'Charmed I'm sure,' Heather said, her voice so acid she could have cut steel with it.

Victor told her he was delighted to meet her but then he rushed to open the car door. Strike while the iron's hot, sort of thing. 'Hop in,' he urged Betty. 'Plenty of room at the back. That's the style! You'll take the passenger seat, won't you Spitfire.'

And as her mother-in-law was glaring at her, she did, chin in the air and face set. I got a right to my own life, her expression said. You hain't my keeper.

So they drove off to the Kinema, and although Barbara made a point of sitting between the little 'uns, she had to admit it was a very good evening. Going with Vic was one in the eye for Mrs Wilkins, the film took their minds off the buzzbombs and he was really good company. Hazel and Joyce were highly taken with him because he gave them so many sweets. His pockets were stuffed with them. Must have been saving his coupons for months. And it was rather a lark to be driven home in that car of his. Bit like Cinderella. Except when they'd dropped the Horner girls off and she was suddenly on her own with him. *That* was a bit embarrassing.

He was as easy as if he'd been taking them all out for months. 'What you doing Saturday?' he asked casually as they turned into Childeric Road.

'I don't know,' she said, equally casual. 'Betty wants me to go out with her.'

'Where to. The flicks?'

192

'No. Dancing. They got a palais next to the Kinema.'

'I noticed.'

'She goes every Saturday. She been on and on at me to go too.'

'Well then, let me treat you both.'

'I don't know about that.' Going to the pictures with him in a crowd was one thing, dancing with him quite another. 'I hain't been dancing since I got married.'

'Why not?'

She answered him honestly. 'Don't seem right somehow. Not without Steve.'

'That's daft,' he assured her. 'There's no harm in dancing, now is there. *Everyone* go dancing these days. Everyone went dancing in Lynn, didn't they.'

She opened the car door, climbed out and stood on the pavement thinking about it, tempted but uncertain. 'Well I don't know.'

Having money in his pocket had given Victor a new and ebullient confidence. He knew she was tempted and he knew what to do about it. He had an ally now. 'Ask Betty,' he suggested, slipping the car into gear. 'See what she says. I shall be there anyhow. Eight o'clock, same as Lynn. I'll see you around!' Clark Gable couldn't have handled it better.

'Good idea,' Betty said, when Barbara called in at Woolworths the next day to test her opinion. 'Take you out of yourself. Bit a' life. Do you good. Can't see no harm in that.'

'Your aunt will,' Barbara said. 'You saw how she went on the other night. An' that was onny the pictures.' It made her feel really pleased with herself to remember how much they'd annoyed her.

'What she say when you got in?' Betty wanted to know.

'Nothin'. She just made a face.' And she gave a fair imitation of Heather's disapproving grimace.

'That's just her way,' Betty said, patting her mounded hair into place and keeping an eye on two potential customers. 'You don' wanna take no notice of her. Steve wouldn't mind, now would he? An' he's the important one. I mean ter say, you're only young once. He wouldn't want you to stay cooped up at home all the time.'

But Steve was the nub of the problem. Barbara couldn't bear the thought that she might hurt him by what she did. She'd written him a long letter that very morning before she went shopping, telling him all about the buzzbombs in Greenwich and how she'd queued for raspberries for over an hour, because they were so rare and she thought they'd be a treat and how the supply had run out before she got to the door, but she hadn't said a word about Victor's reappearance. She'd persuaded herself that there was no point in saying anything because it would only worry him for nothing, but the mere fact that she'd kept quiet about it was significant, explain it how she would. Even so, it *would* be nice to go dancing. Now that the offer had been made so persuasively she knew how much she'd missed it. It made her feet tap just to think about it.

'Tell you what,' Betty said, when she'd served her two customers. 'Why don't *we* go an' meet him in there, sort a' thing? That way we're not exactly going *with* him, are we? We're just sort a' going.'

Put that way it was possible. After all, Betty would be there so that wouldn't be like a date, and she'd been dancing with him so many times it wasn't as if it was anything new. So she looked out her red dress, put on her bold face, and she and Betty just sort of went.

The Palais was a magical place, all gilt and red plush and subdued lighting with blue cigarette smoke wreathing up into the ceiling like incense. It had a sprung floor and a dazzling mirror ball, and up on the stage there was a smart-looking band playing the latest tunes, Glen Miller and everything. There were servicemen everywhere, sailors in their tiddly suits looking glamorous, Yanks doing the jitterbug, a crowd from the RAF base at Kidbrooke, very noticeable in their RAF blue. It was such a crush that they'd been there more than ten minutes before Victor found them. He greeted them so casually that it was obviously not a date. So that was all right.

And oh what a joy it was to dance again! The Saturday hop at Lynn had been fun but this was the best she'd ever known. There was a frenetic energy about the dancers here. The beat was faster, the smell of sweat and dust, cigarettes and musk more intense, the dancers more abandoned. It was as if they were all grabbing at their last chance of fun before the bombs fell.

And whatever else you might say about Victor Castlemain, he was a smashing dancer. He took it in turns to dance with both girls and found himself other partners when they were jiving with the Americans. He bought them cloakroom tickets and kept them plied with cigarettes and chewing gum and, all in all, behaved himself admirably. So naturally when he suggested another trip to the cinema on Thursday, 'All four of you', they agreed at once.

Their outings rapidly acquired a pattern. Flicks Thursday, Palais Saturday. And because it was such fun and they needed fun so much, they soon found they were looking forward to their evenings out. It made the tension of the week more bearable and gave them all a chance to be young and irresponsible and almost carefree. Of course they all knew a buzzbomb could fall on a dancehall or a cinema as easily as it could come down anywhere else, but once they were inside they forgot their fears, cocooned in a warm fug of crowded bodies and cigarette smoke, caught up in a glamorous dream.

The only snag as far as Barbara was concerned was that she still hadn't told Steve about Vic's arrival. On that first Sunday morning, she wrote to confess that she'd been dancing with Betty and to hope he wouldn't mind, but she kept quiet about their other companion.

Then as the weeks went by and it grew more and more difficult to find the right way to tell him, her secret solidified. It made her feel guilty but that was silly, wasn't it? It wouldn't go on for long, and there was nothing in it, it was only a bit of fun. Anyway, she'd earned it, hadn't she, the sort of life she was leading these days.

Heather didn't share that opinion at all.

'Out every night of the week,' she complained to Bob. 'Gallivanting about with that Victor. It's no way for a wife to behave.'

'Not every night,' Bob demurred. 'It's only Thursdays and Sat'days.'

'An' dancing with every Tom, Dick an' Harry, I shouldn't wonder.'

Bob struggled to be reasonable. 'You don't know that Heather.'

His protest was swept aside. 'Of course she is. Don't tell me. You want to see her when she goes out sometimes. She's made up to the nines. You never saw such warpaint. Well you saw the state of her last Saturday, didn'tcher? Disgraceful, I call it. I don't know what she thinks she's doing. And our poor Steve out there fighting the Jerries. You'd think she'd have more regard for his feelings, poor boy.'

'She's young,' Bob tried.

That didn't sway her either. 'She's flighty. I tell you what I think. I think someone ought to tell him.'

Bob's heart was sinking deeper and deeper into his chest. 'But not you, eh? You wouldn't want to upset him, now would you? Not when he's in France.'

Heather had to admit that no, she wouldn't want to upset him. She was much too fond of him for that and much too worried about him. 'But somebody ought to say something to that girl,' she said. 'An' if this goes on . . . .'

But the next Thursday evening, to her surprise and

relief, Victor Castlemain didn't turn up and the four girls went chattering off to the cinema without him.

'There you are you see,' Bob said, when he came in after his night shift and she told him the news. 'He was just a flash in the pan. That's all. You was worrying for nothing.' It had been a bad night, with more than four buzzbombs in their immediate area, and his face was creased with fatigue.

'There's your breakfast,' she said, lovingly. 'Eat it up quick while it's hot, or you won't get the benefit. Then you can get off to bed. You look done in.'

'It's a long war,' he said, rubbing his eyes.

At first, Barbara was rather annoyed to be stood up. 'Thass Vic all over,' she complained to Betty. 'He's too casual. Always was.' But even as she spoke she realised that she was quite pleased about it because he'd revealed his clay feet. Steve would never have stood anyone up. It wasn't in his nature. She remembered how he'd sent his friend Dusty with a note when he was put on jankers. Dear Steve. Wasn't that just typical of him? If only they'd hurry up and get this war over and done with and let them be together again.

That Saturday she and Betty went to the dance on their own and enjoyed themselves every bit as much as they would have done if Victor had been with them. They missed his cigarettes and chewing gum but that was about all. And when Thursday came round again and the black car appeared outside the house, they were both cool to him.

'Thought you'd left the country,' Barbara said, as she opened the front door.

'Sorry about that,' he said, beaming at them. 'Something came up. Had to work.'

Neither of them believed him. 'At night?' Betty mocked. 'I thought you was a salesman.'

'So I am,' he said. 'Matter of fact, I brought you some of my goods.' And he lifted a large cardboard box

197

from the boot of his car and handed it to Barbara, looking smug.

She stood in the doorway holding it in both hands. It was very heavy.

'It's like Christmas,' Joyce said, thrilled by it. 'What's in it? Ain't you going' to open it, our Barbara?'

They could hardly unpack the thing in the hall because there was nowhere to set it down except the floor, so they all trooped upstairs again. Luckily Bob was at work and Heather had gone to the pictures with Sis, so they had the kitchen to themselves. Barbara put the box on the table and all four girls scrambled to unpack it. It was full of tinned food, all of it rationed, peaches, pears, spam, corned beef, three different kinds of jam, stewed steak, powdered egg, even sweets. A cornucopia.

Victor was hovering beside them, watching Barbara's face. 'D'you like it?' he asked.

But she didn't answer him. I can't take all this, she was thinking. Thass much too much. Thass embarrassing. Why couldn't he have brought me a couple of tins? Half a dozen maybe? That would have been acceptable. But this . . .

Betty was stunned by the sight of it. 'Good God!' she said. 'How d'you get hold of all that? It's enough to feed a regiment.'

'Ain't it lovely, our Barbara?' Joyce said, fingering a tin of peaches. The mere thought of such a feast was making her stomach ache to eat it.

Hazel had been reading the labels in her studious way. 'This is American,' she said, holding up a tin of sweets. 'USA, it says here. Have you been to America?'

'Surplus stock,' Vic explained easily. 'War damaged. I work for a middle man. He let me have it. That's where I was last week, as a matter of fact. Seeing as I stood you up I thought I ought to make amends.'

Barbara was thinking hard. It didn't look damaged at all. What if he's a spiv? she wondered. That could be

198

nicked or bought on the black market. Either way it certainly wasn't right. 'I can't take it,' she said at last. 'That wouldn't be fair. Not when everything's rationed. I mean, if I have it, somebody else'll be going short.'

He was quite unmoved by that argument. 'Suit yourself,' he said, shrugging his padded shoulders. 'If you don't have it, that'll only get thrown on the scrap heap.'

That caused an outcry. 'You can't throw it on the scrap heap,' Hazel protested. 'That's good food.'

'Oh have *some* of it,' Joyce begged her cousin. 'A tin a' peaches or something. That wouldn't matter, would it? A little tin a' peaches.'

'Quite right, littl'un,' Victor said. 'If you want it, you have it. I brought it for all of you. Better'n throw it on the scrap heap, that's what I say.'

'Oh it is!' Joyce agreed. 'Ain't it, our Barbara? We couldn't throw it on the scrap heap.'

Torn between their hunger and her own conscience, Barbara came up with a possible compromise. 'Orl right then,' she said. 'We'll share it between us then. Four quarters. Three for you lot and one for me.' That would be fair and it would cut her own share to manageable proportions.

'It's all good stuff,' Victor said, as she and Betty began the division. 'You'll love it.'

Having made her decision, Barbara was cool again. 'I'll tell you when I've ate some of it,' she said. 'You never can tell with tins. Specially when thass war damaged.'

Good old Phossie, Victor thought, as he watched them. He'd said food would be the best present. *'Nobody's gonna turn their nose up at a bit of extra, you mark my words. Not when the rations are so microscopic.'* And he'd been right. She'd only accepted his offering on sufferance, he understood that, but she *had* accepted it. 'Who's for the flicks?' he said happily.

Joyce and Hazel were eager but Barbara's share of

the tins had to be stacked away inside the cupboard before she was ready. To have left them on the table for Heather to find when she got home would have been too like deliberate provocation.

As it was, the goods weren't seen until the following morning, when the kettle was coming up to the boil and Heather opened the cupboard to get the tea-caddy. Then they provoked a quarrel.

'What's this?' Heather said. 'Where did all these tins come from?'

'Victor brought them last night,' Barbara explained, a bit too boldly. 'Thass surplus stock. Betty's got some too. He brought it here for us an' we divided it up.'

Heather sniffed her derision. 'Surplus stock my eye,' she said. 'I wasn't born yesterday. That's off the black market.'

'Thass what he said. I'm onny tellin' you what he said.'

'We shall have the police round,' Heather warned. 'The black market's illegal.'

'Better eat it quick, then,' Bob grinned. 'Before they catch us red-handed.'

Heather closed the cupboard door and busied herself with the tea. 'Well you can count me out,' she told them. 'I'm not eatin' black market food an' that's flat. I don't hold with the black market. Set of crooks they are. You don't want to have anything to do with them. They're just a flash in the pan. Bob'll tell you. Steer well clear of them. That's my advice.'

But her advice wasn't taken and the flash in the pan turned up at regular intervals to escort the girls to the cinema and the dancehall and to provide chocolate and toffees and yet another collection of tins. And as the weeks went by and the tins sat temptingly in her cupboard, she gradually came round to the notion that a steak pie would be preferable to yet another plateful of sausage and mash and that the food might as well be eaten 'now it's here'.

'I still don't approve, mind,' she said, as she dished up the pie. 'I just don't like to see things go to waste.'

'Quite right,' Bob said, holding up his plate.

Joyce and Hazel had no qualms of conscience at all. By the time they broke up for the long summer holiday at the end of July, their share of the loot had long since been eaten and forgotten. When Vic turned up at the cinema with a box of chocolates they were simply and plainly delighted.

'He ain't half nice,' Hazel said, when she and her sisters were out shopping with Barbara the next day. 'Don't you think so, our Barbara?'

'He's orl right,' she allowed. 'He's got deep pockets, thass what t'is.'

'Has he?' Hazel said, and determined to look at them the next time they were out together.

But Heather went on fretting and the more often he appeared at her gate the stronger her disapproval grew. 'She should send him packing,' she complained to Bob. 'She's got no business gallivanting off with another man, not now she's married to our Steve. It's not fair. I still think someone ought to tell him.'

'He'll be home soon,' Bob hoped. 'I mean the war can't go on for ever. There has to be an end to it sooner or later.'

She sniffed her scorn at his naivety. 'You're an optimist!'

'Well maybe they'll let him have some leave then. You never know. Wait till he's home an' let him sort it out for himself.'

Three days later the news bulletins justified his optimism. *'Germans in full retreat'* the headlines yelled. *'Broken army scrambles for Falaise exit.'* *'Chaos as sky armada smash choked roads.'*

201

Chapter Sixteen

'This is more like it,' Steve said, grinning at his mates in the TCV. They'd been travelling at speed all morning and there was no doubt that the Germans really were pulling back at last.

The sudden change of pace had lifted their spirits. They felt like conquerors, as the foreign fields rushed past them and the vehicle yawed excitingly every time it took a corner and rocked like a ship along the empty roads, the whine of its four-wheel drive high-pitched with effort.

'Berlin by teatime,' Dusty grinned. 'This is the life.'

In fact, life in their high-sided vehicle was extremely uncomfortable, even at that moment with the sides down to give them more air. Respirators and packs hung from the roof bars in the ceiling, their rifles were propped against their knees and the tip-up seats grew harder by the mile. But it had been their home since they landed and they were used to it. They'd eaten there, dozed there, smoked, played cards, joked, grieved. They hadn't stopped for anything, not even to answer the call of nature. They'd simply stood on the mounting steps, usually with a mate to hang on to their webbing straps to stop them from falling, unbuttoned their flies and sprayed the road. The first time necessity had forced him to do such a thing, Steve had been embarrassed. Now he was even used to *that*. It was the way things were on active service and nothing compared to being under fire.

'All we need's that port,' he said, 'and then we can really get cracking.' Lack of a proper port had put an immense strain on their supply lines, as they were all aware, because everything they needed was still being brought in through the Mulberry harbours or straight onto the beaches. As they drove along, they'd been speculating about which port would be captured first. Steve favoured Cherbourg, Dusty thought the Yanks would go for Brest.

'Hold on to yer hats,' the driver called out. 'We got a welcome committee.'

They were instantly alert. 'Jerries?'

'No. See fer yerselves.'

They looked out over the open sides of the truck and saw that they were driving between an avenue of pollarded trees towards a small, dusty village. It was run-down and dishevelled but it hadn't been bombed, which was a first, and there was no sign of the Germans, which was another. Instead, standing in line along both sides of the road was a group of local people, mostly women, some kids, a few old men. Two of the women were holding up a large *tricolore* and they were all waving.

The convoy slowed to a crawl and the company hung over the sides of the truck to wave back, blowing kisses and grinning themselves silly. And at that, there was an eruption of sound, a clatter of clogs as more people came running down the village street, carrying flowers, weeping and calling, 'Vive la France! Vive les anglais! Vive la libération!' as they joined the crowd running along beside the trucks. The air was full of petals, rising and falling, like a scented snowstorm, pink and white roses and hundreds of huge white daisies with golden centres. They fell across the bonnet and into the truck, caught on respirators, hung on upturned rifles, carpeted the floor.

Steve found he had a lump in his throat. We're liberating them, he thought, looking down at their joyful faces. We're setting them free. Now we really *are* the British Liberation Army. It was a wonderful moment.

But there wasn't time to dwell on it. It was time for

happy action. One of the village girls managed to clamber onto the running board and leant across to tuck a white daisy into Dusty's tunic, and after that there were girls everywhere, clinging on to the sides, standing on the mounting steps, thrusting gifts of flowers and wine into every available hand, kissing every available mouth.

They were escorted through the village in a triumphal procession and by the time the dusty streets were left behind and the TCV finally picked up speed again, they were all quite dizzy.

'What d'you know about that?' Dusty said, flushed with kisses. 'I reckon I could've clicked with that redhead.'

'Do you think they'll give us flowers an' things at the next place?' the newest recruit wanted to know.

'In this war,' the corporal said, 'there's no telling.'

The next place they came to was a small market town and here they were pelted with fruit as well as flowers. Dusty got hit on the forehead by a large apple, which he said had to be travelling at about forty-five miles an hour, given the combined speeds of truck and projection. It split open on impact and left him with a colourful bruise for which he was teased all the way to the next village. The girls were bolder in the town too and climbed right into the truck to sit on the nearest lap and get down to some serious snogging. And by that time the floor of the truck was like a meadow, completely covered in daisies.

'This is the life!' Dusty said. His face was rosy with lipstick smears and he was grinning so widely it was a wonder he didn't crack his mouth. 'D'you see the one *I* had? What a bint! Another ten minutes an' I could have . . .' And he was off into an erotic fantasy.

The others encouraged him, cheering him on. But Steve was quiet. The girls had fallen into his lap too and being kissed had roused him most powerfully. Now he felt ashamed of his reaction, normal though it was. It wasn't the way he'd intended to go on, not now he was married. He should have been above temptation, true to his darling, not lusting after the first eager woman to wind her arms round his neck. But oh God, the scent of them, after all these months in the field, the lovely warm familiar female scent, the swell of their breasts, the sheer sensation of passionate lips on his. It was irresistible. But it would have to be his secret, he certainly couldn't tell Barbara what he'd been up to. It wasn't something anyone could understand unless they'd been through it themselves – like everything else in this war.

Dusty was still gloating, 'Boy oh boy, what a little cracker! Roll on the next village! This is the life!'

'Make the most of it,' the corporal warned. 'We could be back in action round the next bend.'

In fact their return to duty was a mere three miles further down the road where the truck stopped abruptly and they were ordered to debus.

'We've caught up with the tanks,' the major explained. 'Fun's over for the moment. This road's mined, so we can't go any further until that's dealt with, and we want some snipers flushed. Corporal, take eight men down this side road till you reach the wood, then turn right and there should be a footpath. Go down the footpath. Keep under cover as far as possible. If the cover peters out, come back to the road. Your job is to locate and deal with snipers and find out the enemy strength on the other side, if that's possible. Sergeant Benson, take another eight and clean the snipers out of the wood to the west of the path. You should see the tanks about a hundred yards up. Move off in ten minutes.'

Being back to the old stomach-wrenching fear again after so much joy was very hard to take. But there was a job to do and they got on with it. Brutally.

The first sniper was ridiculously easy to spot. He was up in a tree and they picked him off before he could fire

205

a shot, watching with gloating satisfaction as he fell. The second only revealed his position when he put *them* under fire and he'd wounded the new recruit before they could flush him out.

After the rattle and terror of their exchange it was suddenly very quiet.

'Look after Tosher,' the corporal said to Steve. 'The rest of you follow me. There could be another bugger. Keep yer eyes skinned.'

'They're in the bleedin' barn,' a weak voice said.

It seemed to be coming from the ditch a few yards ahead of them and it sounded faintly Scottish but they approached it with caution, just the same. The Jerries were up to all sorts of tricks. But no, it was a Scotsman, a great big fellow, patiently lying on his side and pale from loss of blood which was seeping from a wound in his back.

They questioned him quickly and he told them all he knew. 'Six, with a machine gun and a *panzerfaust*, covering the entrance.' They'd taken him prisoner that morning. Or he thought it was that morning. He was vague about the time. When he'd tried to make a run for it, they'd shot him in the back.

'Never turn yer back on the bleeders,' he advised, as Steve put a field dressing on his wound. 'They're nae to be trusted.'

'I'll remember that,' Steve promised. And did. Long after most of the other events of the day were blurred by fatigue. It seemed typical of the way the Germans were waging this war, setting up concentration camps, shooting people in the back, sending pilotless planes to bomb civilians. Still, he thought, at least we'll soon be dealing with the launch sites, if we keep up this pace.

And, marvellously, they *did* keep it up. By August 15th, they'd reached the river Vie and once across, they had a clear run along the new Route National to another river called the Risle. There they found that all the bridges had been destroyed by the retreating Germans, which was only to be expected, but the Inniskillings were with them and they discovered a bridge near Montfort and another in a fairly good state at Pont Authou, which was a mile upstream, so by the end of the afternoon, the entire Armoured Brigade was safely across. Then there were only a few miles of rolling countryside between them and the Seine. There were still skirmishes to fight, but there was time to eat and time to sleep. There was even time to write home.

Steve's letters to Barbara were a commentary on the speed of the campaign. By now their progress was so widely reported that he felt he could tell her where he was, if he kept it vaguely general, and what he was doing, if he kept it carefully brief. There were far too many things he couldn't write about, like the bitter street fighting in Lisieux, or the truck that took a direct hit, or the fact that he never passed a day without being afraid, or the fact that he could now kill his enemy without remorse or pity, the way he'd shot that sniper in the tree. I've changed, he thought sadly, as he took up his pen. I'm not the man she married. But he certainly couldn't tell her *that*. All he *could* do was to keep her informed and let her know he was still safe and well. And give her good news whenever he could. As he did that August.

28th August.
We are in the Foret de Bretonne and have reached the Seine. There is a rumour that we have destroyed several of the flying bomb launch sites. Let's hope so. It's too much to hope they'll have stopped but are you noticing a difference?

31st August.
It is pouring with rain but we are still on the move.

207

7th September.
We have crossed the Belgian frontier and are at rest in a town with a beautiful town hall. Belgian civvies came out in their hundreds to welcome us. The girls were wearing the Belgian national colours, which are red, yellow and black. There was a public lavatory in the square and we all used it. Sheer luxury.

20th September.
Still at rest.

7th October.
In Holland. Very flat polder country. Reminds me of East Anglia. Plenty of food because we have taken a German food depot. You never saw so much meat and butter. No wonder Goering is so fat.

The letters were eagerly awaited in Childeric Road and answered at length. In September Barbara and Betty both wrote to assure him that the buzzbombs were slacking off a bit. They hadn't stopped altogether but at least there were fewer of them. In October Heather wrote to say she was glad they were feeding him properly. But at the end of the month, when he wrote to tell them they were at rest again, he ended his letter with a cheerful PS that unwittingly provoked a storm.

We are billeted with Dutch families, who feed us well and are very good to us. I sleep in a barn with seven others, actually on a bed with a real feather pillow. Positively sybaritic.

The letter arrived on a Thursday morning just after Bob and Barbara had left for work and it put Heather in a bad mood because it was addressed to Barbara and that meant she would have to wait until the evening to know how he was. He did write to her and Bob

208

occasionally. She had to admit that. But nowhere near often enough. It was usually Barbara who got the letters. And this one would all be read in a rush because it was Thursday and that damned nuisance would be coming. She'd thrown out hint after hint to the stupid girl that going out with another man was no way for her to behave but she hadn't taken the least bit of notice. And now she'd got to wait all day before she could read her own son's letter.

She brooded about it all day, chopping up meat with vicious accuracy, and when she came home and found Barbara sitting at the kitchen table drinking tea, it was the first thing she spoke about.

'You got a letter this morning,' she said. 'From Steve.' Her voice sounded aggressive but she was too pent up to notice.

'Yes,' Barbara said easily. 'I know. It's by the teapot. You can read it if you like.' Actually she'd had two letters that day but she'd only opened Steve's because the other one was from Becky Bosworth and would only be gossip.

Heather took up the letter and read it where she stood. 'Poor boy!' she said. 'Look at that! He's grateful to be sleeping in a bed.'

'I daresay he is,' Barbara said, smiling at the thought of him. 'He's been out in the fields most nights.'

The smile infuriated Heather. 'It's nothing to laugh at,' she said hotly.

Her annoyance pleased Barbara. It was a chance to sting her mother-in-law for foolishness. 'I hain't laughing,' she said. 'I was smilin'. Thass different.'

Annoyance spilled into hostility. 'Don't be rude,' Heather said and she spoke as if Barbara were a child.

Now the smile was bold and delighted. 'That ain't rude. Thass a fact.'

The attack increased. 'You ought to be sorry he's living in the fields,' Heather said, taking off her coat. 'Not sitting there gloating.'

'Gloating? I was *not* gloating.'

'It's all very well for you, sleeping in a nice warm bed every night, gallivanting about with your fancy man.'

'Doing what?'

'You heard me.'

'I do *not* gallivant. An' he ain't a fancy man. You make it sound disgusting.'

Battle was joined at last. 'It is disgusting,' Heather said, feeling relieved that it was out in the open. 'You're a married woman. In case you've forgotten. You got no business going out with other men. You should stay at home like decent women do. Our poor Steve sleeping in the fields and being shot at all the time and you out dancing with every Tom, Dick an' Harry. It is disgusting.'

'An' I s'pose he'd have a bed provided if I stayed in all the time?' Barbara mocked. 'The Germans would give in then, would they? I can see it all. Oh, Hitler'll say, we got to stop the war, Barbara's not going out this evening. Get on the blower to ol' Churchill.'

Heather was icy with annoyance. 'Try not to be stupid,' she said.

'That ain't stupid,' Barbara told her coolly. 'Thass logical.'

'It's stupid. And rude. You've got no respect for your elders, that's your trouble.'

'An' you're perfect!'

'At least I don't mess around with other men.'

'He ain't other men. Thass just squit. I knew him at school. An' if I wants to go out with him, I shall.'

She's gone too far now, Heather thought, and turned for a furious attack. 'Squit? Squit? What sort a' language is that? You want to watch your tongue.'

Barbara saw that she'd made a mistake but she fought back at once. 'Thass not "language". Thass what we say in Norfolk.' And when Heather made a disbelieving grimace. 'We all say it.'

210

'Then perhaps you'd better go back there. Then you can say it all you like. Because I tell you here and now I won't tolerate language like that in *my* house.'

'Oh I see what this is all about,' Barbara said. 'You want to get rid of me. Thass what t'is. Don't you think I don' understand you. I may not talk same as you, but I hain't a fool. You've never wanted me here, have you? Never. You never wanted me to marry your son. Thass the truth of it.'

We've gone too far now, Heather thought. But it was too late to retract anything even if she wanted to. And she didn't want to. 'You're hysterical,' she said. 'I suggest you go into the bathroom and wash your face and calm down.'

Barbara's temper broke into furious action. She stood up, gathered her letters, glared at her mother-in-law. 'Thass it!' she cried. 'I had enough. I'm gettin' out.' And she kicked out of the room, stamped along the corridor and slammed into her bedroom. She'd pack up and go. She wouldn't stay in this rotten house to be insulted, not for another minute.

It wasn't until the bag was packed that she looked at the clock and realised that Victor was due to arrive in less than five minutes. Well all the better, she thought. He can drive me away. And she put her letters in her coat pocket and went down to wait for him on the doorstep. There was just time to open Becky's letter and read it before he arrived.

It was short and rather odd.

'*I thought you ought to know. Your Ma she say not to tell you. You gone your own way she say. I don't know what your Pa say. He don't speak of it. The boys are very upset.*' Oh God, something awful's happened. '*The funeral is on Friday this week.*' But thass tomorrow. Whose funeral? Please God don't let it be Norman. '*They brought his body home Saturday.*' Becky, for Christ's sake! Whose body? '*I thought you ought to know, being you can't let your own brother go to his*

211

grave an' you not there. I am so sorry to tell you this. All my love, Aunt Becky.'

The shock of the news was so dreadful that it made her shake and she had to lean on the gatepost for support. She could feel the colour draining from her face. He couldn't be dead. Not Norman. He was so strong and such a good swimmer. Everybody said so. They'd made jokes about it. They'd said, even if he was torpedoed he'd get away somehow. He was that sort of feller. He couldn't be dead. It wasn't possible. She must have got it wrong. If she read it again it would turn out to be a mistake. But it was all there in Becky's scratchy writing. Oh Norman, she grieved as the tears rolled out of her eyes, why you? She was bent over the gatepost like an old woman.

Which was how Victor saw her as her came roaring up the road in his black Humber.

'Ready for the off?' he said cheerfully as he jumped out of the car. Then he saw her face. 'What's up?'

She handed him the letter, too far into grief to speak, and he read it quickly. 'Thass terrible,' he said. 'Will you go?'

She nodded. ''Course.'

'I'll take you there,' he said. He'd just about got enough petrol in the tank. 'We'll cut the pictures. Your cousins won't mind.' He was supposed to be meeting the Skibbereen at midnight but that wasn't important now. He'd deal with it later. If he drove fast maybe he could be there and back in time.

Barbara felt as if her mind had stopped functioning. She had to pull at it to respond. It was as though the news had knocked her out of character. She was grateful to have decisions made for her. But there were other things to attend to as well. 'I'll have to change shifts,' she said. 'I'm supposed to be working tomorrow.'

He was full of tenderness towards her. 'Get you in

the car,' he said gently. 'Let me tek that ol' case. Thass right. Now you just leave everythin' to me.'

It was a relief to sit down, a relief that Betty and the littl'uns took the news with such sympathy, a relief that Mr Threlfall was on duty at the depot and said he'd change shifts for her, provided she could take the eight o'clock shift on Saturday morning.

'Don't you worry about a thing,' he told her. 'We'll manage. You just cut off home. You got enough on your plate.' If the war had taught him one thing it was how to cope with sudden death. 'I'm ever so sorry.'

So she and Victor set off for Lynn and into a spectacular sunset. She couldn't speak at all now but he seemed to understand and simply drove on steadily, giving her the occasional smile as she sat slumped and miserable in the passenger seat, watching the sky. The setting sun threw out dazzling shafts of liquid gold from behind a darkening cloud, and as it dropped nearer and nearer to the horizon, the underbelly of the clouds was stained flamingo pink. It was incredibly beautiful and her dear loving brother would never see it again.

CHAPTER SEVENTEEN

Bob Wilkins was late getting home that night and, as Heather was scowling in her sleep, he crept into bed beside her very carefully so as not to wake her. Consequently it wasn't until breakfast that he discovered that Barbara had gone.

He was so upset he lost his appetite. 'Gone?' he echoed, putting down his knife and fork. 'What d'you mean "gone"? What's brought that about?'

'We had words,' Heather admitted. 'Last night. An' before you make that face you'd better hear me out. She said some dreadful things to me. Really dreadful. She was swearing an' cussing the way you'd never believe. The air was blue. I told her I wouldn't have it. You'd've said the same if you'd been here. I said it was beyond human flesh an' blood to stand. So she packed her bag and took off.'

'Where to?'

Heather poured herself a second cup of tea and shrugged the question away. 'No idea.' It had worried her to find the bedroom cleared and the bed unslept in but she wasn't going to admit it.

'You must know,' he protested. 'Good God woman, she's been out all night. Anything could've happened to her. She wouldn't've gone without saying where she'd be.'

'You've got too high an opinion of her,' she said, sipping her tea slowly to keep herself calm. 'That's your trouble. I told you she was a nasty piece a' work, didn't I? Very well then. Now I been proved right. She's gone an' she hasn't told me where to and that's all there is to it.'

'What about Steve?'

'Exactly. What about Steve? Well, he'll have to know about her now, won't he? We should've told him months ago only you wouldn't have it. I shall write this morning.'

It was a very rare thing for Bob Wilkins to put his foot down but he did it then. 'You won't do no such thing,' he said and his face was fierce. 'You'll leave well alone till we know where she is an' what's happened to her. Do you understand me, Heather?'

She recognised that he was giving her an order and that it would have to be obeyed but she went on making her case. 'He'll have to know sooner or later.'

'Wait!' he instructed. 'That's all. I'm not having him upset with gossip.'

'Gossip!' she said. 'Oh that's nice. I get sworn at an' it's gossip.'

He stood up and put on his jacket, buttoning it neatly and brushing the lapels the way he usually did. His face was set. 'You know what I mean,' he said.

She looked from his fierce face to the half-eaten meal on his plate. 'Where you going?'

'Out.'

'But you haven't had your breakfast. You're not going out without your breakfast.'

'Put it in the oven for me,' he said. 'I'll have it later.'

And went, treading the stairs as carefully as usual and shutting the door behind him as quietly. But he didn't whistle as he walked away and the lack of that little chirruping sound distressed her to tears. Damned girl, she thought, blinking angrily. Now look what she's done. Oh why couldn't he have married a nice girl from round here? A nice respectable girl, with good manners, that we all knew, that'ud speak like us instead of all that country burr. That gets on my wick. I'll bet she's been with that awful feller all night. I wouldn't put it past her. Bob'll like *that* when he finds out. She's probably rolling around in bed this very minute, sleeping it off.

*

She was right about that, at least. Barbara *was* in bed at that moment but she wasn't asleep and she was lying perfectly still, trying to gather her thoughts and her energy for the day ahead. She and Becky had sat up till two in the morning, talking and grieving, and now Becky was up and had lit the fire and was clattering about downstairs making the tea, but she was in bed and loath to get up. The trouble was that their conversation had gone round and round over relatively easy ground. They'd remembered how strong Norman had been and what a good swimmer he was and how well he rowed, and said, over and over again, that he'd been cut out for the sea and that they couldn't believe they'd never see him again. Barbara had found out what time the funeral was going to be, and where, and who was coming. They'd even discussed what they ought to wear. But she hadn't asked the one question she really wanted to have answered.

'Come on down, my poppet,' Becky called to her. 'Tea's made.'

Tea. Toast. Quietly going over the same talk, again and again, gradually inching to the question. More tea. Getting dressed in the clothes they'd agreed on. Brown skirt, white blouse and Becky's old navy mackintosh to cover it all because she couldn't wear her red coat. Still inching. Going out of the door, checking in the mirror to see that they looked 'orl right'. Still inching. I must know. I must ask. Do it now or that'll be too late.

'Aunt Becky.'

Becky turned her foxy face towards her. 'Poppet?'

'How did he die?'

The answer was quick and honest and brutal. 'Drowned, my lovey. Burned too bad to swim they do say an' covered in oil.'

The horror of it was like a blow to her stomach, even though she'd half expected it. To die like that, burnt and in pain, out in the middle of the Atlantic, all on his own. She could feel the oil burning on her own flesh, the

216

terror of the water over her head. 'Oh my poor Norman! That ain't fair!'

Becky patted her arm. 'You got han'kerchief, 'ave you, gal?'

Barbara shook away her tears. She had to be controlled. That wouldn't do to let everyone see her in a state. 'Yes. I'm orl right.'

'You're a good brave gal,' Becky said, button eyes full of pity. 'Catch hold of my arm.' And when Barbara hesitated. 'I could do with a bit of support.'

So they walked through the yards to her father's house arm in arm, supporting one another. Her own yard was exactly as she remembered it, dark and cramped and full of clutter, the same worn mangles against the wall, the dustbins and old bikes, the tin baths propped against the brickwork, even the same nets hanging to dry, the same smell of fish, wet boots and dirty clothes, and above it all, the same putrid stink from those awful outside lavvies. After months in the comfort of Childeric Road, she found it appalling and knew it was a slum. But at the moment it was full of relations, who'd spilled out of the house, and were standing around waiting and commiserating. So she had to put on a calm face and go and greet at least a few of them before she went indoors.

The tiny living room was crowded too. Her father was hunched in his chair in the corner with his crew around him and a half-finished glass of whisky in his hand. His mates were all in their sea-faring caps and Sunday ganseys, but he was wearing a blue suit. She hadn't been aware that he even possessed such a thing, leave alone seen him wear it, and the sight of him, so ill at ease and quiet and shrunk into himself, made her feel a sudden rush of pity towards him.

''Lo Pa,' she said. 'You orl right?'

But he didn't look up. Instead her mother swooped across the room and seized her by the arm. 'Whass brought *you* here then?' she said. 'I thought you were working up in Lonnon. On the trams.' Her voice was querulous and aggressive and her face tear-stained. 'I'm surprised you got time for us now, the sorta life you're leadin'.'

I won't be provoked, Barbara thought. Not today. She's upset. She don't mean it. 'Where's the kids?' she asked and looked round to find them.

They were sitting back to back on a low wooden stool in a corner of the room, hemmed in by adult legs and noisy conversation and looking most unlike themselves, with their hair slicked to their skulls – who did that to them? – and their school guernseys clean and pressed. They were so glad to see her it made her want to cry. Instead she knelt on the floor and put her arms round them and told them she'd look after them.

'You stand by me,' she said. 'Then you'll be orl right.'

There was a rustle of movement by the open door and somebody was calling that the hearse had arrived and it was time to go. Her father lumbered to his feet, still not saying a word, and with his mates protectively around him, led them all out.

Afterwards Barbara was puzzled to realise how little of the funeral service she could remember. Her own brother was being committed to the earth and yet she stood at his graveside and didn't feel any emotion at all. She looked away from the anguished faces round that awful pit, because she couldn't bear to see them or to look at the coffin, but then she didn't know where to put her eyes and glanced idly across at the dark walls of the church, thinking how old it was. She noticed the white wings of a flock of herring gulls as they soared overhead calling like cats, found she was admiring the grey backs and the garish yellow bills of the adults, counted the speckled yearlings, thinking what a lot of them there were. Finally she watched the branches of the yew tree swaying in the wind and sniffed the air thinking how salty it was. But she didn't think of her brother at all. There would be time for that later, when she was on her own and it wouldn't matter if she cried. For the moment it was all she could do to get through the awesome words of the service.

But when her father took the proffered spade and shovelled the first load of earth to cover his son and she heard the sharp clods rattling down on the lid of the coffin, she was suddenly pulled to such grief she was afraid she would fall and closed her eyes against the pain of it. At that point, her mother began to wail, standing alone on the other side of the grave, and she went on and on until the service was over and they were all walking back to the yards again. Poor Ma.

'Whass goin' to happen now, Bar'bra?' Jimmy wanted to know. He'd clung on to her hand all through the service and was holding it still, so tightly that his grip was quite painful.

'There'll be a few sandwiches or something,' she told them. 'People generally have a bite to eat after. That won't take long.'

But to her horror, plate-loads of food had been prepared, and were being carried into the house by her neighbours; shrimps, cockles, winkles, fish-paste sandwiches, even a flatmeat pie. And there were boxes full of glasses, and a keg of beer standing in the corner where the kids' stool had been.

'Got to give him a good send-off,' her uncle said cheerfully. 'Come on Crusher, bor, git that down yer. Mek all the difference that will.'

Thass a party, Barbara thought with disbelief. They're holding a party. Feeling returned in a rush of temper. How dare they do such a thing! Hain't they got *any* sense? All those great coarse mouths chomping up bread an' marge an' fish-paste, all that beer slopping over the edge of those glasses an' running down those stupid chins, an' Norman burnt to death.

Her father was hunched in his corner again. He had a full glass but for once in his life he wasn't drinking.

'Best of the bunch,' he said, holding the glass in both scarred hands as though it were a bouquet. 'Well an' away. Best of the bunch. I should of told him an' now he's gone an' thass too late.'

'Never you mind, bor,' his skipper said, comforting him in the only way he knew. 'He'd of knowd it. Just you drink up.'

'Thass a cruel mistress, that ol' sea,' another commiserated. 'All onnus knows that. Thass took many a good un, one way or 'nother. You think of ol' Tanker. Took him.'

'An' Froggie,' one of the uncles put in. 'I 'member when they brought him in, all over slime, an' his face caved in, an' all. You 'member that, don't you Crusher.'

But Crusher could only sigh.

So they went on encouraging him with gruesome tales. 'You 'member when Jiggy fell outta the riggin'. That was a funeral! I 'member the percession. All round Pilot Street an' in ter Chapel Lane.' 'You 'member when we took that ol' corpse out the water. Three mile out that was. The stink of un. D'you 'member? And not one on us knowd un.'

Barbara couldn't believe they were being so insensitive. It was hideous, barbaric. She strode through the throng until she was standing among them. 'Stop it!' she said, the words hissing through clenched teeth. 'Just stop it! Can't you see what you're doin' to him?'

'We hain't a-doin' nothin' to him,' the skipper told her. 'We're cheerin' him up. Ain't we, bor?'

But one of her uncles moved into the attack. 'S'pose you know what's best for us now you're livin' up Lonnon,' he said, sneering at her. 'S'pose you're all high an' mighty now. What you done with that bebby of your'n, eh? You tell us that.'

It was such an unexpected attack that it took her breath away but she fought back at once, bristling at them. 'What bebby?'

'The one you was aspectin' when you went hossin' off with that soldier boy of your'n.'

You vile man, she thought. How dare you say such a thing! How dare you imply . . . In a small honest corner of her mind she knew it could easily have been true but that only made it worse. She drew herself up to her full height and pulled in her stomach so that it was as flat as she could make it. 'Thass just a load of ol' squit what someone's been tellin' you,' she said. 'There ain't a bebby. There never was a bebby. I onny been married five months an' he been in France four an half of 'em. I'll trouble you not to spread wicked rumours, Uncle Ned.'

Her mother was at her elbow, flushed in the face and breathing quickly. But she'd come to defend her cousin, not her daughter. 'That could ha' been true though,' she said to Barbara. 'How was we to know? You went off so quick, you could ha' been in any ol' state, we wouldn't ha knowd.'

It was a shock to come under attack from her own mother but Barbara turned to take her on too. 'Well I wasn't,' she said stoutly. 'So now you *do* know.'

'This is what comes a' marryin' a foreigner,' her mother complained, tears springing to her eyes again. 'You should ha' stayed here an' married one of your own kind, like we all done. Thass what you should ha' done. But no. You would go your own way. There was no tellin' you. Well you made your bed so now you must lie on it. An' your poor brother cold in his grave. You oughtta be ashamed of yourself.'

'So thass a sin to get married now,' Barbara said furiously. 'Is that what you're sayin'?'

'You don' marry out the North End,' Maudie said. 'No good never comes of that. As you'll find out.' She turned to address her relations. 'But no, she won't be told. You'll see. Never would. Always disobedient she was, even as a littl'un. Downright wilful. Go her own way. Say what she please. Break your heart an' damn

221

the consequences.' Grief and drink had tipped her into an anger she couldn't understand or control. 'Well don' you think you can come back here upsettin' us, just 'cause your brother's dead. Poor boy. We don' want you. None of us. You're no daughter of mine. Not now. So you can just clear off. You made your bed an' now you just gotta lie on it . . .'

To be spoken to in such a hateful, harmful way, and right after poor Norman's funeral, was too much for Barbara to endure. She had to get away. Now. Before they said anything worse. She stepped back, her face stiff with pain, stumbled through the crush, pushing bodies away from her to left and right, careless of spilt beer and scattered food, and pelted out of the yard. She had no idea where she was going, she simply ran blindly, but after a few yards she realised that instinct was taking her to the quayside and then she calmed a little and walked instead of running.

I should never have come up here, she thought as she stood beside the river gazing out at the great soothing expanses of water and sky. I got no place here. They don't want me. I been cast off. That was a leaden certainty. '*You're no daughter of mine.*' Wasn't that what she said? I should've stayed in London. Thass where I belong now. But that brought another rejection into her mind. When she went back – and she'd have to go back, they were expecting her at the depot – where would she stay? She couldn't live in Childeric Road any more. Not after the awful way Mrs Wilkins had spoken to her. '*Gallivanting about with your fancy man.*' They all think so badly of me, she anguished. To hear them, you'd think I was a good-time girl, not a married woman. And that hurt almost as much as their rejection. Oh Steve! she mourned. If only you were here and I could talk to *you* about it. He was the only one who would understand. The only one in all the world. If he were here he'd put his arms round her and kiss her and storm off into her mother's wretched hovel, tall and handsome in his uniform, and give them a piece of his mind for being so unkind. Oh if only she could see him just for a minute. It was so lonely without him.

She sat sadly on the wall, perching there the way she'd done as a little girl. The quay was full of fishing boats waiting for the tide, their masts dark against the bright sky, their faded sails set, nets and pots already loaded. On the opposite side of the river she could see the spire of East Lynn church, sharp as a bodkin among the bronze branches of the denuded trees. Was it only last spring they'd made love in that haystack? It seemed a lifetime. Was it only last spring they'd strolled around town with their arms round each other and kissed in the Walks and sat in the back row at the pictures and danced in the old Corn Exchange? This had been her home then and no one had been sent to France and Norman had been alive and everything had been wonderful. Oh Norman! Norman!

Now that the first rush of anger and grief was clearing, she realised that she was sitting in the self same spot where he'd been so good to her the last time they'd been together, where he'd dried her tears and sorted out her problem, getting that form signed, looking after her. She could hear his voice. *'There's more than one way to kill a cat ... I can see another right here on this ol' piece a' paper.'* Dear Norman. He'd been such a good brother, always there and always sensible, and they'd had such fun together when they were little. She let her mind drift back into the past, remembering how they'd gone rowing in the dinghy, and how she'd watched him set out with the fishing fleet that very first time, and how proud he'd been when he came back because he hadn't been sea-sick. And the afternoon gradually gentled into evening around her, holding her safe in a salty haze, the sky amassing lilac cloud, the river darkening from milky blue to brooding brown, a faint grey mist rising from the water to drift dreamily towards the opposite bank. Thass beautiful, she thought, an' thass my home no matter what they say.

She was easier now, aware that there was no need to feel rejected, no need to feel anything if she didn't want to. It was simply a matter of solving her present problems, that was all, the way she and Norman had done that last time. *There's more than one way to kill a cat.* She couldn't stay in Lynn, but then she didn't want to anyway. And if she couldn't live in Childeric Road there were other places. If she was to be in the depot by eight o'clock the next morning, she'd have to catch an early train. A workman's or something. They went very early. Then she'd work through her shift and after that she'd look for a room of her own. There ought to be something somewhere, even in London. If she couldn't find one straight away, she'd go round to Betty's mum and see if she'd put her up for a night or two. Or failing that she'd sleep in a shelter. She just had to get on with it, that was all.

Planning her life made her feel better. Although she wasn't consciously aware of it, she had squared her shoulders and lifted her chin. She would walk back to Becky Bosworth's and see if there was a fire going and something to eat, because she was cold now and quite hungry. Then she'd get cracking.

There *was* a fire. She could feel the warmth of it and hear its comfortable hiss as Becky opened the door. And there was a feast on the table, for her aunt had brought home a selection of the funeral shellfish. And sitting by the fire, as if he belonged there, was Victor Castlemain.

She was really pleased to see him. After being spurned and insulted by her family, it was a pleasure to be able to talk to one of her own kind without fear of criticism. 'I thought you'd gone back to London,' she said, as she held out her cold hands to the blaze.

'Went. Did the business. Came back again,' he told her. It had actually been a good deal more difficult than he made it sound but he certainly wasn't going to let her know that. 'Brought you a tin of peaches. In case you were hungry. I didn't think you'd want much after the funeral.'

'No,' she agreed sadly.

'But peaches might be all right?'

His kindness lifted her spirits. He was so blessedly normal after the miseries of the day. Despite their sadness, the three of them sat up to the table and ate what they could and talked in a gentle, disjointed way, remembering Norman as a boy at school saucing the teacher – 'D'you remember how pink she used to go? All up her throat. Poor ol' mawther' – swimming in the river on a summer's day – 'He was always a good swimmer' – out bird's nesting, sitting in the Saturday pictures cheering Roy Rodgers – 'I can't think what we saw in him.' It was wonderfully comforting and it spun the meal out for over an hour.

But eventually Vic stood up and said he'd have to be leaving. 'I'll be back at five o'clock tomorrow morning.'

'Five o'clock?' Becky said. 'What for?'

'To drive our Barbara to London.'

'You sure?' Barbara asked.

'Thass why I came back,' he said. 'You won't get there in time for work if you go by train. I checked. Could you be ready at five o'clock?'

'He's a good feller,' Becky approved when he'd gone. 'I'm glad you're goin' back with him. I never did like those ol' trains, bumpin' about all over the place. You never know who's on them. He'll look after you.'

Waking at five was very odd and driving out of Lynn along completely empty roads in the pitch dark was even odder.

'I never seen Lynn so empty,' Barbara said as they purred through Tuesday Market Square. 'Thass like a ghost town.' The sight of it was making her shiver.

'Tell you what,' Vic said, 'there's a blanket on the

225

back seat. Why don't you wrap it round you an' have forty winks. I bet you didn't sleep much last night, did you?'

'Sure you don' mind?' It seemed a bit mean to sleep while he was awake and driving.

''Course not,' he said. 'You go ahead.'

So she pulled the blanket through to the front seat and cocooned herself in it, glad of its warmth. 'I shan't sleep long,' she said. 'Just a nap.'

When she woke, they were driving past a tram. It was half past seven and daylight, and they were in London.

'Said I'd have you back in time,' he said. ''Nother quarter of an hour an' we shall we there. How's that for driving?'

She thanked him and meant it. He'd been very good to her these past two days. 'I don't know what I'd have done without you', she told him, 'an' thass a fact.'

She couldn't have said anything to please him better, so he joked to cover his delight. 'Gone by train,' he said.

They were at the depot in a quarter of an hour, just as he'd promised. He leant across to open the door for her and as she gathered her things, he wondered whether he could ask her out. 'I don't suppose you feel much like dancing Saturday?'

'No,' she said sadly. 'Not really.'

'Pictures then? I could call for you Thursday.'

'I shouldn't think so,' she said, as she eased out of the car. 'Thass too soon.' And as the words were in her mouth she had a sudden terrible vision of Norman lying face downwards in a great sea, turning in the wave, burnt black. It was so overpowering that she had to run into the depot to get away from it.

So he drove away.

It was a great relief to Barbara to be back in uniform with her cap on her head and her ticket rack round her

226

neck, taking her tram out of the depot and off to a working day. Having a job to do rescued her from her thoughts and, even if her passengers complained about the rations and told her the same old tales about the doodlebugs, at least she knew when to answer them and when to listen. That day, to everyone's relief, they didn't see any of the horrible things and the only explosions they heard were a long way away. But when the shift was over she was so tired her bones ached.

I'll get away quick, she decided, soon as I've signed off and see if there's anything advertised in the newsagent's. It was already growing dark and she didn't fancy traipsing the streets in the blackout.

Mr Threlfall was standing by the incoming trams with his checkboard in his hand and his pencil behind his ear. He waved to her as she walked towards him and so did another, bulkier figure standing beside him.

It was Aunt Sis. 'Ah! There you are,' she said, as Barbara checked out. 'I come to see you home.'

Barbara retrieved her case and walked with her aunt until they were out of Mr Threlfall's earshot. Then she explained, rather wearily. 'I hain't livin' at Childeric Road no more, Aunt Sis. I've left.'

Sis smiled benignly. 'I know,' she said comfortably. 'Bob told me. I heard all about it. All I need to hear anyway. She's a good woman our Heather but she's got it wrong this time. And while we're at it, lovey, I heard about your poor brother too. A bad business. Our Betty told me. So you don't have to tell me anything if you don't want to.'

After two days overburdened with emotion, it was comforting to be beside such calm. Comforting and soothing, as if the weight of her sorrow were being lifted from her shoulders. They strolled out into the darkening High Street, together but not talking, waited for a tram to emerge from the depot, crossed the High Street, headed off towards Woolworths. They'd walked right past its long frontage before Barbara asked where they were going.

'Why home,' Sis said. 'Where else? You're comin' home with me.'

228

CHAPTER EIGHTEEN

Aunt Sis – or to give her her full and proper title, Mrs Cecily Tamworth – had lived in her cramped flat above the newsagent's ever since Dunkirk, maintaining that now she was on her own, two rooms and an outside WC were more than enough for her to keep clean. 'Just so long as I've got room fer me books an' papers,' she would say, whenever her brother suggested something better. 'That'll do me fine.' As the years passed and her loss became more bearable, she gradually acquired the few creature comforts that were now indispensable to her, a sagging armchair, eased to accommodate her bulk, a padded stool for her aching feet, the bottle of three star brandy on the dresser to cheer and sustain her, the box of Havana cigars beside it to mellow off the day. It was a solitary life but it was what she wanted.

Nevertheless when her brother Bob came round to see her, anxious because Steve's wife had nowhere to live and explaining that Heather had 'been a bit tricky', she agreed almost without hesitation that the kid could muck in with her 'for the time being'.

'Won't be partic'ly comfortable,' she pointed out, 'but we can't have her wandering the streets.'

It was a warning she felt she had to repeat when she and Barbara reached the front door.

'It ain't exactly a palace,' she explained, as they climbed the stairs towards it. 'Just the two rooms. Enough fer me books an' papers. But it'll do you a turn till you can find something better. We got the camp bed for you. Remember? The one you had round Mabel's.'

Barbara remembered only too well. Lying in that crowded bedroom, feeling unwanted. But she went

229

where she was led and didn't say anything. They reached the landing, which was as dark as the stairs, and Sis opened a door and led her into the light of an extraordinarily cluttered room.

At first sight it looked like a cross between an untidy library and an even more untidy newsagent's. There seemed to be shelves above every item of furniture, all crammed with books, leaning into one another, piled on top of one another, heaped upon heaps, and every item of furniture was covered too, in files and newspapers and untidy piles of letters. There was a bureau beside the fireplace, sagging under the weight of the paper it contained, a dresser that was doing duty as a bookcase, an ancient *chaise longue* and a battered armchair with newspapers where other people would have had cushions. And hemming everything in, a vast quantity of dark heavy cloth, brown velvet curtains looped at the window, bronze chenille on the table, a faded draft excluder across the door, once red baize but now blotched and faded, even a wine-red mantel cover above the fireplace, trailing brown tassels and supporting a collection of china knick-knacks, a clock, a brandy bottle, a stone jam-jar full of spills and yet another letter rack. It was overwhelming.

But then she glanced at the third corner of the room and realised that it was a kitchen area with a sink and a cooker and that standing by the cooker, with one of her mother's aprons wrapped around her waist and her dark hair caught up in a blue snood, was cousin Betty. There were two saucepans steaming on the cooker and she'd been prodding the vegetables with a fork, but the minute Barbara stepped into the room, she threw fork and saucepan-lid onto the draining board and rushed to hug her, throwing both arms round her neck and kissing her most lovingly.

'Was it awful?' she asked, brown eyes full of concern. 'I'll bet it was. You poor thing. We was all thinkin' of you. Come up to the fire. Your hands are like ice.'

'Oh!' Barbara said. 'It's so nice to be home.' Then she burst into tears.

They cuddled her and petted her and let her talk. Sis gave her hot milk laced with brandy and Betty removed her shoes and put her 'poor cold feet' on the stool to warm by the fire, crouching beside them to give them 'a bit of a rub' from time to time. And under their loving ministrations, Barbara told them all about the funeral – even down to how unkind her mother had been.

'Grief,' Sis explained. 'That's what that was. You mark my words. Takes us all different ways. Come an' have yer supper. We got hot bacon roll. It's more onions than bacon, to tell the truth, but least it'll warm you.'

But Barbara's grief had unleashed all sorts of anxieties. 'What does your ma think of me?' she asked Betty. 'I mean, bein' thrown out like that?'

'Don't you worry your head,' Betty reassured. 'She don't think none the worse of you. We none of us do, do we Aunt Sis?'

'No,' Sis said. ''Course not. It'll blow over.'

'But what if it doesn't?'

'Then you stay here with me,' Sis said. 'Come up to the table an' eat this while it's hot.'

But Barbara's head was still full of anxieties. 'What am I going to tell Steve?' she worried as she sat at the table. 'I'll have to write to him, won't I, or else he'll send his letters to the wrong address an' I shan't get them. Oh dear! What shall I say to him?'

'Don't say nothing yet,' Sis advised. 'Give yerself a chance to recover. Wait till he's sent a letter to you an' *then* write back.'

'But what shall I say about being here? I shall have to say something.'

'Tell him you've moved in with me.'

'He'll wonder what for.'

'We'll think a' something. Say you come to give me a hand. He knows how untidy I am.'

'But how will I get his letter? It'll go to Childeric Road.'

'We'll collect it for you, won't we Bet? Or we'll get Bob to pop it in on his way to work. Now stop worryin' an' eat yer food or it'll go cold and you won't get the benefit.'

'But what if . . .' Barbara began. But then she made a great effort and stopped. This was a private, superstitious fear and she shouldn't burden them with it, especially when they were being so good to her. But it cramped her chest with anguish just the same and she couldn't put it out of her mind. What if Steve had been killed too? She hadn't known Norman was dead until that letter came. She had always known he was at risk, out there with all those dreadful U-boats trailing him, but she hadn't accepted the fact that he could be killed. He'd gone to sea and she'd assumed he would come home again, the way he always did. And he'd been dead for weeks and she hadn't known. What if Steve was dead too? Now. This very minute. There could be another dreadful letter on its way, and she wouldn't know that either until it reached her.

The food was in front of her and Betty was urging her to eat it. 'You must be hungry. I'll bet you never had nothing dinner time.'

So she ate, although she had no appetite; and slept that night in her narrow camp bed, although she was afraid of what she might dream; and went to work the next morning as though she'd been leaving the flat every day of her life. But the fear continued, niggling even under the steadying routine of work, and the days passed, Sunday, Monday, Tuesday, and Steve's letter didn't come.

Victor Castlemain drove back to Phossie Fernaway's feeling twice the man he'd been when he left the place.

He'd played knight in shining armour to Spitfire's damsel in distress. He'd looked after her and fed her and driven her back to London as if they were husband and wife. In fact he'd done a lot better by her than her real husband, if the truth be told. It was a real feather in his cap. He was still preening when Phossie came strolling back from the pub, self-satisfied and smirking, to tell him that the Skibbereen was in a really poisonous mood and that it was all his fault.

'You en' 'alf annoyed him,' he said, searching for a new packet of fags, 'not turnin' up a second time. Livid he is. Says you're on borrowed time an' you're to remember where your petrol coupons come from. You wanna watch out or he'll dump you.'

Victor didn't care what the Skibbereen said or did. 'I got a life to live,' he said. 'I can't be at his beck an' call all the time. I was with my gal. Your fags are by the clock.'

'Well he's furious,' Phossie said, retrieving the packet. 'I wouldn't like to be you. Once you can get away with but twice you're asking for it. An' I might say, you missed a good'un this time. Nylons. I'm goin' up west to flog 'em.'

'I'll give you a hand, if you like,' Vic offered, although he knew Phossie wouldn't rise to it.

'No fear,' his friend said, enjoying the first puff. 'These are mine. You find yer own.'

I will, Vic thought. That's exactly what I'll do. It's high time I set up for myself. I been dancing to the Skibbereen's tune quite long enough an' he don't treat us fair. Not by any means. Look at the cut he takes. I'll visit a few warehouses on the quiet, watch what goods are coming in, find a docker who'll let a few cases fall my way. There'd be a lot more profit in this business if I could cut out the middle man. And I might find something really choice that I can give to Spitfire. A few expensive presents wouldn't come amiss at this point. Consolidation, sort of thing.

He started the very next morning while Phossie was still sleeping off his night's exertions. And was still trying, without any success at all, late that night when the pubs closed.

The first man he approached said he dealt with the Skibbereen direct, the second, who was a burly docker with a long scar down the side of his face, said he didn't hold with the black market. 'Spivs an' drones. I'd hang the whole bloody lot of 'em.' The third was too drunk to make sense. But the next morning he suddenly struck lucky.

He was sitting in his local, drinking rather morosely, when a small sly man sidled up to him and joined him at the table. At first he thought he was a new runner for the Skibbereen and looked up ready for instructions but he got a surprise.

'You in the market fer sheepskin coats?' the man asked.

It was his opening. Served up on a plate. Just when he wasn't expecting it. Now play it cool. Keep calm. 'Could be? That depends on the price an' the state of the goods.'

'I got one outside,' the man urged. 'Like a look?'

It was a classy coat, full length with a fur collar, probably rabbit but very soft and pretty.

'How many d'yer want?' the man asked.

'How many you got?'

'A score. Sixty quid the lot.'

Three pounds each and I could sell them for four easy. Maybe four ten. Or five. I could give one to Spitfire an' still make a profit. She'd like a coat like that, 'specially in this weather.

Greasy notes changed hands, the deal was done, the boxes handed over, and while Vic was packing them in the boot of his car, the man disappeared, without leaving a name or a telephone number or anything. I should have got that first, Vic thought. I wasn't quick enough. But it didn't matter. Word would get around. Now he'd done one deal, there would be others.

His satisfaction turned to anger when he'd ferried his cargo home and was checking it over in his bedroom. Then, and much too late, he discovered that the four boxes only contained four coats each instead of the five he was expecting, which meant that he'd paid damn nearly four pounds a piece for them. He raged for nearly half an hour, his face dark with fury. What a bloody twister! What a bloody, stinking little twister! If I see him again I'll punch his face in. No wonder he didn't give me his name, bloody little toerag. That just goes to show you can't trust anybody in this game. Not a soul. Well all right. Next time, *I*'ll do the con act an' if anyone's going to be stitched up it'll be the other guy. I'll bloody see to that.

But despite everything they were still gorgeous coats and Barbara would look smashing in one of them. He couldn't wait to see her and hand it over. If he sold the rest for a fiver, he'd still make a profit. I'll go to the Kinema Thursday, he decided. See if she's there. An' if she's not, I'll cut off to the dancehall on Saturday. And the Saturday after if I have to. I won't rush her. Softly, softly, catchee monkey.

As that second cold week progressed Betty was treating her gently too. She suggested a trip to the Kinema on Tuesday but didn't press it when Barbara said she felt too down.

'I reckon it's gonna snow,' Joyce observed, looking out of the kitchen window. 'We had to put our coats on in class this afternoon. My fingers was mauve.'

'Well make sure you take your gloves then', her mother advised, 'if you're going out. Wrap up warm, the lot of you. I don't want you getting chilblains again. We had enough a' that last winter.'

So the three Horner girls went to the pictures and Barbara went home to Aunt Sis. She found her stoking the fire, puffing with the effort she was making. 'Brass monkey weather,' she said to Barbara as she came shivering in. 'Your letter's come.'

Relief turned Barbara's legs to water. 'Oh thank God!' she said. 'He's all right.' And she took the letter from the rack on the mantelpiece and sat down to read it.

Sis watched her. 'You didn't think he would be, did you?' she said, her voice full of sympathy.

Barbara could admit it now. She could admit anything now. He was alive and well and all in one piece. He hadn't been wounded. He'd written to her. 'I was bein' stupid,' she confessed. 'With Norman being killed I thought . . . well I s'pose I was sort of facing the fact that anything could happen to anyone. Still thass all right now. I was just being stupid.'

'We're all the same,' Sis told her, clipping the tongs together and hanging them up. 'We all worry. You can't help it. It's nat'ral if you love someone.'

'Yes.'

'Well there you are then. Now you can write him a nice long letter an' tell him all about everything, an' give him my love. What's he been up to? Does he say?'

Barbara handed the letter across. 'Patrols mostly, an' moppin' up.' The words were soothing. They sounded much less dangerous than fighting. And Aunt Sis was right. Now she could write a nice long letter and let him know where she was.

It was done that evening, four pages of it, describing the funeral and how she'd felt about it and how it had upset her father and how unkind her mother had been. Now that he'd written to her she found she could be generous. '*I know she didn't really mean it,*' she wrote. '*That was because she was upset but she shouldn't have said I shouldn't have married you. That was going too far and I told her so.*' Then having signed her name with its usual pattern of kisses, she added a postscript to tell him that she'd moved '*to give your Aunt Sis a hand with her Union work. I never seen anyone with so many papers and forms and things.*' She felt quite pleased with the way she'd handled it, telling him just enough to keep him informed but not burdening him with tales about his mother and the unkind way *she*'d gone on. There'd be time enough for that when he came home. And he must come home sooner or later. They might even let him back for Christmas. Wouldn't that be wonderful!

Next day, even though it was bitterly cold and spitting with rain, and even though she saw three buzzbombs in the course of the morning, which was quite unusual these days, and was held up for nearly half an hour while the civil defence dealt with the aftermath of one of them, work was almost a relaxation. And when Betty came round in the evening to ask her whether she felt up to going to the dance on Saturday, she was tempted. It shamed her to admit it, but she *was*.

'I don't know,' she temporised. 'That don't seem right, not so soon after . . .'

'No,' Betty agreed. 'Tell you what. We'll leave it till Saturday. See how you feel then. It's early days yet.'

It seemed the right decision. But on Friday morning Barbara had a letter that changed her mind. It arrived after Sis had left for work and just as she was finishing the washing up. It was from Steve and it was addressed to the flat, which showed he'd got her letter.

My own dear darling,

I am so very sorry to hear about your brother. It is a terrible thing to have happened. You must be in a dreadful state. I wish I could be with you. I know exactly how you feel.

His comfort spread up from the flimsy paper, from the warmth of his words and the sight of his lovely, steady handwriting. She felt as if he were standing beside her, wrapping her in his arms, kissing her hair. My own dear darling.

237

Death is always awful no matter how many corpses you see. I remember when Nan died, what a state we were in then. It took ages to get over it. She'd been ill for a long time and we all knew she'd never get better but that didn't make it any easier. We missed her dreadfully. Death in war is much, much worse. People don't die in a war. They are killed and most of them are young and have their lives before them and it isn't just a few here and there, there are thousands of them. I think the worst thing is there's no time to mourn them. We just have to get up and go on. There's nothing else we can do. If we sat down to grieve every time one of our mates got killed, the campaign would grind to a halt and the Germans would push us right back into the sea. It's the same for people at home. If Londoners sat down to grieve every time there was a bomb or a doodle-bug, the city would grind to a halt. That's what Hitler was depending on when he started the Blitz. But it didn't happen because people got on with their work and didn't stop. That's what we do here. We bury the dead and keep going. It sounds callous, written down like that, but there isn't any other option. So don't let this stop you. Keep on going. Live your life to the full. It's the best way to honour our dead.

I love you more than I can tell you. One day soon, God willing, I shall be home to prove it to you. Hold on till then my darling.

Yours,
S.

It made her cry for more than half an hour, and she would have cried longer had she not been due at the depot. It was such a loving letter and so sensible. As she walked through the dusty streets, passing the long modern frontage of their splendid Woolworths, she was agreeing with every word. Keep on going. Live your life to the full. I will, my darling. You just watch me.

That evening, when she heard Betty's footsteps at the top of the stairs, she ran straight out onto the landing to greet her.

'I've decided,' she said. 'I will go dancin' with you.'

'Good!' Betty said and as they walked into the living room, she gave Barbara one of her daring looks. 'I'm ever so glad. The thing is, I got someone to come with us this Sat'day.'

Barbara was instantly and happily alerted. A boy-friend. That had to be. How lovely! That would account for the new softness about her – and tonight's new hairstyle. 'What someone?'

'His name's Lionel,' Betty said, tucking her hand in Barbara's arm, ready for confidences, as they squashed onto the *chaise longue* together. 'He works in the storeroom. We call him Lie. Daft, innit? 'Cause I don't think he would. Ever. Lie, I mean. Anyway, they just come here from Whitechapel. Him an' his family. They was bombed out so they're living with his gran, sort a' thing. He's a smasher. You wait till you see him. He's got really dreamy eyes, all lovely an' blue, an' lovely thick hair. Like Steve's, only sort of fairish. You'll love him. Vic'll be there too, won't he? We can make a sort a' foursome.'

Barbara had forgotten all about Victor Castlemain. Now she felt quite conscience-stricken about him. 'He asked me to the pictures,' she remembered. 'An' I just ran off and left him.'

'He won't mind,' Betty said easily. 'Did I tell you he's got blue eyes? Lie, I mean.'

So that Saturday they put on their dancing shoes and plenty of lipstick, splashed themselves with Evening in Paris and went to the Palais, Betty rather nervously, Barbara determined to enjoy herself come what may.

It was a smashing evening, as they told one another afterwards. To Betty's delight, Lie and Barbara took to one another at once, even though he turned out to be a very ordinary young man, with mousey hair and grey eyes, and not the handsome creature Betty had described. And Victor *was* there and in very good form.

He didn't mention the coats until the lights dimmed for the first waltz. He and Barbara sat it out, as they usually did. He'd accepted the fact that she wasn't going to waltz with him, comforting himself that she wouldn't waltz with anyone else either. They'd get around to it eventually, if he played his cards right. Meantime . . .

'Thass cold enough tonight,' he said.

'Freezing,' she agreed. 'I was perished on the trams this morning.'

'You need a thick coat.'

'I ain't got the coupons for a coat,' she said. 'That'll have to wait till next year.'

It was all panning out as he'd planned it. Couldn't have been better. 'Wait here,' he said. 'I got a surprise for you. I'll be a couple of minutes.'

It took him less. Betty and Lie were strolling back to their table as he returned with one of his splendid coats draped casually over his arm.

'Present for you,' he said to Barbara.

She couldn't help liking it. Who wouldn't? It was a gorgeous coat. She could feel her eyes dilating at the sight of it. But she couldn't accept it. Not even from old Victor. That wouldn't be right.

'Where d'you get it?' she asked.

'Bought it, didn't I? Wholesale.'

'What about the coupons?'

'Never mind the coupons. Try it on.' If he could get it round her shoulders, she'd accept it.

She hesitated, was tempted, and finally put it on, sighing into the luxury of it. It looked as glamorous as he'd hoped, the fur collar a perfect foil for that dark hair of hers, a soft frame for her pretty face. 'It must have cost the earth,' she said.

'Thass a present,' he told her and appealed to Betty for support. 'What'd you think, Betty? Don't it suit her?'

Betty's admiration was unreserved. 'I think it's smashing,' she said and teased. 'I couldn't have one an' all, could I?'

At first he didn't take her seriously. Then he realised what an opportunity she'd given him. If he gave her a coat too, that might swing it. It would cut into his profits but so what. Spend some to earn some, sort of thing. 'Yes,' he told her. 'You could. Matter a' fact, I got another one out in the car. Identical. Hang around.'

There were no complications to hinder Betty's acceptance. She was thrilled with her coat and put it on at once. 'Whatcher think?' she said to Lionel.

'You look glam,' he admired but turned a shrewd face to Victor, aware that there could be a catch in it. 'What's the damage, though? I mean that's a good bit a' schmutter. Like Barbara said, must'a cost.'

'On the house,' Victor said grandly. 'Any friend of Spitfire's is a friend of mine.'

He was rewarded by a rapturous smile from both girls. And Betty flung her arms round him and gave him a smacking kiss on the cheek to thank him. For a second he thought Spitfire was going to kiss him too. She didn't but she could have done. And she'd accepted the coat. Oh yes, he thought, preening with satisfaction as the mirror ball dappled his two expensive gifts with shifting patterns of white light. I've done really well. Started my own firm and given my Barbara a gift she'll never forget. Put a foot in both doors, so to speak.

CHAPTER NINETEEN

Snow was falling on the river Maas, drifting before Steve's eyes in huge irregular flakes that settled on his eyelashes and drifted gently down onto tanks, TCV's and every uniformed figure in sight until everything he could see was blotched and patched in a wintry piebald. It was November and bitterly cold, the flat Dutch polders needled with frost and the roads that traversed them treacherous with ice.

For the past ten days the battalion had been at rest, billeted with the Dutch and usually inside in the warm, unless they were on outpost duty or servicing their vehicles or taking in supplies. Steve had spent most of his leisure time writing letters, for Barbara had written to him every day, long rather muddled epistles telling him about her working day, and how she couldn't believe she would never see Norman again, and that she was still living with Aunt Sis, and what a waste war was, and how she'd gone dancing with Betty and then felt guilty about it afterwards '*so soon after the funeral*'. Squashed at the end of her first letter she'd added a postscript that made him ache with pity for her.

I am sorry to go on and on like this but I got to tell someone and if you were here I would tell you. If that upset you just tell me and I won't do it again. Only I've done it this time, so that's a bit late but you know what I mean.

He wrote back at once to reassure her, saying that she must tell him everything and that it didn't upset him. '*Far from it.*' But answering her letters was more difficult. In that first long letter he'd said all he could bear to say about death, and now he was stuck for words.

In the long slog across France he'd found all sorts of ways to offer comfort to his mates – a fag lit and handed across, a sympathetic thump on the back, sometimes just a companionable silence – but they were all actions. If he could have seen her, it would have been easier. He could have put his arms round her and stroked her face and kissed her and that would have told her everything. Now he felt he was repeating himself, no matter how hard he tried to comfort her, using the same worn phrases over and over again.

He told her he was glad she was back at work, approved when she said she was staying with Aunt Sis for a bit longer. '*I know she's untidy but she's a marvellous politician and a doughty fighter in a good cause. I wish there were more like her.*' And when she wrote to say that she'd been dancing with Betty again, he sensed that she was worried about it and applauded that too. '*She's a good kid, our Betty, even if she's as bad as I am on the dance floor. Don't tell her I said so or she'll give me what-for. Have fun anyway, when you can.*'

Not that there was much fun in his own life. On the ninth rest day they were issued with winter uniforms – leather jackets for the infantry and multi-zippered snow suits for the tankies – so, like it or not, it was obvious they would soon be on the move again. They were war-weary and winter-weary and seriously below strength, and to make matters worse an order called 'Python' had come through to inform them that troops who had served overseas for more than five years were to be allowed home.

Dusty was disgruntled to hear it. 'I could ha' done with another ten days' rest,' he complained. 'Never mind goin' home. Some bleeders have all the luck.'

'Stop bellyaching, you miserable old bugger,' Steve

243

said. 'They've earned it, all they've been through. All across Africa an' all the way up Italy and now this. You'd cut off PDQ if it was you.'

Dusty had to agree with that but he was still discontented. 'What are they gonna do with the rest of us?' he grumbled. 'That's what I'd like to know.' The battalion had taken so many casualties that it was down to a third of its original number – a fact that neither of them cared to think about too often.

'Here's Sergeant Morris,' Steve said, squinting at the bulky figure trudging towards them through the curtain of snowflakes. 'Ask him.'

'Reorganisation,' the sergeant told them. 'The three Queen's regiments are being amalgamated. We're all being informed tonight.'

'An' what's happening to us?' Dusty wanted to know.

'We're being joined up with the 9th Durham Light Infantry and the 2nd Battalion, the Devonshire Regiment. Good lads.'

That was better news. But Dusty accepted it grudgingly. 'Not before time.'

'Wasn't what I come over for though,' the sergeant went on. 'You've waylaid me. No, what it is, I got a notification for Private Wilkins. Official.' And when Steve took the envelope looking puzzled, 'It's your promotion come through, old son. You're being made corporal. Changes all round, you see.'

'Corp, eh?' Dusty said when the sergeant was out of earshot. 'Jammy bugger!'

'It's my hard-earned reward', Steve said, 'for putting up with you all these months.' But although he joked about it, he was proud to be promoted. It was something to write home about. Unfortunately the 9th Durham Light Infantry were driving into camp even as he spoke, so there was no more time for letters. It was all action.

They took to the road at daybreak the next day, back to the familiar pattern of fear and tension, action and

244

reaction. It was a dark, damp, depressing morning. The rising sun was watery yellow and tentative. It flushed the horizon with the faintest pink which faded in five minutes, and once risen it diminished in size and colour until it was simply a dull white disc in a sky the colour of dirty bandages. To the north, where woods rustled and brooded, snow still covered the tops of the pine trees with a white fringe, but it had melted everywhere else, and the roads they travelled were awash with slush and mud from one embankment to the other. To the south there was so much surface water on the polders that they looked like sheets of lead and the dykes that divided them were sullen grey and swollen. It was going to be a hard slog. But at least this time they were up to strength and had two formidable new weapons to support them, a tank adapted to clear mines with long whirling flails and another that was reputed to be capable of throwing out a tongue of flame a hundred yards long.

As Dusty said, 'Can't wait to see *that*.'

The first went into action almost at once. They hadn't made more than half a mile before the leading tanks ran into soggy ground. Two were so badly bogged down, that the remainder were ordered to find firmer ground. And that turned out to be a minefield. Two tanks were knocked out instantly, a third was hit by a 75-millimetre, and at that point, the flails were ordered in to clear the mines. They did it in sensational fashion, blazing along the edge of the field, long flails whirling and touching off mines as they progressed, the noise and colour of the explosions highly dramatic in the grey of the day.

Steve and Dusty and their mates watched it with great satisfaction, but then the first skirmish began and the attack was too immediate for them to watch out for anything except their backs. There was a sudden purple flash, then a call to halt and take cover, and then shells came screaming towards them out of the woods.

A hundred yards ahead, the surviving tanks had halted too and one was blazing away with Besa tracer, left and right, up and down, blasting the whole of the front of the wood. Beads of fire sprayed at the trees, struck them and whirled off again. Steve and his mates lay where they'd landed behind the embankment with their weapons ready and pointing at the trees, as bursts of enemy tracer sailed, a hundred feet up, over their heads.

There was an officer crawling along the embankment towards them, yelling to them to keep their heads down, and as he approached, a sniper's bullet sliced off the metal pip on his left shoulder. Seconds later one of Steve's troop was hit in the hand. Glancing back he could see blood jetting over the stock of the man's rifle and heard him groan as he slipped into the mud.

'Too bloody close!' he muttered as he began to wriggle back to his casualty. Bullets were thumping into the earth all round them and he checked their trajectory automatically, realised that they were coming from a nearby tree and looked up to see a familiar grey-green shape among the bare branches with its rifle cocked towards them. The casualty would have to wait. 'Sniper!' he yelled. 'Two o'clock!' Then things happened at speed and in confusion, as he and the troop let off a volley of fire. The sniper was wounded but struggled to stay aloft, was hit again and fell. And then there was an outburst of machine-gun fire from the distant woods that had them all scrambling back behind the embankment.

Steve was pleased to note that he was still calm. He took out the wounded man's field dressing and bound up his hand. 'It's a clean wound,' he told him. 'You'll be out of it now. Back to Blighty.'

'Thanks, corp. D'you get him?'

'Yep. Won't shoot anyone else.'

But the fire from the woods had them pinned down and *that* was getting worse. It was coming from a concrete pill-box they could just see at the edge of the wood.

'Now what, corp?' Dusty said.

Steve was trying to work it out. The machine gunners had a good range and there was no cover apart from the embankment, so it would be suicidal to run out into the field, and although they could lob a few grenades, they wouldn't do enough damage unless they could get them through the door. But before he could answer, the flame thrower had arrived and was in spectacular action.

The flame it threw was a hundred yards long and spurted from the gun like a dragon's tongue, bright yellow and scorching everything in its path. They could feel the heat of it from where they crouched, smell the wood burning, hear the roar as it engulfed the pill-box. Dark figures tumbled out into the wood, some on fire and screaming. And the guns were silenced. It was the most dramatic thing Steve and Dusty had ever seen. As they told one another much later that evening, standing by the leaguered tanks, smoking and chatting like the old comrades they were.

'S'been a fair old day, all in all,' Dusty observed. 'Snow's stopped. Jerries retreated. Them flame throwers worked a treat. We shan't have so much nonsense with the buggers now. They was giving up in droves. How many prisoners did we take, d'you reckon?'

''Bout forty.'

Dusty gloated. 'That's the style. Lock 'em all up, rotten bleeders.'

They smoked in silence for a minute or two, looking out over the flat dark countryside. I've not done too badly, Steve thought, for my first day as corporal.

''Nother day gone,' Dusty said.

'Marked off?'

'Yep.'

'How many's that?'

'Five months, two weeks and three days,' Dusty said with great satisfaction, and began to sing. '*Oh eleven more months an' eight more days I'll be out of the calaboose. Eleven more months and eight more days they're going to turn me loose.'*

Home, Steve thought, and remembered it suddenly, with a yearning that cramped his guts. Warm chairs by a warm fire, the smell of bacon frying, the wireless playing. The High Street full of crowds, the row of shops, Dad's tobacconist's, Mum's butcher's. The Town Hall. Barbara running down the steps holding his hand. Barbara in bed with those white arms round his neck pulling him closer . . .

There was a muffled roar from somewhere in the distance, immediately followed by three more in quick succession.

'What the hell's that?' Dusty said, as they both turned to look.

Across the river, in German-held territory, four white vapour trails were climbing the sky, two to the left, two to the right.

'Ack-ack?' Steve wondered. But there were no explosions. The trails simply went on climbing, higher and higher, forming four white parabolas in the ink-black sky. They couldn't be buzzbombs because *they* flew straight, once they'd been launched. They weren't planes either because they were climbing too fast. But if they weren't bombs or planes, what the hell were they? There was something sinister about that long trajectory heading out to sea.

'Some sort of gun,' Steve decided, being practical. 'Long range. They're testing it.'

'Good job they ain't firing at us,' Dusty observed. 'That's all I got to say.'

But London was on the other side of the Channel. Oh Christ! They couldn't be firing at London, could they?

They watched until the vapour trails faded and disappeared.

'Ah well!' Dusty said, stubbing out his cigarette

248

under the toe of his boot. 'We shall know soon enough. I'm for a spot of shut-eye.'

Sis and Barbara sat up late that evening too, although they hadn't intended to. Sis had a lot of Union letters to catch up with and took down her writing box as soon as the cloth was cleared. Barbara made up the fire, and sat in the armchair beside it, to darn her stockings and sew a button on her blouse. Then she was at a loss to know what to do next.

'I s'pose I really ought to tidy up some of your papers,' she said, gazing into the fire. 'I keep tellin' Steve thass what I'm here for.'

'You could try that lot on the sideboard,' Sis suggested, without looking up. 'The file labelled Beveridge Report. The dog-eared one. It's mostly newspaper cuttings. I've been meaning to get it sorted for ages.'

'How d'you want it done?'

'Chronological,' Sis said. 'There's dates on most of 'em, somewhere or other.'

So the file was discovered and the sorting out began, with the date rewritten in red ink in the top right-hand corner of each cutting, 'so's you can see it'.

At first Barbara simply restored order without looking at any of the documents. But then she discovered that one of them was a letter.

'You don't want this in with the articles, do you?' she asked.

Sis didn't look up. 'What is it?'

'It's a letter to *The Times*.'

'Who from?'

Barbara looked at the signatories. 'The Archbishop of Canterbury, the Archbishop of York and the Archbishop of Westminster, and the Moderator of the Free Church Council.'

This time Sis looked at her. '*Five agreed standards for social organisation after the war,*' she quoted and grinned. 'I should just say I do. Your Steve gave me that. Read it.'

So, as it was Steve's gift, Barbara sat on her heels and read the list. It was a considerable surprise, for although two of the items on it were what she would have expected from a group of churchmen, that a '*sense of a divine vocation must be restored to man's daily work*' and that '*the resources of the earth should be used as God's gift to the whole human race, and used with due consideration for the needs of the present and future generations*', the other three were not.

'Thass amazing,' she said as she read.

Sis grinned at her again. 'What is?'

'They want to change the world. They say we ought to do away with "*extreme inequality in wealth and possessions*". Wouldn't that be wonderful? And they want every child to have – what is it? – "*equal opportunities for the development of his peculiar capacities*".'

'Quite right,' Sis said. 'At the moment the only kids who get to grammar school are the bright ones who win scholarships and the ones with rich parents who can afford the fees, whether they're bright or not. That's unfair and wasteful.'

The implication of what she was saying made Barbara feel as though her head were swelling. 'So what they're saying is, if you win a place at the grammar school, they think you ought to take it?'

''Course. That's obvious.'

'I won a place an' didn't take it,' Barbara confessed. 'Pa wouldn't let me. He said he couldn't afford it.'

'That don't surprise me,' Sis said, with sympathy. 'I knew you'd got a good head on your shoulders. So there you are, you can see what a waste it was.'

'Yes.'

'So what we got to do is win this election an' see it never happens again.'

'How would you do that? I mean, if they can't afford it, they can't an' thass all there is to that.'

'See that they earn a good wage for a start. Then they'd be more able to afford it. That's one way. An' if the kid wins a scholarship, it should win a grant at the same time.'

That seemed a wonderful idea to Barbara. 'If there'd been a grant when I was eleven I could have gone,' she said. 'But wouldn't that cost a lot of money?'

'Waste costs a lot of money,' Sis told her. 'You leave a house without repairs and in the end it turns into a slum and you have to pull it down and build a new one. Which is another thing we got to do.'

'What? Rebuild the slums?'

'Pull 'em all down, the whole damn kit and caboodle, and start afresh. We got a head start in the East End, thanks to Hitler. One bomb on a terrace in that neck a' the woods an' they all fell down like a pack of cards. Jerry-built you see, nasty bug-ridden hovels. Not fit for human habitation. People live in some terrible places in this country, more shame to us. Houses with no running water, dirty little earth closets out the back, bugs in the wallpaper, black beetles. Nobody should have to live like that.'

'No,' Barbara agreed, remembering the North End. 'Slums *should* be pulled down.' And she thought what a difference it would have made to her life if she'd grown up in a place like Childeric Road.

'Decent home,' Sis said. 'That's the basis of a decent life. An' I know what I'm talking about. I've lived in some pretty crummy places in my time.'

That was a surprise. 'Have you?'

'Very crummy some of 'em, specially when I was a kid. We was always hard up in them days. Used to go hopping to make a bit extra. Steve used to come with us. Picking hops all day an' off to the pub to drink 'em in the evening. An' then back to talk politics round the camp fire till we couldn't keep our eyes open.'

251

'Did Steve talk politics?'

'Not in those days, no,' Sis said. 'He was too little. Used to listen though. All ears he was. I reckon it was the making of him. He knew what sort a' world he wanted by the time he was fourteen, I can tell you that. Very idealistic, your Steve. When the Beveridge Report came out he bought a copy on the day it was published.'

'An' I always thought politics was just about money and taxes and that sort of thing!'

'Depends on your politics,' Sis laughed. 'Ours is about ideas. You should read the Report.'

'Yes,' Barbara said thoughtfully. 'P'rhaps I should, if he bought it the day...' But before she could say anything else, there was a long dull explosion.

It sounded a long way away but it went on for much longer than anything they'd heard in the last few months, and that puzzled them. When the last reverberation had faded, they got up, switched off the light and opened the curtains to see if they could see where it had been. There was a faint glow on the horizon.

'Something's gone up,' Sis said. 'Ain't a buzzbomb though. That I *do* know. Unless they're makin' 'em twice the size.'

'We'll hear about it tomorrow,' Barbara said, as they left the window and went back to their sorting.

The next day the rumours were contradictory. Some people said it was a gas main, others an accident at a munitions factory, others a house struck by lightning. It wasn't until late afternoon that any real news came through and then it was alarming. Whatever it had been, it had happened in Chiswick and had done tremendous damage. 'Knocked down half a street,' the clippies told one another. 'Terrible casualties. Ever so many killed.'

'Then that's no gas main,' Heather said trenchantly, when Sis called in at the butcher's on her way home. 'Don't give me that. It'll be another bomb. You mark my words. An' if there's one, there'll be more of them.'

Sis made a grimace because it sounded all too likely.

'How you getting on with Barbara?' Heather said, very casually.

'OK,' Sis said. 'She ain't a bad kid.'

But Heather had closed her face. 'Handsome is as handsome does,' she said. 'I reserve judgment on that one.'

But she was proved right about the rockets. The next morning they were woken just after dawn by another thunderous crash and during the day there were three more. There were no official statements, but everybody knew that London was under a new bombardment. News of the explosions passed swiftly along the tram grapevines. This was a bomb that arrived without warning. Some said it travelled so fast you heard it coming, with a 'sort of swishing noise' *after* it had exploded. And it was huge. Every explosion caused immense damage and the blast was felt for miles around.

There was still no official explanation. But a few days later there was an explosion in Dairsee Road and three days after that another in Lewisham and by then local knowledge of what was happening left no one in any doubt that these were rockets of some kind. One man had seen one of them, 'like a telegraph pole flying horizontally at about 6,000 feet. It was a brownish colour,' he told the local paper, 'and flying much faster than a buzzbomb. It left a trail of brown oily smoke.'

'Ain't we had enough?' Barbara's passengers asked one another as they climbed aboard her tram the next morning. 'First the Blitz an' then the buzzbombs an' now this. They really got it in fer us!'

'They're evacuating the kiddies again,' another said.

Hazel and Joyce said they'd rather stay where they were. Joyce was only going to be at school another term and then she'd be out at work. 'Like our Betty says,' she told her parents, 'if it's got your number on it, it'll get you wherever you are. Ain't that right, our Betty?'

Betty was more interested in her new perm which

hadn't taken properly. 'I shall look a sight Sat'day,' she complained. 'She ain't half made a mess of it. Lionel'll think I'm a freak.'

Joyce persisted. 'But ain't that right, our Betty?'

'What?'

'If it's got your number on it it'll get you.'

'Oh that. Yeh! No point worrying about it. It's not as if you can get out the way. You can't, can you. Not if you can't hear it coming. Best thing's just to get on with your life an' forget about it.'

CHAPTER TWENTY

The official report on Hitler's new secret weapon made chilling reading when it was finally given.

> Britain's front line at home is under fire again –
> from a stratosphere rocket that is dropping on us
> from 60 to 70 miles up in the air, a rocket that
> travels faster than sound and flashes across the sky
> like a comet trailing fire. Weighing about 12 tons,
> it carries a ton of high explosive, has a range of
> 210 to 250 miles, travelling at speeds of up to
> 4,000 mph, and is probably being launched from
> sites in Holland.

'An' there's no defence against it,' Phossie Fernaway added sourly, when he'd read the paper and passed it to Victor. 'Which they've conveniently forgot to say. We're just bloody sitting targets.'

'I'm off out of it, if thass the case,' Victor said, propping the newspaper against his newly acquired pot of marmalade. 'I shall go down Essex way an' milk a few farmers.'

'For the Skibbereen?'

'Nope,' Victor said easily. 'On my own account. I've made some good contacts. He ain't the onny cock a' the walk. And there's a brickworks I want to see. There'll be some very good pickings from the brickworks with all the bomb damage there'll be.'

'You wanna watch it,' Phossie warned, spreading butter on his toast. 'If he finds out . . .'

'He won't. You worry too much.'

'Anyway, I thought you was courting,' Phossie said. 'What about this girl of yours?'

'She's patient,' Vic told him. He'd made a good impression with those sheepskin coats and he didn't want to waste it, but a courtship was one thing, profit and self-preservation another. 'I hain't stayin' here to be blown to pieces by blazing comets. Sod that for a game of soldiers. I'll come back now an' then to sell the goods an' see if the Skibbereen's got a job for us.' He was doing the odd job on his own but he still needed the Skibbereen if he was to live in any style. I can see her then. 'I mean to say, it'll only be for a little while. It can't go on for ever.'

'I bloody hope not!' Phossie said, as another explosion rattled the windows. 'I'm not cut out fer this sort a' life, am I.'

But cut out for it or not, most Londoners had to accept it. As the weeks and the explosions passed, they settled into a weary resignation, living stoically, one day at a time. Food was in shorter supply than ever, there was always dust in the air, always fear just around the corner. Sis grew angry, Mabel and Heather jittery, Bob and Sid worried quietly, Hazel and Joyce were more quarrelsome. Only Betty and Barbara stayed resolutely themselves. If your number's on it . . .

'We ain't seen Vic for quite a while,' Betty observed. 'D'you reckon he'll turn up to the dance Sat'day?' She and the others had invited Barbara in for a cup of Camp coffee after their cold walk home from the pictures. Now they were sitting round the kitchen table warming their hands on their nice full mugs and gossiping, except for Joyce who was standing in front of the fireplace, putting her hair in curlers for the night.

'Shouldn't think so,' Barbara said. It didn't worry her whether he joined them or not. She was grateful for the coat but that was as far as it went.

'I'm going shopping, Sat'day morning,' Joyce

announced from the mirror. 'It's only a month till Christmas.'

'No it ain't,' Hazel scoffed. 'It's weeks yet.'

'That's all you know,' Joyce said. 'It's a month exactly. 25th of November. N'yer!'

'Why must you two argue all the time?' their mother said, putting her mug down with a sigh. 'It don't matter what day it is. If you want to go shopping, go. Only don't keep fightin' one another in my kitchen.'

'You can come in to Woolworths an' have a cuppa with me an' Lionel,' Betty said, 'if you don't fight. What about you, Bar?'

'I'm at work.'

'What time's your dinner hour?'

'Half past twelve.'

'Come across then,' Betty instructed. 'We'll wait for you, won't we kids. It'll be a laugh.'

So their Saturday was arranged.

It was a horrible day, cold and grey and dispiriting. It had been snowing in the night, so they woke to icy roads and pavements dusted white. Sis and Barbara wore thick jerseys under their uniform jackets, looked out their fingerless gloves and their thickest woollen socks and wound scarves round their necks, on the principle that it didn't matter what they looked like so long as they were warm. And Betty went to work in her new sheepskin coat.

The depot was freezing cold so the trams started sluggishly and, because the points were frozen, every journey took longer than it should have done. By midday all services were running late.

The Saturday shoppers grumbled as they pushed their way aboard, bulky as bolsters in their extra clothes. 'We got enough to contend with without snow an' you lot late all the time.'

'I'm glad it's dinner time,' Barbara said to Mr Tinker, as they turned into the depot after their last run of the morning.

'Snow's gone,' Mr Tinker said. 'That's one good thing.' The white fall of the early morning hadn't settled, cold though it was. 'I'm for a cup a' char. You coming?'

But Barbara didn't get a chance to answer. At that moment there was a sudden roaring, rushing noise and a flash of light so bright and blinding that it hurt her eyes. For a second she stood where she was, leaning against the side of the tram for support as the ground rose and fell under her feet as though it was no longer solid. The roaring noise was so loud it felt as though it was pummelling her eardrums and there seemed to be less air, for she was fighting for breath. She knew it was a rocket but she was too frightened to scream or to move. It was as if her mind had been blown away.

It wasn't until the noise had faded, that she came back to her senses and looked around her. The depot was full of whey-faced people all looking at one another but Mr Tinker was lying beside the tram, groaning. He must have fallen and she hadn't noticed. He had a long cut on the side of his face which was bleeding profusely and he was totally confused.

'What is it?' he asked, dabbling his fingers in the blood. 'What have I done?'

But all Barbara could think about at that moment was that it was a rocket, that it must have gone off close by, that Sis was in the station, that the kids were out shopping and Betty was in Woolworths, and that she had to go and find them. Mr Threlfall was walking towards her, pale but in command. He would deal with Mr Tinker. She had to go out and help at the incident. She found her energy again and ran into the road.

What she saw there was so dreadful that for a few seconds she was too stunned to take it in. The air was thick with dust, clouds of it, thick and brown and swirling like something in a nightmare, and through it she could hear people crying for help and groaning in extremes of pain, and a child screaming, 'Mummy!

Mummy! Mummy!' over and over again. It took time for her eyes to adjust to the lack of light and then she realised that there were things falling out of the sky, tumbling and turning in the air and thudding down onto dirty pavements and a littered road – bricks and bits of concrete, torn rags, half a chair, lumps of flesh. At first she thought they were joints of meat and that a butcher's had been hit, but then, with a shock of such horror it brought the gall into her throat, she realised that they were bits of arms and legs, torn and bloody, but hideously recognisable. And as she watched, a small white hand fell before her eyes and landed at her feet, a baby's small white hand, curved and tender and still in its woolly sleeve. Oh dear God! A baby's hand!

The screams and cries were still going on, and now there were other sounds too, feet running and voices calling, 'Derek! Where are you?' 'Joan! Joan! Joan!' And a man ran past her, heading towards the station.

'Where is it?' she called to him.

'Woolworths,' he called back, his face fraught. 'I can't stop. My old lady's there.'

No, she thought, it can't be Woolworths. It mustn't be. Betty's in Woolworths and the kids. We're going to meet there for our dinner. And she ran towards it, dodging the horrors, her heart beating so painfully it felt as though her chest was going to split.

The dust-cloud was rising ominously right over the corner of Goodwood and New Cross roads and as she got nearer she could see that the traffic had stopped and that both roads were full of bodies, some crawling and crying, some lying still and silent in pools of blood, some running about in a terrible aimless terror, all of them covered in brick dust and with slivers of glass stuck in their clothes and hands and faces. There was blood everywhere, smeared against the kerb and over the tramlines, puddling the road, streaked across torn clothing, gushing from wounds. It was as if there'd been a battle, as if someone had turned a machine gun on the street.

Such an excess of horror seemed to have turned off her emotions. She noted that there was a burnt-out bus in the road. It had been crushed by the blast as though someone had squashed it together like a concertina, its red paint burnt back to the bare metal, and it was full of passengers, all of them dead where they sat and looking more like statues than people because they were smothered in dust. And she hardly felt anything for them at all. She looked across at the Town Hall, broken glass crunching under her feet, and saw that there were bodies spread-eagled across the steps, but she felt nothing for *them* either and she couldn't stop to help them. She had to get into Woolworths and get Betty out. And the kids. That was all that was important. She had to get into Woolworths.

But when she reached the corner she saw with a renewed shock of total stomach-churning terror that there was nothing left to get into. Nothing at all. Just a vast crater ringed by enormous piles of bricks and rubble that spilled out over both roads. She could see right through the dust to the houses in the street behind and the looming shape of Childeric School, huge and stranded like a beached ship. But even though the familiar smell of a bombing was filling her nostrils and she could hear people screaming underneath the wreckage, she couldn't, wouldn't believe it. 'Oh please!' she said. 'Please don't let this be happening. Please don't let them be dead.'

There were men and women rushing past her, clawing at the rubble, hurling chunks of masonry aside. Yes, she thought, get them out! Quick! And she joined the scrabble, pulling at the nearest pile of brick and concrete, frantic with grief and shock. There was a fire blazing in the crater and she knew it was right over where the cafe had been and that she would have been there herself if the tram hadn't run late. But that was

260

nothing to the terrible need to find Betty and the kids and to get them out alive.

More people were arriving, clambering over the rubble, calling and crying. She could hear the bricks slipping away from their feet and the crunch of glass. And then, immediately beneath the rubble she was lifting, she heard the faint sound of someone crying for help.

'I'm coming!' she called. 'I'm coming, Betty! Hold on!' But the next lump of masonry she seized was too big for her to shift on her own. 'Help me please!' she cried to the nearest shape. 'Thass too heavy for me.'

Worn hands moved into her line of vision, pulling and tugging. She could see a trodden-down shoe pressed against the wreckage, taking the strain, and then a pair of black boots, coated with dust.

'There's a bit a' wood there,' a man's voice said. 'We could use it as a lever.'

Someone collected it and handed it down, and then they were all pushing it under the mass of brick and concrete, struggling to get it into position, heaving together – 'One, two, three, heave!' – their hands covered in grime and brick dust. And the lump shifted, moved, was lifted up. They could see a shoulder, covered in filth and streaked with dark blood. And at that they worked like wild things, hauling and pulling, until a woman's head was uncovered, pushed down against her chest by the weight of the brickwork that had fallen on her. It wasn't Betty but that no longer had any relevance. She was a neighbour and she was injured, in pain and so shocked she simply stared at them and couldn't even tell them her name. They dug until they'd uncovered her entire body and lifted her out, limp and floppy, as though she were a doll. And by then the ambulances were arriving and two nurses ran to take over.

Barbara was still full of frantic energy. She'd found one casualty. Now she had to find another. She had to find Betty and the kids. She wiped the sweat out of her eyes and looked across at the nearest person, ready to thank her and ask her to help again. And found herself staring into the anxious blue eyes of her mother-in-law.

She was too fraught to feel any surprise. Their quarrel was a petty irrelevance now. There was only this dreadful driving need, this dreadful aching terror. 'Oh Mrs Wilkins!' she said. 'Betty's in here. An' the kids.'

'I know they are,' Heather said briefly. 'I came straight across.'

'We must find them,' Barbara said, urgently. 'I was going to meet them in the cafe. They were in the cafe.'

Someone was yelling on the other side of the crater. 'Over here! We've found something!' It was a young man in RAF uniform and there were others digging beside him. What are *they* doing here? she wondered as she ran. Whatever it was she was glad they'd come. There was something reassuring about a man in uniform and they were all working hard, shovelling the bricks aside with spades, and tossing great lumps behind them as they dug deeper into the mass.

And they *had* found something. Just underneath the concrete there was a torn shred of heavy cloth. She could see it as soon as she reached the pit and it wasn't long before they pulled it out. It turned out to be the empty arm of a winter coat – but underneath it was the long brown edge of Betty's new sheepskin.

'Oh quick!' Barbara said, reaching for the nearest chunk of masonry. 'That's my cousin. Is she breathing? Can you see?' The relief of finding her was so acute she was weeping. She was there. Inches away. They only had to dig and they'd get her out and she'd be all right. Oh please, please God, let her be all right.

'Take it easy!' the RAF man said, holding out a restraining arm. 'We don't want to crush her.'

'Can you see her?'

'Not yet. If we can just get this shifted I might be able to get down to her.'

But when the rubble was shifted, it was obvious that they hadn't found her after all. What was lying among the rubble was just her coat, filthy dirty and so torn it would never be worn again, and still with half a hanger stuck into the shoulder. They'd found the remains of the staff cloakroom. Barbara's disappointment was so crushing she sank to the ground with the anguish of it.

There was a police sergeant climbing over the wreckage towards her and looking round she saw that the fire brigade and the men of the light rescue service had arrived and that the road was full of ambulances.

'I'd go home if I was you,' the sergeant advised as he reached her. 'You can't do no more here. We're going to rope off the area.'

Barbara waved towards the fire. 'My cousins are in there.'

The sergeant winced his sympathy. 'Give their names an' addresses to the constable,' he said. 'The one on the corner down there. See him? We'll let you know the minute we have any news. I promise.' And when she frowned at him. 'It's fer the best, miss. We'll get 'em out quicker when the site's cleared.'

She recognised the truth of what he was saying but she couldn't bear to walk away. The RAF men were still digging, so why couldn't she?

Heather was by her elbow. 'He's right,' she urged. 'They'll make a better job of it than we will. They're bringing cranes in.'

'How do you know?'

'They just said. Come on.'

'Where to?'

'To tell poor Mabel. She won't know.'

Yes, Barbara thought, they ought to tell Mabel. So they gave the names to the constable and headed off to her house. But before they'd gone more than twenty yards, they saw her standing on the corner of Batavia Road. Her face was so wild that at first sight Barbara didn't recognise her, but then she saw that she was holding Joyce by the hand and shaking it as if she were trying to pull it from her arm. She was shouting, 'You bloody little fool! You bloody stupid little fool!' and both of them were weeping. It was the first time Barbara had ever heard her swear.

'Oh thank God for that,' Heather said. 'Our Joyce is all right at any rate. Come on!'

They ran, calling, 'Mabel! Mabel!' but she didn't hear them or see them until they were standing beside her. Then she looked up. 'Have you seen her?' she begged. 'D'you know where she is?'

'Not yet,' Heather told her, gently. 'They're digging them out now. I've given her name to the policeman.'

'What, Hazel's?'

'And Betty's.'

Mabel was too stunned to take in what they were saying. 'We don't know where she is', she said, 'thanks to this stupid fool. Let go of her, didn't she? Sid's out of his mind.'

'I didn't know there was going to be a rocket,' Joyce wept. 'She wen' off with Molly. She always goes off with Molly. I didn't know there was going to be a rocket.'

'Right here, she left her,' Mabel wailed. 'Right here. She could ha' been blown to pieces. Did you say they were digging them out? Has anyone seen our Betty? Oh my God this is awful! Awful! Sid's out of his mind.'

'Where is he?' Heather asked.

'Gone round the hospitals. We couldn't think what else to do.'

'Go and see that young copper,' Heather advised. 'Tell him where you're going to be, in case they hear anything, then come home with me for a little while. You're done in. What we need's a nice cup a' tea. We can't do nothin' here.'

'I had one from the WVS,' Mabel said, but she allowed herself to be led away.

Heather turned to her daughter-in-law. 'You coming,

264

Barbara?' It was a genuine invitation, given affection-
ately, and Barbara was touched by it. But at that
moment she heard a tram squeaking along the lines in
the road above them and the sound brought her back to
the moment. She had a job to do.

'I'd like to,' she said, her voice as full of affection as
Heather's had been, 'but I got to get back to work. My
shift's till six. Thanks all the same. I really would have
liked to. I'll call in later, if thass all right. Thing is,
people'll want to get here won't they? If they've got
someone . . . They'll need the trams.' She was remembering Steve's letter. '*We just have to get up and go on.*'
'I must go.'

'Yes,' Heather said. ''Course. You're a good girl.
Look after yerself.'

The dust was beginning to settle and the light had
almost returned to normal. Out in the street the WVS
were dispensing tea from their huge teapots and the
civil defence were clearing the road. The dead had
already been wrapped in shrouds and laid out in a
terrible neat line on the pavement and teams were
carrying them into Pearce Signs. She couldn't bear to
give them more than a glance in case one of them was
Betty or Hazel.

It'll be better at work, she thought, as she hurried
along the road. And it was. Mr Threlfall was so
obviously relieved to see her that she felt easier as soon
as she got inside the depot. Mr Tinker was in hospital
having his head stitched, so she worked with another
driver called Scottie and, although the ache of anxiety
scrabbled in her belly all afternoon, she was glad to
have something to occupy her mind. Every time they
got back to New Cross she looked out anxiously in case
someone had news and was waiting to tell her. But it
wasn't until past four o'clock that she heard anything
and then it was Mr Threlfall who told her.

'Some feller came with a message for you,' he said.
'Sid or some such. I wrote it down. Ah here it is. Hazel

is in Lewisham Hospital. Sis is coming to pick you up at six o'clock.'

Thank God, Barbara thought. If she's in hospital at least she's alive. There's hope. 'Anything else?'

'No. That's it. Sis at six o'clock. Have you seen Mrs Phipps? She said she'd come in an' help us out.'

So they haven't found Betty, Barbara thought. She knew they were still digging and still getting people out because she'd seen the cranes and the ambulances. They were still hard at it when she finally finished her shift, even though it was dark. They were working by floodlight, which was a thing she'd never seen before. Oh they must have got her out by now, surely.

Sis was waiting for her by the entrance. But she shook her head when Barbara asked her if there was any news.

'Only about Hazel,' she said. 'But you've heard that ain'tcher?'

'How is she?'

'Cracked her ribs, poor kid. They're keeping her in overnight. Sid's seen her. Said she wasn't too bad all things considering. We're all going up this evening. You an' me are going to Bob's for the night. The flat's in no fit state.'

Until that moment Barbara hadn't given their home a thought but now she realised it must have been damaged. It was too close to Woolworths to have escaped in one piece.

'Is it standing?' she asked.

'Just about,' Sis told her. 'You'll see. We're going there to collect our things. It's OK to go in if we're careful. We'll have to watch out for glass.'

The further end of the terrace was dark and empty and already smelt dank. The doors had been blown out, the windows were smashed, there was no electricity, the curtains had been torn to shreds and their once-warm, cosily-cluttered rooms were full of icy air, darkness and debris, which they saw when Sis switched on her torch

266

– the *chaise longue* covered with ash, the floor littered with papers and broken ornaments.

'Don't look at it,' Sis advised. 'Just find what you can of your things an' we'll get out of it.' There was half a loaf in the bread bin, and a scraping of butter in the butter dish but the food cupboard had been blown open and, except for a battered tin of custard, nothing else was still edible. She found a shopping basket, tipped the dust out of it and began to pack her necessities, cigars, brandy bottle, three files. 'I'll get me nightgown an' a change a' clothes an' we'll be off.'

So Barbara followed the dancing beam of the torch and retrieved her own treasures – Steve's letters in their shoebox, her best blouse and her green skirt, her old scarlet coat. And there was the sheepskin, covered in dust but otherwise intact. The sight of if brought the horror of the bomb-site roaring back into her mind. 'Oh Betty!' she said. 'Betty! Betty! Betty!'

Sis was at her elbow, patting her back. 'Come on, duck,' she said. 'No use staying here. They'll get her out if they can. Don't touch the door as you go out. It looks dangerous.'

So this is what it's like to be bombed out, Barbara thought, as they set off to Childeric Road. You're down to what you can carry away. She felt proud of them both for making so little fuss about it. But then it was the least of their worries with Betty still under the wreckage.

'Perhaps they'll have heard,' she hoped, as they reached the gate.

But there was no news. Little Mrs Connelly came bustling out into the hall to say how sorry she was. 'Tell Heather I got a soup on the go,' she said. 'You'll need something to keep you going. It's all nice an' hot, so it is.'

Not that any of them were in a fit state to eat anything. Sid had gone to work, because 'the papers had to be printed', but the rest of the family were gathered in the kitchen, Joyce prowling and miserable, Mabel sitting by the fire, next to her brother, her face grey with fatigue and anxiety, Heather in her own chair, knitting furiously.

'We just been up the site,' she said to Sis. 'They reckon they're goin' on all night. Bob's gonna stay here while we nip up to the hospital. Just in case. D'you want a cup a' tea before we go?'

They had tea and struggled through a plate of Mrs Connelly's soup and then they were off again, wrapped in their scarves and woolly hats, and hoping they wouldn't find Hazel in too bad a state.

In fact, she was remarkably cheerful, even though her chest hurt her and she had several angry cuts on her hands.

'That was the glass,' she told them proudly. 'My balaclava was cut to *shreds*. You should'ha seen it. They're gonna let me have it as a keepsake. Me an' Molly was blown right down on the pavement, an' we was *miles* from Woollies, up by Kennedy's. We was gonna get some bloater paste. We never got it though. She's got a broken arm. They've put it in plaster. Show 'em yer arm, Mol. We're all gonna write our names on it. The nurse said.'

'Young you see,' Sis explained, when they'd all been in to see her, two by two according to hospital regulations, and were comparing notes on the way home afterwards. 'They don't see the danger.'

Mabel was tearful. 'It breaks my heart to see her,' she said. 'The state she's in. Her poor little hands!'

'They'll get better,' Heather assured her. 'They look worse than they are. Well you know yourself, cuts always do.'

But the person they were really thinking about was Betty.

'We'll stop at the site on our way back, just in case,' Mabel said. 'You never know, they might have found her by now.'

But there was still no news.

'Come back with us,' Heather said. 'You won't sleep till you know. None of us will. Least it's Sunday tomorrow. That's one good thing. We shan't have to get up for work. We can sleep on once we've heard.'

So they all went back to Childeric Road and sat up all night and waited, making endless cups of tea, and saying over and over again that no news was good news, although none of them believed it. Occasionally they dozed off in their chairs and woke with a start to the sound of traffic in the New Cross Road or a train passing at the bottom of the garden. But when the morning finally came, they still hadn't heard anything and the rescue teams were still digging.

'It's a nightmare,' Mabel said. 'It just goes on and on. We must hear something soon, surely to God.'

But Sunday dragged by and nobody came. By this time they were all in such a state that none of them could settle to anything. They went to visit Hazel in the afternoon, taking care not to tell her what was going on, and were told that she'd be home the following day. Barbara and Sis went back to the flat to sort out their shoes and clothes, and discovered that the bomb damage teams weren't coming in till Thursday to repair the doors and windows, so they'd have to go on living in Steve's room for a bit longer. But for the rest of the time there was nothing but endless waiting and diminishing hope. And at the end of the day, another night to sit through.

This time the Horners went back home and waited there because Sid had gone to work again and Mabel wanted to be ready for him in the morning. But he'd been home for nearly an hour and Sis and the Wilkins had all gone to work themselves before news finally came.

It was brought by a policeman, who shuffled his feet and looked so desperately embarrassed that they knew it was bad before he said a word. He was ever so sorry, he said, but they'd found part of Betty's identity card stuck to the steps of the Town Hall. Did she always carry it?

Sid saw the implication at once, with such a sinking of heart that it took all colour from his face. 'Yes,' he said. 'She did. It was in her uniform pocket.'

'Ah!'

'Then she's dead. That's what you're saying.'

'I'm afraid so.'

'You ain't found – nothing else?'

'No. I'm ever so sorry. You *could* go to Pearce Signs an' see if you recognise anyone there. Well not anyone exactly. The bodies have all been identified but they got – well, bits. Arms an' legs an' that sort a' thing, if you could face it.'

Sid couldn't bear to do such a thing. The mere thought of it was making him shake.

'If she's dead, she's dead, poor kid,' he mourned. 'That's bad enough without seein' her in pieces.' Then he realised another implication. 'It'll mean we can't have a funeral or nothing.' And at that Mabel began to cry. She wept so bitterly that he stopped talking about it and simply put his arms round her. And the policeman went tactfully away.

'They might find her,' Mabel cried, clinging to his jacket. 'They might. Mightn't they? I mean there's always hope. We mustn't give up.'

Sid couldn't answer her. What could he say? He kissed the top of her head as his tears fell into her grey hair, and rubbed her spine for a very long time, lovingly and automatically, because they both knew there was no hope at all.

It was Monday afternoon before the last battered body was lifted out of the wreckage in New Cross Road. At the final tally, a hundred and forty-four people had been killed, hundreds more were injured and there were still twenty-four unaccounted for, and listed among them were Lionel Korczowski and sixteen-year-old Betty Horner.

270

CHAPTER TWENTY-ONE

News of the New Cross rocket filtered through to the general public in the haphazard way of the bush telegraph. It reached King's Lynn more than four days after the event, and was passed through the North End from house to house as yet another example of the barbarity of the Germans. Until it reached Maudie Nelson. She was so alarmed by it that she went straight round to Becky Bosworth, her eyes strained with concern.

'Thass where our Bar'bra lives,' she said. 'New Cross. I meanter say, she could've been hurt. Bein' New Cross. I mean, I wouldn't want her to be hurt, not after young Norman.'

'She'd write if she was,' Becky comforted.

Maudie shook her head. 'She hain't writ since the funeral. We had words.'

'I know,' Becky said in her blunt way. 'She tol' me. Well then, write you to her, gal.'

'I don' axactly know her address,' Maudie admitted rather shamefacedly. 'Thass why I come round.'

'Ah!' Becky understood. And went to find it.

Maudie's letter took a long time to write and when it was finished it was so long-winded and muddled and so much of it was crossed out and corrected that she was none too sure she ought to send it. But concern for this wayward daughter of hers proved stronger than the fear of exposing herself to ridicule for her lack of learning and it was committed to the post.

Barbara's reply was short to the point of brutality.

Dear Ma,

*I am alright. Steve's cousin worked in Wool-
worths and she was blown to bits. We couldn't
even have a funeral on account of there was
nothing left of her. That is what rockets are like. I
hope you are well. Give my love to the boys.*

Barbara.

'Oh dear,' Becky said, when she saw it. 'Thass a bit
sharp. You gonna write back, are you?'

Despite her bland expression, Maudie could be
perceptive. 'No,' she decided. 'Thass her way of
hollerin', I reckon. She don't want me to write. I got the
address, in case there's some other time.'

She had understood her daughter's state exactly. A
good long holler was just what Barbara needed – and
just what she couldn't allow herself. After the first
terrible waves of shock and disbelief and anger, Betty's
family were gradually moving into the second stage of
mourning, easing the perpetual ache of loss by deliberately invoking happy memories. Naturally, most of
them were of Betty as a little girl and that left Barbara
out of things, because her memories were restricted to
the last six months.

It was extremely hard to feel outside the family again
and just when she needed their warmth and contact so
very much. By keeping busy, she could just about cope
by day, but her nights were shattered by hideous
nightmares in which she walked endlessly down terrifying streets as bits of torn bodies fell out of the sky to
splatter her with blood. She woke two or three times
every night sobbing with terror and went to bed afraid
of what the next night would bring.

It would have been easier if there'd been anyone to
confide in. But there wasn't. Betty had been the only
one who had really understood her. The only one she'd
loved. And she *had* loved her, very much. Almost as
much as she'd loved Norman. But who would understand that? Even if they had time to listen to her, which

272

they didn't. Sis was on late turn and slept heavily, Hazel and Joyce were so upset they kept to themselves, and the other adults had too much to contend with to notice that she'd become a thing apart. She couldn't even write to Steve, not yet anyway, and certainly not when she was so angry and so vulnerable. Her letter to her mother had shown her that. After she'd sent it, she'd felt ashamed of it, but when she'd been writing the thing, it had been a quick angry response and she'd hardly thought about it at all. If she wrote to him like that, she would upset him terribly, and that was something she'd promised herself never ever to do. If she could have seen him she could have told him everything, gradually, watching his face to be sure she wasn't going too far or too fast, but writing was too distant and, in her present state, much too difficult.

In the end Heather brought the matter to a head.

'It's nearly Saturday come round again,' she said. 'We'll have to write an' tell Steve. He ought to know. I thought Mabel was going to do it, but she says she can't face it. An' Sid's in such a state I can't ask *him*. He ought to know though, poor boy. They were ever so fond of one another. Oh dear, it doesn't seem right for her to be killed. She was always so full a' life, larking and mucking about. I shan't know how to begin to tell him.'

Barbara spoke up before she could think better of it. 'I'll do it,' she offered. If she started by telling him his mother had asked her to write, it would alert him before she got to her awful news and then it mightn't be quite such a shock.

It pleased her to see that Heather was grateful. 'Would you?' she said. 'That's ever so good of you. It's not an easy thing, a letter like that.'

So that night, while Sis was at work, Barbara sat down in Steve's now overcrowded bedroom and wrote to him at last. It was a very long letter, telling him all she could remember of the explosion and moving carefully on towards the worst. Once she'd begun to write it, tears and words flowed together.

She described their long wait and told him how the policeman had come to break the news and how many deaths and injuries there had been.

It makes me so angry I don't know what to do with myself. If I could find the men what made that rocket or the men what designed it, I would tear them limb from limb or shoot them until they were dead or tie explosives all over them and blow them to pieces. I never hated anyone the way I hate them.

Then, having reached the bottom of the first furious page, she turned it over and told him that she and Sis had been bombed out and were now sharing his room.

We brought the camp bed over. That's a bit of a squash but we don't mind. What's a squash compared to what other people are suffering?

Which led her to the state they'd been in ever since. She described everything, from Mabel's tears to her own nightmares, and ended with an explanation.

We are all still in shock, I think. We all loved her very much and that's hard to believe she's gone. Your mum and dad say they're sorry they can't write to you at the moment but they know you will understand. So do the others. Your uncle Sid and aunt Mabel and Hazel and Joyce.

I'm sorry to be so angry but I can't help it. It wells up in me every time I think of her. Please, please, take great care of yourself. If you got hurt or anything I wouldn't be able to bear it.

The letter was delivered three days later when Steve

returned to base after a long day on foot patrol. It was bitterly cold in the Netherlands and the advance there had more or less ground to a halt. The Germans had withdrawn to defences alongside a small stream called the Vloed Beek and the 131st Brigade was holding a ridge to the north-east at a place called Sittard which was little more than a village but had plenty of cellars to give them shelter when they came under artillery fire.

The line had been held by both sides for several weeks and even though the fields between them were waterlogged and heavily mined, they ran frequent patrols, for there were bridges to be watched and gun sites to be pinpointed and both sides knew how important it was to be watchful. The Germans had good positions on the banks of the canal and used their searchlights with unpleasant accuracy, and now that they were closer to home, they were better supplied than they'd been in the entire campaign, especially with artillery and ammunition. They even had some heavy railway guns to the rear of the line. But at least the gunfire was spasmodic and at least there were no pitched battles, which was a relief to Dusty Miller.

'Let some a' the other buggers get stuck into the big battles,' he said. 'We done enough.'

Steve agreed with him until he read Barbara's letter. Then he was so overwhelmed with anger he could have done with some action.

'She was sixteen,' he said to Dusty, pale with shock and grief. 'Bloody sixteen an' they've killed her. They want their fucking heads shot off.'

'We'll bring in the flame-throwers,' Dusty promised. 'Don't you worry. They'll get theirs. They won't get away with it.'

'But they have,' Steve said. 'They've killed all those people. Hundred and forty-four, she says, and twenty-four missing. Women and children. Little children. Our Betty. Bloody sixteen. I'll have to write.'

'Do it now,' Dusty advised. 'We could be on the go again tomorrow.'

So the letters were written. The first two, to his parents and his aunt and uncle were simply to tell them how very, very sorry he was, and what a lovely brave girl Betty had been, and to assure them that the Germans would pay for what they'd done. But the third took longer because there'd been so much anger in Barbara's letter and there was so much he wanted to say to her.

You are right to be angry, my dear, dear darling, Don't apologise for it. Anger is natural. Be as angry as you want. We're angry here. It's what keeps us going. That and knowing that when the war is over we are going to build a better world. None of us has any doubt about that. We used to talk about it a lot while we were training. We don't so much now, there isn't the time, but we did then and I can tell you there's a hunger for change that is getting stronger and stronger. For a start, we won't have a useless organisation like the League of Nations next time round. We haven't fought and died to let a bunch of fools throw it all away for a second time. But that's only part of it. The really serious business is to make changes at home. Political changes. We're not coming out of the army to go on the dole and see our families starve. If we can have full employment to wage a war, we can have full employment to wage the peace. Nobody should be afraid that they can't afford the doctor when they're ill. Never again. Everybody who wins a place to a grammar school like you should be able to take it. It still makes me cross to think how you were wasted. You should have gone to that grammar school of yours.

Then he realised that the letter had become a rant and paused to consider what to say next. At last he wrote:

276

*I think what I'm trying to tell you my darling, is
that when someone you love has been killed, it
helps to have something positive to plan for. It
keeps you going. We have to keep going no matter
what happens. We must never give in. Aunt Sis
would tell you the same. You ask her. She joined
the Union and the Labour Party when Uncle
Percy was killed. It gave her something to hang on
to. I'm not saying that was the only reason she did
it but it was the first one. Talk to her my darling
and see if she doesn't agree.*

*Tell the others I will put in for some compas-
sionate leave but I'm not optimistic about getting
it. It's usually only given for close relatives.*

*Take the greatest care of yourself. I couldn't
bear anything to happen to you. I love you more
than I can tell you.*

He'd never written to her at such length before, nor
with such passion. And for once he didn't print
SWALK or BOLTOP on the envelope. He was too
serious for that.

Which Barbara noticed as soon as it arrived.

She was rereading the letter when Sis came home
from work late that evening. Heather and Bob were
round with Mabel, as they often were these days, so
they had the kitchen to themselves.

'How is he?' Sis wanted to know.

'He don't say,' Barbara realised. 'Thass mostly about
politics. I think he's as angry as we are.'

'Naturally.'

'You can read it if you like,' Barbara said, handing it
over. It would be interesting to hear her opinion of it.

'Very sensible,' Sis said, when she'd finished reading. 'But then he always was.'

'You think thass the answer then? Politics? Getting
involved?'

Sis looked at her for a long thoughtful second. 'Why

277

don't you come along to our next meeting?' she said. 'Then you could see for yourself.'

'Depends when it is,' Barbara said cautiously. 'I might be working.'

But as it turned out, the next meeting was on Thursday evening when she was working days again. So she put on her sheepskin coat – partly for warmth and partly to remind herself of Betty, painful though that was, and partly as an act of a private bravado to spite the Germans and show them she wasn't defeated and that she'd wear whatever she wanted – and she went with her aunt.

It wasn't a bit what she expected. She'd always imagined that socialists were wild-eyed revolutionaries who met in attics and drank brandy – or coffee at the very least – young men and women with tatty clothes who made passionate speeches and manned barricades with flags in their hands.

Instead she was ushered into a musty front room where nine middle-aged men sat hip to haunch around a narrow table, smoked pipes, drank tea and coughed. The chairman was a small, grey-haired man, who was called Mr Craxton and took an interminable time to say the simplest thing, and there was only one other woman, who was tall and skinny, wore her hair in a bun and was even older than Aunt Sis. All ten of them were burdened with paper and they all spoke in the same peculiar language, about 'conference' and 'the manifesto' and 'motion 29' and something they referred to as a 'possible composite'. In short they were a disappointment.

But they made her welcome and called her love and provided her with a cup of tea, and the woman, whose name was Christine, said it was nice to have someone young in the group.

'We're choosing a parliamentary candidate for Bellington South tonight,' she confided, when they paused to refill their cups. 'It's a safe Tory seat so the Labour

278

Party's a bit on the small side. There are only six people on their management committee at the moment and none of them are willing to stand, so they've asked us to help them out.'

Barbara said, 'Oh,' which seemed to be all that was expected of her and wondered who they would choose. To her amazement, it was Mr Craxton.

'But he's so boring,' she said to Aunt Sis as they walked home. 'No one'll elect *him*.'

'Well not in that seat, no, they won't,' Sis agreed. 'But this is just a run-in, to give him experience. He'll make it next time round. He's a good man.'

'He's boring. They should have chosen you.'

Sis laughed. 'I'm not in the running.'

'Why not?'

'Buggin's Law,' her aunt explained. 'He's the chairman. It's his turn.'

'Thass daft!' Barbara said trenchantly. 'You'd make a much better candidate. He'll send people to sleep.'

'He writes a good pamphlet,' Sis said. 'Come round the flat tomorrow an' I'll show you one.'

'Have they repaired it then?'

'Not yet. There's still no gas but it's got windows and the light works.'

It also had new door jambs and a new door, which was a tight fit and, as such, a great improvement on the old one.

'We'll get the fire lit,' Sis decided. 'No point working in the cold. Is there any coal in the scuttle?'

There was. So they lit the fire, took down all the shredded curtains and began to sort through the debris on the floor. Sis was ruthless. 'Chuck it out if it's broken,' she said, when Barbara held up a battered figurine. 'I ain't got time to fix it. Nor the patience neither, if the truth be told.'

But she found the file she was looking for. It was full of leaflets, headed 'Education', 'Health', 'Housing', 'Nutrition' and 'Pensions'. Most of them were crammed

279

with small close print but one was much simpler. 'There you are,' she said to Barbara. 'Read that.'

The Five Giants on the Road to Recovery: Giant Want. Giant Disease. Giant Ignorance. Giant Squalor. Giant Idleness. We must organize now to provide full employment; to rebuild a better Britain; to provide social services to secure adequate health, nutrition, and care in old age, for everybody; to provide full educational opportunities for all.

It was almost exactly what Steve had said in his letter.

'So what d'you think?' Sis asked.

'Sounds good,' Barbara allowed, 'but can we do it? Thass the thing.'

'Oh yes,' Sis told her. 'We can do it. Providing we win the election. If the Tories get in, it'll be the mixture as before.'

'Will they?'

Sis sat back on her heels with another tattered file in her hands. 'Not if we can stop 'em,' she said. 'That's what we're all working for. To be ready when the election comes and to give 'em a damn good run for their money.'

That night Barbara wrote another long letter to Steve telling him she was going to join the Party and that they were going to win the election. And he wrote back to tell her he wasn't a bit surprised, that he loved her more than ever – *'I can just see you waving the red flag!'* – and suggesting that she ought to read the Beveridge Report. *'It's on the third shelf. Write and tell me what you think of it.'*

So the weeks passed and although the family were still grieving, and Steve didn't manage to get any leave, Barbara's immediate sorrow began to ease. She still missed Betty terribly, especially on the days when they would have gone to the pictures or the Palais, and her nightmares continued as terrifyingly as ever, but now she woke herself up, switched on the bedside lamp without disturbing Sis and read the report to take her mind from the horrors. Which, for most of the time, it did, for it outlined the possibility of a new way of life which was exactly to her taste; work for everybody, free education for every child up to the age of fifteen, free health care paid for by a national insurance, a pension when you retire. What a weight of worry would be lifted from everybody's shoulders if they could make that happen.

She and Steve wrote to one another whenever they could, she every evening, he duties permitting, long detailed letters, discussing the report section by section and looking forward to the future they would build together 'when this lot is over'. The buzzbombs and rockets went on, there was never a day without a difficulty of one kind or another and the weather grew worse and worse, with frozen pipes and icy roads at home and thick fog in Holland and Germany, but they had their dream to keep them going, and writing about it made them feel they would both survive. Even when the war suddenly took a turn in the wrong direction and the papers headlined the news that the Germans had thrust fifteen miles into liberated territory, they were undeterred.

'It is a set-back,' Steve admitted, 'but it won't last. We shall soon have them on the run again. They wouldn't have got away with it, if it hadn't been for the fog keeping the RAF grounded. Real Hitler weather.'

'The papers say they're trying to retake Antwerp,' Barbara wrote back, 'and split the British and American armies in two. That says this morning there is a twenty-five mile gap in the Allied line.'

But Steve's confidence was justified. The campaign, which came to be called the Battle of the Bulge, was long and bitter but the Germans *were* driven back.

In the second week in December Sis had a letter to tell her that her flat was fully repaired and ready for occupation. She packed her 'bits and bobs' that evening, as soon as she got in from work, asking Barbara casually, when they were alone together in the bedroom, 'You coming back with me then, kid, or are you stayin' here?'

'I think I shall stay here,' Barbara decided. 'Thass all right, hain't it?'

'Looks all right to me,' Sis said. 'See you at the meeting Thursday then.'

So Barbara stayed in Childeric Road, where she helped with the housework and shared the queuing and felt she was almost one of the family again. And although the peace between her and her mother-in-law was fragile, it was at least a peace.

Bob was delighted to have her back and said so happily, and even Heather approved, especially now she'd become a fully paid-up member of the Labour Party and spent so much time with Sis.

'It's not *me* that's different,' she said, when Bob teased her about her change of heart. 'You've only got to look at her to see how she's altered. Look how sensible she's being. Oh no, there's a lot a' good in her now. She was ever so good writing to Steve like that when we was all in a state. An' we don't see anything of that Norfolk feller anymore, I hope you notice. We got that fly right out the ointment.'

CHAPTER TWENTY-TWO

'What've we got?' Victor said. The Skibbereen's limousine had just pulled up alongside his Humber and as he and Phossie had been waiting at their appointed rendezvous for more than half an hour, he was impatient to get started.

'Cloth,' the Skibbereen told him as he and Phossie stepped out of the car. 'Just arrived. Eight rolls. Marked with a black star.'

His driver, who doubled as look-out, was already in position at the corner of the street and the others were arriving now. Mog and Tiffany had parked on the other side of the road and were running across to join them. 'You'll have to cut the wire to get in,' the Skibbereen said. 'Cutters in the boot, Mog!'

Mog flicked his dog-end into the rubble of the nearby bomb-site and groaned. 'Not wire again, Skibbers,' he complained. 'That's death to a good suit, is that.'

'Give 'em here,' Vic said, taking the cutters. 'I'll do it.' It wasn't a job he particularly enjoyed but at least if he did it himself, he would make the hole big enough to get through in a hurry – and *he*'d got enough sense not to wear his good clothes.

It was a very cold night and a surprisingly quiet one. There'd been no rockets for nearly twelve hours and all they could hear were late-night trams buzzing in the distance and the occasional splash of a passing tug on the river below them. The warehouses were dark and unguarded, the streets completely empty and there was no traffic in the docks at all, but that was to be expected at this state of the tide and this time of the night.

Phossie held the torch and Vic started work on the

wire fence, his breath streaming before him like white smoke. It was exciting to be breaking in like this but the quicker it was done, the less the risk.

It was a doddle. One of the easiest jobs they'd ever tackled. No guard dog, no police, rolls at the end of the line, clearly marked. They were in and out and the cars were being loaded in less than three minutes. But as he picked up the last roll, Vic saw a possible extra.

'There's two bales of stuff over there on the floor,' he whispered to Phossie. 'Looks as if they've fallen off the shelves. What say we roll them too?'

'What are they?' Phossie whispered back. 'No good nicking stuff you can't shift.' They'd had a hard time with the last lot Vic had stolen on spec because it was army surplus and badly stained.

But this, as Vic discovered when he tore away the wrapping, was silk. 'That'll sell like the proverbial hot-cakes,' he said. 'Wait till the others have gone an' we'll come back for it. Go an' keep cavey. I'll wait here.'

Luck was still going their way. 'They're packing,' Phossie reported from the doorway. 'Mog's off. The Skibbereen's getting into his car.'

Vic could hear the cars being driven away. 'Right!' he said, picking up the first roll. 'Cop hold! Now run for it!'

It isn't easy to run when you are carrying a full roll of cloth between you but they went as fast as they could and reached the wire, where Phossie stood the roll on end and balanced it while Vic climbed through.

Then and without any warning at all, everything changed. The look-out hooted a warning, a police whistle shrilled, somebody was running, and the Skib-bereen emerged from the shadows like a bad dream, took the silk and was gone without a word.

'Christ!' Phossie said.

But Vic was running towards their car, hissing at him to follow, 'Scarpa! For Chrissake!'

Seconds of panic and frantic activity, struggling to

284

scramble into the car, driving off with the door open and swinging, a vague impression of struggling figures at the corner of the street, one helmeted, no sign of the Skibbereen or any of the others, and then they were round the corner and heading for home along a blessedly empty street. Vic was aware that the sweat was running into his eyes, that his heart was beating in an odd lop-sided way, and that he was flooded with exhilaration and triumph. 'Anyone after us?'

Phossie checked. But there wasn't. They'd escaped. They'd got away. 'We made it!' Vic yelled. 'We made it!'

'Only just,' Phossie warned. 'An' we're not out the wood yet.'

'Then I tell you what,' Vic said, slowing down. 'We'll drive like good citizens from now on,' he said. 'No point speedin'. That'ud only draw attention to ourselves.' He was thrilled to realise how competently he was handling this situation. 'Oh there's no flies on me, bor.'

But when they reached the house, the Skibbereen's limousine was waiting by the kerb and the boss himself rose out of the driving seat and stood on the pavement, massively, barring their way.

They followed him meekly into the house, senses prickling, closed the door behind him, stood in front of the empty hearth and waited for retribution. It came at once.

'Don't you never do that to me again,' the Skibbereen warned. 'Not if you want to stay healthy.'

Vic tried to brazen it out. 'Do what? We only took an extra roll. I mean, it was lying on the floor, asking to be nicked. You'd have said so yourself if you'd been . . .'

The Skibbereen pushed his face so close to Vic's that they were almost nose to nose. 'You do *not*', he snarled, 'nick nothing on your own account. You take what I tell you. Understand? No more no less. Just what I tell you. Is that clear?'

They agreed that it was, Phossie fearfully, Vic defiantly bold. ''Course.'

'You damn nearly fucked everything up,' the Skibbereen said. 'My driver's been nicked because of you, I hope you realise.'

'He won't grass,' Phossie tried to reassure. 'Not him.'

'No, 'course he won't. That ain't the point. The point is I got to get another driver. You've broke up my team.'

Victor thought of a solution at once, a chance to make amends and earn a bit of extra cash at the same time. 'I can drive,' he offered.

'You', the Skibbereen said scornfully, 'can keep your trap shut and do as you're told for a change. I've had a damn sight too much of you.'

'I only thought . . .'

'I don't pay you to think,' the Skibbereen said, harshly. 'I'm the brains behind this outfit an' don't you forget it. Ever. I give the orders, you do as you're told. You're just a gofor. Expendable, that's what you are. Two a penny. Common as muck.'

'I only offered,' Vic said stiffly. But he was talking to his boss's back.

'We're still working for you, ain't we?' Phossie asked. 'I mean . . .'

'If I want you,' the Skibbereen said, 'I'll call for you.' And left with a flourish.

'Now look what you've done,' Phossie said.

Victor was burning with anger and humiliation. 'Don't you start,' he warned. 'I've had enough for one evening.'

But Phossie opened his mouth to speak again, 'I told you there'd be trouble . . .'

'Christ Almighty!' Vic roared. 'Hain't I had enough? Shut your stupid fucking face!' And he turned and stormed out of the house. He had to put a distance between himself and degradation, to get up and go.

Anywhere. It didn't matter where. The car was waiting by the kerb. There was petrol in the tank.

He was halfway to Ipswich before he could think coherently and realised where he was going. How dare he put me down like that, he raged. I'm the best worker he's ever had, worth all the others put together. I ought to leave him, here and now. I would too, if it wasn't for the money. It wouldn't take much after being treated like that. I could set up a warehouse job just as well as he does. Better probably. Thass just a matter of getting contacts. Thass all 'tis. Getting contacts. Once I can do that there'll be no stopping me. I know all the ropes. I hain't green no more. Shan't get conned a second time the way I was over them ol' sheepskin coats. I learnt my lesson there. The road stretched before him, long and dark and full of possibilities. He wasn't going to be put down like that, ever again. There had to be a brickworks somewhere that would sell off old stock. This time he'd search until he found one. And then he'd give the Skibbereen the heave-ho.

It was morning by the time he reached the first brickworks on his list and he was unwashed, unshaven and unfed. But he squared his shoulders, pulled up his coat collar to hide the grime on his shirt, and set off to find the foreman.

He was a total waste of time and effort. 'Bricks?' the man said, looking round at the piles in the yard. It was beginning to snow and the wind was lifting the little flakes and tossing them about, so that the space between the two men was speckled and full of confusion. 'You're joking, mate. We ain't got enough to go round. Gold dust bricks are. Anyway it's all government contracts now. We can't sell 'em private, even if we wanted to. More than my job's worth, that'ud be. Whatcher want 'em for?'

'Build a house.'

'You a builder then?' the foreman asked, looking at Vic's overcoat. 'Don't look like one.'

287

'Buyin' for a friend,' Vic explained.

'Try the dumps,' the foreman said. 'There's plenty a' *them* around. Where they put all the pieces. Bomb clearance an' that.'

Vic muttered that he might well.

'Tell you what though,' the foreman said, flicking his cigarette end into the nearest unfrozen puddle. 'Bricks is a thing a' the past.'

Vic pricked up his ears. Something new. Something to supersede bricks. It could be just the thing he was looking for. 'Yes?' he asked.

'Straight up,' the foreman said. 'Once this lot's over, it's all going to be pre-fabricated houses. You mark my words. They got 'em already. Delivered in cardboard boxes they are, straight from the factory, the whole kit an' caboodle. 'Course you still have to dig foundations, plumbing an' electrics an' that sort a' thing, but then you just open the boxes, fit it all together, and four hours later, Bob's yer uncle, there you are, brand-new house, kitchen, bathroom, fitted cupboards, roof, every mod con, ready to walk in.'

It sounded wonderful. One in the eye for the Skibbereen. 'Thass just my style. Where can I get them?'

'You'll have to wait a couple a' years,' the foreman warned, amused by his eagerness. 'They ain't come on the market yet. Still experimental. Try the dumps. That's my advice.'

It was such a disappointment that Victor could feel his face freezing. 'Well thanks for your time,' he said, stiffly. 'I 'preciate it.' And he trudged back to his car. His feet were so cold he couldn't feel his toes and if he didn't have something to eat soon his stomach would think his throat had been cut.

The snowfall was thickening. The Humber already had a white dusting and the apprentice standing by the bonnet was wearing a mottled cap and white tweed shoulders. 'This yours?' he asked, as Vic swept the worst of the snow from his windscreen.

It was a chance for Vic to vent some of his ill humour. 'Hain't you got work to do?'

The boy wasn't abashed. 'Don't get shirty,' he said. 'I come to ask you sommink. You works for the Skibbereen, don'tcher.'

It was a statement, not a question and could be answered with a nod.

'I seen you in the pub,' the boy went on, gazing at the bonnet as if it were the font of all truth. 'Last month. Blue Boar.'

'So?'

'My uncle's got a few things might interest.'

A break. Could it be? Now and so easily. 'Oh yes. What sort a things?'

'Butter. Eggs,' the boy said casually. 'Side a' bacon. Turnaround Farm. Two miles down the road. You can't miss it.'

'I'll call in,' Vic said, equally casual.

Which was how he drove back to London with a boot full of dairy produce and two sides of bacon, singing all the way. Now Mr High-an'-Mighty Skibbereen, sir, you'd better watch out.

It took him the rest of the day to sell off the goods. He knew there were plenty of restaurants in the West End that bought on the black market but he had to be careful to avoid the ones that were already supplied by the Skibbereen. It was past midnight before he got to bed and by then he was totally exhausted but he'd done a good job and made a healthy profit. There was no sign of Phossie so he had the house to himself. Despite the dust and dirt of the bedroom and the intense cold of the night, he slept the sleep of the justified.

The next evening, washed, shaved, dressed in his best suit, fed to capacity, and with his last half dozen eggs and half a pound of butter in the glove compartment, he drove to New Cross.

It was a clear night so the blackout wasn't as much of a nuisance as usual, but, even so, he drove down the New Cross Road slowly and carefully, avoiding the tramlines so as not to crack the eggs. He hadn't seen Barbara for weeks, so the food was something of a peace offering and had to be perfect.

A tram loomed past him, like a great dark ship, whirring and clanking, and it occurred to him, a bit late, that she might be at work. He ought to have sent her a letter or a postcard, to warn her he was coming and arrange things properly. Still not to worry, he'd knock on her door first and see if she was there and if she wasn't he'd park outside the depot and wait for her there. He could handle it. Smiling to himself, he drove towards Woolworths and the flat.

Like everyone else, he'd heard rumours about the New Cross rocket but he hadn't given them much attention. Rockets were two a penny these days. You heard them going off all the time but, of course, when you heard them, they were over and they'd fallen on someone else, so you soon forgot about them. Suddenly being confronted by that huge bomb-site gave him quite a turn. Bloody hell! he thought, slowing to look at it. That *was* a bad one. It occurred to him that Spitfire must have seen it. Now he remembered that she'd moved to her aunt's flat and looked along the road to see if the aunt's flat was still standing, and was relieved to see it, with curtains at the windows, and smoke coming out the chimney, perfectly all right and perfectly normal. Bit close though, he thought, looking back at the space. I shall have to sympathise. And he parked the car and picked up his presents.

Barbara had had a bad day. It was dark and cold, there were more rockets than she could count, and her passengers had been full of gloom and depression.

'Them things are beginning to get on my wick,' one old lady confessed, after a particularly loud explosion.

'Bleedin' Jerries. Pardon the French, dear, but they just go on an' on an' on. Never any end to 'em. Just when you think you got 'em licked they come up with summink worse. An' our poor lads out there fighting the beggars. It don't bear thinking about.'

But how do you stop a thought once it's in your head? Barbara remembered Steve all through the day, aching to have him home, racked with anxiety in case he was hurt, fraught with the terrifying knowledge that he could be killed just as easily as Norman and Betty and that there was nothing she could do to prevent it. The sound of those double explosions, echoing and re-echoing across the London streets, pushed her back again and again to the nagging, brutal fact that she would rather have avoided – that good people were killed in this war every single day and in the most evil ways. She yearned for her brother, for Betty, for all the other dead and dying she'd seen on that November morning. By the time her morning shift was over, she was aching with grief.

Fortunately Sis came strolling in during her lunch break to tell her she'd be a bit late for the meeting that evening and to ask if she'd nip across to the flat to pick up her blue file. 'You still got the key, ain'tcher?'

Barbara said yes so wearily that Sis looked at her with concern.

'Bad day?' she asked.

'Too many rockets.'

'Never mind,' Sis comforted. 'It's Thursday. Dreamers and schemers day. See you at the meeting. Keep yer chin up. Don't let the buggers grind you down.'

So Barbara struggled on through the rest of the day, keeping her chin as high as she could, and at last the long shift was over and she could get ready for the evening and cut across to Sis's flat and hunt for that blue file. She lit the fire ready for Sis's return and washed the breakfast things and tidied the newspapers into a pile, and then it was only the file to find and she could be off. At that moment the doorbell rang.

She was too weary to feel surprised or pleased that it was Victor on the doorstep.

'Oh,' she said flatly. 'Thass you.'

He was so thrilled at the sight of her, bright and bold in her scarlet sweater and the navy-blue slacks she used to wear at the Saturday hop in Lynn, that he forgot about the rocket. 'Brought you a little present,' he said, holding out the carton of eggs and the butter.

She recognised the value of the gift but she hadn't got the energy to respond to it. 'Thanks,' she said in the same flat voice. 'You'd better come in then I s'pose.' It was too cold to stand and talk on the doorstep.

He followed her, worried by how down she was. 'You all right?'

She said yes, but it was as if she hadn't heard the question.

'Thought you'd like to go to the pictures,' he offered as she led him up the narrow stairs.

'What?'

'Pictures,' he repeated. 'You an' me and the others. That's Thursday.'

She'd forgotten that Thursday used to be their night out. 'I got to look for a file,' she said as she led him into the kitchen.

He put his presents down on the table and tried a joke. 'Oh well then, if you got a file to find, I'll tek Betty an' leave you behind. Hark at me! I'm a poet an' I don't know it.'

'I'd rather you didn't talk about Betty,' she said, and now her voice was cold. 'If you don' mind.'

'Oh my!' he said, his face bold with the success of his joke. 'Don' tell me you're a-gettin' jealous. Not of our Betty. Naughty, naughty!'

She was stung, suddenly and to such rage it made her shake. 'You're so stupid!' she roared at him. 'No, I hain't jealous. You just leave her right out of it, thass all. Right out of it!' And when he grinned at her annoyance, 'You hain't to talk about her! I won't have it!'

He wagged a finger at her, still teasing. 'Naughty, naughty!'

It was too much. 'Oh!' she roared at him. 'You're so stupid. You're so bloody stupid. She's dead. Don't you understand? Dead! I shan't never see her again.'

Now he was confused but he fought back automatically. 'Don't holler at me, gal,' he bristled. 'It hain't my fault. I didn' kill her.'

'I never said you did. Just don' talk about her.'

'But how did she . . . ? I mean . . .'

'That bloody rocket,' she shouted. '*Now* d'you understand?' And she burst into tears.

Tears he could cope with. He hadn't watched B movies all those years for nothing. He sat her down, produced a clean handkerchief, gave her a shoulder to cry on, found her a cigarette and lit it for her. 'I'm ever so sorry,' he said. 'That's awful.'

She cried for a very long time. 'First Norman and now her. There'll be nobody left. An' they're planning Christmas as if everything were normal. I can't bear it. We're going to have a goose with one leg, if you ever heard of anythin' so ridiculous.'

He couldn't see why they didn't get an ordinary goose with two. So she explained what it was, smiling for the first time that evening. 'Thass a leg of mutton with some stuffing in it,' she said. 'Heather's trying to cheer us up.'

'Tell you what,' he said impulsively. 'How about if I got you a real goose?'

She was impressed by such an offer. And tempted. A real goose, she thought. Imagine that! A real goose an' apple sauce. A proper Christmas dinner. That *would* cheer them up. 'Could you?'

'Oh yes,' he said with just the right blend of modesty

and importance. 'I got contacts. I could bring it over Christmas Eve.'

'Not here though. I'm living in Childeric Road now.'

'I'll bring it there then. And then you an' me could go dancin' up West maybe. The Lyceum's a good place.'

'No,' she said as she blew her nose on his handkerchief. 'I can't face dancing. Not yet.'

He didn't push her. 'No,' he said. ''Course. I can see that. What about the pictures then? Not here, 'course. Up West. Somewhere you ain't been before.'

She thought about it. She hadn't been out since ... An outing *would* be nice if it was well away from New Cross. She'd have to keep it a secret from Heather, of course, because she couldn't face a lot of arguments about it. But they could meet at the corner of the road and she could say she was going with a friend from work. I'll give these eggs an' things to Mabel, she decided, otherwise they'll know he's come back and there'll be ructions. I'll think of some explanation for the goose later on. 'Thanks,' she said at last. 'I'm not promising, mind, but I might like that. It's possible.'

So the deal was done and he was as good as his word. That Christmas Eve, when Bob and Heather were out doing their last minute shopping and Barbara was giving the kitchen a last minute sweep through, he arrived at the corner, as they'd arranged, and sounded his horn. And when she went down to signal to him that the coast was clear, he walked in with the biggest goose she'd ever seen.

She left it on the kitchen table with a note propped up against the white feathers of its breast.

My contribution to the feast. I have gone to the pictures. Will buy apples for the sauce on my way out. Will help you pluck and pull it in the morning.
    Love, B.

Then she and Victor went up to Leicester Square to the pictures. And there, in the anonymous crowds and swept along by the loud, improbable fantasy on the screen, she lost her unhappiness for an hour or two and forgot the rockets and the rations and didn't think about Norman or Betty until she was out in the dark of common night again.

'That takes you out of yourself, the ol' pictures,' Vic said, as they walked back to the car.

'Thass what Ma say,' she remembered.

'She got a lot of sense, your ma,' he said. 'Leave your troubles behind for an hour or two. No harm in that.'

'No,' she agreed. 'There hain't.' That was just a rest, time off, a bit of fun. What she needed.

'How about next week?' he hoped, encouraged by how relaxed and happy she seemed to be. Strike while the iron's hot, sort of thing.

This time she didn't hesitate. 'Yes,' she said. 'Why not?'

CHAPTER TWENTY-THREE

The essence of roast goose pervaded the house that Christmas morning, rising in every room in a succulence of promised pleasure, sending luscious traces down the stairs to entice the newest arrivals, at its most mouth-watering in the kitchen, where it roused hungry anticipation and delectable memory in equal measure. But it didn't do Barbara any good at all.

She and Heather had been up at six, to pluck, pull and stuff their precious bird, and when Mabel and the girls arrived just after nine to see if they could give a hand, they were busy cooking vegetables and running back and forth to keep an eye on the pudding which was boiling in the copper in the bathroom. But despite their hard work, there was an uneasiness between them, a determination to be sensible about this Christmas, an awful enforced jollity that was as sharp as thorns in a holly bush.

The Connellys were spending Christmas with their daughter and, before they left that morning, they'd told Heather she must feel free to borrow anything she needed, so Joyce and Hazel were set to work at once to carry four extra chairs upstairs, with strict instructions that Hazel was to take care of her ribs. And Heather tried a joke.

'Just as well they've gone away,' she said, 'or God knows where we'd have all sat. We'd've been in one another's laps.'

Ordinarily a remark like that would have led to all sorts of suggestions and a lot of happy teasing but this time it fell so flat they didn't even smile at it. Mabel said 'yes' bleakly and the two girls simply turned away to set the table, with a sheet for a tablecloth and every piece of glass and china that Heather possessed. Then they did their best to make amends for not appreciating her joke and spent a long time telling her how pretty the room looked, until the men came back from the pub and rescued them, bearing two whole bottles of wine 'to add to the feast'. And the goose was served.

It was a splendid bird and cooked to perfection, but just as Bob was carving the first slice, Mabel sighed and said, 'Our Betty would have loved this. She was always a one for poultry.' And before they could comfort her, her eyes were full of tears.

Sid leant towards her to pat her hand. 'If she can see us now, she'll be saying "What a lot a' porkers!" D'you remember her on that picnic? "What a lot a' porkers!" '

It was a vain attempt. They were all too cast down to enjoy the meal, rich and special though it was. 'Not too much for me,' they said, as slices of goose were offered. 'Just a little.'

That was a mistake, Barbara thought, looking at their meagre portions. I thought it would make a lovely meal and cheer them up but I've made things worse. And she ate, feeling as bleak as all the others.

As the plates were being cleared, Sid tried to cheer them with praise. 'Best dinner I've had in ages,' he said, patting his stomach. 'An' we got our Barbara to thank for it I hear.'

'Yes,' Mabel agreed, making her own effort. 'It was lovely, Barbara. I never thought I'd be eating goose this Christmas. Where on earth did you get it?'

The question jerked Barbara from her unhappy thoughts but cautious with grief and disappointment, she didn't tell them the truth. She was aware that Heather was looking at her quizzically and that Bob was looking at Heather uneasily and the two glances alerted her. She couldn't tell them it had come from Vic. Not now, when they were all so ill at ease. Not ever probably. 'I'm a country gal, don' forget,' she temporised. 'I got friends.'

'Well tell 'em we appreciate it,' Sid said. 'Best dinner we've had in ages.'

'Was that where you got the butter, our Bar'bra?' Hazel said.

'What butter was that then?' Heather asked, her face suddenly sharp.

'Half a pound a' butter an' six whole eggs,' Hazel told her. 'Real eggs with shells. Not dried. We had 'em fer supper. They was lovely.'

'Fancy!' Heather said, looking a challenge at Barbara. 'You'll be setting up as a grocer if this goes on. We shall have to register with you.'

'Time to put the wireless on,' Sis said, intervening before they could start to quarrel. 'Or we shall miss the King.'

'You're right,' Bob said, thankful for her good sense. 'Look at the time.'

So the difficult moment passed, because they only just had time to tune in before the Christmas broadcast began. The announcer was Frank Gillard, the BBC correspondent. 'Lovely voice,' Sis approved. 'I like a man with a good voice.' He began by telling them he was with the British Liberation Army 'somewhere in Germany' and then revealed that he was actually the guest of the famous Desert Rats.

The announcement electrified everyone in the room. 'That's Steve's lot,' Heather cried. 'That's the 21st Army. Oh Bob! He's with our Steve.'

Bob held up a calming hand. 'Shush! Let's listen.'

'... *in a local* Gasthof,' the announcer was saying. '*A fine hotel, typical of the sort of building you find in this region. The battalion has commandeered it for the festivities.*'

At that point there was a burst of cheerful laughter in the background, young male voices, guffawing and giving an ironic cheer.

One of them could be Steve, Barbara thought, yearning for him. Hearing their voices like that made him seem suddenly close to her, as if she could put out her hand and touch him. Oh my dear, dear, darling. If only . . .

The announcer was still speaking. It was a signal honour to speak on the wireless just before the King's speech, especially as this could be the last Christmas of the war – more cheers – so the soldier who had been chosen *had* to be one of the Desert Rats, one of the men who had fought through Africa and Italy and were now blazing their way into Germany. It gave him great pleasure to introduce Corporal . . .

Corporal? Could it be?

'Corporal Pass of D company. Corporal Pass.'

Barbara's disappointment was momentary. Not Steve, but it could be one of his mates. And if it was the 21st Army, he could be there. He could be one of the men who were cheering. If she listened hard she might hear his voice. Oh what a wonderful thing that would be, to hear his voice again.

Lusty cheers preceded the corporal's speech, beer mugs were waved until the beer slopped over, flushed faces shouted encouragement, the wooden tables were thumped until they were in danger of toppling.

'You tell 'em, corp!' Dusty called out. And he was cheered too.

A full day's holiday, away from the campaign, inside a warm hotel, with nothing to do but eat and drink and sing a few carols to pay for the privilege, was such luxury they were quite light-headed. They'd explored the place as soon as they took it over, decked the walls with great branches of holly and evergreens, rearranged the furniture, commandeered the bedrooms and found so many kegs of beer down in the cellars that they couldn't have drunk it all if they'd been there till doomsday, although they'd put a fair bit away while they were waiting for the broadcast to begin. Now, with the regimental band playing and the smell of cooking rising pungently from the kitchens and everybody saying this was the last Christmas of the war, they were drunkenly and ridiculously happy. It didn't matter what Corporal Pass was saying, nor what the poor stuttering King was trying to stumble through, it was Christmas and the war would soon be over and they were alive and winning.

The band had struck up the introduction to the first carol and the producer had appeared to urge them on. 'Now then chaps. "Hark the Herald" on the count of three. Lots of sound. Belt it out.'

And belt it out they did, bellowing the words as if they were a battle cry and not a Christmas hymn. *'Peace on earth and mercy mild. God and sinners reconciled.'*

The deep-throated sound rolled up into the beams of the dining hall. *'Born that man no more may die.'* Amen to that, Steve thought. We've had quite enough killed. Now let's get it over as soon as we can. March maybe. April. It couldn't be long.

Dusty was sniffing the air. 'D'you reckon it's turkey?' he asked under cover of the next intro.

'I'm easy,' Steve told him. 'It's proper food, that's the great thing. It's not coming out of a tin and we're eating it off a plate.'

'How many more've we got to sing?' Johnnie Musgrove complained. 'I'm starving. I could eat a horse.'

'Don't tempt them,' Steve warned, laughing at him.

'When's the cabaret?' Tom Ferguson asked.

'Later,' Steve promised. 'After the grub.'

And later it was, when the broadcast was over and forgotten and they were all so well fed that their stomachs were distended. As the dirty plates were carried away, the band took up their positions again, the drummer gave an impressive drum roll and the doors at the far end of the hall were flung open to reveal a troop of extraordinary dancing girls, dressed like Carmen Miranda with dishcloths tied round their heads, crowned with huge bundles of camouflage in lieu of fruit, wearing bright red lipstick and huge paper earrings, and costumed in battle-tops and army boots and an inventive collection of skirts, made of old curtains, old camouflage nets and old bits of parachute in every colour going, green and gold and pink. When they were four paces into the hall, the band struck up with 'Hands Knees and Boomps-a-daisy' and they began to dance, crashing their multicoloured hips into one another as though they intended to break bones. They were cheered to the echo.

Dusty was sloshing beer into all the mugs on the table with cheerful and drunken inaccuracy. 'More for you Tom? Johnnie? Whet the ol' whistle.' But most of his mates were on their feet and scrambling to join the dance in an uproar of high spirits and sudden abandon.

They danced until they were exhausted, Hokey-Kokey, Lambeth Walk, drunken jive, as the heat in the hall increased and the band played until the sweat ran into their eyes. At eleven o'clock they ended with a long trailing conga, round the dining room and out into the reception hall and all through the rest of the *Gasthof*. By the time the leaders got back to the dining room the band had packed up their instruments and were enjoying a well-earned drink.

'What a night!' Tom Ferguson said. 'They done us proud.'

'So they should,' Steve told him, handing cigarettes round. 'We're winning the war for them.'

'How long d'you reckon, Corp?' Johnnie Musgrove asked.

'Late spring, early summer,' Steve told him. 'Once we're over the Rhine, one more push should do it.'

'An' then home,' Dusty said. 'Can't come soon

enough fer me. Find mesself a bint, put me feet up, settle down. Just the job.'

'One more push,' Johnnie Musgrove echoed, 'an' then home.'

The pianist was back at the piano, playing the introduction to another carol. 'We done that!' they called to him. 'It'll be Boxing Day in half an hour.' But he just grinned at them and went on playing and after a while a group of his mates strolled across to sing along. It was a gentle carol and made a peaceful end to their hectic day.

> *'In the bleak midwinter, frosty wind made moan,*
> *Earth stood hard as iron, water like a stone,*
> *Snow had fallen, snow on snow, snow on snow . . .'*

Outside the high windows, snow was falling still, in huge heavy flakes, steadily and persistently. Beneath it, in the quiet fields, the guns were wearing white shrouds, waiting; tanks stood in line, wearing their new white camouflage, waiting; TCV's were in position like huge white boxes, waiting; the only colour in that white landscape was the blood red of the crosses on the ambulances, waiting. One last push.

In King's Lynn, Victor Castlemain was in the Three Tuns drinking with his cronies. They'd been at it for over an hour and in the last ten minutes they'd moved from beer to whisky and from reminiscence to confusion.

Spikey was lugubrious with self-pity. Christmas was the last thing he was thinking about. 'Call-up papers, bor!' he said to Victor. 'I ask you.'

'You knew they were coming,' Vic told him reasonably. 'You should have got out the way.'

'Thass a bit late now,' Spikey sighed. 'They come. I got 'em. Report in six weeks.'

'That could all be over on six weeks, bor,' Tubby tried to comfort.

'With *my* luck?' Spikey gloomed. 'You'll be next, Victor.'

'Not me,' Vic said happily. 'Any why? I'll tell you why. They don't know where I am.'

'Your ma'll forward it, bor.'

'She don't know where I am neither,' Vic said and when his friends looked at him with drunken admiration, 'No flies on me, bor.'

'You're a one, Victor!' Tubby said.

Spikey was feeling disgruntled and decided to change the subject. 'See anything of Spitfire these days, do you, bor?' That wouldn't hurt to remind him he'd lost his girl. Take the wind out of his sails. Cut him down to size.

But Victor was looking smug. 'Spitfire?' he said, leaning back in his chair and grinning at them. 'Oh yes. I see her. Quite often actually.'

'Lucky beggar!' Tubby said enviously. 'How d'you swing that then?'

'Charm,' Victor told him and laughed. 'No, between you an' me, I think she's bit lonely up there in London. They're a funny lot. Not like us. So I take her out, show her a bit of life, dancing, the flicks, that sort of thing.'

They were drunkenly impressed, Tubby openly, Spikey despite his annoyance.

'What about that ol' soldier?' Spikey wanted to know.

'While the cat's away,' Vic said, gazing at his image in the pub mirror. He was really rather pleased with himself. The good food of the past six months had put flesh on his bones and made him look older and more mature. More than a match for a stupid soldier. They think I'm having an affair, he thought, enjoying the grudging admiration of his cronies. Well let them. If I play my cards right, it could be an affair. Plenty of women take lovers while their husbands are abroad. In

303

fact, if I could get a flat or a house or something, I reckon I could tease her away from him really easily. After all, she's only known him a couple of months and *I*'ve known her for years. And he's been away a good long time now. When he comes back he'll be a stranger. When you think about it, I hold all the best cards and I've run a brilliant campaign so far. Now it just needs one last push. That's all. One last push.

CHAPTER TWENTY-FOUR

January is a bad time of year to embark on a new endeavour. Darkness glooms away the warmth of celebration, snow hunkers over our hopes, ice stops the breath of our dreams. It takes a strong will simply to get on with our everyday work and the effort required to wage war is superhuman. Steve and Dusty grumbled that they could quite understand why soldiers in earlier generations simply packed up and went home at the first sign of bad weather. 'They'd got their heads screwed on!' But a world war continues no matter what the weather. Armies simply have to adapt to it. And at least the BLA was well equipped, even if it couldn't match the careless abundance of the Americans.

By the beginning of the year, every bit of military equipment had been painted white, including their rifles, and they and the tankies had been issued with new winter uniforms which turned out to be padded white snow suits that made them look like amiable snowmen as they plodded between their vehicles. For most of the time the infantry wore their usual motley collection of clothing, issued and scrounged, layers and layers of it, topped by leather jerkins and heavy greatcoats, but when they were out on patrol they were glad to be camouflaged, even if their special clothing *was* bulky, for underneath the padding they were still sweating with fear. Blood runs crimson in a field of snow.

The new campaign began with the usual massive bombardment. After seven months of more or less incessant fighting, Steve could hear it without a tremor, thankful for its power and relieved that the enemy would be thoroughly softened up before the brigade was ordered in to push them to retreat.

They moved off in the usual way too, in the early morning, before first light and under cover of a creeping barrage. It was bitterly cold and the snow was thick underfoot, which made the going heavy, and to make matters worse their smokescreen had frozen in the air so that they were surrounded by fog. The whole battalion was on the move but Steve could only see the handful of men immediately around him. And at that point things went wrong. The barrage crept too slowly and the shells fell short and began to explode among the brigade.

There was an outburst of violent swearing. 'Fucking hell, corp! Now what?'

The only possible place to take cover was a dyke which Steve could see a hundred yards ahead of them. It was about six feet wide and was probably six feet deep too and half full of freezing water but it was better than standing out in the open waiting to be killed by friendly fire. 'Make for the dyke!' he yelled, waving them on, and he bellowed at their signaller as he ran, 'Tell 'em – lift the stonk one hundred, for Christ's sake!'

The water in the dyke was covered by a sheet of ice. It broke as they jumped in and then they were up to their waists in freezing water and gasping with the cold of it.

'Bloody hell fire!' Dusty shivered. 'We'll get fucking frost bite.'

But Steve's message had got through and presently the shells began falling further ahead so they were able to scramble out of the water and press on, as well as their wet legs would allow them.

'Bad enough we got to fight the bleedin' Jerries', Dusty grumbled, 'without fighting the bleedin' weather an all.'

'No choice,' Steve said succinctly. 'We can bellyache all we like, it won't stop the weather.'

But in fact, the next stage of the operation had already been postponed for twelve hours because of the fog which was thickening by the minute. Steve and Dusty weren't the only ones to recognise that the weather was a second enemy to be watched as closely as the Germans. The brigade needed at least partial visibility if they were to advance without taking too many casualties, and the state of the ground required careful observation too, for tanks could only be used if the going was firm enough. After their long hard slog from Normandy, they'd all learned to be resourceful, to cope with changes of plan, and not to take any risks that could be avoided.

The brigade's first task that day was to bridge the Vloed Beek, which was a twenty-foot stream which was now blocking their advance. When they reached it, they found, as they expected, that the original bridges had all been blown, but they managed to get across by using specially constructed ladders, grappled together across the width of water. Not an easy job because they were very exposed, even with the continuing fog as cover, and they came under heavy enemy shelling and some small arms fire and took too many casualties. But it was done, and the foothold was enough.

The fog thickened during the day and was made worse by the smoke from their twenty-five pounders. By afternoon, vision was reduced to a few yards. Then, as if that wasn't enough to contend with, there was a partial thaw which left the snow thick in the fields but filled the roads with half frozen mud. The Gebroek road to their supplies in the west was soon impassable even to tracks and it wasn't long before they heard that the supply lorries were bogged down.

'What fucking next?' Dusty growled.

'Night,' Steve told him.

'Smashing!' Dusty said sarcastically. 'Ain't we the lucky ones!'

That night was pitch dark and it was snowing as they

307

set off, but the advance continued nevertheless. Each company could only take one Jeep and a carrier with them for essential stores and ammunition, it was impossible to manhandle the six-pounder anti-tank guns across the dykes in the dark and, naturally, they had to cope with a counter-attack. It came from the direction of Susteren, and began just as the leading Company and Battalion HQ were crossing the stream and at their most vulnerable. The column dropped off Bren gun teams at once to return fire and after a while the 3rd Royal Horse Artillery joined in with a heavy bombardment on the flank of the leading company. Their fire was so massive and so accurate that the attack petered out. But presently it began to snow again, this time heavily. By the time morning came, they were chilled and irritable and wearily apprehensive about what they would have to cope with next. Or as Dusty put it, 'bitched, buggered and bewildered'.

It was a sharp cold morning and surprisingly quiet, the landscape shrouded with drifting fog, the fields freshly covered with snow. They were rested and fed and, towards afternoon, advanced to the next dyke, watching out for snipers and holding themselves ready for another counter-attack. But none came. The dyke was crossed without a shot being fired and the field before them was empty.

They advanced with caution, line abreast, rifles cocked, breath streaming before them, boots leaving deep pits in the snow, one yard, two, three . . .

The first mine exploded with a crack that made them all jump. There was a man down – Percy was it? – both feet gone, blood spurting into the snow. But before Steve could open his mouth to call a halt, there were two more explosions and two more down.

'Stand still, for Christ's sake,' he yelled. 'Don't move!' And when they'd all stopped and there were no more explosions, 'Follow your footsteps back.'

So they retreated by way of their own footprints,

carrying their mangled casualties with them. The mines had been a matter of inches underneath the snow.

'Crafty sods!' Steve said to Dusty as they regrouped to await orders. 'They've just laid the fucking things down and buggered off and let the next fall cover them up. They must've done it last night when it was heavy.'

Dusty was thinking about their casualties. 'Was it both feet?' he asked.

'Who?'

'Poor old Percy.'

'Yep.'

'That's him out of it then.'

And we're still here, Steve thought as the stretcher bearers carried their wounded away, and apart from the odd flesh wound now and then, *we*'re in one piece. He'd been shaking with fear and fury as the mines exploded but now he was too tired to feel glad about their escape. It was a fact, that was all, like coming under fire as you crossed a stream, and being shelled by your own side, and watching your mates die, and everything else in this god-forsaken war.

It was deceptively peaceful out there in the snow for there was still no sight or sound of the Germans. As they waited, a sharp wind began to blow. It stung their unprotected faces and swept the newly fallen snow into drifts against every obstacle, from tree stumps to the wreckage of the exploded mines. But at least it blew away the fog. Now they could see that the sky was that peculiarly colourless white that follows heavy snowfall. What trees there were stood gaunt and black against the horizon, some shattered by shells, some bearing crows like burdens. And about a mile to the east, there was a lone farmhouse, crouched under its roof of snow, the brown smoke from its chimney smudging the empty sky. For the first time since his arrival Steve thought about the local inhabitants and what the war was doing to them.

'It must be hell for people living here,' he said.

Dusty was lighting a cigarette. 'It's hell, full stop,' he said, drawing in the first sharp drag. The smoke was hot in his throat and made him cough. He turned his head and spat into the snow. '*That* to war!'

Steve was still thinking about the locals. Left alone to lead their lives in peace, they would have drowsed out the winter, quietly indoors. Now everything they knew was being smashed, their houses gutted, their livestock killed, their fields littered with the debris of war, the burnt-out tanks, broken vehicles, smashed guns, empty tins and bottles, spent cartridge cases, fag-ends, used dressings, vomit and shit and every conceivable kind of filth, miles and miles of it strewn across the countryside. He was drawn with pity for them. Even when the war's over, their lives will never be the same again. Any more than ours will.

Orders were coming through. 'Corporal Wilkins, take six men . . .'

The atrocious weather had frozen the British Isles as well as Europe, and according to the papers, London was the coldest place in the country. On January 6th, the *Mirror* reported that it had been 18 degrees below freezing at Kew overnight, and by the end of the month there were rumours that down in Dover the sea had frozen over.

'Great sheets of ice, it says here,' Joyce told her family, reading the paper avidly. 'I wouldn't half like to go there an' see it.'

'With your chilblains!' her mother laughed at her. 'You'd be hobbling for months.'

'At least it's put paid to the rockets,' Sis said. 'We ain't had nowhere near so many a' the beggars these last few days. *An*' they've lifted the blackout. It ain't all bad.' It was a relief to her to be able to walk to work or to go visiting without having to carry a torch.

Heather was more interested in the war reports. The only way she could cope with the winter was to ignore it – snow, icy roads, burst pipes, the dilapidated state of the town, standing in a biting wind in those endless back-breaking queues, Barbara's perpetual gadding about, which was a weekly source of nagging irritation, even though she knew she was only going to the pictures with her friends from work. As the cold days passed, she buoyed herself up with the thought that spring was coming and that the war would soon be over, no matter how hard life might be at the moment. And it *was* hard. Food had never been in such short supply nor such poor quality, potatoes so full of eyes they were no bigger than marbles once they'd been peeled, bread grey and much adulterated, bacon limited, eggs a thing of the past.

As Victor was told by one of his farming friends. 'No good asking fer eggs,' he said, a bit too cheerfully. 'Hens won't come into lay till the spring. Tell 'em they'll have to make do with powdered.'

Victor didn't think much of that for an answer. 'Might as well be eating rubber,' he said.

'It's rubber or nothing!' the farmer told him. 'Roll on peacetime, eh?'

It was galling to have customers waiting and no goods to sell them, especially as the Skibbereen had just talked his way into opening the gate on a consignment of tinned peaches and had then sold them on himself without offering anyone else so much as a single tin. From time to time he called on the entire gang to assist, including Victor and Phossie, so they were obviously still in his employ – but he did them no favours.

'We can go hang, you notice,' Phossie grumbled, as they mooched round the corner to the pub. 'He don't care. No skin off his nose.' Then his tone changed abruptly. 'Oh Christ!'

'What?' Vic asked, following his friend's frightened gaze. 'What is it?'

It was two military policemen, red caps bold in the

light from the pub windows, striding along the road in their menacingly purposeful way.

'I'm off!' Phossie said, and disappeared into the darkness of the nearest alley.

Now who's going to pay for the beer? Vic thought crossly. With few goods of his own to sell and the Skibbereen providing fewer opportunities, he was rather short of cash at the moment and he needed every penny he could scrape together now that he was taking Spitfire out. The final push he'd promised himself at Christmas was still eluding him, although they went to the pictures at least once a week. We're all grinding to a halt, he thought as he walked on to the pub, and that's bad for trade. People won't buy things when they're feeling low. What we need is something to give us a lift. A victory or something. In the meantime, he'd have to find someone else to stand the round that evening.

But the lift they needed didn't come until the beginning of March, when the snow had thawed and spring had finally arrived. Then and at last, the news they all wanted to hear was blazed across the front page. The US 3rd Army had crossed the Rhine. Now, with the Russians over the River Oder and within forty miles of Berlin, the Allied trap was closing around the hated Third Reich at last.

'Great stuff!' Bob said, when he'd read it. 'The beginning of the end.'

'Can't be more than a few months now,' Sis agreed. 'We could have our general election by the summer.'

And Steve will be home for it, Barbara thought. Oh it *was* good news. Just keep him safe till it's all over, she prayed. Thass all I want.

Even Heather raised a smile.

And in his dark kitchen in the Isle of Dogs, Victor was delighted. But once he'd scanned the headlines, he went on to read an article lower down the page, his attention caught by the new and exciting word 'pre-fabricated'.

*We have a chance to rebuild 1,000,000 damaged
homes, or to replace them with new pre-fabricated
houses. Now what about these emergency houses?
What are they like? Work will start on them as
soon as the war is over and there are plans to
build more than a million. I have seen the full-
sized model myself and steps are being taken to
make sure that a good number of housewives have
a chance of expressing their views about them.
Currently on view at the following sites . . .'*

This is it! he thought. This is the push I need. I'll
promise her a home of her own. She'll never be able to
resist *that*. Not after living in the North End. That's a
clincher. More than that stupid soldier will *ever* be able
to offer her.

He read on, avidly, hoping they'd give some indica-
tion what the rent would be. But they only said it was
'*likely to be reasonable*' and hinted that there would be
a list for prospective tenants. He wasn't deterred.
However much it was, he could afford it. He'd take her
to see one of them the minute he could arrange it and
he'd put his name on the list the minute it was opened.
I'll write and ask her to the Lyceum, he thought. If I
play my cards right, I bet she'll come dancing now.
Then I'll tell her about the houses while we're on the
floor.

It was a cunning letter.

*Good news about the Rhine crossing. I bet you are
all pleased as Punch. Me and a few friends are
going to the Lyceum dancing on Saturday to
celebrate. Would you like to join us? It is a good
place. I told you about it before if you remember.
It is in the Strand where the GI's go. I think you
would enjoy it. I shall understand if you do not
feel up to it yet. I do not want to put you under any
pressure. I shall be at our usual meeting place at*

313

eight o'clock and if you would like to come with us
I would be happy to take you.

It was delivered by second post the next afternoon
when Barbara was in her bedroom rereading some of
Steve's letters, the way she often did when she was
feeling low or lonely – as she was at that moment
because the good news had made her too aware of how
much she missed him. It was nearly time for her to go to
work, for she was on late turn that day, but there was
just time to read one more. The bundle lay on his brown
counterpane with its red ribbon untied, and naturally,
the letter in her hand was his one-and-only love letter. '*I
could never forget you*,' she read, eager for the words to
warm her. '*You are under my skin. I remember
everything about you, how you look, how you smell,
how you feel . . . You are my own dear darling . . .*' But
oddly, and for the first time ever, the warmth didn't
begin, the familiar, necessary magic wasn't working,
and what was worse, when she tried to remember him,
the details of his face were vague, as if the memory of
him was fading like the ink on the page. It was so
horrible the tears stung in her eyes. I can't be forgetting
him, she thought. Thass not possible. Not when I love
him so much. Not when the war's nearly over.

Their wedding album was still standing on his
bookshelf, white as snow among the blues and oranges
of his collection. She took it down quickly, and opened
it to gaze hungrily at his recorded face, but there was
distance in that image too. It seemed an age ago, as if
they were two different people. She turned the page,
hoping for better with another photograph, and there
was the group picture, with Aunt Becky holding on to
her hat, and Mr Wilkins smiling sheepishly, and Mrs
Wilkins with that awful disapproving look on her face.
She didn't like me then, Barbara remembered, and she
don't like me much more now. Not if the truth be told.
We put up with each other, thass all, but deep down she

314

ain't changed. She give me just the same look every time I go out, as if I got no right to enjoy myself. If it wasn't for the odd trip to the pictures now and then I reckon I'd go potty living here. Oh if only they'd let Steve home for a day or two.

And at that moment she heard the letter fall through the letter box and rushed down the stairs at once to pick it up, thinking of Steve all the way. It was quite a surprise to find that it was from Victor Castlemain, for although they went to the pictures every week, he never wrote to her.

But she was glad of the letter just the same. The thought of going dancing again was very tempting and they'd certainly got something to celebrate. She knew it would annoy Mrs Wilkins – if she ever found out about it – but Steve wouldn't mind. He'd told her to go out and enjoy herself. She'd read the letter just a few minutes ago. '*Live your life to the full,*' he'd said. And there was no harm in going out with old Victor. He never tried anything on, no kissing or saying silly things. He didn't even hold her hand, although they walked along arm in arm sometimes. It was really rather noble of him when he was still attracted by her. She'd been a bit worried about that at first, but now she took it as proof that she hadn't changed, that she would still be attractive when Steve came home. That wasn't fair to Vic but it wasn't as if she was encouraging him, and anyway he didn't seem to mind. He was a good friend.

Even so, she *did* feel a bit guilty as she walked in through the tall columns of the old theatre in the Strand. Perhaps she was being heartless. Perhaps she shouldn't be out dancing, when Norman was drowned and poor Betty'd been killed and Steve was still in France. But then they were inside and the band was playing 'Pennsylvania Six Five Thousand' and the place was so loud and frenetic and overcrowded that she couldn't think of anything except the excitement of the moment and the fun of dancing again.

315

There was no sign of any of Vic's friends but she had partners in plenty for the floor was packed with servicemen and Vic was an attentive companion. After the first hour the bandsmen began to mop their foreheads and the GI's threw off their tunics as the beat grew faster and faster. Barbara's hair was stuck to her forehead with sweat and her shoes were covered in dust.

'What an evenin'!' she said to Vic, as she came back to join him after an energetic jitterbug with a cheerful GI.

'Glad you came?'

Her answer was rapturous. 'You bet!'

It was the perfect moment. 'I got some news for you,' he said.

She wasn't terribly interested. After all, what could he say to beat the news she'd been reading that week? 'Have you?'

He leant towards her until he could see the reflection of his face in the pupils of her eyes. 'How would you like a home of your own?'

She laughed at him, teasing, 'You got one to sell then?'

'Not exactly,' he admitted. 'But I could find you one for rent.'

'Really?' She was still teasing but her curiosity was roused.

'Really. They're the latest thing. Pre-fabricated. They can build one in four hours.' And he showed her the cutting, walking her across to the nearest wall-light so that she could see to read it.

She was very interested but she saw a drawback straight away. 'I wouldn't be eligible though, would I?'

'Why not?'

'That says here, Londoners an' their families. I hain't a Londoner for a start. Nor a family.'

'They're for couples as well,' he told her. 'Service-men and their wives are gonna be top priority. People on war work. Things like that. You'd be just the sort of person they're looking for. They're putting them up on the commons already. They want to know what people think of them. I could get you a preview ticket if you'd like.'

Yes, she would, very much. 'When?'

'You tell me.'

'I hain't got a day off till Monday week,' she said. 'An' I promised to go to Bellington South in the afternoon with Aunt Sis. Would the morning be all right?'

'I'll fix it,' he said. 'Wanna dance?' And was thrilled by how happily she stepped into his arms.

CHAPTER TWENTY-FIVE

The prefabs stood in a row along the edge of the
common, between the pavement and an avenue of
limes, each with its own plot of garden around it,
defined by a tiny picket fence, each with a flat roof, a tin
chimney, walls made of plain grey panels and green
doors and windows, neat and new like a line of well-
wrapped parcels. One of them had net curtains in the
windows and a long queue of people waiting on the
front path.

'What d'you think?' Vic said happily, smiling
towards them as if he'd designed and built them
himself.

'They're smashing,' Barbara said. 'Look at all the
trees 'longside. Thass like bein' in the country.' They
reminded her of the trees in the Walks in Lynn, so
straight and tall and shapely and all putting out new
leaf, pale green and tender in the gentle sunshine, the
way things ought to be. And that made her think of
Steve and the way they'd kissed under the trees all those
long, long months ago. More than a year. 'What a place
to live!'

'Wait till you see inside,' Vic said, leading her
towards the queue. 'By all accounts that's first rate.'

It was a long wait, but the sunshine was warm and
the air balmy and they had plenty to talk about –
schooldays in Lynn, the characters they'd met at work
there, the awful houses in the North End, how different
it was from London – so the time passed pleasantly.
Barbara noticed that people were being allowed into the
building six at a time so there was obviously plenty of
room inside. The queue shuffled forward at steady

intervals, and eventually it was their turn. Victor produced two tickets from his inside pocket and they were in.

If the outside of the house was like a well painted box, the inside was a dream. Barbara walked from room to room in a daze, living room, bathroom, three bedrooms and all so neat and uncluttered and easy to keep clean. Most of the furniture was built into the walls and came with the house, drawers and wardrobes in the bedroom and cupboards in the living room on either side of a gas fire that would keep the place warm without all that filthy business of raking ashes and blackleading a grate. There was even a built-in table that you could fold back into the wall when you weren't using it. Wouldn't Aunt Becky like *that*!

But it was the kitchen that set the seal on the place. It was the cleanest, neatest kitchen she'd ever seen, with a brand new gas cooker, a modern copper for washing the clothes, a geyser to provide hot water whenever you wanted it, an entire wall of shelves and cupboards where you could keep enough food for a family and still have room left over, and wonder of wonders, a small white cupboard that turned out to be one of those new refrigerators. The young woman guiding them round explained how useful it would be. 'No more runny butter in the summer. Nice fresh eggs – once they're off the ration. Meat and fish as fresh as it was when you bought it. You can't get flies in a refrigerator. I think it's the best thing that's ever been invented.'

'So do I,' Barbara agreed. 'Thass really hygienic.'

'Are you putting your name down?' the young woman asked Victor.

'That's up to the lady,' he said, looking at Barbara. 'Would you like to live in a place like this?'

The sunlight was streaming in through the kitchen window, warming the nape of her neck, enriching the scarlet of her coat, spangling her dark hair with sharp white highlights. 'Wouldn't I just!' she said.

319

'In that case,' their guide told them, 'follow the arrows to the next house along. If you'll give your particulars to the gentleman there, he'll see to it. His name's Mr Fishpool.'

'I'll do it for you,' Vic offered, giving Barbara the full force of his most charming smile. 'You stay here. See all you want to.' And was gone before she could thank him.

She was loath to leave the place, even though she knew she was holding other people up by staying. She could imagine herself living there, sitting on that comfortable sofa of an evening, in front of the fire, with Steve beside her, listening to the wireless, with his books on those shelves, and the table folded away; sleeping with him in that neat bedroom, making love in that bed. Oh to be in his arms again! It made her yearn so keenly she had to walk out of the bedroom into the bathroom to recover. She looked at the white geyser on the wall, deliberately turning her mind away from thoughts she couldn't handle. Imagine having hot water on tap, she told herself. There'd be no more boiling kettles to wash up if we rented a place like this. We could have a bath every day. It would be like living in a palace.

The next group of six was drifting in through the door, all wide-eyed and open-mouthed. She would have to go. But I'll be back, she told herself. I'll be back with Steve. *This* is the sort of house we're going to live in, the minute they say we can, the minute the war's over, the minute he's out of the army. The thought of it made her so happy that she danced out of the house, turning her face to the sun like a child, eyes widened and lips parted. She couldn't wait to write and tell him about it.

Victor was loitering under one of the lime trees. He'd unbuttoned his jacket, and pushed his fedora to the back of his head, and he was wiping his forehead with his handkerchief. He's getting hot, she thought, poor ol' bor, and he's been really kind fixing all this up for me, getting the tickets and giving them the particulars and everything.

'All set?' he asked, as she smiled towards him.

'Yep. Did you give them my address or Steve's?' she said.

It had been such a casual question that she was surprised to see how shifty it made him look. 'Oh, home address, I think,' he said vaguely. 'Anyway, that's all taken care of. What say we go an' have a bite to eat? You got time, ain't you.'

'Thass no good giving them my address,' she told him. 'Thass got to be Steve's. He'll be head a' household. You always have head a' household on the rent book. Wait there. I'll see to it. I won't take long.'

He caught at her coat, trying to prevent her. 'There's no need, Spitfire. You can tell them when they write, can't you. Let's go an' have dinner, eh?'

But she shook him off. 'In a minute,' she said, on her way to the office. 'I must see to this first.' A mistake had been made and it had to be put right there and then. She couldn't walk away and leave the wrong name on the application form. Especially when it was Steve's name that was missing.

Mr Fishpool was small and precise and agreed that the alteration should be made. 'What was the name, madam?' he asked.

She told him and he searched through his list. But he couldn't find a Mrs Wilkins. 'Not on today's list, I'm afraid.'

Barbara couldn't understand it. She looked round for Victor and an explanation, but he hadn't followed her into the office. 'That was onny a few minutes ago,' she said. 'That must be there.'

Mr Fishpool turned the address book towards her. 'I can't see it,' he said. 'Perhaps you'd like to check.'

He was right. There was no Wilkins on the page. The name that jumped into her eyes, bringing irritation with it, was Castlemain. And Mr and Mrs Castlemain what's more. What's he playin' at? she thought furiously. I told him to put *my* name down, mine an' Steve's. Not his.

But she kept calm. 'I can see what 'tis,' she said. 'Thass my friend. Mr Castlemain. He was supposed to give you my name as well as his. He must have forgot.'

Mr Fishpool remembered Mr Castlemain. 'Ah yes,' he said. 'The young man on war work. We had quite a chat. Is your husband on war work too? It makes a difference to your application.'

'My husband', she said with immense pride, 'is in France with the 21st Army. He's one of the Desert Rats.'

'In that case,' Mr Fishpool told her courteously, 'allow me to say that I hope you will be allocated one of the very first houses we have to offer.'

So Steve's name and army address were written in the book with his home address beneath and a new application form was completed in every detail and signed with a flourish. Then she strode out into the sunshine, to have it out with Victor Castlemain.

He was standing on the common, biting his nails, and feeling horribly apprehensive. When she'd gone rushing off he'd been in two minds whether to go or stay, knowing she was bound to find out what he'd done and fearing her wrath. He'd decided against such cowardice and had hung on and thought up an excuse, but he was very uncomfortable. It had never occurred to him that his carefully laid plans could be wrecked so easily. He'd planned the conversation they were going to have, right down to the last sentence, when she was going to agree to share the pre-fab with him, and now, here she was striding across the grass, scowling at him, and despite the brave face he put on, he was inwardly quailing.

'What's all this squit about you bein' on war work?' she said.

To be attacked from such an unexpected quarter made him huffily defensive. 'Well so I am. That *is* war work. Food for the front line, sort of thing. Supplies for the citizen army. If that wasn't for people like me you'd all be half starved. We're morale boosters.'

'You're a spiv!' she said, cutting him down to size. 'That got nothin' to do with boosting morale. I never heard such a load of ol' squit. You nick things an' sell 'em to make money.'

'I got you a goose,' he defended himself.

'Yes, all right, so you did,' she allowed, mellowing towards him. 'Which I 'ppreciate.'

'Well there you are then.'

But her attack wasn't over. 'I got another bone to pick with you though, Victor Castlemain. I thought you were going to put *my* name down on that list. Thass what you said, wasn't it? An' what do I find when I get there?'

'I had to give them my name to get the tickets,' he explained, using his prepared defence. 'They were like gold dust. You wouldn't believe how many people were after them. I had to sign for them. Never known that before. And when I got into that office I had to hand them over, first thing they asked for, so I couldn't make the application in another name, could I, or they'd have smelled a rat.'

'But you signed it Mr and *Mrs* Castlemain,' she said, only partially placated. And teased him, 'Who's this missus? Why hain't we been introduced?'

'That was all married couples on that list,' he explained. 'I couldn't just put my name. They'd never have considered it.'

'I don' know what you thought you were playin' at,' she rebuked him. 'You should have put my name an' Steve's. Thass what you should've done. I could've lost it altogether if I hadn't gone back. They didn't teach you much sense at that ol' grammar school uv yours.'

'It would've all come out in the wash,' he said. 'I mean, I'd have changed it when they wrote to me, if that's what you wanted. You only had to say. I mean, you wanted to come here, didn't you? You wanted to see them.'

'Not if I had to pretend to be married to you,' she said, half teasing, half cross.

He drew himself up to his full height, his face serious. 'There was a time when you *were* going to be married to me,' he said.

It hurt her to be reminded. 'That was boy an' gal stuff.'

'I meant it,' he said passionately. 'I still do.'

This was getting too intense for comfort. 'Oh come on, Vic,' she demurred. 'Thass all over now.'

He took a breath before he answered her, calculating the risk. 'It needn't be,' he urged. 'I mean what's to stop us moving in together if I got one of these houses? Would that be such a bad thing?'

She was shocked. 'You hain't seriously suggesting it, surely?'

'I don't see why not,' he said. 'Lots of gals do.'

'I hain't lots of gals.'

'Look,' he urged. 'Times are changing. That ain't like the old days. People do all sorts of things now they'd never have dreamed of before the war. I could give you a much better life than you got at the moment. Good food. Place of your own to live. Pretty clothes. A car. I could look after you. It won't be for ever. I know that. But for a little while, just till the war's over. We're both on our own an' we ain't exactly strangers, now are we?'

The changing expressions on his face told her more than his words could ever have done – hope in the widening of his eyes, affection in the softening of his mouth, a shadow of vulnerability. Poor Vic, she understood. That *was* what he planned. He really thought I'd move in with him if he got me a house. And she knew that it wasn't just that she attracted him, he loved her, and this situation was as much her fault as

324

his, because she'd been going out with him as though
they were courting, and she'd never told him how she
felt about Steve. I should have explained everything
before I got married, she realised. I hain't been fair to
him.

'I'm Steve's wife,' she told him, surprising herself by
how gentle she was being. 'I belong to him now. Even
if I wanted to move in with you – which I don't, I must
be honest – I couldn't. You do see that, don't you?'
And she put out a hand to touch his arm, to calm him or
reassure him, she wasn't sure which. And was upset to
discover that he was trembling.

'I'm as good a man as that soldier,' he said, pulling
away from her, stiff-necked and offended. 'Any day of
the week. Better probably.'

She had a sudden searing vision of that soldier,
walking towards her across Tuesday Market Square,
long legs striding, arms outstretched to catch her up and
hold her close, brown eyes smiling, lips parted. Those
dear soft lips. She could feel them kissing her, could
remember the taste of them, the smell of his skin as they
lay cuddled together in that ferny bed. Oh my dear,
dear, darling.

'But he's the one I love,' she said. 'I'm so sorry Vic.'

To be rejected was bad enough but to be pitied was
worse. Much, much worse. 'You're a fool!' he shouted
at her. 'You hain't got the sense you were born with.
Anyone else would've jumped at an offer like that.
Jumped at it. What's the point of staying with your in-
laws when you could have a house of your own? Thass
just false pride. I thought better of you than that. Think
about it, Spitfire! I'm offering you a really good life,
dancing, pictures, good food, anything you want. But
no! What do you do? You turn round an' kick me in the
teeth. Treat me like dirt.'

His anger upset her. 'No,' she tried. 'I hain't. I just
said . . .'

325

But now that his fury had broken, he roared on. 'Kick me in the bloody teeth. Treat me like dirt. Well I ain't dirt. I'm as good a man as he is any day of the week. Dammit I won't be pitied!'

She knew he'd get worse if she tried to argue. This was a North-Ender's temper and she just had to let him holler it out. 'I got to go,' she said. 'Tram to catch.' And set off at once across the common, striding like a man, dark hair bouncing, red coat bright against the new green grass.

Her departure stopped him in mid roar. 'Where are you going?' he called.

'Bellington South,' she called back. 'I told you.'

'Well sod you then!' he growled. 'See if I care. Thass your loss. I made the offer. Can't do no more than that.'

As he growled, a tram came buzzing along the rails on the road below and she saw it and began to run towards it. There was no bringing her back now. No making her see sense. He couldn't understand how this had happened. This is all her fault, he thought, watching as she darted into the middle of the road. She behaves as if she's queen an' everybody else is dirt. She hain't got an ounce of gratitude in her body. She got too big for her boots up here in London. She need taking down a peg or two. Showing who's boss. Anger against her reinstated him a little, restoring his self-worth. She needn't think she can put me down. I'm more than a match for *her*.

The Humber was waiting for him by the kerbside. Nice obedient cars, Humbers. He got in, turned on the ignition, enjoyed the hum of the engine, patted the leather of the passenger seat, noticing that the sun had warmed it, preened in the pride of ownership. I'd like to see that soldier of hers in a Humber, he thought, as he drove off. I bet he hain't even got a pushbike. An' he'll never get her a good house. Never in a thousand years. Well she can live in a slum for all I care. Serve her right for turning me down. How could she do such a thing? His thoughts were in such a turmoil of rejection and frustration that he had no idea where he was going. He was driving away and that was enough.

CHAPTER TWENTY-SIX

Heather Wilkins had spent that Monday morning doing the weekly wash all by herself and getting steadily more irritable. By the time she stopped for a slice of toast and a nice little pot of tea, she was hot and sweaty and her back was playing her up something rotten. She could have done with some help or at least a bit of company but Bob was on nights so he was still in bed getting his sleep, and Barbara was out visiting some friend or other. Wouldn't you know it! She'd had the grace to rinse through her own bits and pieces before she left but it wouldn't have hurt her to stay in and lend a hand with the sheets and towels. She was getting more and more selfish these days.

Now that the weather was warmer, the steam from the copper permeated the flat. She'd hung the washing in the garden – for the first time in months – but the bathroom walls were streaming with water and the air on the landing was dank and unpleasant.

Better open a few windows, she thought, and tiptoed into the bedroom to do it while it was in her mind. Bob was lying in a hump under the covers, sound asleep and snoring, so she raised the sash very gently so as not to wake him. As she did so, she looked down idly into the street below – and there was that horrible black Humber cruising towards the house. Not the fly in the ointment again, she thought, glaring at it. That's the last straw on a washday. I thought we'd got rid of him long since, damned nuisance. Well she's not here so he'll just have to go away. Maybe he won't stop.

But no. He parked the car, leant across the passenger seat, rolled down the window and looked out. He'd seen her before she could step back from the window. So when he waved and called hello, she had to go down and answer the door to him or he'd have woken Bob.

She wasn't particularly gracious. 'What's brought *you* here then?' she said, blocking the entrance.

Until she spoke he'd had no idea. He simply followed his anger and the car had brought him to her house. But at the sound of her voice his confusion cleared and he knew exactly why he'd come. It was to be revenged. That's what it was. To pay Barbara out for turning him down. To put her in her place. 'I got something to tell you,' he said.

'She's out,' she told him brusquely.

'I know. Thass *you* I come to see.'

There was something about his expression and the tone of his voice that stirred her curiosity. 'You'd better come in then, I suppose,' she said. 'Don't make a noise. My husband's asleep.'

It was quiet in the kitchen and there was a pleasant breeze blowing through the half-open window. She gave him tea and indicated that he should sit at the table. Then they both waited.

'Well?' she said at last.

'Thass about your daughter-in-law, Mrs Wilkins,' he told her.

'I gathered that,' she said impatiently. 'What about her?'

'She hain't what she ought to be.'

He was gratified to see that she looked pleased to hear it. 'Tell me something I don't know.'

'She was out with me this morning. Did you know that?'

'No,' Heather said grimly. 'I didn't but I might have guessed.'

'We went to see a house.'

That shocked her. 'You did *what*?'

'That was her idea,' he said quickly. 'I didn't plan it, to tell the truth. I was against it. But you know how she

329

go on. I thought she'd holler if I didn't take her. She's a rare one for hollerin'.'

Heather could believe that too. But she'd thought of something else. 'I suppose you're the one who bought the goose.'

He admitted it with a self-deprecating smile.

'And the one she's been going to the pictures with.'

He admitted that too, this time assuming an apologetic expression. 'I'm ever so sorry. You weren't supposed to know. She made me wait for her round the corner, so's you wouldn't see the car.'

'Artful baggage! And you've been to see a house, you said.'

Her response was so encouraging he was beginning to enjoy himself. 'She *would* have me put my name on the tickets,' he confided. 'Well not just *my* name actually. I had to pretend we were married. Thass what I came to tell you. Look, I'll show you.' He took the two stubs from his pocket and laid them on the table in front of her.

She read them and grew pink-cheeked with anger. '*Mr and Mrs Castlemain.*' The effrontery of it. Didn't I say she was a bad lot? Hard as nails and bold as brass.

'An' thass not all,' Vic said, when she looked up, 'I'm afraid.'

'Have another cup of tea,' she said kindly, 'and tell me all about it.'

So Victor took tea and revenge and they went on enjoying his confidences. He described how worried he'd been to be going out with a married woman – 'I mean, I wouldn't have done it if it hadn't been her. Knowing her all these years, you see. We been like brother an' sister' – how concerned he was in case people assumed he'd been two-timing Steve – 'I met him when he was in Lynn, a fine man' – how shocking it was that she'd put her name down for a house without consulting her own husband – 'An' not even in her own name.'

'Whose then?'

'Well . . .' he pretended to dither. 'Look I'm sorry to have to tell you this. I wouldn't if it wasn't for . . .'

She insisted. 'Whose?'

'Well mine actually. Mr and Mrs Castlemain, same as on the ticket.'

She was enraged. 'I can't understand it. I really can't. I mean, what's she playing at?'

'I probably shouldn't say this, Mrs Wilkins,' Vic said, leaning towards her earnestly and enjoying the drama of what he was going to say, 'but I think she wants a second string to her bow. Just in case, sort of thing. I think thass all I am. A second string to her bow.'

The implication of it made Heather widen her eyes in anger but before she could answer she became aware that Bob was standing beside them, yawning and scratching his grey hair. They'd been so absorbed they hadn't heard him walk in. 'Any tea, Mother?' he said.

Heather looked up at him, her face full of satisfaction. 'You'll never believe what I've just heard,' she said.

Vic stood up before she could start the story. 'I'd better be off,' he said. 'Time for work, sort of thing.' There was something about Mr Wilkins' expression that made him uneasy. He'd done a good job with the old girl. No point running risks and spoiling everything. 'I'll see myself out. Thanks for the tea.' And went at once.

'What was all that about?' Bob asked, settling into his chair and reaching for the morning paper.

'I got a nice little lamb's kidney for your breakfast,' Heather said, getting up to cook it. 'There's tea in the pot. I'll tell you while it's cooking.' And did, in furious detail.

Bob heard her out patiently but with a sinking heart. 'Done to a turn,' she said setting the kidneys before him. 'Just how you like 'em. So what d'you think a' that?'

'What I always think. You're a very good cook. First rate. I dunno how you do it.'

'You know what I mean,' she rebuked him, as she sat down again. 'What d'you think of all this carry-on?'

He chewed his first mouthful thoughtfully. 'Don't let's be hasty,' he advised. 'Let's hear what *she*'s got to say before we judge.'

'She can't say anything,' Heather told him with bitter satisfaction. 'Not now. Didn't I tell you she was a bad lot? All that secrecy. I knew there was something going on.'

'You've only got his word for it,' Bob pointed out. 'I wouldn't trust him particularly. He's got an axe to grind. An' he's a spiv.'

'That's right,' Heather said crossly. 'Take her part. I should!'

'Somebody's got to,' he said, giving her his wry grin. 'She's not here to answer for herself.'

'Wouldn't make any difference if she was. There's no answer she can give.'

'Well wait an' see, eh? Give her a chance.'

'I've given her a darn sight too many chances, if you ask me,' Heather said, looking fierce. 'We should've spoken out right at the start, when she would go off dancing with every Tom, Dick an' Harry. I knew it wasn't right. I told you so at the time if you remember.'

'Yes,' he admitted, 'you did. You told me she was a good brave girl as well.' And when she scowled, 'You came back here after the rocket an' you said she was a good brave girl.'

She had to agree, although she didn't want to. 'Oh she's brave enough. I grant you that. But she's flighty. Off with other men. There's our poor Steve out there being shot at an' here she is mucking about with other men. That's what *I* object to. Any mother would.' Her cheeks were flushed with righteous indignation, her mouth a determined line, her eyes daring him to disagree.

It was politic to change the subject. 'You got any more tea?' he asked, holding up his cup. 'I'm dry to me boot-straps this morning.'

Outside in the garden their poor scuffed lawn was springing green again and there was a crop of London pride putting out purple flowers down by the shed. He could just see it through the bellying sheets and shirts on the washing line. 'It's a lovely day,' he said.

That was Victor's feeling too as he drove happily back to the Isle of Dogs. What a triumph! he thought. That'll teach her. She needn't think she can put me down and get away with it. I'm more than a match for her. I'm a match for anyone. I had that stupid old mawther eating out of my hands back there. Eating out of my hands. Which reminded him that he hadn't had any dinner. I'll open a tin of that American steak, he decided, the minute I get in.

But in the event the steak had to wait, for when he got to the house, Phossie was in the living room packing a suitcase. He was wearing his best suit, his hair was fairly dripping with brilliantine, and his ferrety face was closed and drawn. There were clothes strewn all over the room. The horsehair sofa was covered in shirts, the rocking chair held a pile of brand-new underwear and his spare shoes stood on the rag rug in front of the empty grate, looking as if he'd just jumped out of them.

'What's this?' Victor asked, strolling into the room. 'We goin' somewhere, are we?'

'Too many a' them bleedin' redcaps,' Phossie explained, scooping up the shirts and stuffing them into the case. 'I'm off, aren't I.'

'Off?'

'Got to get away,' Phossie said, trying to cram his shoes into the case on top of the shirts. 'One a' the buggers nearly got me. Hardly put my head out the door, had I, an' there he was.' He despaired of the shoes. 'You can have these if you like. They won't go in.'

'They're too big for me,' Vic said, visibly turning up his nose at them. 'Put them in a carrier bag. Where you going then?'

'North,' Phossie said, opening the cupboard. 'There's redcaps everywhere you look down here.'

'What about the Skibbereen? Does he know?'

Phossie pulled an old carrier bag out of the cupboard and tipped its collection of ancient wires and rusty tools onto the floor. 'Nope. You can tell him if you like. An' while you're about it, tell him them macs was perished. Right load a' rubbish they are. I haven't managed to shift one of 'em, have I, never mind twenty.'

'Thass nothing to do with me,' Vic said. 'You bought the bloody things. You tell him. Do your own dirty work.'

'Sod that fer a game a' soldiers,' Phossie said, pushing the last of his underwear into the case. 'Like I told you, it's every man fer himself in this lark.' And he bolted up the stairs.

He was going to run before I got back, Vic understood. I wasn't supposed to find him like this. I was supposed to come home to an empty house. How underhand! And I'll bet he's taken all the food. That'ud be just his style.

There were bags and cases all over the room but it didn't take him long to find the one he wanted. He tipped the contents out behind the sofa where Phossie wouldn't see it – tins, sugar, butter, tea, coffee – and stuffed the empty bag with an old cushion. Bloody thief, he thought, surveying the hoard. He wasn't gonna leave me a mouthful.

'Well best a' luck!' Phossie said, reappearing at the top of the stairs. 'I'm off now.' His case was so full he was bent over sideways by the weight of it. But he

334

gathered the rest of the bags in his other hand, found his balance and staggered for the door. 'See you around.'

'I doubt it,' Vic said, adding with heavy irony. 'Sure you ain't left nothing behind?'

Nothing but the stink of his sweat and his sodden fag-ends all over the floor and a pile of filthy clothes in the bedroom. I'm not staying here with all his rubbish, Vic told himself. He's turned it into a bloody slum. I'll go down the pub and have a liquid lunch. I've got the cash for it. There was something to be said for not taking Spitfire to dinner after all.

As he walked to the pub, he thought of the pre-fabs and remembered how neat and clean they'd been. Thass the sort of place for me to live, he thought. Not in this dump. He glowered at the street, hating it. More than half the rotten houses were empty and the terrace next to the bomb-site was just a shell, no tiles on the roof, no glass in the windows, just those horrible black walls, still standing and covered in dust. At one point he could see right through to the terrace in the next street. All right for Phossie but I'm a darn sight too good for it. I shall find somewhere else, first thing. Squaring his shoulders he strode into the pub and ordered himself a beer and a whisky chaser.

'Victor!' a voice boomed. 'Is Phossie with you?'

It was the Skibbereen. He'd recognised the smell of his cigar even before he turned and saw those broad shoulders and the bulge of that great bull-neck. The Skibbereen, sitting at the corner table with two of the gang, the tall scraggy bloke called Tiffany on his right and Mog, looking dour as ever on his left.

'He's scarpa'd,' Vic said, taking the fourth seat at their table. 'Gone north. Too many redcaps.'

'Pity,' the Skibbereen said, wiping his mouth with the back of one plump hand. 'I had a job for him.'

In his present self-satisfied mood, Vic offered his services at once. 'Give it to me then,' he said. 'I'm as good as Phossie any day of the week. Better in fact.'

335

The Skibbereen noted his boldness but wasn't impressed. 'I need someone dependable,' he said.

'That's my middle name,' Vic said.

The Skibbereen raised his eyebrows. 'You could've fooled me.'

'I know *when* to be dependable,' Vic explained. 'Which you can't say for everyone.'

'True,' the Skibbereen admitted. And considered. 'If I cut you in,' he said at last, 'I shall expect commitment.'

'You'd get it. Total.'

'Day an' night. You won't get home much.'

'That'ud suit me down to the ground,' Vic assured him. 'There's nothing to keep me here. So what's the score?'

'Hatton Garden,' the Skibbereen said. 'Diamond rings. They got an assignment coming in from Paris in a day or two. Could be big.'

Vic was very impressed but he bent his head to his beer and tried not to show it. He'd handled this too well to want to risk losing face. 'Paris, eh?'

'They're running the boat trains again, mate,' Tiffany explained, scratching the stubble on his chin. 'Started last Saturday.'

'I need a team of three,' the Skibbereen said, 'to keep an eye on the place. Visit the pubs. Chat up the locals. Tiff's in charge. He knows the form. We need all the information we can get – when it's coming in, what it's like, who's gonna be there to receive it.'

It was the chance of a lifetime. A different league. A step into the big time. Diamond rings. It would make a difference to everything. Now that he'd cut Spitfire down to size, he could start over again with her, and what better way to do it than to give her a diamond ring. A great big solitaire, like you see at the pictures. He could imagine her face as he put it on her finger. That would put him in her good books *and* knock that stupid soldier right out the equation. Oh that couldn't be better.

She'll be a bit upset with me hollerin', he thought. This will put it right.

It would have upset him to know that Barbara was writing to that stupid soldier at that very minute and that she'd forgotten all about his hollering and all about *him* as soon as she jumped aboard the tram. The clippie had turned out to be little Mrs Phipps which was a pleasant surprise and the passengers had all been on good form now that the sun was shining and the war was nearly over. One of them had missed her stop because she was so busy reminiscing about the fruit she'd enjoyed before the war and looking forward to eating it again.

'Bananas now. I like a nice banana. I'll bet you can't remember them, can you, dear. 'Course they have them dreadful dried things fer the kiddies but I can't abide 'em. Look like doggie do's, if you ask me. Puts me right off.'

'You'll 'ave your young man home soon,' another woman said to Mrs Phipps as she came darting down the stairs. 'Then I suppose we shall have to do without you.'

'You won't get rid of me as easy as all that,' Mrs Phipps said. 'Nor you, eh Barbara? She's got a young man coming home an' all, ain'tcher, duck? Any more fares pliz!'

By the time she ran across the road to Sis's flat, Barbara was singing. The placard outside the news-agent's said, '*Rhine crossing latest*' and the sun was making the shop windows dazzle and gleam all along the street. '*You'll 'ave your young man home soon.*' Oh yes. Yes please. And we can live in a pre-fab and walk on the common every evening and make love every night.

Sis met her at the top of the stairs.

'You're happy,' she said.

It was true. It was true. She was almost too happy to

explain why. 'I've just put our names down for a house. Me an' Steve's.'

'Good for you,' Sis approved. 'I'm just off to get some fish an' chips. D'you want some?'

'Yes please,' Barbara said. 'I'd come with you onny I must write and tell Steve. Oh Aunt Sis, you should have seen it.'

Sis laughed at her. 'Tell me when I get back. An' look sharp with the letter. We've got half an hour and then the others'll be here.'

'I'll be ready,' Barbara promised and she took the stairs two at a time, steep though they were, and rushed to the dresser to find pen and paper.

She was still writing when Sis returned with their meal. She couldn't stop. There was such a lot she wanted to tell him that the words tumbled onto the paper, detail after detail, while they were fresh in her mind. She put the plate of fish and chips at her elbow and wrote and ate at the same time, laughing when Sis warned her she'd get indigestion. She'd only just signed off with a row of kisses when Mr Craxton arrived to say that the others were waiting downstairs and hoped they were ready. Then naturally once she'd posted her precious letter, she spent the entire journey to Bellington South telling them all about her discovery.

'What a difference good housing is going to make,' Mr Craxton said, smiling at her.

'What a difference these pre-fabricated houses will make,' Christine agreed, patting her bun to make sure it was still neatly pinned. 'If they really *can* erect them in four days it will be the answer to the housing problem. I wouldn't mind one myself.'

The bus was pulling up. 'We're here,' Sis warned. 'Now we'd better be serious. This is Bellington South don't forget, not New Cross.'

It was hard for Barbara to be serious that afternoon, particularly as she couldn't see the point of it. If this was a safe Tory seat, the way everyone said, and they were going to lose it, no matter what any of them did, why not lark about and have fun?

But they were all rearranging their faces. Christine was trying so hard she looked quite solemn, Sis was wearing her stern expression, the two men from the Union were pulling at their ties and Mr Craxton looked as if he was going to make a speech and was memorising his notes. As she followed them from the bus Barbara wondered what it was about this place that was making them so ill at ease.

It didn't take her long to find out. The main street was the most affluent she'd ever seen, wide and tree lined and full of classy shops, and the side streets were enough to make *anyone* feel out of place. No old-fashioned terraces here and no soot-blackened walls, but big houses in semi-detached pairs, looking new and prosperous, as though they'd just been built, their roof-tiles clean of lichen and their paint hardly faded at all. Each one had two wide bow windows, one above the other with very white nets and, here and there, the occasional aspidistra in a fat pot, and they all had big front gardens, as spruce as parks, each with a square of green lawn and carefully attended shrubs, holly and lilac and spotted laurel and forsythia in full bloom, yellow as butter.

I can see what Sis means, Barbara thought, taking it all in. You'd need a really good income to live in a place like this. That's as far above New Cross as New Cross is above the North End. And she wondered why people as wealthy as this would have anything to do with the Labour Party and felt quite apprehensive as they stood on the doorstep waiting to be allowed in.

Carpets on the floor, so thick that she couldn't hear a footfall, velvet curtains at the window, plump sofas covered in chintz, bone china on the table, very pretty and horribly delicate, and the lady of the house, who was called Pauline, wearing a twin-set and pearls. But she welcomed them kindly, saying how good it was of

339

them 'to come all this way to make our acquaintance'. And she'd made a carrot cake for the occasion.

'We're a very small group, as you see,' she said as she signalled to them to sit in her sumptuous armchairs. 'Eight in all, but Mr and Mrs Coome Merton couldn't join us. Pressure of business.' And she began to make the introductions.

Barbara tried to be sensible and pay attention – saying hello to Sophie Something-or-other, a librarian, a teacher called Brian, a very old man who wore spats and said he was a chemist – but it was too hard and after a while her mind simply swam back to the pre-fabs and she was off in a dream again. She drank tea, ate a very small slice of the carrot cake, answered questions and made conversation as well as she could, and finally followed her hostess out into the road for the 'short walk to our community hall' where Mr Craxton was to be formally accepted as the Labour candidate for the constituency.

The dream lasted all through the meeting. She woke from it twice, to applaud Mr Craxton and to say goodbye, but for the rest of the time she was striding across the common, arm in arm with her darling, kissing under the lime trees in the Walks, far away in the hop fields, making love in their tile-hung cottage, back together again, living and loving in their nice new pre-fab.

She was still in her own world when she put her key in the lock at Childeric Road and drifted up the stairs to the flat.

There was no sign of her father-in-law. He must have gone to work. But Mrs Wilkins was sitting in the armchair by the fire, sewing a patch onto one of his work shirts. Her work-basket stood open on the table and the arm of the chair was stuck with pins.

'Oh,' she said coldly, 'there you are!'

Barbara was still so happy she missed the warning

signs. 'Thass been a lovely day,' she said. 'You'll never guess what I did this morning.'

'That's where you're wrong, young lady,' Heather said, biting off her thread, and now there was no mistaking the disapproval in her voice. 'I know exactly what you did.'

Barbara decided not to be daunted. She'd obviously done something to annoy – not staying in to help with the washing probably – but it was trivial compared to her news. 'I put my name down for a house.'

Eyes narrowed. '*Your* name?'

'No. All right. *Our* name then. Thass where I was this morning. Wait till I tell you about it.'

'I know where you were,' Heather told her sternly. 'And who you were *with* which is more to the point. Our name indeed! A fine thing! I always said you were a flighty piece, and I've been proved right. Our name!'

Barbara couldn't understand why she was under attack. Proved right? she thought. Our name? What's she on about? Proved right about what?

Her puzzled expression exasperated Heather. 'Don't start putting on an act,' she warned. 'Don't pretend you don't know. He's told me all about it.'

The fury of her words made Barbara feel panicky. 'What am I supposed to have done?' she said, her heart racing.

'You know perfectly well.'

'No. I don't. I don't know what you're on about.'

'Gadding about with your fancy man for a start. Off dancing all hours with every Tom, Dick an' Harry and the car hidden round the corner where I can't see it. That's nice, isn't it. *Very* nice!'

Understanding dropped the pieces into an ugly picture. 'Oh I see,' Barbara said. 'Thass Victor Castlemain's doin'. He been here telling tales. Well let me tell you thass all squit what he say. You don't want to tek no notice of *him*.'

'So you didn't go dancing with him. Is that what you're saying?'

The question made her feel cornered. 'Well yes,' she had to admit, 'we went dancin'. There's no harm in that.'

'No harm?' Heather roared. 'No harm? An' my Steve out there being shot at. He could be lying dead this moment, all on his own out there. Lying dead, and you say there's no harm.'

'Don't say that!' Barbara cried, anguished by the awfulness of the image she was conjuring. 'You hain't to say it. I won't have it!'

'You won't have it! You? How dare you speak to me like that! You got no right to open your mouth in this house. Carrying on with your fancy men. You're just a little tart. That's all you are! A little tart. A trollop!'

To be called names at the end of such a day was such a shock it made Barbara shake. She fought back at once and with all the force she could muster. 'Oh I see whass goin' on,' she cried. 'This is because I married your son. Thass what 'tis. Thass got nothin' to do with dancing. You never wanted me for a daughter-in-law in the first place. Did you? Never. Well let me tell you, there's nothin' you can do about it. He's married me an' thass that. If you don't like it you can lump it.' And because she was very near tears, and she certainly wasn't going to give this woman the satisfaction of seeing her weep, she ran from the room.

Left on her own, Heather picked up the shirt and finished off the last hem, pulling the cotton through the cloth in sharp rasping tugs. She was taut with anger and her stitches were all over the place. Lump it! she thought. How bloody rude! I'll make you swallow those words my girl. Lump it indeed. We'll see about *that*. I shall tell my Steve. You needn't think you can shout at me like that an' get away with it.

The flat was very quiet. As far as she could tell, her adversary seemed to be locked away in her bedroom for the night, so she got up and found pen and ink and writing paper. I should have done this months ago, she thought, as she arranged the paper on the table. I should have put paid to it then. We wouldn't have had all this trouble, if I'd written sooner. And she began while her anger was still high.

Dear Steven,
    I am sorry to have to write to you like this. I would not do it only I think you ought to know. It is not fair to be doing this to you behind your back, that is what I think anyway. I have kept quiet about it for months for fear of upsetting you. What would you say if I did not tell you? Of course there might not be any truth in it, you will have to make up your own mind. Your father says not to tell you but I do not think that is fair to you. The thing is what you ought to know is your Barbara has been messing around with another man. He says you met him in King's Lynn. His name is Victor Castlemain. I have spoken to her about it.
    I hope this finds you in good health as it leaves me,
    Your loving mother,
    H. Wilkins.

CHAPTER TWENTY-SEVEN

Steve's two letters were delivered to him just as the brigade was preparing to cross the Rhine. There was so much to do he knew he would never find time to read them both so he stuffed his mother's letter unopened into his breast pocket next to his fags and skimmed through Barbara's quickly where he stood. Her enthusiasm rose from the page like sunshine. *'A home of our own! Think of it!'* But there was too much going on – Jeeps darting about on either side of him, sergeant majors roaring, trucks being inched into line, the tankies chafing to be off – and he couldn't concentrate on anything except the job in hand. Good though her news was, it would have to wait until he was over the river.

The crossing was a massive undertaking, almost as complicated as the landing had been, and it was organised with the same attention to detail and the same air cover, for the Rhine at this point was more than a quarter of a mile wide and still a hazard. The mere sight of it was enough to show them what an obstacle it had been. It reduced all the other rivers they'd encountered to mere streams, from the Seine to the Maas. But now that the initial assault was successfully over, the Allied armies had it well under control.

The meadows leading down to the water's edge had been marked out into assembly areas, with the usual white tape, and there were redcaps everywhere directing the traffic, which was endless and complicated, for it wasn't just troops and armoured vehicles and tanks and guns that were being shipped across, but supplies and support groups too, trucks carrying blood-banks, long lines of Red Cross ambulances, lorries piled with ammunition, crates full of food. There were Jeeps jauntily bouncing down the slope beside the convoys, even a bulldozer sent to scour out another exit route on the further side, but only one hastily constructed pontoon bridge to take it all across.

Downstream the engineers were constructing a second bridge, working with difficulty against a strong-running current. It was a bright spring day and the river looked totally peaceful, sky-blue and olive-green and spangled with sunlight. Above it, a cloudless sky was criss-crossed by the white contrails of the Spitfires and Typhoons that were taking it in turns to patrol, just in case the Luftwaffe should dare to put in an appearance.

Not that anyone in the brigade seriously thought they would. Not now. Not in the face of such fire power. No matter how many doubts they'd secretly entertained during the ten-month slog to this crossing, now that they'd arrived they were sure of their victory. The slogans they'd painted on the sides of their vehicles were evidence of that, cocky and cheerful and full of confidence. *'And you'd never have thought it would happen!' 'Rhine Ferry – No Charge, No Sandwiches and No Risk!' 'Montgomery Express, London to Berlin'.*

Their good spirits were infectious. Even Dusty was cheerful. 'Here we go!' he said, as a redcap waved their TCV towards the pontoon. 'Next stop Berlin!'

The crossing went smoothly and so did the drive inland, for the assault troops had obviously established a wide front all along the river bank. They passed several riverside farms but most of them had been shattered by artillery fire and those that were still intact had prominent white flags draped from their remaining windows. It was plain that the civilians in the area had been thoroughly cowed and when the column turned off into a belt of woodland, they could see the reason why. As well as the river crossing, there had been a massive airborne landing here too. The fields were still full of

345

gliders, lying where they'd landed, some tipped over on their wings, some crumpled like paper, as if they'd been flung out of the sky. There were containers littered in every direction and the trees were hung with discarded parachutes. They dangled from the branches, green, yellow and white like exotic fruits, bright bold evidence of the terror and excitement of their fall. And in the middle of the litter, half a dozen farmworkers were standing together, cowed and quiet, watching the tanks and guns as they roared through.

About an hour along the road they reached a village, where there were more white flags draped across the front of the houses and no sign of any civilians at all. By this time they were actually feeling bored, for there was nothing for them to do but sit and smoke and wait to arrive.

Dusty had run out of cigarettes and was cadging from his mates. 'Anyone got a fag? I'm gasping.'

'You're a pain in the neck,' Steve told him. 'Never mind gasping.' But he reached into his pocket to find him a cigarette. And as he did so he touched the sharp edge of his mother's letter. Time to read my mail, he thought and he picked up Barbara's first because he'd skimmed it that morning and his mother's would only be chit-chat.

Now he could take his time and enjoy her every word. How dear and close she seemed, describing this house they were going to live in. He'd have been content to live in a barn, providing he could be with her, and here she was telling him of a house with a garden and built-in furniture – even a refrigerator, he noticed. We *are* going up in the world. He read it all through twice and then, as their journey was still proceeding and still uneventful, he took out his mother's letter and read that too.

The shock it gave him was so intense it drained the colour from his face. If it had been anyone other than his mother he wouldn't have believed the words he was

346

reading. But there they were, in her familiar looping handwriting, stark and uncompromising. '*Your Barbara has been messing around with another man.*' It was like being punched in the stomach. She couldn't have been. Not Barbara. I'd have known.

Dusty was leaning towards him, sharp face concerned. 'You all right, corp?'

'Yep,' he said. 'My mum rabbiting on, that's all.' Mustn't make a fuss or I shall let the side down. 'How much fucking longer are they gonna keep us on the road?'

'Up an' at 'em, eh corp,' another man grinned at him.

'That's the ticket,' Steve agreed. But he didn't want to do anything except make sense of the letter. It couldn't be true. She wouldn't do such a thing. Would she? Not Barbara. It was as if his mother's words had opened up a picture-show in his head, flooding his mind with images whether he wanted to see them or not – Barbara's face in close-up, drowsy with kisses, the long line of her body gilded with firelight, her hands, setting a fire, pouring tea, weighed down by that heavy bouquet, receiving his ring, those quick feet tripping down the Town Hall steps, leaping towards the cottage, running across that market square, those gorgeous sea-green eyes, looking straight at him, smiling and loving. Oh she couldn't do such a thing. Couldn't. He wouldn't believe it.

And yet as the TCV purred on along the German roads, other images pushed into his mind too. His mother had given him the name of the man. Victor Castlemane, she'd said. Wasn't that the name of the feller Dusty'd flung out of the dancehall on the night they met? The one who'd shouted at her. He could hear his voice. '*You come here with me,*' he'd said. '*You're my gal!*' Had she been? Was there something going on, even then? He'd been violently possessive. In fact I thought he was her boyfriend. I asked her. And she said no. But was she telling me the truth? Oh God, she couldn't have been lying to me, could she? Not my Barbara.

The images intensified. Now she was dancing with other men, doing the jitterbug with a whole series of Americans, all chewing gum and handing her on from one to the next, now she was walking towards him arm in arm with that horrible Victor. Oh yes, he *did* remember him, in sharp, painful focus, a short handsome boy with a bold face. Just the type to take someone else's girl. Oh for Christ's sake, this is awful.

They stopped and struck camp and he did everything that was required of him but the images didn't go away. They got more insistent. He ate what was set in front of him as taunting pictures filled his mind – Barbara and that foul creature whispering together, dancing together, kissing . . . No, no, no! Even in sleep the torment didn't stop and at five he woke with a start from a nightmare of such exquisite misery that he was glad to be awake, even with a day's fighting ahead of him.

That day the advance was quicker than they expected, although most of the old hands moved guardedly. There was still no sign of any opposition but that was no reason to take chances.

They passed through two villages, checked over a series of empty farmhouses, and finally, just as the light was fading, they came to another rather larger village, tucked between two slight hills, with a sizeable farm about half a mile to the east, built of red brick like all the other buildings in the area and looking solid and prosperous. The villagers were waiting in the square with a white flag, more than ready to surrender, and Steve and his team of six were detailed to check the farm.

There were three main buildings, the farmhouse, which was intact and would be relatively easy to flush out, and two barns set at right angles to one another, both badly damaged and both capable of harbouring a sniper.

Steve made a quick judgement. 'We'll check the barns,' he said, looking at Dusty. 'You lot clear the farm. Keep your eyes skinned for any more dug-outs.' Lots of the locals had been hiding in dug-outs and they would make a ready hiding place for troops.

The four men gave him the thumbs-up and headed off for the farmhouse. He and Dusty watched until they were out of sight. No ambush. No snipers. No gunfire of any kind.

'Right,' he said. 'Let's deal with these barns. Slow an' steady.'

They stalked towards the nearer of the two buildings. It was so quiet they could hear one another breathing. The barn door was tightly closed.

'Kick it in?' Dusty whispered.

'Yep,' Steve whispered back and he suddenly remembered how he'd kicked open the door to his honeymoon bungalow and how valiant he'd felt and how impressed Barbara had been. He could see her now, looking up at him. Oh she couldn't have betrayed him. Not when they loved one another so much.

Then boot met wood, there was a crash and the door burst open. And to his horror, he found himself looking down the long barrel of a Spandau. It was pointing straight at him and the soldier stooped over it was wearing the familiar field grey of the German army. Jesus! Now, and disastrously too late, he remembered his training. He should have told Dusty to cover him, hidden his approach, entered by the prescribed stages. How could he have forgotten anything as elementary as that? But he had and now they were both facing capture or worse and it was all his fault. Jesus!

There was a long pause while the three men stared at one another. Nobody fired and nobody moved. Then, with a suddenness that made them all jump, there was a burst of fire down by the farmhouse and the German began to shout.

Steve and Dusty sent rapid eye messages to one

another, reaching the same decision in the same split second. They were caught. It was over. If they ran they'd be shot in the back like the Scotsman. How vividly Steve remembered the Scotsman! They threw their rifles onto the barn floor and raised their hands in surrender. It was ignominious but there was nothing else they could do. The firing at the farmhouse was still going on but the German had picked up his machine gun and was waving it at them, pointing into the next barn and shouting at them angrily, '*Mach Schnell! Mach Schnell!*' Steve realised he was still analysing the sound of the exchange as he went where he was ordered. Three rifles – or was it four? – and then the long rattle of a German machine gun. Get the hell out of it, he urged his mates. But they were beyond his help now. They would have to fend for themselves. He was deserting them. Oh God! The shame of it! He was deserting his men.

There was a battered truck standing in the second barn and they were pointed into the back of it. Then the German climbed into the driving seat, slinging his Spandau down beside him, and they were off, with a squeal of tyres and a cascade of dust.

Now they'll hear us, Steve thought. But the exchange of fire was still going on and they were out of the yard and tearing along a sunken road, where they couldn't see the farmhouse or the village or anything at all expect a tunnel of branches. And the chance for a counter-attack and rescue was gone.

They drove for over an hour as the darkness fell, heading east and using totally deserted roads. Steve and Dusty sat on the floor of the truck among packets of food and piles of old uniforms and dozens of petrol cans. It was extremely uncomfortable for the roads were in bad repair and they were thrown about at every turn. But the physical discomfort was nothing to the turmoil in Steve's mind. He felt stunned by his stupidity, and deeply, horribly ashamed to have been so cowardly. He should have followed the procedures, and then none of this would have happened, and he shouldn't have given in so quickly. How could he have made so many mistakes? The more he thought about it the more miserable he became. He shrank into himself, saying nothing, staring at the side of the truck, a failure, giving in at the first threat, a bad soldier, a worse husband, nothing but a total, God-awful, fucking failure.

Presently Dusty plucked up the courage to move. He took his cigarette packet from his tunic, very carefully, watching his captor all the time, and offered it to Steve saying, 'Smoke?' To his surprise the German turned towards him and put out a hand towards the packet too, saying, '*Ja*.'

So they smoked together and as the German wasn't shouting or waving his gun at them, Dusty began to talk – very quietly.

'Where d'you think we're going, corp?'

It took an effort for Steve to answer him, as if he were pulling a great weight into his head. 'East,' he said at last.

'I'm dyin' for a jimmy riddle.'

'So am I,' Steve realised.

But neither of them thought it would be possible to stand up and relieve themselves out of the back of the truck so they sat on in discomfort and Steve fell back into his misery. More time passed and Dusty was just observing that they 'must be there soon' when the German suddenly pulled up and climbed out.

It was pitch dark and they seemed to be alone in the middle of a field. The German was piddling against one of the trees in a small copse about a hundred yards away. So they got out of the truck too and followed his example. Then they weren't sure what they were supposed to do and stood by the truck awkwardly ill at ease.

Their captor was standing at the edge of the field, smoking and looking out into the darkness.

351

'What's he doing?' Dusty whispered.

Again that enormous effort for Steve to pull his thoughts into his mind. 'Waiting for someone?' he ventured. 'Maybe it's a rendezvous.'

But nobody arrived and presently, the German flicked his dog-end into the copse and walked briskly back to the car. He took a pressure stove, a coffee pot and two billycans out of the truck and signalled to his prisoners that they were to prepare a meal. It was most peculiar. And what followed after the meal was even more peculiar. The German climbed into the back of the truck, motioning them in ahead of him. Then he produced an army blanket from under the pile of clothing, wrapped himself up in it, pulled his revolver from his belt and lay down to sleep with the gun in his hand.

'Run?' Dusty mouthed.

Steve shook his head. Weighed down by misery he couldn't see the point of it. They were miles into German territory and unarmed. They'd only be picked up again in the morning. They might as well stay where they were and wait to be handed over. He pulled a greatcoat from the pile, huddled into it and settled to sleep too. The German could be lost – he'd been driving without any reference to a map – or he could have come here to meet up with his unit. Either way he'd hand them over tomorrow and then they'd be registered as prisoners of war and sent to a camp somewhere and the whole thing would be out of their hands. No soldier would drive about the countryside with two prisoners. Not for long anyway.

But the next day, they drove on further and further east, using the minor roads and avoiding the towns, and they weren't handed over. And in the evening they stopped in another empty field, ate and drank as before and bedded down for yet another night.

'It don't make sense,' Dusty whispered when the German seemed asleep. 'What's he playing at?'

But whatever it was he had very good hearing, for at that point he sat up, threatened them with the revolver and bellowed at them, '*Halt die schnauze!*', obviously telling them to shut up. He was an ugly-looking man with a long horsey face and small eyes and his anger was making him look cruel, so they did as they were told, looking away from him in the sullen way of all captured soldiers.

So another night passed and the three men slept fitfully, the German irritably watchful, Dusty cold and puzzled, Steve more and more depressed.

CHAPTER TWENTY-EIGHT

On the morning after her quarrel, Barbara got up at half past five. Her sleep had been broken by bad dreams and when Steve's alarm-clock trilled her awake, she was so weary it was an effort to open her eyes, but she had no intention of being in the house when her mother-in-law woke. So she got up at once, had a lick and a promise in very cold water, made a cup of tea, ate a slice of bread and marge and was gone before the kitchen clock struck six.

It was a bright, clear, empty morning and she had the street to herself. Being out in the open restored her spirits, and especially at that moment, in that town. She walked past the dusty privet hedges, enjoying the mottled yellow of the brick walls, the gull-grey of the tiles, the stolid bay windows, still curtained and sleeping. She felt she belonged there and was glad to be alive, despite her stupid mother-in-law. This is such a brave town, she thought, such a good, solid, dependable sort of place. We been bombed an' buzzbombed, we've had rockets dropped on us, an' people we love have been killed, an' we've put up with everything. We hain't the sort to give in.

But at that moment she saw a familiar figure trudging along the road towards her. She'd forgotten that six o'clock was the time Bob came home when he was working nights. Oh dear! she thought. I really don't want to talk to him, nice though he is. Not now. What shall I say? But she couldn't avoid him, not without being deliberately rude, which would hurt his feelings and she didn't want to do that. So they met at the bend of the road.

They were both embarrassed, he because he knew there'd been a row, she because she knew that he knew. But they made light of their meeting and their embarrassment.

'You're up early!' he said, smiling at her.

She made an excuse. It sounded feeble even to her ears. 'I promised to see Mr Threlfall,' she said. 'Before work.'

He kept so calm that he didn't register any emotion at all. 'Ah!' he said and walked on. But once he was indoors, his annoyance couldn't be contained.

Heather was in her dressing gown in the kitchen, setting the table for breakfast and looking anxious but for once her fraught expression roused no pity in him at all.

'I've just met Barbara,' he said.

She closed her face. 'Oh yes,' she said dismissively. 'Bacon an' fried bread be all right?'

'What's she doing out this time a' the morning?'

Her answer was truthful and aggressive. 'Keeping out a' my way I expect.'

'You went for her.' It was more a statement than a question.

'Somebody had to say something,' she told him. 'You can't let things go forever. We've got our Steve to think about.'

'And this is going to help him?'

'She shouted at me, Bob. She was horrible.'

He didn't doubt it but there were other things that were more important at the moment. 'What she say about the fly in the ointment?'

'As good as admitted it.'

He'd hoped she would have denied it. No, more than hoped, he'd expected her to. Was there truth in what that boy had said then? He sat down wearily in his chair before the fire and unlaced his boots.

'Did you ask her? Straight out, I mean.'

''Course. She couldn't deny it.'

So there's real damage been done, he thought. Whatever possessed her, silly girl? She might have known there'd be trouble. 'So now what?'

Heather turned the rasher of bacon in the frying pan and reached for the slice of bread. 'Don't ask me,' she said. 'You know more than I do. She went rushing off without a word to me. I wasn't even up. I suppose she'll move back with Sis, if she'll have her. I can't keep pace with her, coming an' going all the time. Poor Steve.'

In fact Barbara had no intention of moving in with Sis. It wasn't something to make a habit of and, besides, she had no reason to run away, not having done anything wrong. I'll sleep there and eat there, she decided, and I'll keep my head down and stay out of her way and wait. Sooner or later she'll have to eat humble pie. On which comforting thought, she reached Sis's flat.

Sis had just lit her first fag of the day when the bell rang. Spluttering and coughing, and with the cigarette stuck to her bottom lip, she trailed her dressing gown cord down the stairs to let her visitor in.

'Don't surprise me a bit,' she said, when Barbara told her what had happened. 'There's no one like our Heather for gettin' hold of the wrong end a' the stick. You done the right thing getting out of it. You 'ad any breakfast?'

'Not much,' Barbara admitted. 'I was in a rush.'

So they made a big pot of tea and scrambled up some powdered egg and settled down to talk politics among the newspapers just like old times. Sis was full of plans for a political meeting at Bellington South.

'There's got to be more supporters there than we seen at that meeting,' she said. 'I mean, that stands to reason. Mr Craxton's gonna suggest we call a public meeting. He says he'll propose it on Tuesday week. Week today. Why don'tcher come with us? Be a nice evening out for you.'

So it was agreed. And they went on reading the

356

papers. And Sis found an article about the new pre-fabricated house. 'Look at that,' she said. 'Just up your street. In every sense a' the word.'

Engineering experts, the paper said, were being released from airfield work *within the next few months* to switch to preparing roads and drainage systems for building sites. *'In the first two years after the end of the European war, there are plans to build up to 300,000 houses – 100,000 in the first year and 200,000 more in the second.'*

'You'll be in your pre-fab before you know where you are,' Sis promised.

Yes, Barbara thought, happily. I shall. The war'll be over, an' he'll be home, an' we'll have a place of our own right away from everybody, an' all this silly nonsense will be put in proportion. Oh I can't wait. It wouldn't be hard to keep occupied in the meantime, not when there was so much going on.

Sis looked at the clock and gave a squawk. 'Land-sakes! Look at the time! We'd better look sharp or we'll be late.'

So they went their separate ways to work. And the spring sun shone on them both. 'See you next Tuesday!' they called to one another.

But that Tuesday didn't turn out the way they expected.

Barbara passed the rest of the week in almost the way she'd planned. She worked afternoons and evenings until her day off on Sunday, which she spent with Sis, and by Monday morning, when she returned to the day shift, she and Heather had established a speechless truce that didn't require either of them to communicate beyond a simple good morning. Heather cooked the breakfast, Barbara made the tea and washed the dishes, and as it was washday, she washed her clothes too, by hand, and hung them in the garden before she left for work. And that evening she and the two girls went to

357

the pictures and then sat talking until it was very late so that she came home after Heather had gone to bed.

Bob had sat up to see her in, but tactful soul that he was, he didn't say anything about the way she was behaving. He simply asked her what the picture'd been like, and hoped she'd enjoyed it.

She kissed him goodnight, glad of his discretion and unaware that he was secretly wondering how much longer she and Heather would keep up their quarrel. Neither of them could have foreseen that it would come to a conclusion the very next morning.

They were eating their silent breakfast when Mrs Connelly called up the stairs. 'I've a letter for you, Barbara, so I have. Shall I be bringing it up to you?'

There was something so strained about her voice that Barbara left the table at once to go and see what was the matter. She met the old lady halfway up the stairs and one look at the envelope in her hands told her the worst. It was an official letter. OHMS. The sort that brought bad news.

She opened it where she stood and pulled out the letter, heart thudding and hands shaking. 'Oh dear God! Dear God!'

Bob and Heather were on the landing, leaning over the stairwell, alarmed and anxious. 'What is it?'

'He's missing,' Barbara said, and as she moved her head to look up at them she began to cry.

Heather ran down the stairs so precipitately it was a wonder she didn't fall, grabbed at the letter and read it aloud. 'Oh my Steve!' she cried. 'My poor dear Steve. It's not true!'

But the words were inescapable. '*Missing in action.*' There was even a date.

Bob tried to comfort them, his face strained. 'It don't say killed,' he pointed out. 'Missin' ain't killed. It just means they don't know where he is.'

'They didn't know where our Betty was either,'

Heather said wildly, 'an' look what had happened to her.'

It was too much for Barbara, for wasn't that exactly what she was thinking herself? She knew if she stayed in that claustrophobic stairwell a moment longer she'd be screaming. She had to get away. 'Work,' she said, struggling past them all. 'I got to go to work.'

'Is that a good idea?' Bob asked, putting a hand on her arm. 'I mean . . .'

But she shook him off, pushed on up the stairs, grabbed her red coat from its hook on the bedroom door, snatched up her handbag and ran headlong down again and out of the house. Work! It was the only thing.

But for once in her life keeping busy didn't help her. Her anxiety was so extreme and her fear so terrible that it was as if the news had punched a hole right through the centre of her body. Every time she thought of him, or remembered the letter, her heart dropped down and down into the pit. Missing. Like Betty. Blown to pieces and never found. She tried to be sensible, to persuade herself that missing *didn't* mean dead, but the most she could hope was that he might be injured somewhere and that they might find him. And imagining him wounded brought back all those awful memories of the dead and injured lying in these streets and bits of body falling from the sky. Oh please God, not that! Not that!

Barbara cooked her usual meal that evening, although none of them had the appetite for it. They sat round the table saying the same useless things over and over again without comforting one another in the least. 'Missing don't mean killed.' 'We'll just have to hang on and wait, won't we.' 'Mustn't give up.'

'I told Sis and Mabel,' Heather said as they were clearing the table. 'They came into the shop. Sis says not to worry about the meeting if you don't feel up to it.'

Barbara looked at the clock, checking the time. She'd forgotten all about the meeting. 'Thass all right,' she said, sadly. 'I'll go. That'll give me something to think about.'

'They'll understand if you don't want to,' Bob said.

But Barbara felt she had to go. Life didn't stop because you were worried. There were things to do.

Sis was waiting at the bus stop with all the rest of the committee except Mr Craxton.

'You all right?' she asked, giving Barbara a hug. But although Barbara nodded, she couldn't smile and she couldn't think of anything to say.

'Don't give up heart,' Sis advised, still cuddling her. 'Missing could mean any number a' things. Try not to think the worst, eh.'

'I can't think of anything. Thass like a nightmare.'

'I know,' Sis said, her round face wrinkled with concern. 'I know.'

Christine was preoccupied, fidgeting from foot to foot, gazing down the street. 'I hope Mr Craxton's OK,' she said. 'It isn't like him to be late.'

Barbara didn't care if he was. He was the least of her worries that evening. But the others said they were sure he'd turn up and the two Union men declared that they'd never known him miss a meeting. Ever. Regular as clockwork he was. But there was still no sign of him when their bus arrived.

'What are we to do?' Christine asked, as it juddered to a halt beside them. 'Are we to go without him or what?'

'We'll go on ahead,' Sis decided, shepherding her into the bus. 'No point in all of us being late. He'll follow on.'

But at that moment she saw a woman running down the street towards them, calling to her, a short stout woman with bottle-blonde hair. 'Mrs Tamworth! Cecily Tamworth!' And she turned, with one foot on the pavement and the other on the platform and waited for her.

'I'm so glad I caught you,' the woman said,

breathlessly. 'It's Mr Craxton. Oh dear! I don't know how to tell you this. I'm his niece, Joan. I'm afraid he can't come. He's ill.'

They were all alarmed. 'How ill?' Sis said. 'What is it?'

The answer was a shock. 'He's had a heart attack. He's in hospital.'

They stood where they were, some on the pavement, some on the platform, staring at her. 'Is he very bad?' Sis asked.

'Well he ain't going to die, if that's what you mean, not according to the doctor, but he won't be standin' for Parliament, that's for sure. He's got to take things easy. They ain't even sure about the shop.'

The conductor had walked down the bus to see what was causing the hold-up. 'You gettin' on or off, lady?' he said to Sis.

'Off,' Sis told him. 'We'll catch the next one.' And she and the committee returned to the pavement so that they could give their full attention to Mr Craxton's niece.

'Came on all of a sudden,' she told them. 'We thought it was indigestion. Mrs C gave him Rennies.'

'I'm *so* sorry,' Sis said.

And Christine asked, 'How is he now?'

'Not good. They got to watch him for twenty-four hours in case he has another one.'

They were still questioning and commiserating when the next bus came round the bend.

'We'd better go now,' Sis said. 'Thanks for lettin' us know. Give him our love. Tell him not to worry. An' say I'll come up an' see him tomorrow.'

'My word!' Christine said, when they were all on the bus and settled into their seats. 'Poor Mr Craxton! Who'd have thought it? What will they do at Bellington South?'

What indeed? To be without a candidate with the election so close was, as Pauline said she hardly needed

361

to point out, 'a real blow'. She looked round at their concerned faces, as they sipped coffee from her elegant bone china and spread their files and papers across her elegant polished table. 'It's a bombshell,' she said. 'Here I've been thinking we were going to plan our first public meeting in years – he wrote to me about it only last week and we thought what a good idea it was – and now this.'

'What are we to do?' the schoolteacher asked.

'Oh dear, Brian,' Pauline said. 'I really don't know.'

'You'll have to choose someone else,' Sis told her.

'Choosing was the problem in the first place,' Pauline said. 'We thought and thought, you know, and there's absolutely nobody. It's a big commitment and we're all such *busy* people. The Coome Mertons would be the ideal people, naturally, but they've always got so many business matters to attend to – they send their apologies, incidentally.'

The librarian stirred his coffee and hastened to assure them all that he'd be only too glad to offer his services, 'but working the hours I do, I'd really be too much of a liability. You need someone absolutely reliable.' The old man in spats excused himself on the grounds that he was really a little too long in the tooth. The teacher admitted, modestly, that he was good at public speaking but doubted whether he could carry off a parliamentary candidature. 'If push comes to shove, I'll weigh in but I'd rather you found someone else.'

In her present fragile state, Barbara was irritated by the way they were taking the news. Not a word about poor old Mr Craxton, she thought, and what a lily-livered lot they are. Whass the matter with them? I bet they'd stand quick enough if they thought there was any chance of getting elected. The longer the excuses went on, the more irritated she became. In the end she was stung to speak.

'I tell you what I think,' she said, at a pause in their catalogue of excuses.

They turned polite faces towards her.

'You're lookin' for someone with commitment. Thass right, hain't it?' It was. They were agreed on that. 'A good public speaker.' Oh yes, that was essential. 'Someone who knows the facts an' can put them across.' Indeed. 'Strong socialist. Fighter. Good personality.'

'You are describing the ideal candidate, my dear,' the spatted gentleman said, smiling at her paternally. 'Would we could find him.'

'That hain't a him,' Barbara told him, 'thass a her. You got the ideal candidate sittin' right here in this room. She don't miss a trick. There hain't a thing she don't know about this area. She got files an' folders on every subject under the sun. If any on us wants information, she's the one we go to.' She looked round at her fellow committee members, who'd worked out who she was talking about and were grinning at her and nodding. 'Hain't that right? Well then, I'd like to propose Mrs Cecily Tamworth. Any seconders?'

The proposal caused such a stir that for a second she was afraid she'd gone too far, too soon. But then all five members of her committee raised their hands in support and Sis laughed out loud and thwacked her on the shoulder. The spatted gentleman was nodding, the teacher looked perky, the librarian was clapping his hands, and Pauline, who'd been startled at first, changed her mind when she saw what a positive reaction she was getting.

'Would you consider it, Mrs Tamworth?' she asked.

'If you're sure you know what you're letting yourselves in for,' Sis said, 'and on mature consideration, yes I would.'

After that, the meeting became quite light-hearted. And very busy. Sis showed them all the material she'd been gathering about the planned National Health Service and outlined the sort of thing she'd like to see in their local literature, 'providing I'm accepted by the party'. By the time they parted company late in the evening, they'd organised another local meeting, planned their public meeting, designed leaflets to advertise both of them, and costed the entire enterprise.

'An inspired proposal,' Pauline said to Barbara as they parted. 'I wish the Coome Mertons had been here to see it.'

Sis chuckled about it all the way home, puffing a cigar and wheezing with smoke and delight.

'You're a case,' she said to Barbara, as they parted at the top of Childeric Road. 'I never thought you'd spring something like that on me.'

'I wouldn't have done if I hadn't been worried about Steve. I just couldn't sit there an' hear them makin' all those silly excuses an' him . . .'

Sis grew serious at once. 'No good telling you not to worry,' she said. 'I know that. But, like I said, don't face the worst until you have to. Missin' don't always mean dead. Keep your pecker up.'

Barbara kissed her goodbye and said she'd try but she knew it would be impossible. Just the thought of going back into the house where his parents would be sitting up worrying was making her heart drop into the pit again. But in fact, as she discovered when she got in, both her in-laws were in bed and she had the place to herself.

She crept away into Steve's bedroom, and eased into his bed, lying on her side with her head on his pillow, looking at the three neat lines of his books in the moonlight, remembering him. It had been a terrible day and an extraordinary evening and she was very, very tired. But she couldn't sleep.

After a couple of hours, she gave up trying and sat up and switched on the light. She was desperate for someone to talk to, someone who would listen and understand what she was saying, someone who spoke her language. Sis was a dear but she was too caught up in her politics, Mr Wilkins was grieving as much as she was herself and so was Mrs Wilkins, to give her credit. But as she sat there, with her arms round her knees, listening to the sounds of the sleeping house – somebody snoring downstairs, bedsprings creaking, timbers shrinking and cracking the way they used to do in Lynn – she suddenly remembered her aunt Becky. That was it! She'd write a letter to Aunt Becky. At one remove, it would be possible to say everything she wanted to. Aunt Becky could take it.

It was another hour before the letter was written but then she slept at last, and the next morning, although she was very tired, she felt she was able to cope. Breakfast was horribly difficult because they were all in such a state but they got through it, somehow or other, and then there was the bustle of clearing the table and washing the dishes, and then at last she could leave them and go to work. It was a relief to be on her own again and another to post her letter.

Becky Bosworth was setting off to the baker's when the letter arrived but when she'd read it, she decided the bread could wait and walked straight round to Maudie's place to tell her the news, her sharp face dark with distress.

Maudie was standing on her doorstep gossiping with Vera Castlemain.

'He done marvellous up in Lunnon,' Vera was bragging. 'He got hisself a new job. Did I tell you? With a di'mond merchant. Imagine that. 'Course I always knew he'd get on. Even as a little lad. He was so brainy. Well you remember how brainy he was. Never thought he'd get a job with a di'mond merchant, though. Never in a thousand years. You think of the money he'll make.'

Maudie was very impressed. 'Always knew he'd do well,' she said. 'Thass a great pity he didn't marry our Barbara, if you ask me. They'd ha' made a good pair. When he comin' up to see you then?'

'Not yet awhile,' Vera admitted. 'He say he got to stay on guard. Every evenin' he say. 'Course with di'monds I s'pose they got to watch out for thieves. Stand to reason.'

Becky breezed into their conversation and pushed it to a halt. 'You seen this, have you?' she said to Maudie. 'You heard the news?'

Maudie took the letter and read it slowly, at first with interest and then with growing distress. 'Oh my dear heart alive!' she said. 'My poor Bar'bra. That hain't fair! What a thing to go an' happen!'

'Shall you go up an' see her then?' Becky asked.

'That ol' boat's a-comin' in,' Maudie said, frowning to be caught between two needs. 'Aspected this marnin'. Don't want him hollerin'. He ain't axactly in the best of moods. Leastways he weren't when he set off. Reckon I'll write to her.'

Vera was looking puzzled. 'Whass goin' on?' she asked, her round face perplexed. 'Who you gonna write to?'

'Becky'll tell you,' Maudie said. 'Hassen you up an' get home or you'll hev the boat come in an' you won't be ready.' She turned to Becky, holding up the letter. 'Can I keep this fer a day or two, while I'm writing?'

'Long as you like,' Becky told her.

So the letter was kept and answered – at length and ungrammatically but with more affection than she'd shown her poor daughter for a very long time.

And the next morning Barbara had two letters from Lynn. There was nothing else, and she *had* so hoped there would be, but she encouraged herself that two letters from Lynn would do to be going on with. And they *were* a comfort, Becky's so sensible and her mother's so loving.

I know I was not keen on you getting married but I would not have had this happen for the world. Your pa dont know on account of he is at sea at

present. I have not told your brothers on account
of they are too young. I do so hope you get better
news soon which you will write and let me know
wont you. I shall be thinking of you all the time.

If only she could have written to me like that when I
got married, Barbara thought bitterly, instead of all that
hollering. It's dreadful that I got to lose my husband
before my ma will write to me properly. But then she
checked herself. Missing hain't dead. Don't face the
worst until you have to. And she offered up one of her
quick, heartfelt prayers to make amends for her black
thoughts, 'Please God, don't let him be dead. I'll write
back to Ma this afternoon and I'll be really nice to her,
and I'll be really nice to Mrs Wilkins too, only please
don't let him be dead.'

CHAPTER TWENTY-NINE

'This is beginning to stink,' Steve whispered, holding his nose and grimacing.

'Speak fer yerself,' Dusty whispered. 'We all stink.'

Which was true. After two days without washing, their hands and faces were seamed with grime, their chins covered with an ugly uneven stubble and they smelt like tramps, filthy-sour as though they were rotting.

But Steve was referring to the situation they were in, which was steadily becoming more and more bizarre. They'd been travelling about the German countryside for more than forty-eight hours now, and in a most peculiar way, using minor roads and farm tracks and doubling back on themselves whenever there was any other traffic in the area. Their food stocks were low, there was hardly any water, they were down to their last two cans of petrol, and their captor was hideously bad-tempered but he still showed no sign of handing them over to anyone else.

From time to time, his two prisoners attempted a shorthand conversation, pretending to look at one of their letters, or at Dusty's calendar, and communicating in unfinished sentences and army slang, backing up what couldn't be said with nods and frowns and changing expressions, for fear of being overheard and understood. Now the truck was lurking under a clump of trees at the edge of a field while a convoy passed noisily on the road below them and they were making the most of the cover the row gave them.

'Sounds like tanks,' Steve whispered.

'Ours or theirs?' Dusty asked. ''Ave a shufti.'

Steve couldn't see anything from where he was crouched on the floor of the truck. He wondered if he could move into a better position but decided against it. Their driver's shoulders were too tense to run risks. 'Can't.'

Sure enough the German turned to spit orders at them, his eyes narrowed, pale brows scowling. '*Halt die schnauze!*'

So they had to shut up. But Steve mimed peeing against a tree and Dusty nodded to show he understood when they would continue their conversation. Which they did when the convoy had passed and they all went off into the copse. There was no sign of any more traffic but the tracks the convoy had left were clear in the dust of the road. They were the long zippered marks of passing tanks.

'I don't reckon he meant to take us prisoner,' Steve said from his side of the tree.

'No. I been thinking that too.'

'I reckon he's doing a bunk.'

'A deserter?'

'Yep. He'd've handed us over straight away if he'd been on the level. I don't think he's a Jerry either.'

'He speaks the lingo.'

'Two lingos.'

'Straight up?'

'I reckon. He's got two ways of telling us to shut up. You listen. I reckon he's Polish or something like that.'

'So?'

It was time for a bit of courage. They'd been prisoners for long enough. 'I think we should grab some food and make a run for it.'

Dusty put his head round the tree to grin agreement. 'When?'

'Tonight. When it's dark. If those tanks were ours we ought to be able to find them. If they weren't they can't be far away if the Panzers are in the area.'

369

'He's coming back,' Dusty warned, glancing over his shoulder. Could they do it? Was it possible?

The noises of the day were certainly encouraging. Something was going on and not too far away. Heavy artillery fire which had to be Allied. All the sounds of a tank battle. And eventually, towards evening, they saw a squadron of heavy bombers, heading east and not more than ten miles away.

'Catching up with us,' Steve whispered, looking skyward as the roar of their engines continued. 'Grab that liver sausage while he's not looking.'

That night they made camp just inside a thick wood that covered a long sloping hillside. They ate their meagre rations hungrily, drank their coffee, which was particularly bitter that night, getting down to the dregs. Then all three of them ambled off into the trees, in what was now their customary way, to relieve themselves before settling down for the night.

It had been a warm spring day – too warm to be cooped up in the smelly fastness of that truck – and now the sun was setting in a blaze of sumptuous colour, scarlet and orange and gold striped by long lines of lilac cloud. The fields below them were darkened with blue shadow and there wasn't a sight or sound of another living soul but from where they were standing they had a good view of the road they'd just left and a clear panorama of the open countryside around, with a sizeable town to the south-east and at least four villages beyond that. Plenty of cover and good observation. It couldn't be bettered.

They watched as their captor strolled back to the truck. He was lighting a cigarette as he walked and the smell of its smoke drifted up to them most temptingly. They'd run out of their own supplies that morning but he obviously had a secret cache somewhere.

'Trust him not to share it,' Dusty whispered. 'I'm dyin' fer a fag.'

Steve told him to shush. This was a crucial moment

370

and they needed their wits about them. 'Move up,' he mouthed, tossing his head to show the direction they should take.

They moved with caution, treading very carefully and wincing at what a lot of noise they were making as they crunched through the dead leaves. But the German was walking on, still smoking and didn't hear.

Bit further. And a bit more, slipping from tree to tree so that they could dodge for cover if he turned round. There were birds calling in the copse below them and they could hear a horse nickering somewhere. But he still didn't look for them. Instead he sat with his back against one of the wheels and went on smoking.

Dusty peered round the side of his tree. 'What now?' he mouthed.

At that moment there was a roar of heavy vehicles and three armoured cars appeared in the road below them, travelling fast and too far away to be identified. The German jumped to his feet, glanced at the woods, hesitated for a second and then climbed into the truck and drove it at speed across the field, following the hedgerow and heading in the opposite direction. Within minutes they'd turned a bend and disappeared and he was bumping into the next field, driving like a maniac.

'Christ!' Steve said. 'He's going without us. He's leaving us behind. Didn't I tell you.' It was too good to be true.

'He'll be back,' Dusty said sourly.

But he wasn't. They watched until the dark shape of the truck had disappeared into the shadows and they listened for a long while after that in case they heard him returning. Soon, even the sound of his engine was gone. They were on their own and they were free. They wanted to jump about and shout but that wasn't possible in enemy territory. So they thumped one another on the back instead, grinning like Cheshire cats. It was too easy.

What followed was not.

They decided to stay in the woods that night and to sleep if they could. 'There's no point trying to get anywhere tonight,' Steve decided. 'Once the sun goes down it'll be too dark to see. We'll make a bed in the leaves and stay here. Good insulation, leaves.'

'Bleedin' babes in the wood,' Dusty mocked.

'We'll sleep like tops,' Steve told him. 'I betcher.'

But in fact neither of them slept at all. As the last light faded, the woods gave an ominous shiver and the shadows under its thick branches began to lengthen and distort. It was as if it were returning to some older, more primitive, savage existence and the return brought a new fear with it, equally primitive and equally savage. Every swaying branch concealed a danger, every speckled trunk a threat, every shifting space was live with half-seen, irrational terrors. And when the last of the sunlight was gone, the terror intensified, for now the darkness was total and impenetrable and every sound was magnified. The harmless wood had become a menacing forest and the old dark forces of evil and horror were stalking in its depths.

They fought their fears for nearly an hour until Dusty couldn't stand it any longer. 'Sod this fer a game a' soldiers!' he whispered. 'I'm off out of it.'

'It's only superstition,' Steve whispered back.

'Then why are we whispering?'

'In case they hear us,' Steve admitted. 'OK. You're right. We'll get out.'

But even at the edge of the wood, it was still hideously dark and the demons were still waiting.

'We'll take it in turns to keep guard,' Steve said. 'I'll take first watch.'

But neither of them slept until first light and then they sank into such heavy slumber that it was some hours before they woke, drenched in dew, stiff-legged, much too far out in the open and parlously hungry.

'I'm fucking perished,' Dusty complained. 'How the hell are we going to get back to the unit?'

Steve produced the liver sausage from his tunic and cut off two large chunks. Now that the night was over, he was his reasonable self again. 'Quit bellyaching,' he ordered. 'Least the goblins didn't get us. If we head west, we'll be going in the right sort of direction. Eat up!'

So they breakfasted on liver sausage and dry biscuit, washed down with water. Then they set off along the edge of the wood, heading west, or west-north-west, and keeping their eyes skinned for any movement on the roads. None came. They saw a tractor and a farm wagon and a gang of labourers in the fields – and there was plenty of activity in the air, all of it Allied but none of it near enough for them to hazard a guess as to where it was coming from.

Towards afternoon they found a stream and crouched beside it, scooping the water into their hands to drink. It restored them a little for it was cool and sweet-tasting and they'd both been extremely thirsty. They filled their water bottles, rested and went on. But there was still no military traffic of any kind, Allied or German.

That night Dusty crossed off another day on his calendar and they slept under a hedge, taking it in turns to keep watch. At sunrise they set off along a completely empty road, still heading west. But after another long day they were still in enemy territory and no nearer to finding the British army or to knowing where they were.

'How much longer can we keep this up?' Dusty wanted to know.

'While there's food, there's hope,' Steve told him. But the days went by and the food gradually ran out, even though they were rationing it carefully. By the fifth day they had nothing left but water and they were both very hungry.

'We should've stayed with the Jerry, you ask me,' Dusty grumbled, as the morning trudged away. 'At least he fed us.'

373

'We'd've ended up in Poland,' Steve said. 'And he wouldn't have fed us once his supplies ran out.'

'Six days we been going, an' we ain't seen a soul.'

'Five and a half,' Steve corrected. 'It's midday.'

'Five, six, what's it fucking matter? We're finished. We got no fucking food, no fucking maps, we don't know where we fucking are. I say we ought to walk to the nearest farm an' give ourselves up. Call it a day. That's what I say.'

'Well I don't,' Steve said, and tried to encourage him. 'They could be just over this hill.' It was a very slight incline but it hid their view of anything ahead of them.

'Or they could be sixty miles away. Face it, Steve, for Christ's sake. We're finished. We might as well give up. I'm for the farm. Next one I see . . .'

'We're not going to fucking surrender a second time,' Steve said fiercely. 'I'll tell you that for nothing. Where's yer guts?'

'Bleedin' empty. That's where they are. Bleedin' empty an' killin' me.'

'Listen!' Steve ordered, holding up his hand.

'Bleedin' killin' me!'

'Listen! Listen!'

'What?'

They'd been so angry with one another they hadn't heard the sound of engines. Now they realised that there were armoured cars approaching and scrambled behind the hedge just as the aerial of the leading car trembled over the brow of the hill. They watched, breathless with fear and hope, as the car gradually rose into their view, first the gun turret, then the driver – wearing the familiar black beret – then the chassis, clearly numbered and bearing its wonderful, unmistakable badge, the bright yellow rectangle with the charging black bull of the 11th Armoured Division.

Dusty leapt out of the hedge in a moment of pure joy.

And they opened fire. Sweet fucking Jesus! They opened fire.

There was a moment's total confusion, as both men flung themselves on the ground and Steve screamed, 'We're British for Chrissake! Don't fire!'

Then there were boots running towards him and a sergeant beside him and he was being picked up and dusted down and sworn at for a fucking idiot, 'jumping out on us like that. You could've been killed.' And then they were both looking at Dusty who was still lying in the road with his hands over his head.

'Oh fuck!' the sergeant said. 'Did we hit him?'

'No!' Steve roared, running towards him. 'No! Not now!' It was too dreadful. To be killed now, just when the war was so nearly over, when they'd come so far and endured so much, and by his own side. His own fucking stupid side! He was torn with grief and shock and fury, raging at the sergeant. 'Fucking idiots! You've killed him an' he's on your fucking side. How could you be so fucking stupid?'

And Dusty rolled over and grinned up at them. 'Rotten shot!' he said.

Then they were all laughing and whacking one another across the shoulders, and Steve and Dusty were hauled aboard the second armoured car and back with the British army again. They were given cigarettes – the bliss of a smoke after all that time – and iron rations to take the edge off their hunger, promised a shower and a good slap-up meal, brought up to date on the news of the war.

'Can't take you back to base just yet,' the sergeant explained. 'We've got to liberate some bloody concentration camp. Jerry's packing it in all over the shop. This lot just came out of nowhere with a white flag, would we take over the camp. They got typhus there apparently. You'll have to come for the ride.'

Steve didn't care where they went. Dusty was alive.

They were back with their own side. That was what mattered.

The three armoured cars turned off the minor road to follow a track between a forest of pine trees. Long beams of sunlight plunged like shining swords through the tall trunks, touching the branches with rich bright green, and striping the sides of the three war-worn vehicles with dappled patterns of white light and blue-green shadow. They could hear a bird singing high in the branches, peep-a, peep-a, peep-a. It was blissfully peaceful.

At first the smell was just a minor irritation, something that they were passing, something that would pass. But as they drove on, it grew steadily stronger and more putrid, like a combination of rotting meat, stinking rubbish and foul drains, a miasmic stench that penetrated to the inmost corner of the cars and filled their mouths and throats until they were retching.

'What the hell is it?' they asked one another. There was nothing in the woods to cause it, as far as they could see. Yet the further they drove, the stronger and more repulsive it became. It even blocked out the scent of the pines.

Then their journey came to an end and they saw what it was. The camp lay directly ahead of them and scattered on either side of the track were scores of dead bodies, men and women, some in convicts' striped suits, some in rags, some half naked, their arms and legs stick-thin, their heads shaven, all of them blotched with purple bruises and smeared with blood.

The men of the 11th Armoured looked out at them in horror, all thinking the same thing. Why were they so desperately thin? Why had they been left where they fell? It must have been an execution of some kind, because they'd been shot from the front and fallen face upwards or onto their sides. Had they been starved and then shot?

'Dear God!' Steve said. 'What sort of place is this?'

The gates were being opened. It was time for them to enter.

'It's called Belsen,' the sergeant said.

CHAPTER THIRTY

The commandant of Belsen concentration camp was waiting at the gate. From their vantage point beside the leading armoured car, Steve and Dusty had a good view of the proceedings and the man. He was exactly the sort of creature they expected – thickset, stocky, arrogant, cruel – and he dominated their attention, dressed in the immaculate, be-medalled uniform of a high-ranking officer, with a well-brushed cap and brightly polished jackboots, his face a mask of brutal insolence, heavily jowled and fleshy, with small eyes and beetling eyebrows. He showed no sign of fear at all and had turned his back on the camp and his prisoners, as if they were nothing to do with him, as if they didn't exist.

Behind him, the camp spread out its stinking and obvious presence, lines of cheap wooden huts, an expanse of bare, flattened, long-dead earth – where was all the grass? – and hundreds of prisoners, waiting, still and terrible, like half-clothed skeletons, stick-limbed and filthy, their skin the pale yellowish-white of old parchment, heads shaven, faces gaunt and scabby, eyes sunk into purple sockets. Some were standing, their arms dangling at their sides as if they no longer had the strength to lift them, many more were lying on the ground, too weak and ill even to sit up. And the stench cloyed around them, sickening and pervasive.

The troops at the gate were so appalled at the sight of them that they were bereft of speech. They looked from their own sturdy bodies and well-fed faces to the emaciated skulls and weary eyes before them and couldn't believe that they were seeing such things. How could anyone be reduced to such a state and still stand?

How could anyone be reduced to such a state? They didn't look human. But that thought, true though it was, was too shaming.

The commandant was the only person who wasn't abashed by the filth and starvation behind him. He clicked his heels to greet the brigadier and introduced himself as Joseph Kramer, looking as though he was proud of himself. Then he introduced his companions, a line of SS men and another of SS women, chief of whom was a pretty blonde, young and plump and looking most attractive in her trim uniform. 'Irma Grese.' It was all polite and proper and pompous, as if they were at a garden party.

The brigadier's way with such people was cold and absolute. He turned to the military policemen who were waiting behind him. 'Arrest them,' he said and climbed back into his staff car.

'Now what?' Steve asked the sergeant.

'Now we escort the food truck in,' the sergeant said.

'Poor bastards!' one of his privates said, looking at the prisoners with anguished pity.

'Don't let any of them touch you,' the sergeant warned. 'If you get lousy, you'll get typhus an' I'll bet they're crawling alive.'

It was true. They could see the lice, walking across those bare bony backs, climbing an exposed arm, squatting on a child's forehead, evil, disgusting creatures, large as thumbnails and dark with blood.

'He'll get the hygiene section in,' the sergeant said, nodding towards the brigadier's car. 'De-lousers, medical corps, casualty clearing station, the lot. The wires'll be red-hot now he's seen this.'

They inched into the compound, driving very slowly because the prisoners who could stand were staggering towards them, holding out withered hands and calling to them, '*Shalom! Shalom!*' signing, taloned fingers to cracked lips, that they needed food, their eyes imploring.

379

'It's coming,' the sergeant called to them. 'Quick as we can.'

But there's so many of them, Steve thought, as they drove gently on. There must be thousands here. How can we possibly feed so many? What will we give them? They're much too weak for ordinary food. To his shocked eyes the problem seemed insurmountable. The men squatting by the roadside or propped against the kerb with their heads lolling on their chests – their pitifully sunken chests – weren't even bothering to ask for food. They looked as if they'd crawled there to die, already more like corpses than human beings. They must have been starving for ages, Steve thought. That foul commandant has been watching them starve to death, poncing about in his fancy uniform and his bloody jackboots with that fat female of his, and all the time he's been watching these people starve to death. How could he do such a thing? The cruelty of it made him ache.

They found the cookhouse, which was empty of everything except cooking utensils, and there was a rush to fill it with supplies and get it operational. Steve and Dusty, having no other duties, joined the teams who were carrying in the food. The most important items were sacks of flour, dried milk and sugar, which were unloaded first so that the cooks could set to work right away.

'Bengal mixture,' they explained when they were asked what they were making. 'Invalid food. It's all they can take when they're as bad as this lot.'

It looked like gruel and Steve grimaced at it. 'And we thought *we* were hungry out on the road,' he said.

Dusty was gazing into the distance. 'What's that under the trees?'

'What trees?' Steve asked, looking round. He hadn't thought to see anything growing in such a place, but there they were, three miserable trees, covered in dust and drooping for lack of sustenance like everything else

380

in that hellish place. Heaped in their shade, too terrible
to be believed, too grotesque to be comprehended, was
a pile of dead bodies, all naked and rotting and all so
thin that they were nothing more than long bones
covered by strips of yellow skin, stretched and creased
like old chamois leather and glistening in the spring
sunshine.

'Jesus!' Steve said. 'Jesus Christ!'

Dusty was estimating the size of the pile, sixty yards
long at least, probably more, thirty yards wide, four feet
high. 'Fucking hell, Steve! There must be hundreds of
'em.'

'It's monstrous,' Steve said. 'To let them lie there
like that. Like rubbish.' He wanted to weep and scream
at the obscenity of it, but he couldn't. He had to stay in
control. 'How could they do such a thing?'.

It was a question all the troops were asking and they
went on asking it all evening, long after they'd left the
nightmare of the camp behind and returned to their
own, clean, hygienic headquarters, where they were
well fed and given beer to drink and water to wash in
and extra supplies of cigarettes for that much needed
smoke.

Steve and Dusty scrounged clean clothes, had a
shower and a shave and a very good meal, and listened
to the latest news on the wireless, but even then,
restored to themselves, they couldn't shift the smell of
the camp from their nostrils or the memory of its horror
from their minds and that night it was hard to sleep for
the appalling images that swelled in their dreams. Being
shot and killed in battle was horrific enough but it was
something they could accept. It was the way things
were in a war and as bad for one side as the other, a
matter of odds and luck, eased by the knowledge that
some of it could be avoided by pre-planning and quick
thinking. But to be starved to death, unarmed and
defenceless, men, women and children, was too cruel to
be comprehended. How could they do such a thing?

And early next morning, they had to go back to it.

'It'll get better', the sergeant reassured them as they drove towards the camp, 'once we get things sorted out.'

But the smell was worse and it didn't take long to discover why. The engineers had arrived and the terrible business of burying the dead had begun. They'd already dug a huge pit and were using a bulldozer to push the pile of rotting corpses into it, scooping them up in a tangle of arms and legs, torn skulls and rat-bitten bodies. The driver of the bulldozer was vomiting into his face mask – poor sod – but it had to be done. There was no time for individual funerals, even if such a thing had been possible, given how many dead there were. There was no time for dignity or pity. They had to be buried quickly before the entire camp died of typhus and dysentery. The only satisfactory thing about the whole revolting business, in the troops' opinion, was that the people being made to assist at the graveside were the captured SS guards.

Lorries arrived in rapid succession all day. Among the first were the hygiene teams, who brought supplies of DDT and cases full of flit sprays, and were soon busy spraying the walking inmates who queued in long patient lines to be relieved of their unwanted livestock, scratching and waiting. One of the huts was being scrubbed clean ready for use as a temporary hospital as soon as the medical teams arrived. And there was another delivery of food, mostly bread-flour and potatoes.

The cooks were despondent. 'Fat lot a' good mixing up all that Bengal mixture,' one of them told Steve. 'It just made 'em sick. Poor buggers couldn't keep it down. MO reckons it was too rich. We got to give 'em potato soup.'

It had been a bad night too. Some of the walking inmates had tried to raid the food stores and the guards had been ordered to fire over their heads to keep them

out. 'Wouldn't've done 'em no good if they'd got the
food,' the cook said. 'If Bengal mixture's enough to
make 'em sick, bread an' bacon would kill 'em.'

The fresh supplies were already being unloaded.
Dusty rolled up his sleeves and got down to it, but Steve
couldn't face it. To be told that these poor devils were
so weak they couldn't even digest invalid food upset
him almost as much as the sight of the mass grave had
done. He had to get out of the cookhouse or he'd be in
tears.

'I'm going to see if there's something else I can do,'
he said to Dusty. 'I feel stifled in here.'

'Try the major,' the cook suggested. 'He's organising
everything. He was down by the de-lousing section last
I see of him, checkin' 'em in.'

Being a major he was easy to find.

'7th Armoured?' he said, when Steve had explained
who he was and what he wanted. 'You're a bit off the
beaten track, aren't you?'

Steve explained quickly and with a touch of pride.
'Captured and escaped, sir. There's two of us. Private
Miller's unloading supplies.'

'This is a bad show,' the major said. 'Can't send you
back, you know. Not for the moment. No transport.'

'No, sir. I understand that. I came to see if there's
anything I could do.'

'We shall be pulling out in a day or two ourselves,'
the major said, still solving the first problem Steve had
presented. 'So you've got two options. You can come
with us, or you can wait here until you know where
your lot have got to. It's up to you.'

'We'd rather stay here, sir. We'd like to rejoin our
lot, if that's possible.'

'Righto,' the major agreed, and turned to the second
problem. 'Now you want a job to keep you occupied
pro tem. Is that right?'

'Sir.'

'I'll detail you to assist Captain Kennedy. He's

drawing up a list of all the bed bound. Trying to get a bit of order into the place.' He sighed. 'Anyway. He'll be glad of some help. The Prof will show you the ropes.'

'The Prof, sir?'

'Some sort of professor,' the major explained. 'Speaks about ten languages, or so I'm told. Captain Kennedy's found him terribly useful. Wait here. I'll send him over.'

The person who came stooping across to the delousing section some twenty minutes later was slow and shuffling and looked like an old man. The stubble on his chin and his shaven head was grey and his nose had the beaked look of extreme old age. But his eyes were the rich brown of someone in his twenties and when he spoke his voice was young too.

He addressed Steve in immaculate English and very politely. 'I believe you would like my help. You are to join Captain Kennedy's team, is that correct?'

Steve agreed that it was and asked what he had to do.

The Professor showed him a file full of names and addresses. 'There are six of us now,' he said. 'We go to each hut in turn. We complete a form for each inmate. I have lists of the phrases you will need. We wrote them yesterday. You see. "What is your name?" "How old are you?" "Where do you come from?" That one is German. This is Dutch. French. Yiddish.'

Apart from the French, which Steve recognised, the words were baffling. 'I'll have to write them out phonetically,' he said. 'Otherwise I'll never be able to pronounce them. I haven't got your gift of tongues.'

The Professor's gaunt face lifted into a smile. 'I was professor of modern languages in Berlin,' he explained. 'Once upon a time.'

That was rather a surprise. 'What brought you here?'

Again the smile. 'I said rude things about Hitler. A capital sin.'

That took courage, Steve thought, because he must

have known what he was letting himself in for. He was full of admiration for the man and concerned that he had suffered so much for such a trivial offence. 'Are you all right?' he asked.

'I have been eating gruel for the last twenty-four hours. And weak tea. Today I graduate to soup and bread, so I am told. I have not eaten so well in months. It is unimaginable luxury.'

They compiled a new list of the three phrases, the Prof pronouncing them as Steve wrote them down. Then they were both sprayed with DDT, to protect them while they were working, they collected pencils and erasers and two camp stools from Captain Kennedy's headquarters, and then they walked down the camp to the hut where they were to start work. It was a relief to Steve that he would be usefully occupied and away from that terrible mass grave.

But the hut held horrors too. It was dark and airless and the bunks were simply wooden shelves ranged in three tiers along both side walls, and hideously over-crowded, each one containing three sick and starving men, feet to the wall, shaven heads to the centre of the room. There was an odd rustling sound going on, which made Steve wonder whether there were rats in the place, and the smell inside was foul in the extreme for there was obviously no sanitation. One man was crawling out to the latrines on his hands and knees as they arrived, but others had not been able to make it and lay in their own filth.

It took a few seconds for Steve's eyes to adjust to the darkness and a few more before he realised what was making those odd sounds. Some of the men were trying to clap. They peered from their bunks, touching their emaciated hands together, shush, shush, in ghostly applause.

'They are pleased you are come,' the Prof said.

The two men worked in the stink of the hut for as long as they could endure it, patiently asking questions

385

and writing down the answers. At first Steve found it impossible to spell the names and had to turn to his companion for an interpretation of what was stammeringly said. But he gradually improved, the lists were gradually filled and towards noon, the orderlies arrived with weak soup and medicines, followed soon after by a medical officer.

To Steve's horror, two of the men he'd just questioned were certified dead.

'They can't be,' he protested. 'I was talking to them a few minutes ago.'

'They're dying like flies,' the MO said. 'We took more than a hundred out the last hut.'

'They're not going to that awful pit are they?'

'No,' the MO reassured. 'There's another one dug. They'll be buried properly. We've got a rabbi here now.'

Even so, it was searing to see those poor empty bodies being wrapped in shrouds and carried away. And worse when he went out of the hut for a smoke and realised what was going on in the hut.

While he'd been busy taking names, he'd assumed that the MO was simply examining his patients to see which of them needed medicine; now, watching from the door of the hut, he saw that he was pinning an identification mark on some of them and spending very little time with the others. He wondered what the chosen ones were being identified for and it wasn't long before he found out. More orderlies arrived, this time with stretchers. The identified inmates were lifted from their stinking bunks and carried away.

'Where are they going?' he asked as two of the orderlies passed him with their burden.

It was to the hospital hut. They were to be de-loused and washed and given a clean blanket to lie on and then the medics were going to take care of them.

'What about the others? Are you taking them later?'

The answer was chilling. 'There's no hope for the

others,' he was told. 'These are the ones who might survive.'

'But . . .'

'Look, mate,' the orderly said roughly. 'There's no room for all of them. These are all we can manage. The others are dying. We can't save them.'

'But you must . . .'

The orderly exploded into temper. 'Must!' he said. 'Who are you to tell us we must? There's no must about it. We're just the poor bloody infantry, mate. Not gods. We do as we're told. It's all we bloody *can* do. Oh get out the way for Chrissake.' And he signalled to his mate to carry on.

Pity and anger stalked the camp side by side. Steve couldn't think of anything else except the state of the prisoners. Their faces wept in his dreams and filled his waking moments with an almost perpetual anguish.

Dusty seemed to be able to set them aside. He got raucously drunk, told filthy jokes, and drew another line on his calendar every evening, counting off the days, as if he were still on active service. 'You just got to get on with it, ain'tcher,' he said. But Steve found every hour more difficult than the last.

He and Dusty were sprawled under the trees after their evening meal on the second evening, smoking and resting, when three of their new mates came bouncing up in a Jeep.

Dusty woke up at once. 'Nice work!' he admired. 'Where'd you get that?'

'Commandeered it.'

'Where are you off to?'

'To town. We're moving on in a day or two so we thought we'd see the sights. Wanna lift?'

'Why not?' Dusty said cheerfully. And after thinking about it for a moment, Steve agreed. Anything was better than sitting there with the smell of the camp eating into their brains and those endless awful faces rebuking and rebuking.

387

So they went to town, which turned out to be a small place called Celle.

It was like stepping into another world. It was such a pretty town that if it hadn't been for the horror a few miles away, they would have called it charming. There was no sign of destruction, no shattered buildings or shell-pitted roads. Here the streets were clean, the shuttered houses proper and provincial and at the centre of the town there was a green park, surrounded by prosperous houses and fine gardens, where magnolia trees were in full and magnificent bloom, their heady scent wafting into the Jeep with every turn of the evening breeze.

Many of the citizens were out taking the air after their working day, as if there were no such thing as war. They didn't seem to be the least bit abashed to be sharing the streets with their conquerors. They were all well fed to the point of plumpness, and very well dressed, the men in good suits and elegant hats, the women draped with fox furs. It was more like a spa than a town under occupation.

'And there's the difference,' Steve said, as he and his mates parked the Jeep and joined the promenade. 'They kill their prisoners and torture them to death, we live and let live.'

'Maybe they don't know what's been going on,' one of his new mates suggested.

'They couldn't be off knowing,' Steve said. And as if to prove him right, the wind suddenly changed direction, the scent of magnolia was blown away and the park was full of the ghastly stench of the camp. 'Oh God yes. They knew. And they didn't do anything about it.'

Pity and anger again, stirring in him like something alive and struggling to be free. 'I can't bear this,' he said. 'Let's go back and have a drink.'

The next morning they all had sore heads but there was still work to be done and that day the reporters started to arrive. It was almost a comfort to the army to see somebody else being shocked. They watched with satisfaction as men from the BBC prepared to film the burial of the dead, for the huge pile of corpses was only half cleared and another mass grave had been dug to accommodate the rest.

Dusty and two of the cooks came out to watch the cameras at work.

'It don't seem fair to film them, poor buggers,' one of the cooks said, as the bodies were shovelled towards the grave. 'Ain't they suffered enough?'

But Dusty understood the necessity. 'They got to film them,' he said. 'Otherwise no one'll believe it's happened. I wouldn't've done, if I hadn't seen it for mesself. Would you? No. Well then. People have got to see with their own eyes, like we're doing. There's got to be a record.'

'I seen enough,' the cook said, turning away. 'Come on, you lot. Let's be 'aving yer. We got people to feed.'

That morning Steve and the Prof started work in the hospital huts. 'Start with the women's hut,' Captain Kennedy instructed. 'Some of them haven't been interviewed. It's getting a bit complicated now the MO's shifting them about.'

For a hospital, it was pretty basic. But at least it was cleaner than the other huts had been – there was even a faint whiff of disinfectant – and at least the patients had a bunk to themselves and a blanket to lie on and were obviously being kept clean. But they were very sick and it took almost as long to coax information from them as it had done in the filth of the men's hut.

It wasn't until he'd patiently filled in seven or eight forms that Steve saw the significance of the date he'd been writing at the head of each paper.

'I've just realised something,' he said to the Prof as they walked on to the next bunk. 'It's my birthday. I've come of age.'

The Prof knew the right English response. 'Many happy returns,' he said.

And as Steve was thinking how incongruous it was, another English voice suddenly spoke from the next bunk. 'May the next one be in peacetime.'

It was one of the prisoners and this one was sitting up, with her back propped against the upright between the bunks and her knees bent to accommodate her length. She was a tall woman and, even in her present state, they could see she was young and had been pretty, with high cheekbones and large well-spaced blue eyes.

'I am Hannah,' she said to Steve, still speaking in English and she smiled at the Professor. 'Him you vill not need.'

'She speaks better English than I do,' the Prof agreed, patting her hand but he spoke to her in German to ask if she was well and she answered him in the same language, coughing into a piece of rag.

Her fragility worried Steve. She seemed too gentle to survive in this gross place. But he asked her name and religion, wrote down her last address, and then ventured to discover how she had learnt English.

'I vas teach,' she explained. And corrected herself, 'Teacher. I am sorry. It is a long time I do not speak your language.'

There was so much he wanted to know about and he sensed that she might be willing to tell him, if he didn't tire her too much. The Prof had moved on to the next bunk, so he stayed where he was, perched on his uncomfortable stool and asked if she wouldn't mind talking to him.

No, she would not mind at all. What did he wish to talk about?

So much, he hardly knew where to begin. 'Have you been here long?'

Again that sweet smile, lighting her blue eyes. 'For ever, I think.'

'It must have been dreadful.'

Sadness clouded her face. 'Yes. It has been dreadful.'

'Did they starve you deliberately?'

The answer was calm and all the more terrible for that. 'Oh yes. They meant to kill us all, you see. It vas planned. There vere to be no more Jews. Did you not know?'

He was impressed by her composure and horrified by what she'd just said. 'We heard rumours,' he told her. 'I never imagined it could possibly be anything like this though. I mean, this is beyond belief.'

'This is peaceful,' she corrected him. 'Now ve are fed. Ve have medicine. Nobody beat us.'

'Beat you?'

'Oh yes,' she said patiently.

'Who beat you?'

'The SS. The girl, Irma Grese. She especially.'

The commandant's plump female, Steve remembered. 'But she's young. I mean she's not much older than me.'

'You think the young are not cruel,' she said, coughing again. 'I tell you about Fraulein Grese. She kick us and hit us mit clubs. A dog she had. You have seen it, *ja*? If ve fell, she say to the dog, "Bite. Bite. Bite the dirty Jews."'

Steve thought of the plump, pink cheeks of Fraulein Grese, the thick fair hair, the bright smile. 'She'll pay for it,' he promised grimly.

But Hannah shrugged her thin shoulders. 'Vhat payment could she make', she asked, 'that vould undo one blow? Vould ve come back from the dead because she is killed?'

'You don't forgive her, surely?'

'I vill not play their game of hatred,' she said. 'Hatred hurts the hater.'

'But to be so cruel. That was evil.'

She considered for a long while, leaning back against the post. 'She is ignorant,' she said at last. 'A foolish girl. She is poor, probably. A poor, ignorant, foolish girl, and to her they say, "Come mit us. Good uniform ve give you. Good food ve give you. Important ve make you. You guard the dirty Jews." And here she comes and ve *are* dirty Jews. You see how dirty ve are. No vater to vash, rags to vear, no hair. Inhuman you are mit no hair. Dirty Jews. So naturalich, she hit us.'

It was impossible to believe that she could be so forgiving, so understanding, after all she must have seen and endured.

'I've got to move on now,' he said, and his voice revealed how regretful he was. 'May I come and talk to you again?'

'That I should like,' she said.

It was an extraordinary way to spend a twenty-first birthday.

In the next few days, Steve discovered that it doesn't take long to become institutionalised. By his fourth day in the camp, he had developed a curiously lethargic patience, as if nothing mattered except the work he was doing, as if there were no world beyond the gates of the camp, as if he no longer had any will of his own. On the fifth day, the last of the 11th Armoured pulled out and he and Dusty were left behind with the military police and the medical teams, to work on and wait for orders. But the days passed and the orders didn't come and although he should have been concerned about it, it didn't worry him. From time to time he remembered his mother's hurtful letter and Barbara's glowing account of the pre-fab, and knew that when he was back with his unit again he would have to write to them and let them know what he thought, but for the moment they were no more than echoes, and trivial compared to the daily reality of what was happening in the charnel house of the camp.

The obscene pile of corpses was cleared and buried but there were still other burials every day for, as the MO had predicted, most of the prisoners had gone too far to be saved. The place still stunk but the survivors were fed, the sick made marginal improvements, the huts were gradually cleaned, new latrines dug, new medicines delivered, and they could all see that order was gradually being restored.

Routines were a necessary comfort. Steve got into the habit of visiting Hannah twice a day. Her good sense and kindness sustained him and it encouraged him to watch her gradually getting better.

Sometimes she was too tired to say much and then he simply sat beside her and told her the latest news of the war. But sometimes she spoke at length about her family and friends and the school she'd taught in and what a reward it was to see children learn. He told her he'd gone straight from school to the army.

'So young,' she sighed. 'Your life you have before you.'

But he couldn't think about the future. The present was too pressing. 'I still can't understand how this could have happened,' he said. 'I see so many things, every day, awful, sad things, and they don't make sense to me.'

'You should write them down,' she advised. 'Writing makes clear.'

So he scrounged a notebook from one of the orderlies and began to jot things down – the number of people buried, the grief of the rabbi reciting the Kaddish at the graveside, the German proverb 'one louse, one death', the discovery that there was no grass growing in the camp because the prisoners had eaten it. But the thing he returned to over and over again was Hannah's refusal to seek revenge.

'*I cannot understand her,*' he wrote. '*If it had been me I would have been screaming for revenge. That vile commandant should be shot and so should Irma Grese. Evil should be punished. I used to think we were born good but the longer I stay in this camp the more I doubt it. Tomorrow I shall ask Hannah what she thinks.*'

393

But the next morning, when he strolled across to her hut, he found another patient lying in her bunk. He was quite annoyed to find she'd been moved and went off at once to look for a medical orderly.

There was one down at the far end of the hut, washing a very old lady and when he saw who was standing before him, he looked embarrassed and ducked his head.

'Ah yes,' he said. 'Hannah. Look I'm ever so sorry about this. She died in the night.'

Died? She couldn't have. She was getting better.

'She had TB,' the orderly explained. 'It was a haemorrhage. There was nothing we could do.'

Grief rose in Steve's throat like a tidal wave. He had to get out. Now. Anywhere. Or he'd be crying in front of this man, weeping in front of all these people. He ran from the hut, blindly, his boots kicking the supports, hurled himself into the sunshine, ran and ran, away – he didn't care where – until he reached the wire and had to stop because there was nowhere else to go. By then he was crying aloud, weeping for all the deaths he'd seen and endured and never mourned – for Taffy gunned down on that first day and for all the other mates he'd lost, good men, cut to pieces and gone for ever – for the tankies burnt to cinders – for Betty and all the others in that rocket – for Hannah who forgave her enemies and was dead because of them – hot, terrible tears that made him groan with the anguish of too much grief held in check for far, far too long. He was out of control but too wild with weeping to care. When Dusty came wandering over to see what was going on, he was beyond speech. But his old mate was a sensible soul, despite his rough ways, and had seen enough grief in the long campaign to know when to make himself scarce. He simply patted his oppo on the shoulder and left him to get on with it.

The afternoon wore away, the shadows lengthened, and at last the weeping was done. He dried his face on his sleeve, lit himself a cigarette and, after the first few comforting drags, stood up. He felt totally exhausted.

Dusty was walking across the compound towards him and there was a redcap with him.

'We got a message,' Dusty said, but checked before he passed it on. 'You all right?'

'Yes,' Steve said wearily, and asked, without much interest, 'What is it?'

'You're in luck,' the redcap said. 'You're getting out of here. Your lot are at Fallingsbostel. We've just got through to them. There's transport coming over for you at 09.00 hours tomorrow.'

'Back to the real world,' Dusty said, when the MP had marched away again. 'An' about time too. My ol' lady'll be wondering where I've got to. I ain't sent her a letter for three weeks.'

Nor have I, Steve thought. I haven't written to anyone. But he was too numb with grief to be troubled by conscience about it. I'll write and explain when we're back with the division, he thought. She'll understand.

'I shall be glad to get shot of this place,' Dusty said.

Steve looked round at the awful compound, at the mound where so many pitiful corpses were buried, at the hut where Hannah had died. 'I don't think I shall ever get shot of it,' he said. 'It'll be with me till the day I die.'

CHAPTER THIRTY-ONE

The last three weeks had been the longest and most anxious that Barbara had ever known. As the days passed and the letter she worried for didn't arrive, she withdrew deeper and deeper into herself. She went to work, as usual, and did her best to be cheerful to her passengers; she took her share of the housework; and true to her vow, she was polite to her in-laws and answered her mother's letters religiously. But her heart was a lead weight and there was little joy in her world.

After the first shock of the official notification had passed, Bob endured the long wait in his usual patient way but that was because he was afraid that a second letter would tell them the news they didn't want to hear and he preferred to go on in ignorance for as long as he could. At least that left him with a little hope to cling to.

Heather had found a kind of hope too, but hers was superstitious and private. It would be his twenty-first birthday soon. If he was alive – and he had to be alive, she simply wouldn't accept the possibility that he could be dead – then *that* would be the day he'd write to her. The letter would come that morning. '*Dear Mum, Just to say I'm thinking of you . . .*' the way he'd written last year when he was on Salisbury plain. The belief kept her going. Even if he'd received that last awful letter of hers – and oh she *did* wish she hadn't sent it – he would write to her on his birthday. He was bound to. But the hope was too flimsy to prevent her from being miserably jealous of any letter that was sent to Barbara.

'Two more again this morning,' she said to Bob, when the third pair arrived. 'Nothing from the War

Ministry and she gets letters from everywhere else, every damned day.'

'Every other day,' Bob corrected mildly, as he put on his cap.

'Nothing from the War Ministry,' Heather went on. 'Every day that damned postwoman comes up that damned path an' every day I think maybe this is it, maybe they've found him.' Her eyes were glistening with tears in her fierce, taut face.

He put an arm round her shoulders. 'I know.'

She was thinking of her Dear John letter again, and that made her too irritable to respond. 'No you don't. Nobody knows. Day after day. It's not right. Why should she have letters and we don't?'

'They're from her mother and her aunt,' he said. 'You don't begrudge her *that* surely. A bit of comfort.'

But in fact, although Becky Bosworth wrote briefly and more or less to the point, Maudie Nelson's letters were no comfort to Barbara at all. After the kindness of the first one, they'd degenerated into gossip – Jimmy had been *'ever so bad with the croup'*, Mrs Cromer's bunions were worse, Vic Castlemain was *'working for a jewler and doin ever so well'*. Now they were simply a regular reminder of how far apart they'd grown. We got nothing in common no more, Barbara thought sadly. I hardly know what to say to her. She don't even follow what's going on in the war.

If it hadn't been for Aunt Sis and the General Election, it would have been an impossible time. But Aunt Sis was a life-saver. There was plenty to do and she made sure that Barbara was involved in all of it, calling for her after work and leaving notes for her at the garage. Barely a day went by without a job being found. There were letters to write, leaflets to draw up, agendas to compose, and on the first Saturday in April there was a public meeting in Bellington South at which she had to make her first speech as parliamentary candidate.

Mr Craxton looked out a booklet on how to compose such a speech and walked to her flat to deliver it in person. It was his first outing since his heart attack and he still looked frail, so she thanked him for it very kindly and said she was sure it would be invaluable. But when she came to read the thing, it was worse than useless.

'I can't write a speech this way,' she said to Barbara later that evening, and quoted, '*Opening proposition. Development. Further development. Concluding paragraph.* It'ud end up dull as ditch water. No one'ud listen to a word of it.'

Barbara's mind was still sharp, anxious though she was. 'What do you really want to talk about?' she asked.

There was no doubt about the answer to that. 'The welfare state. That's what this election's going to be about. The welfare state an' the five giants we got to conquer.'

'Well thass it, then,' Barbara told her. 'You've written the opening proposition already.'

It took them until two in the morning to write the speech and even then Sis wasn't completely happy with it. But it had taken their minds off their worries and it turned out to be a huge success, unfinished or no. After the meeting she and Barbara and the Bellington South management committee went cheerfully off to the nearest pub trailing half the audience with them. The debate continued until closing time, and Barbara was in the thick of it and glad to be there.

It was only on the rare occasions when she was at home and on her own that her misery was too much for her. Sometimes she took out her precious shoebox and reread some of Steve's letters, so that she could hear his voice again. But the comfort they brought was complicated by an underlying anguish, because so many of them led her straight to the situation she was in now.

398

. . . People don't die in a war. They are killed and most of them are young and have their lives before them . . . I think the worst thing is there's no time to mourn them. We just have to get up and go on . . . there isn't any other option. So don't let this stop you. Keep on going. Live your life to the full. It's the best way to honour our dead . . .

And wasn't that what she was doing? Keeping on. Working hard. Planning for the future. But how would she manage in the future if he didn't come back to share it, if he'd been killed like the others, and she was never going to see him again? It would be his birthday in a week's time. Oh Steve, she mourned, my own dear, darling, darling Steve, that'll be your twenty-first birthday and I don't know whether you're alive or dead.

Meantime the papers were full of the great advances that were being made on all fronts. The tanks were 'swanning' across Germany. Hanover was captured. Vienna was liberated. The Russians were storming towards Berlin. There was even news of success against the Japanese, with American marines landing in a place called Okinawa. The rations were down again but they'd come to expect that. Cheese had been cut from three ounces a week to what Sis called a measly two. But the war was nearly over. They'd started work on the new electoral register. Better times were coming, even if success *was* tinged with sadness. As it so often was.

A piece of sad and rather unexpected news broke on April 12th. President Roosevelt, the stalwart of the American war effort, was dead.

'Poor ol' feller,' Barbara's passengers said. 'To come all this way an' work so hard, an' then die just when it's almost over. Don't seem fair. 'Specially in all this lovely weather.'

And it *was* lovely weather, the hottest April on record. 76°F in the shade, so the papers said. A real heatwave. But there was still no letter from Steve and he'd come 'all this way' too. What if he's dead like the President? What if they write to tell me that? Oh please God don't let them write and tell me that.

'His birthday tomorrow,' Heather said to her reflection that evening. 'Then we shall see.'

But although it was another beautiful day, no letters were delivered at all. That evening, when she finally had to face that there was no possible chance of any more mail that day, she sat down and cried for over an hour.

Barbara was out, at a committee meeting with Aunt Sis, but Bob was on late turn and caught the full impact of her grief.

'Try not to cry so,' he implored, patting her heaving shoulders. 'You'll make yourself ill.'

'I don't care!' she said wildly. 'He's dead. I know he is. Didn't I tell you right at the start? And I never got to say goodbye to him. Not so much as a word. It's the same as our Betty. They said missing then. But they knew she was dead all along. They had to come an' tell us in the end, didn't they. He's not missing any more than she was. I *would* be a fool to be caught out by the same line twice. He's no more missing than I am. It's always the same. They start by saying they're only missing. Missing isn't dead, they say. And we fall for it. It makes no odds *what* they say. They all end up dead in the end.'

He tried to reason with her. 'We don't know he's dead.'

But she groaned. 'We do! We do!'

He offered tea but she groaned at that too. 'And here we are stuck with that awful girl. Why doesn't she go home and leave us in peace?' It wasn't fair and she knew it but grief was making her too bitter to be fair and she needed someone to sting.

Bob didn't know how to answer her. 'Oh come on, Heather,' he said. 'She's as worried as you are. She loves him. Anyone can see that. I mean, we're all in the same boat. You, me, her, all of us.'

'No we're not. She got to say goodbye. I didn't.'

'We are,' he said reasonably and tried to persuade her. 'We're his parents, she's his wife. You can't get closer than that.'

It was a wasted effort. His calm exasperated her. 'Will you stop being so bloody reasonable,' she cried, flouncing about the kitchen. 'You're driving me up the wall.'

He grew touchy the way he always did when she was too wild for him to understand. 'I'm pointing out the truth,' he said, standing stiffly beside the table.

She turned on him, her face blazing. 'Truth!' she said wildly. 'Truth! What's truth got to do with it? You don't know anything about it. You didn't write him that letter.' Then she stopped and put her hand to her mouth, angry and miserable and afraid, knowing she'd gone too far.

For a split second she hoped he might not notice but he was instantly alert and alarmed, understanding that this was serious and that she regretted what she was telling him. 'What letter?' he asked.

'Nothing. It's not important.'

He took two strides towards her, caught her by the shoulders, insisted, 'What letter?'

She was caught. She would have to tell him now. 'I wrote to him,' she said, her voice sullen with distress. 'Just before he went missing. I told him she was carrying on.'

He was wearied with disappointment. 'Oh Heather.'

'Don't oh Heather me,' she said. 'I can't bear it.'

'I told you not to.'

'I know. Don't go on about it.'

'What a thing to do!'

'Look,' she said, her face imploring. 'It's not the way you think. I couldn't help it. I thought . . .'

'Maybe he didn't get it,' he hoped.

401

That plunged her into despair. 'Oh he'll have got it,' she said bitterly. 'Sod's Law he'll have got it. And now he's dead and I can't take it back or say sorry or explain or anything. And we're stuck with that awful girl. Well now she can hook off and marry that fancy man of hers. I don't care.'

'She won't do that.'

'That's what he said. Second string to her bow. In case.'

'No,' he contradicted. 'She won't. She ain't that sort a' girl.' That much he was certain of.

'You should talk to that Victor feller,' she said bitterly.

'You didn't tell our Steve all this, did you?'

She was too distressed to remember *what* she'd told him. 'I don't know. I could have. I was upset.'

And that could have been the last letter he got from us, Bob thought. Poor kid. 'I'm sick to death a' this bloody war!' he said.

Victor had been fully occupied for the last three weeks keeping the 'Hatton Garden' jeweller under observation. He and his two companions had done their work well, as the Skibbereen admitted, although grudgingly. They knew when the local bobby walked his beat and how long he stayed in the area and they'd found out virtually everything there was to know about the jeweller, who to their disappointment, didn't operate in Hatton Garden at all but had a small lock-up premises in a dusty cul-de-sac quite a long way behind that prestigious road.

They knew his name – Ebenezer Jones – and where he lived – in a house in Clapham with his mother – what he had for dinner – sandwiches wrapped in plain white paper – what and where he drank – a double scotch at the end of the day in the Three Tuns. They knew the name of his dog, the colour of his shirts, the size of his shoes, the newspaper he read, even when he went to the toilet. More importantly, they'd discovered where he kept his keys and his safe, and knew exactly how to get in and out of the backyard behind his shop, and from there into the workroom where all the choicest pieces were kept. There was a toilet window that could be easily forced, because he left it ajar now that the weather was so warm.

During their long vigil, Victor had found out quite a lot about his companions too, that Mog had been turned down by the army because he was seriously undersized and that he was very touchy about it, that Tiffany was forty-two and an old lag, a professional burglar who'd met the Skibbereen in the Scrubs. He reckoned that was the turning point in his life. 'Been with 'im ever since, except when we was doin' a bit a' bird. Never looked back, from that day to this.'

But for all their accumulating knowledge, they were no nearer to knowing when the diamonds were being delivered than they'd been at the outset. The April heatwave continued and Vic put on his best suit and visited the shop pretending to be a prospective buyer. 'I'm looking for an engagement ring.' But it was all the old stuff they'd seen in the window for the last two weeks and when he demurred that he couldn't find anything he really liked, nothing else was forthcoming.

'Maybe he's changed his mind,' Mog said, as he and Victor were drinking their customary evening beer in an obscure pub just round the corner. 'I mean, we can't keep this up fer ever. I ain't seen a bit a' skirt in weeks.'

'Nor me!' Victor said. Although in his case the long wait could be an advantage. Give old Spitfire time to get over the hollering. You always left a gal alone for a bit when you'd hollered at her. That was only sense. Meantime he had to admit he'd enjoyed himself pretending to be a customer. He thought he'd done it rather well, with just the right amount of superiority, which had been easy enough because he'd been anticipating the moment when he would slide one of those sparkling diamonds onto Spitfire's finger and put everything right again. The job *was* taking a long time. But it would all be worth it in the end.

The end came with a suddenness that took them all by surprise. Vic and Tiffany were strolling into the cul-de-sac one warm afternoon when a taxi pulled up outside the shop and a foreigner got out, wearing a beige suit and a very French hat and speaking in wonderful broken English as he paid his fare.

He was in the shop for over an hour and when he finally emerged into the sunshine, he looked extremely pleased with himself and went briskly off towards Hatton Garden leaving a strong smell of French cigarettes behind him. The two observers waited until he was out of sight and then Tiffany sent Victor into the shop to try his luck again, while he shot off to ring the Skibbereen.

Mr Jones was delighted to see him. 'Yes, sir,' he said. 'I do remember you. An engagement ring, wasn't it? You're in luck. I've just had a new consignment. Very fine rings. You won't find better in all Hatton Garden, though I say so myself. I'm sure you'll find something to suit today.'

It was a dazzling collection, three rows of very grand diamond rings, all of them shooting fire against the black velvet of their tray – tray 32 – and enough to make anyone yearn with greed. Vic was entranced by them. He didn't have to act when he said there were at least three that would suit very well. And it was pure joy to make his final choice and to be told that he'd selected the finest diamond of the lot.

''Course, I can't make a decision now,' he said, when he'd made as many mental notes as he needed. 'I mean, my fiancée must see it too, you understand. I'll come back tomorrow and bring her with me.'

Mr Jones said it would be a pleasure to see them and smiled his customer out of the shop. And Victor stood on the doorstep and lit a cigarette, very slowly and thoughtfully, while he noted where tray 32 was being taken. Back into the workshop and a turn to the right, where the bench is. Couldn't be better.

The Skibbereen was waiting in their chosen cafe. 'That's it then,' he said, with great satisfaction. 'Midnight. As planned. I'll go out in the garden and *see to my fence.*'

But at midnight everything went wrong.

They got over the back wall easily enough although rather more noisily than Vic thought necessary. But then Mog protested that he didn't think he could get through the toilet window.

'I'll never do it, Tiff,' he whispered. 'It's too small. I shall get stuck.'

'No you won't,' Tiffany told him, sternly. 'We've measured it. That's all took care of.'

'Let Vic do it,' Mog begged. 'You'll do it, won'tcher Vic.'

Victor scowled at him, his eyebrows pulled together into a straight dark line of annoyance. 'You always do this to us,' he hissed. 'I won't. Thass your job. Get you on with it.'

'Push him in,' Tiffany whispered.

Which they did, and presently he opened the back door and let them in. So far so good.

But there was nothing on the workbench at all. And no keys on the hook either.

'That's a bugger,' Tiffany said. 'He must've taken 'em home with him. We'll have to blow it. We need some padding. I don't suppose the old fool's got any cushions.'

He hadn't, so they had to take the curtains down and use them instead, which made Mog feel exposed. 'Anyone could look in an' see us,' he complained to Victor.

Victor was nervous himself but he cloaked it with anger. 'Don't talk squit,' he said crossly. 'There's no one out there.'

405

'Stand back,' Tiffany ordered. And the safe blew up.

The noise of the explosion in such a small space was shattering. Vic could feel his eardrums vibrating as if they were gongs and there was so much dust in the air that for a second he couldn't see anything else. Then he became aware that there was somebody shouting in the street and that Tiffany was grabbing trays and boxes from the safe and throwing the rings into a velvet bag. And he put his own hands into the wreckage and tipped the rings from tray 32.

'Scarpa!' Tiffany said, throwing the trays to the ground and belting towards the door. The shouts were getting louder and now they could hear running feet.

So Mog and Vic ran too, out of the open back door, over the wall, along the alley, panicking that they'd be arrested at any moment. But the alley was empty, Tiffany had vanished, there was no sign of the coppers and all the noise seemed to be coming from the street. And presently they emerged into Farringdon Street and a train went chuffing past making such a racket that it gave them a chance to catch their breath and calm down.

'Now what?' Mog asked, as he leant against the wall, gasping and spluttering.

'Home,' Vic gulped. 'I need a drink.'

'You going back for the car then?'

'No I hain't!'

That worried Mog. 'What if the cops pick it up?'

'Let them,' Vic said, heading for the nearest tram stop.

'They'll trace you.'

'I'll tell 'em it was stolen. Are you coming or not?'

'What about the Skibbereen? You still got some a' the rings ain'tcher?'

'He'll find us,' Vic said. 'He knows where we are. He won't expect us to hang around here, now will he?'

So they caught the tram, which was a bit of a come-down after staging a successful jewel robbery but better than walking. They'd have been horribly conspicuous on foot in the City at that time of night. And after a complicated journey they came safely back to the Isle of Dogs and Phossie's soot-dark house. It smelt sour and filthy, a combination of Phossie's old socks, stale food, and the reek of that clogged lavvy. But there were two bottles of whisky in the sideboard, where Vic had left them before he set out that morning, so they settled down to drink and wait. And day-dream about how they would spend their cut.

'I shall rent a decent house,' Vic said. 'Something with a bit of style.'

'You'll be lucky,' Mog said. 'They're all bomb damaged.'

'Not further out. What'll you do?'

'Buy a Jag. I'm sick a' driving other people's. How much d'you reckon we'll get?'

'There's fifteen rings on a tray,' Vic said, 'that's two hundred if it's a penny. Say four trays, maybe five. Could be a grand. Which reminds me, I'd better get my lot wrapped up. They're still rolling around in my pocket an' he won't think much of that. Shan't be a tick. I'll just go and find a box or something.'

And sort out the rings he intended to keep. He chose three, a half hoop, the biggest cluster and the solitaire he'd fancied in the shop. She could take her choice and he'd sell the others. Then, having hidden them away among his shirts, neatly tucked up in a clean sock halfway up a sleeve, he arranged the rest of his haul in the smallest box he could find and went back downstairs.

Mog was sprawled in his chair, shaking out the last drops from the first bottle as Vic put his box on the table. They'd only just filled their glasses, when they heard two cars drawing up outside. Mog got up, rather unsteadily and peered through the curtains. And there, looming towards the door, with Tiffany sloping behind him like a shadow, was the Skibbereen.

He filled the room, like a bull in a stall, massive and aggressive as if he was about to paw the dirty lino and snort down those wide nostrils, a barrel-chested, iron-fisted, threatening hulk. 'You got a lot to learn, son,' he said to Vic. 'Never leave yer car. That's a mug's game. Tiff's brought it back for yer. Swap it for another one first thing tomorrer. Where's the ice?'

Mog quailed into his chair but Vic stood, ready to fight back. He caught the keys Tiffany tossed to him and pointed at the box. 'Right here,' he said. 'All present an' correct.'

'Twelve,' the Skibbereen counted as he opened the lid. He looked suspiciously at Vic. 'Where's the other three?'

'That's all there was,' Vic said boldly, and when the Skibbereen glowered, 'He must've sold some.'

'Don't mess me about,' the Skibbereen said. 'All the other trays was full.'

'That's right,' Tiffany endorsed. 'Fifteen apiece. We counted.'

'Well that one wasn't. Straight up.' And he turned his pockets inside out to demonstrate his honesty.

The Skibbereen calculated, narrowing his eyes. Should he have Tiffany ransack the place or put on the threateners? If he *had* taken the other rings they'd be stashed well away by now. The boy was dishonest but he was no fool. And at that point Mog spoke up and made up his mind for him.

'When d'we get our cut?' he wanted to know.

'That', the Skibbereen said, 'is entirely up to your friend here. I'll think about it when I get all the loot. All of it mind! D'you wanna lift or are you walking back?'

Mog scrambled to his feet, gratefully obedient.

'Get that car switched,' the Skibbereen said to Vic. 'You owe me rent for next month don't forget. Tiff'll collect on Friday. You know the score, don'tcher. If I was you, I'd do a bit of searching. Try yer conscience for a start. See if you can't find what I want. If you want to stay healthy, that is. I ain't a man to be double-crossed. Makes me disagreeable. An' when I'm disagreeable, I cut up rough. You wouldn't want that.' And with a last menacing scowl he was gone, trailing Mog and Tiffany behind him.

Left on his own in the dust of the empty room, with whisky sour on his tongue, and the stink of the house filling his nostrils, Vic realised that he was panting. Annoyance of course, not fear. No man alive could frighten *him*. But it was unpleasant just the same. He sat on the *chaise longue*, thinking as hard as the whisky would allow. If he didn't come across with the rings, the Skibbereen would have the place torn apart. Mentioning Friday had been a threat as well as a date. They'd all understood that. So he'd have to get rid of them first thing tomorrow morning. And everything else that hadn't come the Skibbereen's way. That case of nylons for a start and quite a bit of the tinned food. I'll have to move it all out, he thought. I can't sell it, or someone'll snitch. But where could he take it? There were plenty of empty houses in the street but if the Skibbereen owned them all, there'd be no point in trying to hide anything there. No, when it came down to it, there was only one place he could go to. It cheered him to see himself distributing largesse, putting things right, reinstating himself.

I'll go there tomorrow, he thought, finishing his nightcap. Or I suppose I should say, later today. When I wake up.

CHAPTER THIRTY-TWO

The first thing Heather did when she got home from work that afternoon was to open all the windows. It had been a very hot day and the flat was stuffy. Then she put the kettle on for a cup of tea and went back downstairs while it boiled to see if the second post had arrived.

'Not yet,' Mrs Connelly said, hobbling out of the front room to join her. 'I've been keeping an eye out for her, so I have. I'll give you a call when she comes. Don't you fret.'

And at that very moment a shape appeared in the frosted glass of the front door.

'Well there she is!' Mrs Connelly cried. 'Now wouldn't you know it! Right on cue.'

But to their great disappointment, it wasn't the postwoman on the doorstep, it was Victor Castlemain, carrying a battered old carpet bag and smiling broadly.

'Hello!' he said to Heather. 'Long time no see. I've brought you some presents.'

Heather gave him one of her shrewd looks. She wasn't at all pleased to see him after all the trouble there'd been. Even the sight of him was troubling her conscience. She'd believed him so readily the last time they spoke but now with Steve missing and Barbara's misery so obvious, she was beginning to have doubts. Was he really Barbara's second string? Maybe Bob was right, maybe she wouldn't ... And yet here he was standing on the doorstep as if he had every right to be there and he'd hardly be doing that if there hadn't been something in it.

Her silence was rather disconcerting. 'Is Barbara in?' he asked.

'I wouldn't have thought you'd have wanted to see *her* again,' she said rather acidly. 'After the way she went on.'

Vic had forgotten about his last visit. Now he remembered it and felt uncomfortable. 'Oh we're old friends,' he said, deciding to brazen it out. 'Take the rough with the smooth an' all that sort of thing. Is she back yet? I asked at the depot.'

'Not yet,' she said. And she made up her mind. Let him come in. Let them meet up again where me and Bob can see them and hear what they've got to say for themselves. Then we shall know what's been going on. He'll be home in a minute. Might even be back before she is. 'Come in.'

He was encouraged. 'I brought you a few presents,' he repeated, carrying the carpet bag into the hall.

She was walking ahead of him up the stairs. 'Oh yes.'

Her tone was too non-committal for him to gauge her mood. 'Some more tinned stuff,' he said, following her into the kitchen. 'Thought you could use it.' He took a tin of American sweetcorn out of the bag and put it on the table.

But he never got the chance to find out if it was welcomed, because at that moment Barbara came up the stairs like a hurricane. Her face was flushed by sunlight and exertion, thick hair bushy, green eyes blazing and she was wearing her clippy's uniform with the jacket unbuttoned to reveal a very pretty blouse, white with little flowers embroidered on it. She looked so delectable it made him feel dizzy.

'You got a nerve, Victor Castlemain,' she said. 'Coming here after what you done.'

''Lo Spitfire,' he said, giving her the most charming smile he could contrive. 'I brought you a present.'

She hung up her jacket. 'Well now you can tek it away again,' she said.

'Don't be like that,' he coaxed. 'Hain't you glad to see an old friend.'

411

'Not if thass you, I hain't. You done enough damage last time you was here.'

'Oh,' he said grandly. 'Thass all forgot.' And he turned the charm on Heather. Let's put this right straight away. 'Forgive an' forgot, eh Mrs Wilkins.'

Heather gave him a steady look and turned away from him to attend to the salad. It pleased her to see how cross Barbara was and how furiously she was attacking. But then again, this could be a lover's tiff. Either way, it was best to keep out of it.

Barbara snorted. 'Not by me it hain't.'

Vic realised that he was screwing up his eyes with apprehension and paused for a second to rearrange his expression. This wasn't going according to plan. Better get on with the presents. 'I thought you could use some tinned fruit,' he said to Heather's back. 'I brought a selection.' He pulled the rest of the tins from the bag like a magician pulling rabbits from a hat, and laid them at one end of the kitchen table, enticingly, but neither of the women paid any attention. Heather was standing by the sink washing a lettuce, and Barbara was at the other end of the table topping and tailing a bunch of radishes. 'Peaches,' he offered. 'You like them.'

'Black market,' Barbara said without looking up from the radishes.

'Well,' he allowed, 'you don't get food like that in the shops. I mean to say. Stands to reason.'

She snorted at that too. 'Reason!'

He moved on, recognising that food wasn't going to work this time. 'Wait till you see what I got for *you*.'

She reached across the table to pick up a cucumber. 'Shift yourself,' she said. 'You're under my feet.'

'Nylons!' he said, opening the box.

She merely glanced at it. 'There's enough of 'em,' she said.

'Take your pick.'

'I s'pose they're black market an' all.'

He'd expected a bit of a rough reception – after all he

had hollered at her – but he hadn't imagined she would block him at every turn. What was the matter with her? He was doing his best. Look at all the things he'd brought her. He smiled again, but she turned her back on him which left him smiling at the air and feeling foolish. There was nothing for it. He'd have to play his trump card. He'd intended to keep it for the really dramatic moment but he would have to play it now. It was the only thing he could do.

He took the solitaire from his pocket and held it up in front of her so that it sparkled in the sunshine. 'What d'you think of *that*?' he said.

She looked at it, her eyes widening. Yes, Yes. She's impressed. She likes it. 'Well?' he asked.

Somebody was coming up the stairs. Heavy feet, trudging and knocking the treads. Oh not now! Not now! 'Well?'

It was Mr Wilkins. Wouldn't you know it? Mr Wilkins just at the wrong moment and both women turning to greet him, all smiles, and the ring lying on the table ignored.

The atmosphere in the room was so marked that Bob picked it up at once but before he could open his mouth to ask what was going on, Barbara took full command.

'Right,' she said looking straight at Victor for the first time since her arrival. 'Here's Mr Wilkins come home. Now we're all here. We'll wait till he's comf'table an' then you got some explaining to do, bor.'

Bob hung up his cap and took off his jacket and lowered himself into the comfort of his armchair to loosen the laces on his boots.

'I brought you a few tins,' Vic said, ingratiating himself quickly. But if he thought he could wriggle out of trouble by holding up tins, he was mistaken. Now that she'd opened her attack, Barbara was remorseless.

'Not that sort of explaining,' she said sternly and she put her hand on the tins as if she was going to push

413

them out of the conversation. 'You got some questions to answer.'

He was alarmed by the force of her attack but he had to face it out. What else could he do? He assumed a jaunty air. 'Fire away!'

'We'll start with those ol' pre-fabs,' she said, picking up her knife and returning to the cucumber. 'You told Mrs Wilkins I put our name down for a pre-fab. Hain't that right?'

'Our names were put down. Yes,' he agreed and he essayed a smile at Mrs Wilkins. 'We went there together.'

Oh no, my lad, you needn't try that, Barbara thought. And she pounced on him, sharp as the knife in her hand. 'Whose idea was that?'

He took refuge in vagueness. 'Don't remember.'

'Oh what a load of ol' squit,' she mocked. 'Don't remember. I bet you don't. So shut you up an' let me remind you since you got such a bad mem'ry. That was *your* idea. You got the tickets an' you wrote the names on the tickets. Mr and Mrs Castlemain. An' you never said a word to me about it. Hain't that right?'

What a fighter she is, Bob thought, admiring her, and wasn't I right about her? I knew she wouldn't play our Steve up. He looked across at Heather to see how she was taking it and was pleased that she was standing quite still at the sink, potato in hand, listening like a cat at a mouse hole.

Barbara threw the chopped cucumber into the salad bowl as if she were hurling a grenade. 'Well?' she insisted. 'Hain't that right?'

'Probably,' Vic said uncomfortably. 'I don't remember. That was weeks ago. Water under the bridge. That hain't important.'

'No?' she said, giving him the coolest stare. 'Hain't it? Well, try this for size then, bor. Whose name you put down for a house?'

414

He was losing the argument. 'I don't know, gal. How d'you aspect me to remember that far back?'

She went on grilling him relentlessly. It was as if they were in a court of law and she was a barrister. He could almost see the wig on top of those dark curls. 'I'll tell you what I'll do,' she said. 'Since you got such a bad mem'ry. I'll ask my mother-in-law to tell us what you told *her*. I'm sure she remembers.'

Oh yes, Heather remembered very well and it was a relief to speak out and challenge him. 'You said Barbara told you to put down *your* name for a pre-fab. You said you didn't want to do it and she made you. You said she wanted a second string to her bow. I remember the very words. No mother'd ever forget a thing like that. You said she wanted a second string to her bow in case our Steve got killed.'

The fury on Barbara's face was so violent that the entire room was fired with it. Sunshine stabbed the windows with red shards of light, knives glinted, gas jets roared in the geyser, diamonds flashed their intermittent spotlights like sharp distress signals. Even the kettle boiled with such fury that its lid jumped up and down.

'You rotten little toerag,' she roared. 'How dare you say such a thing. As if I'd even look at you after Steve. You! Tek a look at yourself, bor. You're nothin' but a cheapskate, a spiv, the lowest of the low. You don't begin to compare with our Steve. Eleven months he's been out there, fightin' in all weathers, sleepin' in the open, riskin' his life day after day, never a word of complaint, a brave, wonderful man. An' now he's missing an' we don't know whether he's alive or dead. An' you dare to think I'd even look at you. Second string to my bow! You make me spit! You don't begin to compare!'

He fought back frantically, forgetting to dissemble, beyond caution or discretion. 'No I don't,' he shouted, 'because I'm better in every respect. Better educated,

415

better looking, richer. Much, much richer. I mean to say, what's a soldier's pay?'

He could hear Mrs Wilkins' sharp intake of breath, was aware of the anger on her face, but it was Barbara who answered.

'Death!' she said, green eyes blazing. 'Bein' shot down. Thass a soldier's pay. You hain't fit to lick his boots. You hain't fit to breathe the same air. An' you think I'd leave him an' set up home with you.'

'Look!' he tried. 'I didn't think . . .'

'No,' she roared. 'You don't think. Thass just your trouble. Always was. Look at that bloody ring! You thought you could buy me! Thass what you thought. You thought, I'll wave a diamond at her. Then she'll come a-runnin'. Well let me tell you somethin', Victor Castlemain. I hain't for sale! I belong to Steve an' no one else. Even if he's dead I shall go on belonging to him. Always! For ever an' ever!' She was weeping with anger and grief and the pent-up misery of all those weeks of waiting. 'I'll show you what you can do with your presents.' And she grabbed the ring from the table and hurled it out of the open window.

He was horrified. 'Thass worth money!' he cried. 'Thass over twenty pounds worth of ring.'

But she didn't care about twenty pounds. She was cleaning him out of the house, removing every sign of his obnoxious presence, quick and strong and unstoppable, like an avalanche. First, three of the tins, crashing down one after the other, then the box of nylons, which sprang open in mid-air and distributed its contents as it fell.

It was wonderfully dramatic. The long stockings were lifted by the breeze and drifted down slowly and gracefully, turning in the air like silken pennants, landing gently all over the garden, on the lawn, on the path, on every shrub and plant, draped and curled like long buff ribbons.

Mrs Connelly, watching and listening at her kitchen

door, was quite taken with them. 'Will you look at that now,' she said to her husband. 'There must be hondreds and hondreds of the things.'

'He *is* a spiv,' Mr Connelly observed. 'She's right about that. If you ask me, those are stolen goods, so they are. I don' wonder she's shoutin' at him. He's a bad lot.'

Upstairs in the Wilkins' kitchen, Barbara was hurling tins again, throwing them from the window with a bold overarm swing, like a bowler.

'For God's sake!' Vic begged. 'What if they land on the ring? You could smash it to bits.'

She didn't care. 'You come here', she said, 'puttin' my family at risk, insultin' my husband. You wanna think yourself lucky I hain't a-throwing you out the window an' all.'

'All right, all right,' he said, backing to the door. 'I'm going. You win. Onny don't throw any more tins or you'll do me a mischief.'

She picked up another one and brandished it at him. 'Good!' she said, eyes blazing. 'I hope I do!'

At which, recognising total defeat, he grabbed his carpet bag and ran, precipitating down the stairs, hurtling into the kitchen.

The funny old woman who'd let him in was standing by the door. 'Just off!' he said. 'Something to find in your garden. Fell out the window. You don't mind if I go an' look, do you?'

She made a grimace at him. 'I don't know about that, at all, at all.' But he was already out of the house and down on his hands and knees, grovelling about in the flower beds. He *had* to find it. Had to. He scoured the little garden, gathering the nylons, cramming the dented tins into his carpet bag, poring over every plant and combing every shrub with tense frantic fingers. Come on! Come on! It must be here!

He was aware that the old biddy and her husband were watching him from the doorway and that there were curious faces peering out of most of the upstairs windows but he couldn't stop, even though he knew he was making an exhibition of himself. Twenty pounds was twenty pounds. And suddenly there it was, flashing fire among the wallflowers. Thank God for that! He picked it up, examined it carefully, polished it on his handkerchief, his legs suddenly weak with relief.

Heavy footsteps on the path behind him. The old feller? Mr Wilkins? Time to be off whoever it was. 'I'm just going,' he promised. And turned his head to find himself looking straight into Tiffany's long sardonic face. The shock sent him into a panic, his thoughts skittering in all directions like shards of broken glass. Christ Almighty! How did he get here? Has he come from the Skibbereen? Or is he on his own? What the hell am I going to do?

'Quite right, sunshine,' Tiffany said, smiling sourly at him. 'Never a truer word. You're coming with me. An' we'll have that nice little sparkler fer starters.'

Victor struggled to control himself and the situation. 'That's mine,' he said, speaking softly, mindful of the listeners. 'Legit.'

Tiffany didn't bother to argue, although he spoke quietly too, his words hissing. 'That's ours. Illegit,' he said. 'Hand it over. Skibber's orders.'

Victor's heart sank to the depths, a cold stone. 'He hain't here, is he?'

'What d'you think?' Tiffany sneered.

Vic's mind was still spinning, but now he was searching for an escape, remembering the Skibbereen's warning. *'See if you can't find what I want. If you wanna stay healthy!'* He tried wheedling. 'Look, Tiff. Give us a break, eh. I know I should have passed it over but it's only the one. I mean to say, look at it this way. You could take it as part of my cut. I mean to say, I've earned it.'

Tiffany was as implacable as Spitfire had been. He held out his palm. 'Give!' he said.

418

'No God damn it,' Vic said. 'I won't. I nicked the thing. That's mine.'

'Tell that to the Skibbereen,' Tiffany mocked. 'He'll be very pleased to hear that. I *don't* think! An' what's all this stuff?' He seized the carpet bag and pulled it open.

The thought of what the Skibbereen would do to him was furring Vic's mind, but he dredged up enough energy to fight. 'Thass mine, you silly bugger. Leave off.'

'That's ours!' Tiffany said, and he suddenly seized Vic by the scruff of the neck and began to haul him down the path towards the house. For a few undignified seconds they struggled like wild things, Tiffany straining forward, Vic pulling away, red in the face and aiming kicks and blows. Then Vic gave a great heave and managed to free himself. He pulled the bag away from Tiffany's hand and made a bolt for it, tearing down the garden and flinging himself at the wall. There was nothing in his mind now except the need to get away from the Skibbereen. But it was a waste of effort. As he pulled himself up the brickwork, clinging to the top of the wall, feet scrabbling, another mocking face grinned above him. Mog! Of all people. Climbing without being urged. Oh for Christ's sake! How many more has the Skibbereen sent?

'Naughty, naughty!' Mog rebuked, and swinging a leg over the wall, he pushed Vic violently back into the garden and Tiffany's waiting clutch. Within seconds the struggle was over. They had his arms pinioned behind his back and were frogmarching him through the house and out into the street, dragging the carpet bag with them.

The watchers rushed from the back of the terrace to the front, eager not to miss a second, and Bob and Heather and Barbara followed them, Bob cheerfully enjoying Victor's come-uppance, Heather anxious about what the neighbours would think, Barbara caught

419

between emotions. She was still angry at the lies he'd told and glad to think that he was getting pushed around, but even so, he was still a North-Ender and she didn't want to see him injured.

By now and to Heather's chagrin, the entire street seemed to be involved, for the noise of the fight had gathered attention and besides, there were three huge black cars standing in a line by the pavement and nobody had ever seen three cars in the street before. Avid heads peered from the open windows, groups congregated on the pathways, the kids left their games to watch, as Vic was pushed along the pavement towards the Skibbereen's huge limousine. Even the postwoman was caught up in the drama. She'd been cycling slowly along the road from the opposite direction when the second car arrived, languidly delivering the afternoon post and looking forward to her tea, but now she stopped her bike and leant on the handlebars to enjoy the spectacle, intrigued by the sight of all those cars and by the fear on Victor's face.

Oh God! he was praying, give me a break. Let me find a way out. But his mind was full of hideous images, of being set on late at night, as he stepped out of a pub, dragged up some dark alley and beaten unconscious, or, worse, driven off here and now to be thrashed in the country where there was no one to help him.

By the time he reached the Skibbereen's open window, he was frozen with fear. His mouth dry, he tried to ingratiate himself. 'Look,' he said. 'I made a mistake. I admit it. I mean it could have happened to anyone.'

'Not to me,' the Skibbereen said coldly and he leant forward to glare at his victim. 'You got two minutes to hand those rings over and get out a' my sight. If you're still around after that, God help you!'

It was a reprieve. They were going to let him go. Wet-palmed with fear, he pulled the two other rings from his pocket and put all three on the Skibbereen's palm. Then he ran, hearing the clunk of his tins as the carpet bag was slung into the Skibbereen's car, a buzz of voices from all those upstairs windows, a gust of horrible gloating laughter from Mog. Into his car and into gear, doing a three-point turn – very badly because his hands were slippery with sweat – but then away, watching his rear mirror, afraid of being followed.

His heart didn't steady until he'd been driving for some time. Then relief washed over him, making him feel quite weak. He'd got away, unhurt, scot-free. So OK, he'd got to move on and he was down to his last shilling, so OK they'd skinned him out, so OK Spitfire had given him a bollocking, but he still had contacts, people still needed food, there was still rationing and what's more he still had another case full of nylons in the boot. They'd do to get off the ground again. I'll make a fresh start, he promised himself, and then I'll come back and find Spitfire again. Now that his mind was working more easily he remembered that she'd said something about that soldier being missing. All right then, if he's missing she could be a free woman by the time I find her again. Oh I'm not beaten. Not by a long chalk.

Back in Childeric Road, it was so quiet that Heather could hear every sound in the street, from the blackbird sweet-singing in the garden to the happy chorus of their neighbours' voices.

Their next-door-neighbour was leaning across the hedge to question Mrs Connelly. 'And what was all that about?'

'Well that's seen *him* off and no mistake,' Bob said, stepping back from the window.

And at that, as if his voice had released her into action, Heather turned to catch her daughter-in-law in her arms, tearful with relief and admiration and affection. I was wrong about her, thank God. Quite, quite wrong. She's a good loyal wife. A good loving loyal wife. 'Oh Barbara!' she said. 'My dear, dear girl! You were splendid back there!'

'I meant every word of it,' Barbara told her, stepping back so that they could look at one another.

'I know. I know.'

'I put *Steve*'s name down for that house,' Barbara said. 'Steve's an' mine.' They had to be quite clear about that.

'I know,' Heather said again. 'I don't know why I ever thought you hadn't. I shouldn't have believed him for a second. Lying hound! Oh Barbara! I've been so wrong about you. I thought you were too young. I mean, I didn't think you could love him the way... And you did, all the time. So much!'

'Yes.'

'I'm so sorry for all the things I said.'

This time it was Barbara's turn to hug. 'I know,' she said lovingly. 'It's all right. Really.'

And at that Heather burst into tears, remembering that dreadful letter and wishing with all her heart that she hadn't written it. 'I couldn't want for a better daughter-in-law,' she said. 'And I'm not just saying that. I mean it. I can't get over the way you saw him off. You were splendid. Wasn't she splendid, Bob?'

But Bob didn't answer, although he'd been watching them both with yearning affection. 'What's that noise?' he asked, turning his head towards the landing. There was an odd knocking sound coming from the kitchen, a rhythmic sound like someone using a wooden mallet.

Heather jumped out of Barbara's arms and gave a shriek. 'It's the kettle.'

Which it was, burnt dry and filling the kitchen with tinny grey smoke. 'Quick! Quick! Get some water in it.' But the water spat and hissed and ran straight out through the hole in the bottom. 'Oh for heaven's sake!' She was so flustered that Bob and Barbara began to laugh and once they'd started they couldn't stop.

'It's no laughing matter!' Heather said, laughing too, despite herself. 'Look at the state of it!'

They were stupid with relief, chortling and chuckling until they were short of breath. They were making such a commotion that they didn't hear Mrs Connelly coming up the stairs.

'It's only me, Mrs Wilkins dear,' she said, looking askance at the smoke. 'Only this letter's come for Barbara an' I thought you'd want to see it.'

Everything else was forgotten at once, burnt kettles, diamond rings, fighting men, wicked lies and all. 'It's Steve!' Barbara cried, recognising the writing. 'Oh God! It's Steve! Give it to me! Give it to me!'

The excitement then, the trembling hands as the letter was opened, the tears as it was passed from hand to hand and read and re-read, its news being too good to be taken in at a single reading. 'He's all right. He was took prisoner.' 'Oh thank God for that!' The day was instantly and totally changed, their lives lifted, proportion restored, quarrels forgotten, Victor forgotten, all misery smoothed away. He was alive and they would see him again.

'Oh thank God!' Heather said. 'Just let him stay safe and well till it's all over. It can't be much longer.'

'They'll give him leave, won't they,' Barbara hoped, green eyes shining.

Bob and Heather had no doubt about it. 'Bound to.'

The thought of seeing him again was making Barbara breathless. 'I wonder what he's doing now,' she said.

CHAPTER THIRTY-THREE

Steve and Dusty were sun-bathing, lying on their backs in a German orchard just outside Hamburg, tunics tossed aside, boots off, shirtsleeves rolled up as far as they would go, taking their ease as if the war were already over. As well it might be for all they knew, for good news was coming in with every bulletin. The Americans had captured Genoa. The Russians were in the outskirts of Berlin. Mussolini had been shot and hung up by the heels in a public square. There were rumours that Hitler was dead too. But there, in the orchard, it was simply and amazingly peaceful. There was no sound of gunfire even in the distance, no planes roaring across the sky, no snipers, no orders, no alarms, just a slight wind that ruffled the blossom in the apple trees so that pink and white petals dropped in a silken fall to dapple the weary faces and young brown arms below them.

Since they'd rejoined the division at Fallingbostel, Steve and Dusty had been kept so fully occupied that they'd barely had time to talk, let alone sit in the sun and dream. The Germans had fought most bitterly and at every turn, through peat bogs, along the edge of their endless forests, over the long wild moor of Luneburg Heath, but the British advance had been steady. They'd taken Soltau in flames and Hollenstedt in ruins, and by the 29th of April they'd crossed the River Elbe and reached the woods south of Harburg. And there, just when they were within sight of Hamburg and gearing themselves up for a major assault, everything had come to a halt.

There was a rumour that a citizens' deputation had

come out to meet the advancing troops waving a white flag and offering to surrender – and another that Monty himself was in the area. Nobody knew for certain, so for the moment they were just lying under the trees waiting to see what would happen next and hoping that the rumours were true. They'd lost seventy-eight men since the Rhine crossing and if they could occupy Hamburg without taking any more casualties, that would suit them fine.

'I reckon this is the end,' Dusty said, happily. 'If old Monty's here.'

Steve smiled at him.

'The minute it's over, I shall put in for a spot a' leave,' Dusty observed, squinting up at the branches over his head. 'We got enough owing! Back home, mate. Imagine it. Nice little bint. Home-cooking. I can't wait.'

Steve smiled at him again but he didn't answer. He'd spent the last half-hour rereading his mail and now he was lying with the letters on his chest, brooding. Barbara had sent him a letter every day since he'd written to her again, and while war dominated his thoughts and he was obeying orders and living an hour at a time, he'd simply been pleased to see her familiar writing and to know that she was safe and well. Now, when he had plenty of time to answer her, he was too confused to do it. The trouble was Belsen had made a nonsense of one of the great certainties of his life, and left him with no way to organise his thoughts and no base from which to work. He wasn't at all sure how he felt about these letters of hers, nor, painful though it was to admit it, how he felt about her.

It troubled him that she hadn't said a word about that Victor feller. And she hadn't mentioned the war much either. True, she'd told him how glad she was that he was alive and well – '*We been so worried about you, no letters all that time. We knew it must be something dreadful. I never thought it would be one of those*

425

concentration camps. That must have been awful' – but apart from that she spent most of her letters telling him about Sis and the management committee of Bellington South. *"Course we know she can't win. That's a safe Tory seat. But she says the experience will come in handy and she might get a good seat next time. We think the election will be called pretty soon once the war's over.'*

He had a vague, disturbing feeling that there was something underneath the letters that wasn't being said, or that he couldn't understand, especially as his mother had only written one letter to him in all that time and hadn't said anything about *that* letter at all, but he no longer had the capacity to think his thoughts through and every time he tried they slid away from him as if he had holes in his brain, or tailed off and were lost in terrible images. Even when he was reading Barbara's letters, he could see those poor, stinking, broken bodies being shovelled into the pit and the smell of death rose into his memory until he was overwhelmed by it and couldn't see the words on the page. After a while he gave up trying. He couldn't read her letters and he couldn't answer them either. It was easier to write in his notebook, for his own eyes and no one else's. Sighing, he put her letters away, and picked up his pencil.

I always thought human beings were the same. I know we are different to look at but I thought we were basically the same. I knew we all did stupid things. I knew we could be unkind, jealous, spiteful, greedy, just plain silly, all those things, but I believed we were basically good underneath it all, that when it came down to it, we'd be moral, our basic humanity would win through. I was wrong.

Oh how painful it was even to write the words.

426

*We are not basically good and we are not all the
same. Some people are evil. Those guards enjoyed
hurting people, they felt justified in what they were
doing. Irma Grese became a torturer and was
rewarded for it, Hannah was tortured and was
punished by death.*

The death-pit gaped under the words, pulling him
down towards it but he had to go on. If he wrote this
down he might make sense of it. And oh, how much he
needed to make sense of it.

*If some people are evil, maybe there is evil
inherent in all of us, maybe the early Christians
were right, maybe we are born evil. If that is so, I
am evil, and so are Dusty and Aunt Sis and my
mother and father and Barbara.*

But at that point he had to stop. What if Mum was
right and she really *was* playing around with someone
else? Was that evil? Or just foolish? How can I be
certain? The question made him sigh with distress. How
could he be certain of anything now?

Sergeant Morris was walking towards them through
the trees. 'Come on then, boys, let's be 'aving you.'

They sat up slowly, pretending to groan. 'Where to,
sarge?'

'Hamburg in a day or two, my lovely lads. And we
won't have to fire a shot.'

'Is it true then, sarge? Have they surrendered?'

'They're surrendering,' the sergeant said. 'Just come
through, which you'd've heard if you'd had the wireless
on instead a' rolling about on your backs out here. I
never saw such a lot a' dozy tarts!'

'No peace for the wicked,' they joked as they
scrambled to their feet.

'Shouldn't be wicked,' the sergeant told them, giving
the well-worn reply. 'What you been up to?'

They parried that in the usual way too. 'Chance'ud be a fine thing!'

The careless words echoed in Steve's mind all evening, congealing his thoughts. He was still brooding over them when news came through on the camp radio that had the entire regiment cheering.

Adolf Hitler had committed suicide. No rumour this time. There was no doubt about it. The German radio had made the announcement itself – after playing Wagner's 'Death of Siegfried' to forewarn their listeners. They hadn't admitted that he'd killed himself, naturally, but had claimed that he'd *died fighting to the last against the Bolshevik Hordes*'. It was the Forces network that had revealed that it was suicide. But what did it matter how he'd gone? He was dead. That was the great thing. And now the Germans would surrender. It didn't clear Steve's mind, but it lifted his spirits.

At four o'clock the next afternoon the division set off to occupy Hamburg. It was raining heavily when they started but by the time they reached the river Elbe the sun had come out. It was a new experience to cross a bridge they hadn't built themselves and an even better one to be entering a German city without having to fight for it. It was only a matter of minutes before the tanks were rolling through the empty streets towards the main square.

The population had been put under curfew so there was no one about except the local police, who stood lining the pavements as they drove past, sullen and subdued and obviously defeated. 'Serve the buggers right,' Dusty said.

They passed the docks where several U-boats stood in their pens, half-built and burnt black. The damage here was spectacular. The enormous cranes and gantries above the docks had been knotted into grotesque shapes by the blast and the heat of the fire-storm had even melted the steel girders, huge though they were, leaving them red and black and drooping.

'They won't be building any more of those damned things in a hurry,' Steve said, looking at the burnt-out U-boats with satisfaction. It was a justified revenge. The submarine builders had had it coming to them for a very long time.

Then they were heading for the city centre where the roads were full of potholes and the destruction was total. In street after street the buildings had been reduced to piles of rubble and, even when they found a terrace of houses, it turned out to be a facade with nothing behind it. Steve was surprised by how quickly the Germans had tidied the place up. The streets had been cleaned and cleared, the tramlines mended although there were no trams running. They'd even restored the telephone wires although there couldn't be a phone left under all that rubble. He couldn't understand their passion for neatness and order when they'd produced a place as foul and disorganised as Belsen. Does evil run by opposites? he wondered. Neat bureaucracy and cruel behaviour.

In Adolf Hitler Platz the garrison commander was waiting to meet them outside the Town Hall, which was about the only building still intact. He was fat and wore glasses and an incongruously tidy uniform. Steve disliked him on sight, hating his superfluous flesh and remembering Joseph Kramer and his immaculate attire. He was delighted when their colonel arrived dressed in an American combat jacket, a pair of corduroy trousers and an 11th Hussars' cap, looking every inch the conqueror and totally himself. And when he ignored the fat German and pulled a packet of army biscuits from his jacket to feed the pigeons, Steve cheered as raucously as all the others.

But his thoughts fell into the same holes no matter what he saw or how pleased he was to see it.

The next day news came through that Admiral Doenitz had sent an envoy to Montgomery's HQ on Luneburg Heath. And that night the announcement they'd all been waiting for was finally broadcast. The Germans had surrendered unconditionally. More than a million Germans in Holland, Denmark and north-west Germany were to lay down their arms at 08.00 hours the following morning. The war in Europe was over.

Dusty Miller put in for leave the very next day. But Steve was still locked in misery and indecision and he stayed where he was.

'You're barmy,' Dusty told him. 'Don'tcher want ter go home?'

'Not yet,' Steve had to admit. 'I got things to sort out. And besides,' managing to grin at his oppo, 'someone's got to keep the army running.'

CHAPTER THIRTY-FOUR

At three o'clock on the following afternoon Whitehall was so full of people it was impossible to walk in any direction except the one the crowd was following. Many had been there since early morning, jostling and dancing and cheering, with paper flags in their hands and London dust on their shoes, and more were arriving by the minute to join the celebration. Barbara had come up on the tram as soon as she finished work, with Sis and Mabel and the girls. Now they were wedged in the mass, waiting for the Prime Minister to declare the war officially over. There were loudspeakers on all the lamp standards and Union flags draped from every window and the sense of happiness and relief that rose on every side was as palpable as incense.

'What a day!' Sis shouted above the racket. 'What a day!'

'Our Betty should've been here to see it,' Mabel said, sadly. 'Poor kid. I keep thinking about her. An' all the other poor little devils. There's been a lot a' good people killed. I don't think I ought to have come.'

Poor Betty, Barbara thought, remembering her with a sudden surge of anguish. And poor Norman. She could see his brawny arms and that rolling walk of his and the way he'd gone whistling off to sea. We got peace at last but *they* paid the price for it.

'It'll never happen again,' Sis said, patting her sister's arm. 'We'll make sure of it this time.'

There was a whirring noise from Big Ben as the great clock began to sound the hour, booming out across the crowded streets in the steady familiar way that had been such a comfort over the last six years. As it struck, the

431

crowds gradually shooshed themselves quiet and at the last stroke, the loudspeakers spluttered and a voice spoke tinnily over their heads announcing the Prime Minister.

There was a cheer and shouts of 'Good old Winnie!', then a pause, and then there was that fruity, unmistakeable voice with the news they'd all been waiting to hear for such a long, long time. Although Japan remained to be subdued, he said, the war in Europe would end at midnight. It was a short speech and ended with a flourish, 'Advance Britannia! Long live the cause of freedom! God save the King.' And at that there were tears as well as cheers.

Barbara was thinking about Steve. Now he'll get leave and come home. Now I shall see him again. In a few days. A week maybe. It made her yearn to imagine it. Steve, Steve, after all this time.

The crowd was on the move again, inching down Whitehall, and looking up she saw that there were people coming out onto one of the balconies and that one of them was a short, stout man wearing a dark siren suit and a Homburg hat and waving a cigar. Churchill himself. At the sight of him such a roar went up that it made her ears ring, and when it died down, a band began to play 'For He's a Jolly Good Fellow' at which they all cheered again and began to sing, waving their paper flags in time to the music. And Churchill held up his cigar at them and nodded and smiled. After the song, the cheering went on for a very long time and it didn't stop until the band played the first chords of 'Land of Hope and Glory'. Then they all settled and stood very still to sing the words while Churchill conducted them, using his cigar as a baton.

'I feel almost sorry for him, poor old beggar,' Sis said, when the patriotic hymn was over and the balcony was empty again and the crowds were wandering off in their various directions. 'He'll take it hard when we vote him out a' power.'

432

'D'you reckon we will?' Mabel wondered.

Sis had no doubt. 'It'll be a close run thing,' she said, 'but we'll do it.'

Now that they'd heard the official announcement, Mabel said she thought she ought to be getting back. 'I haven't got the heart for it. Not really.'

And Sis, having seen what she'd come to see, decided to go home too. But Barbara and the two girls stayed on to join in the fun, for as Joyce declared, 'We'll never see nothink like it again, will we? An' Betty wouldn't't've minded.'

It was an extraordinary evening and they spent most of it in Piccadilly Circus, carried along by the excited euphoria around them. They sang themselves silly, were hugged and kissed by perfect strangers, and danced and danced – the conga, the Lambeth Walk, the hokey-cokey – until their heads were spinning and their feet were sore. At the end of it all, they missed the last tram and had to walk all the way home, so they didn't get to bed until past two in the morning. But they didn't care. The war was over, Steve was coming home at last, life was going to get back to normal.

The next morning Barbara wrote him a long letter describing what an amazing occasion it had been and asking him when he thought he'd be getting leave. She was rather disappointed by his answer for although he agreed with her that it was wonderful for the war to be over at last and told her that the German troops were surrendering in thousands, he didn't say anything about coming home.

'I don't expect he knows,' Sis comforted. 'They'll have to take it in turns for leave, now won't they, or there'll be no one left to look after things. He'll come home sooner or later. We'll just have to be patient, that's all.'

But after a year without him, patience was impossible. I'll get everything ready for him, she decided, and

433

I'll write and tell him. I'll buy a double bed for a start. We can't sleep in that narrow one of his. Which she did.

> *'Thass so big that fill the room,'* she wrote when it had been delivered. *'And so comfortable. You wait till you try it. Oh I can't wait till you're here to try it. You will get leave soon, won't you. That's such a long time since you went away.'*

But his next letter was all about grey paint and a Victory parade that was going to take place in Berlin.

> *There is a rumour that we are to go to Berlin in a week or two. They've given us masses of paint. It is battleship grey and comes from the German naval stores at Lubeck, so they say. We are sprucing up the tanks and the TCV's. Lots of rain recently.*

And still not a word about coming home.

'Keep yer chin up,' Sis advised. 'It's bound to take time. I'll bet he comes back for the election. He wouldn't want to miss that.'

Three days later, on May 23rd, the General Election was called. Polling day was to be on July 5th, and because there were so many men who couldn't possibly get home to vote because they were still on active service all over the world, the election was going to be taken to them. They would cast their votes at special polling stations wherever they were and there would then be a three week interval between the vote and the count while their papers were collected and returned to the relevant constituencies. It was the proper and admirable way to run this election but it didn't help Barbara at all.

'Never mind, duck,' Sis said. 'He'll come home in the end. I shouldn't think about it too much if I was you. We got a job to do.'

Which was true enough. For although they thought they'd prepared themselves for this election, now that it was upon them there was more work than they could cope with, even with an eight week campaign. Sis arranged to take the early morning shift so that she and Pauline could go out canvassing every evening. And Barbara joined them whenever her own work pattern would allow, giving herself up to campaigning so that she didn't have time to brood about Steve. It was a revealing experience.

From the very first evening she was surprised by how much sympathy there was in these affluent houses for the plight of the unemployed and the needs of the sick. For denizens of a safe Tory seat, the people she met were impressively radical. At first it took quite a bit of courage to knock on such important doors and the first two householders she met were fierce ladies who sent her packing, one saying, 'No thank you. Not today,' the other, 'We never reveal our voting intentions. Secret ballot you know.' But the third door was opened by a gentleman who welcomed her and stood on the doorstep talking for nearly a quarter of an hour.

'Sir William Beveridge is quite right,' he said. 'We must tackle these problems. We cannot go on as we were.' And when she asked, almost tentatively, whether the Labour candidate could count on his vote, he said he thought the time had come for change and yes, they could indeed.

'Put the other two down as Tory,' Sis advised, when they met up at the end of the cul-de-sac. 'When in doubt count them against us. It's better to underestimate.'

Even allowing for underestimation, the number of voters who said they were ready for change seemed encouragingly high. And when Sis held her second public meeting, the hall was packed and the questions were fast and passionate.

'We ought to have a card with our address on it and hand them out to fellers like that,' Sis said to Pauline

435

after one particularly heartfelt offering. 'He'd join us if we asked him.'

'I'll ask him now,' Barbara decided. And when the next questioner was on her feet and taking attention away from the platform party, she got up quietly and walked through the hall to do just that, returning to her aunt after ten minutes, with a new member and another canvasser, feeling very pleased with herself.

By the end of the first fortnight they'd acquired over thirty new members and Sis was cock-a-hoop at their success. By the end of the second, they'd settled into such a steady routine that they were canvassing twice as many houses in an evening as they'd done at the beginning. The newspapers kept them provided with ammunition and they were steadily honing their arguments. In the sixth week they all went to a big meeting in New Cross and saw how an established candidate could hold an audience. In the seventh, Sis spoke to a packed meeting of her own and used some of his tricks to excellent effect.

'I'm learning,' she said to Barbara as the bus took them home afterwards. Her voice was husky after all the effort she'd been making but she was beaming with satisfaction. 'We ain't half done well this evening. D'you see that bloke with the Homburg? He was from the *Mirror*. Doin' a piece on first-time candidates, so he said.'

It was a lively article and she was the last and most colourful candidate to be featured in it. '*Mrs Cecily Tamworth, railway worker by day, ebullient candidate by night.*'

Barbara was so impressed by it that she cut it out and sent it to Steve. Maybe that would provoke a bit of interest in what they were doing. And, to her great delight, it did. He wrote back almost at once, to send his congratulations to his 'political aunt'. '*Tell her I've shown your cutting to all my mates,*' he wrote, '*and we're all rooting for her.*'

436

But his next letter was all about the army again and now it was just a little too obvious that he was avoiding Barbara's question about leave. She sat in her lonely bedroom on their new comfortable double bed and wondered bleakly whether they would ever share it. If he hasn't said anything by polling day, she decided, I shall tell Aunt Sis and see what she thinks about it.

In the meantime there was too much work to do to sit about and mope. Pauline and Sis were busy setting up local committee rooms to keep an eye on the turn-out on polling day and to knock up promised voters. There were voting lists to prepare, teams of workers to organise, supplies of tea and biscuits to be laid in. They were all up until past midnight on the eve of the poll and by the time the polling stations were finally closed the next day, Pauline declared that she was too tired to keep her eyes open.

'I suppose you're going straight home,' Sis said to Barbara as they got off the bus at New Cross.

'Not if you can stand my company a bit longer,' Barbara said.

'Let's have a nightcap,' Sis decided. 'We've earned it today.'

So they had a nightcap – whisky and a cigar for Sis, tea and a cigarette for Barbara – and they sat one on each side of the empty fireplace with their feet on stools, the way they'd done all those months ago. And for several seconds they smoked and drank and said nothing. Then Barbara plucked up the courage she needed.

'Aunt Sis.'

'Um.'

'I got something I'd like to ask you.'

Sis was relaxed and easy. 'Fire away.'

'Thass about Steve.'

'You've heard from him,' Sis said happily. 'He's coming home. Is that it?'

'I wish he was,' Barbara said, stubbing out her

437

cigarette. 'Thass just the point. He hain't. The thing is, I'm beginning to think there's something the matter.'

Sis looked at her quizzically. 'What sort a' something?'

'Thass been nine weeks since the war was over,' Barbara said. 'I'm beginning to think he hain't coming home.'

Sis was fully alerted now. This was serious. 'Why's that then?'

'You seen his letters,' Barbara said. 'I mean they hain't axactly love letters, now are they?'

No, Sis admitted, that was true, but it mightn't mean anything. 'My Percy never wrote me a love letter in his life. Some men are like that.'

'Not Steve.'

'He *does* write to you?'

'Oh yes. He writes.'

'Then what's the matter?'

Barbara thought for a few seconds, her face perplexed. 'Thass hard to put a finger on,' she admitted. 'He tells me all sorts of things but they're all about the army an' the tanks an' parades. He never say things like, I can't wait to get home, or I can't wait for us to be together again. Not like I do. I mean, look at this one.' And she took his latest letter from her bag and handed it to her aunt. 'He could be writing to anybody.'

We drove down the autobahn. It was a long drive to Berlin. We went through the Russian occupied area past Magdeberg. It was pouring with rain for most of the journey. We passed a park full of burned out buses, and drove into the Charlottenburg district. We stopped at the Olympic Stadium. Berlin is in a terrible state. I should say over half the buildings have been totally destroyed. There is no electricity and no water and when the sun shines the stink is awful. We keep being warned about the danger of polluted water, and there are

438

*plagues of mosquitoes and rats everywhere you
look. It is not a good place to be.*

'Yet he don't say, I'll be home the minute I can,'
Barbara said, 'which I know I would if I was there.'

'No,' Sis agreed, considering the letter. 'He don't.'

'I don't think he's going to come home,' Barbara said
sadly. 'I don't know why, but I think he's decided not
to. Something must have happened. Don't you think
so?'

Sis gave her an honest answer. 'It could've done,' she
said.

Barbara wanted to cry but she surprised herself by
staying calm. 'You did this once before,' she said. 'Told
me the truth, I mean. When he was recalled. D'you
remember? When we came back from honeymoon. You
knew he was going to be sent to France an' they
wouldn't let him home and you said maybe I ought to
find myself a job just in case.'

Sis remembered. 'I was sure of it that time,' she said.
'I ain't so certain now. There's a lot a' pride in our
Steve. I mean, all sorts a' things could have happened.
He could've asked for leave an' been refused. Could be
in some sort of trouble an' they won't let him home yet
awhile. Could be all sorts a' reasons.'

In the quiet of the flat, after the effort and emotion of
the day, it was possible for Barbara to ask the question
that had been troubling her since the election was
called. 'You don't think he's found someone else, do
you?'

'No,' Sis said, decidedly. 'I don't. He'd've told you
straight out if he had. You mustn't think that.'

'The thing is, there's a sort of atmosphere at home
when I try to talk about it. Mrs Wilkins won't let me say
anything about him not coming home. She sort of shuts
me up every time I mention it. She says, "He'll be
home. You got to be patient," as if I'm making fuss

439

over nothin'. I hain't, am I Aunt Sis? You'd tell me if I was.'

Her face was so woebegone, that Sis put down her cigar and leant across to pat her hand.

'Tell you what,' she said, 'we'll get this election over an' out the way and then if he's still writing like this an' he still ain't come home, I'll write to him mesself and ask him what's the matter. Straight out. How would that be?'

It would be very kind, Barbara said. But her heart was shrinking at the thought that such a letter might have to be written, and she knew she was afraid of the answer he might give if it were.

'We'd better get to bed,' Sis said, 'or we'll be fit for nothing in the morning.' And as she kissed her niece goodbye she made up her mind to say something about this to Bob. If anyone ought to know what was going on, he was the one, and she could catch him at the station in one of his breaks.

It didn't seem to surprise him. 'I been wondering about it mesself,' he said. 'I mean, he ought to have come home by now. Most of the others have had leave. Kenny's son's been home twice.'

'So you reckon I should write?' Sis asked.

'No,' he said. 'Leave it to me. I'll see to it. I should've done it ages ago, but with the election an' everything . . .'

'Can't have our Barbara fretting,' she said, as she left him to go back to the ticket office.

And he agreed that they couldn't.

That night, when he and Heather were in bed, he broached the subject he'd been putting off for far too long.

'You never wrote to him about the Dear John, did you?' he said.

Heather looked away from him. 'I couldn't,' she said.

'An' now he's not coming home.'

'He'll come home,' she said, but there was no

440

conviction in her voice. 'I mean, they can't send them *all* home, can they. Not all at the same time. I mean, not if he's in Berlin.'

'Write tomorrow,' he instructed. 'First thing. Or d'you want me to do it for you?'

That would be too shaming. 'I can manage,' she said. 'There's no need for that.'

'Well see you do.'

She turned her head into the pillow, sighing. 'You don't know how difficult it is.'

He looked at her averted head. 'The longer it goes on the more difficult it'll get. Do it tomorrow. Promise me?'

She answered with a murmur that could have been a promise or an argument.

But she didn't write because the next morning the newsagent's little boy arrived while they were in the middle of their breakfast to say that Daddy thought there was something the matter with Mrs Tamworth. 'She ain't come for her paper,' he explained when they questioned him. Could they come and see?

'I'll go,' Barbara said at once. 'I got a key.'

But Bob and Heather were so alarmed by the urgency in the child's voice that they all went together.

Sis was still in bed in a room frowsy with fever. She was plainly very ill, her cheeks unnaturally red, her breath laboured and wheezing.

'I'll get up presently,' she said, when they trooped into her bedroom, but even those few words reduced her to such a paroxysm of coughing that Bob went out at once to call the doctor.

'Stay with her till he comes,' he told Heather. 'I'll have to go straight on to work or I'll be late. Let me know what he says.'

The doctor didn't come until past eleven o'clock, by which time, Heather and Barbara had gone to work too and Mabel had come over to sit with their patient. There was no doubt about his diagnosis. 'Your sister has

441

bronchitis,' he said to Mabel. 'I'll give you a prescription for some M and B tablets to bring down the fever and some linctus for her cough. A steam kettle would help when the cough is bad. She will need careful nursing, day and night. Can that be arranged? Good, good. Keep her in the warm. I'll call in again tomorrow.'

'That's this damned election,' Heather said trenchantly when she heard what he'd said. 'Taken it right out of her. It's not a job for a woman. I've always said so . . .'

'We'll have to take it in turns to sit up with her,' Bob interrupted, before her complaint could get out of hand. 'Rota, sort a' thing.'

So they drew one up and took it in turns to stay in the flat and feed her pills and cough medicine and do what they could for her. And the letter that Heather should have written to her son was thankfully forgotten. On the second evening, Barbara cleaned the living room while her patient slept, on the fourth afternoon Heather and Mabel gave her a blanket bath, and were alarmed when it exhausted her. She got no worse but she didn't seem to be getting better either. Her voice was so hoarse they could barely hear what she said to them, the cough racked her, her fever returned every night. At the end of the second week, the doctor prescribed another course of tablets. But on the sixteenth day she declared that she was well enough to sit up and struggled out of bed and into her now tidy living room to sit by the window and read the papers.

'Any news of the election?' she wanted to know.

'What news can there be?' Heather said. 'They've all voted I suppose. It's all gone quiet these last few weeks. We shall know in a day or two.'

'I must get better,' Sis said, as if being determined about it could make it so. 'Wouldn't do to miss the count.'

'Nobody would blame you if you did,' Heather told

her. 'I mean it's not as if you're going to win. It's solid Tory.'

'That ain't the point,' Sis said. 'I can't let the side down. I got to go.'

'If you're not up to it, the doctor won't let you go,' Heather warned.

Sis snorted at that. 'He won't be here to stop me,' she said. 'If I say I'll do a thing, I do it.'

Chapter Thirty-Five

By the time Sis and Barbara arrived at the Town Hall on that historic Thursday morning – Sis determined, Barbara in serious attendance – the count was well under way. Three long lines of trestle tables had been set up in the body of the hall to accommodate the sorters and tellers, who were working steadily in their usual purposeful way, and the Mayor was ready on the platform, bulky in his robes of office and looking cheerfully important. As the safe Tory seat, their constituency had been given pole position just below the stage, with the safe Labour seat at the back of the hall and the marginal votes being counted in the middle. There was less excitement in the place than Barbara expected and what little there was was subdued and controlled, more like the throb of a machine than the mob roar of a revolution. Barbara watched as the piles of counted voting slips grew taller and more and more people ambled in through the double doors. If thass really going to be a revolution like Sis say, she thought, thass a far cry from the French one.

Most of the other candidates had arrived by this time too and were standing about trying to appear nonchalant, with their followers and supporters all around them. Barbara was intrigued to see that Sis was the only woman candidate and that the Tories were obvious from their classy suits and the boom and bay of their upper-class voices. She'd never seen Tories *en masse* before and the sight and sound of them was a revelation.

'They're so full of theirselves,' she said to Sis. 'You'd think the whole world belong to them, the way they go on.'

444

'It does,' Sis grinned at her. 'For the moment.'

'Steve should be here to see this,' Barbara said. Oh how much she missed him. 'He'd love it. You here as a candidate and everybody waiting to see what's gonna happen, an' the count goin' on.'

But Sis was smiling into the crowd. 'Here's Mr Craxton,' she said, and plunged towards her old colleague, holding out both hands in greeting. 'Nice to see you, Mr C. How're you keeping?'

'Never mind me,' Mr Craxton said, 'How are *you*? That's more to the point. I hear you been in the wars.'

'Fit as a flea,' Sis told him, coughing to prove it. 'So what's the news?'

'Nothing yet,' Mr Craxton said. 'We got fidgety waiting, so I thought we'd come and watch the count. Pauline's here somewhere. Have you seen her?'

She was just behind him, looking dashing and rather hot in a blue tweed suit and more nervous than Barbara had ever seen her.

'It can't be long now before we get a few results,' she said to Sis. 'I'd say we've given them a good run for their money, wouldn't you? We've left Brian to man the wireless. Strict instructions to come down and tell us if anything exciting happens. I don't know about you, Cecily, but this waiting is wearing me out.'

'Not long now,' Sis reassured her.

'If only we knew which way it was going to go,' Pauline complained. 'The papers are so discouraging. They don't think we've got a chance.'

'The *Mirror* does,' Mr Craxton pointed out.

'Ah yes, the *Mirror*. Granted. But they've been on our side all along. You can't count the *Mirror*. Oh dear! If we could just hear one or two marginals we might have more idea. I do wish they'd hurry up.'

'There's a marginal in this hall,' Sis said. 'Take a look at that.' But there was no way of knowing what was happening on the central table. The piles of voting papers were changing by the second. 'Be a turn-up for the books if there was two Labour seats in *this* borough.'

'We shall just have to hold on to our hats,' Mr Craxton told them in his dry way, 'and have a bit of patience.'

But it was very difficult. Especially when Christine arrived, breathless and dishevelled, to bring her own anxieties into the group. Her snub nose was beaded with sweat, her bun half out of its pins and trailing loose strands of hair. 'Has anyone heard anything? Oh they *are* taking a long time. We *must* have a new government this time, mustn't we.'

There was movement on the platform. The Mayor was tapping his microphone – 'Testing, testing. One, two, three.' Had they got their first result? Yes. At last. The candidates were gathering round him, rosettes to the fore. There was a throb of impatience, a shifting of feet, a buzz of excited voices.

It was the safe Labour seat, won as they expected but with a majority that brought a gasp from everyone in the hall. It had risen from six thousand to nearly eighteen.

'Now that *is* a victory,' Pauline said clapping rapturously.

And Sis said, 'What did I tell you?'

Mr Craxton was cautious. 'One swallow doesn't make a summer,' he warned, as the new Labour MP stepped up to the microphone to make his acceptance speech.

It was a very long one, thanking the returning officer, the mayor, the tellers, the police, his supporters. 'An' Uncle Tom Cobley an' all!' Sis mocked happily.' But at the end of it he was handed a paper and after a pause he told his audience that one or two other London results had come in and proceeded to read them. There was a Labour gain in Dulwich, both the Lewisham seats had been won by Labour and at Peckham, which was one of their closest marginal seats, the Labour majority had

446

risen from 'one hundred last time' to seven thousand. 'I think you'll agree,' he said, 'there's nothing marginal about *that*.' The applause was deafening.

'What price swallows now?' Sis said to Mr Craxton. The excitement was making her cough but she was massively happy.

The young man called Brian was pushing through the crowd towards them. 'They've been coming in fast for the last twenty minutes,' he reported. 'I brought you the latest. Look!'

They crowded round him to read the results.

'I've marked the Norfolk ones for you, Barbara,' Brian said. 'They're really good. We've taken King's Lynn, Norfolk North and Norfolk South. That's where you're from, isn't it?'

'If Lynn's voted Labour we shall win,' Barbara told them, green eyes wide with surprise.

'I'm beginning to think that too,' Pauline said. 'I mean, it could be possible, the way things are going. I mean . . .'

'Hold on!' Brian said. 'They're going to announce the marginal.'

Another group of rosettes around the microphone, more papers fluttering from hand to hand, another set of candidates wearing decorous expressions, the hall bristling with anticipation. Has this one swung too? Oh come on! Come on!

It was another Labour victory and a good one.

Even Mr Craxton was excited. 'If this goes on,' he said, 'I think we shall see a Labour government.'

Results were coming in fast. Every new arrival brought news of another victory. Deptford's Labour majority had doubled to fourteen thousand. Labour had one hundred and seventy-two seats, one hundred and eighty, two hundred and counting. The marginals were falling like flies.

But the vote in Bellington South was still being counted.

'You don't have to wait,' Sis said to her supporters. They were all so thrilled by what had happened up to that moment that she was afraid her result would be a disappointment to them.

'Of course we do,' Pauline said. 'I want to see how big your share of the vote turns out to be. I said we'd give them a run for their money, didn't I? Well then. We're all going to stay.'

So they stayed as more and more results came in and the excitement in the hall grew until they felt as though they were in the middle of an electric storm.

Eventually a teller came over to ask if Mrs Cecily Tamworth would join him at the tables.

'This is it,' Sis said, grinning at her friends.

So they wished her luck and watched as she and the Tory stood beside the teller, listening to what he had to say. Telling them the result, Barbara thought, and in a minute they'll go up onto the platform and we shall hear it too. But they didn't. Instead, the conversation went on and the Tory was beginning to get agitated. And Sis looked flabbergasted, her plump face so pale that Barbara was quite worried about her. What *is* he saying? Are they arguing? Surely not. Has something gone wrong? The suspense was holding her ribcage in a vice.

They were still talking when Heather and Mabel came puffing through the crowd with Joyce and Hazel trailing after them.

'How is she?' Heather asked, plunging straight into the concern that had kept her anxious all through her journey. 'I heard her coughing as we came in. I said to Mabel – didn't I Mabel? – that's Sis an' I don't like the sound of her at all. She shouldn't be here.'

The cough was approaching at that moment, hoarse and rasping, but Sis was beaming despite it, the colour back in her cheeks. 'He's asked for a re-count,' she said, her voice high with disbelief. 'Apparently Bellington South is a marginal now. What'cher think a' that?'

They were stunned. 'Good God!' Pauline said.

'D'you mean you might win?' Joyce asked her, eyes wide.

'You never know,' Sis told her. 'Keep your fingers crossed.'

Oh these brown eyes, Barbara thought, caught by their intensity. They're so like Steve's. And she looked round at them, Sis and Mabel and the two girls all looking at one another with his eyes, reminding her. Then she gave herself a shake and tried to be sensible. It was silly to be thinking of him, especially now, in the middle of all this. But she couldn't help it. You don't stop loving someone because they don't come home. And oh, she did love him. So much. He ought to be here, if Sis is going to win. *If* she's going to win.

'How long will that be before you know?' she asked.

'Too long!' Sis told her.

And she was right. It seemed an age before the second count was completed. The two girls fidgeted, Sis coughed, Heather grumbled, Christine lost all the pins from her hair, Mr Craxton told stories of previous elections, which his wife corrected, Pauline prowled and bit her lips. But at last the two candidates were called over again and this time there was no discussion, just a few words and they were on their way to the platform, the Tory bland-faced with his wife in attendance, Sis, pale and coughing, signalling to Barbara that she should come and join her.

It felt exposed up there on the platform, with the Mayor fussing and the microphone waiting for the final speech. The hall was so crowded that Barbara couldn't see to the other side of it and the heat of such a great mass of people rose towards her as though she were breathing fire. She looked down at the rows of expectant faces, hundreds of them, pale as flowers, bobbing and turning. The tension was so extreme it was like waiting for thunder to break.

The Mayor waited for calm and took a long time to

get it. 'The total number of votes cast in the Bellington South constituency is as follows . . .' It had been a very close vote indeed but the result, by a mere one hundred and thirteen votes, was, as he hereby declared, that 'the said Mrs Cecily Elizabeth Tamworth has been duly elected to serve as Member of Parliament for the said constituency.'

The thunder broke in a cheer that made Barbara's ears ring. Joyce and Hazel were jumping up and down, Heather clapping, Mabel blowing kisses. It was an impossible, unbelievable victory. And Sis stepped forward, smoothing down her old cotton jacket, clearing her throat, ready to make her acceptance speech.

She began it stylishly, thanking the returning officer and his team, the people who'd worked for her and the people who'd shown their desire for a Labour government by voting for her, but then she paused, seemed to be catching her breath, coughed once, tried to continue and was caught up in such a paroxysm that she had to retire to the back of the stage, spluttering and choking, to be given a glass of water.

Her audience waited anxiously, murmuring and watching. 'Bar!' she said, handkerchief to her mouth, struggling to speak. 'You'll – 'ave – to do it – for me. I can't . . .'

Nor can I, Barbara thought, I hain't never spoke in public in my life. She felt such panic she wanted to run away. But she couldn't do that. Not now, with all this going on. The Mayor was nodding and saying it would be all right, and Sis's eyes were pleading, and the audience were shuffling their feet.

'All right,' she said to Sis. 'Thass all right. I'll do it for you.' And she walked up to the microphone. Her heart was beating so heavily it was like a lead weight in her chest and her throat was so taut she was afraid she would start coughing too. She put her hand on the microphone, as much to steady herself as to signal that she was about to speak, moistened her lips and began.

'My aunt, Mrs Tamworth, has asked me to finish her speech for her,' she said, rather quaveringly. 'She hain't been too well these last weeks. She's recoverin', as you see,' – Sis was waving and smiling – 'but not quick enough for a long speech. What she want to say to you is this – or somethin' like this.' Then she paused because she wasn't sure what she ought to say next. Her mind was too full of memories, of Betty laughing in that sheepskin coat, of Norman striding through the North End in his blue gansey, of Steve saying goodbye to her on the platform at New Cross. So many memories and all to do with war. All to do with war. And then her thoughts came together and made sense to her and she knew what she had to say.

'We come a long way in this war,' she began, aware of her own voice echoing back to her through the loudspeakers, but stronger now and more assured. 'We learned a lot, how to cope with death and injury, how to look after one another, how to share. We put up with rations an' shortages, an' bombs an' buzzbombs an' rockets, an' we never give in. We dug our casualties out the rubble. We looked after our wounded. We buried our dead. We never give in.'

She knew that her audience was listening to her with such rapt attention that there wasn't a sound in the hall. Even the echo had changed. 'Thass made us different people to the ones we were before,' she said. 'Different people with different ideas. We don't want to go back to the old way, the way things were. We want our children to grow up in a fairer world, where people hain't afraid to be unemployed or take sick or grow old, where we all work together to protect one another. Thass what this election has been about. A fairer world. Thass what this new government you've just elected will start to create. My aunt would like to thank you for choosin' her to be a part of it.'

At which Sis waved again and their supporters cheered and waved back. And Barbara knew she'd made her first political speech and that it had been a good one.

Oh, she thought, standing on the platform, looking down at all the happy faces below her, if only Steve could have been here. He'd have loved all this, seeing his aunt elected and the Labour Party winning. And she looked across the packed heads to the back of the room and suddenly there he was, tall and auburn haired, with his tunic unbuttoned and his cap on his shoulder, standing there, looking straight ahead of him as if he didn't see her. She was caught between shock and disbelief and overwhelming happiness. I'm seein' things, she thought. Thass all the excitement. My eyes are playing tricks on me.

And then he took a cigarette packet from his tunic pocket and lit up. And the movement of his hands was so familiar that she jumped from the platform, calling his name, 'Steve! Steve!' and ran, plunging through the crowd, all memory and all instinct, with nothing in her mind but the need to reach him. Steve! My dear, dear, darling Steve! She was in his arms before he had time to look up, covering his face with kisses, her cheeks flushed and her green eyes bright as the sea in sunshine. Oh Steve!

The impact of her body was so powerful that it took away his power of speech. It was as if she'd knocked him over, as if he was falling through space, as if he were waking from a long, long sleep, stunned and unsteady. He put his arms round her, leaning back so that he could see her face. 'Hello,' he said, huskily.

And at that she burst into tears. And he found his old easy tenderness again, and put his arms round her, and kissed her forehead, and smoothed her tousled hair and brushed away her tears – such hot, passionate tears – with trembling fingers.

'I thought I'd never see you again,' she wept.

'I know. I know.' How *could* he have waited so long? How could he have been so foolish?

452

The rest of the family were crowding in on them, reaching up to kiss him and pat him, questioning and clamouring. 'Where've you sprung from?' 'Were you here for the count?' 'We're winning! We're gonna have a Labour government. Ain't it wonderful, our Steve?' And he stood with one arm round Barbara's waist and her head on his shoulder and agreed that yes, it was. But what was really wonderful was that he was home and loved and aware that there was good in the world after all. After being stuck in indecision for so long it felt like a miracle.

Presently he saw that his mother was in the crowd too, but standing apart from the others, her face wrinkled with anxiety. With Barbara still held closely to his side, he walked across to kiss her. But he didn't pick her up in his old loving way, as she was quick and pained to notice, and once the kiss was given he stood back and looked at her in a most disconcerting way.

She took refuge in scolding. 'Why didn't you say you were coming?'

'Snap decision,' he told her. 'I didn't know myself till last night.' And he went on looking at her.

His scrutiny made her feel anxious. He looked so much older, so much the soldier, tough and shrewd with all that lovely boyish innocence of his quite gone. And his look was a question that had to be answered. 'Did you get my letter?' she faltered.

Now I shall hear the truth of it, he thought. But did he want to hear the truth of it? 'Which one?' he asked her, stern-faced. 'I haven't had any letters from you or Dad since we crossed the Rhine. No. Tell a lie. One. You wrote me one.' And he made a joke of it to help her, because she was looking so distressed. 'I was beginning to think you'd left the country. Which letter are you talking about?'

She was confused and more anxious than ever. If only she'd written to him and explained. Bob was right. She should have written. 'The letter I wrote when . . . I

453

mean, my last letter . . . The one . . . No, I suppose not. I suppose some of your letters must've gone astray, what with one thing and another.'

'You'd be surprised how well they got the mail through,' he told her. 'They knew how important it was to us.' And he repeated his question. 'Which letter are you talking about?'

She certainly couldn't answer such a direct challenge. Not here, in front of Barbara and all the others. 'It doesn't matter,' she said, ducking her head and looking away from him. 'It's not important. It was only a letter. I mean, there was nothing in it.'

He looked straight into her eyes, daring her. 'Then it wasn't worth writing, was it?'

I've lost him, Heather thought. He's not my boy any more. He's a grown man and I've hurt him and now he's angry with me and I've only got myself to blame. 'No. It wasn't,' she admitted and came as near to an apology as she could in such a public place. 'Trouble is, you say silly things sometimes.'

'And then regret them?' he asked, his voice insistent but more gentle.

The gentleness made her want to weep. 'Yes,' she told him, miserably. 'And then regret them.'

He smiled at her, but it was an odd, sad smile. Forgiveness? Understanding? She couldn't tell.

'Then we don't need to worry about it, do we?' he said. He was aware that Barbara had grown tense during their exchange and he turned to look at *her* again, caught the query on her face and answered it with a kiss, full on the lips, public and committed. 'I love you,' he said.

To be kissed in such a way in such a public place made her blush. Luckily Sis moved in to rescue her. She'd been talking to Mr Craxton and Pauline and had missed most of the conversation but she'd caught the gathering atmosphere and knew she had to deal with it.

'I reckon this calls for a celebration,' she said,

beaming round at them all. 'What say we go down to the Goat an' Compasses? They got a garden for the kids. Be nice out in the sun.'

General agreement, a rush of movement towards the door, Heather and Mabel leading the way, Sis turning to ask her nephew, 'You coming?'

He stood where he was with his arm round his wife. 'We'll follow you,' he called and added quietly to Barbara, 'slowly.'

So they walked out of the hall together, their arms about each other, and strolled along the affluent, crowd-filled streets of Sis's new constituency, stopping to kiss whenever they felt like it, which was more and more frequently. And there, away from the eyes of their relations, alone in that euphoric crowd, it was as if they'd never been apart. They were older, wiser, sadder, but love was pulling them together with every step, binding them close, closer, breathlessly together. He looked down at her face, drinking in the sight of her, re-learning her, aching with the old love for her.

'Will I do?' she teased, smiling into his eyes.

'Oh, I think so,' he teased back. And then grew serious. 'You've changed though.'

'Thass been a long time,' she said. 'A lot's happened.'

'That's what it is,' he agreed. 'We've grown older. You have to grow up fast in a war. You don't have any option. Anyway, it suits you. You're very, very beautiful. And that was a terrific speech you made.'

'You've changed too,' she said. Now that they were out in the sunlight she could see how much. There was no boyishness about him at all and the open innocence of his face was gone. Grown older, she thought, and wise in the ways of a very cruel world. His hair was cropped short, there were lines on his face that hadn't been there the last time she saw him and his eyes had a weariness about them that made her yearn with pity for what he must have seen and endured. 'Was it very bad?'

He gave her an honest answer. 'Yes,' he said. 'I'll tell you about it some time. But not now.' Now it was enough to be getting back to normal, holding her close, breathing in the familiar smell of her skin, recognising that flowered blouse and the green skirt she'd worn a lifetime ago, that day in the haystack, that week in the hopfields. 'Oh my dear, darling girl! You do still love me?'

'Oh, yes, yes, yes,' she said, kissing him with every word. ''Course I do. More than ever.'

The crowd parted to pass them and two schoolboys gave them a wolf whistle.

'I suppose we ought to join the others,' he said.

So they walked on, talking of victory and victories. 'Why didn't you get leave before?' she asked. 'As soon as the war was over. You could've done, couldn't you?'

He gave her another honest answer. 'I couldn't face it I suppose.'

They were so easy with one another now that she could ask, 'Why not?'

'All sorts of reasons,' he said. 'I was afraid of disappointment, scared of the changes I'd find. I think I needed the army routine. I was trying to work things out.' He shrugged, growing impatient with his inability to tell her how it had been. 'Oh I don't know. I don't understand it myself.'

He wasn't making much sense to her but she was full of tenderness towards him. Whatever it was that was troubling him it needed careful handling. She stood on tiptoe to kiss him again, holding his face between her hands. She knew instinctively that this had something to do with his mother, that it was the reason why he'd treated her so sternly back in the hall, but she knew she couldn't ask him about it yet.

He was still struggling to explain why he'd hesitated for so long, as much to himself as to her. 'They offered me leave,' he told her. 'You mustn't think they kept me there. They offered but I just sort of said no, put it off. And then it was hard to say yes.'

'But you said yes in the end.'

'Fortunately.'

She could be curious about that. 'Why?'

'It was your snapshot,' he told her. 'I've been keeping a sort of diary, since Belsen, and I took it out and your snapshot was caught between the leaves. And when I turned it over . . . You'd written on the back of it, do you remember?'

'No,' she had to admit. 'I don't. Thass a long time ago.'

'You said, "*Just in case you've forgot what I look like!*" '

She smiled at that. 'And thass what made you come home?'

'It made me think of home,' he said, 'think of you. I suppose thinking made me want to be here with you. It seemed the right thing.'

'Does it still?' It was a serious question and he answered it equally seriously.

'Oh yes. I might not be sure of many things these days, but I'm sure of that.'

They were nearly at the pub. 'How much leave have you got?' she asked.

'Ten days,' he said, suddenly realising how happy he felt. 'And more to come. I tell you what, how would you like to go back to the bungalow? I'll bet I could arrange it.'

She smiled into his eyes. 'If there's one thing this war's taught me,' she said, 'thass you can't go back. Only forward.'

He stopped to kiss her again. One last kiss before they went in and joined the celebration. They were both changed but he was home, they were together, love was possible. 'Then that's where we'll go,' he said.

457